FIFTH
A FURY

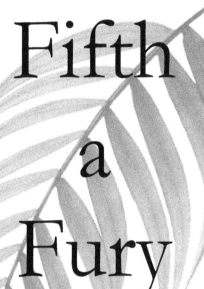

Fifth a Fury

Goddess Isles
Book Five

by

New York Times Bestseller
Pepper Winters

Fifth a Fury
Copyright © 2020 Pepper Winters
Published by Pepper Winters

Published: Pepper Winters 2020: **pepperwinters@gmail.com**
Cover Design: Ari @ Cover it! Designs
Editing by: Editing 4 Indies (Jenny Sims)

Dedicated to:

The survivors of the world.
Through hardship, heartache, health, and hell.
You are the true heroes and heroines.

Sullivan

Prologue

FURY.

Red hot.

Scalpel sharp.

Motherfucking *fury*.

I was its prisoner, master, and king.

It bowed to me, crippled me, and twined around my veins as I sank deeper into the sea.

Fury.

An emotion as familiar to me as the warm ocean sucking me down. A feeling I'd always tried to harness, expel, and ignore. I'd failed on multiple occasions. I'd kneeled beneath its sinister sufferings and existed with silent loathing within my heart, but now…

Fuck.

Now…I no longer turned away from the shooting shards of hate. I welcomed the acidic contempt. I turned my back on humanity and permitted fury to strip me of everything I'd been. To delete my failures. To erase my past. To leave me empty apart from one deeply dangerous thing.

Eleanor…

I jerked beneath the sea.

He took her.

Fury!

I welcomed the poison.

The heinous howl for blood.

Eleanor!

My fury grew again.

My bones snapped with it.

My heart smoked with it.

My entire world was soaked in rage-dripping **FURY!**

It mutated the water around me.

It sent shockwaves through the sea, no longer living within me but surrounding me, choking me.

Eleanor…

I opened my mouth and screamed.

Bubbles shot from my lips.

Oxygen poured from bruised lungs.

And another kind of darkness encroached.

A darkness that promised to strangle me if I didn't find her, free her, *kill him.*

That was my only purpose now.

Kill.

Kill my brother.

Kill Drake.

Drake.

Motherfucking *Drake.*

He has her.

He took her.

He'll DIE.

The surface twinkled above, showing me the way to my vengeance.

My fists curled underwater.

My wounded eyes blinked in the salt.

And my fury morphed from emotion to element.

Blazing fire and howling gales—a tsunami beneath me, churning up the sea floor. I was mayhem. I was unchained.

I'm free.

Fury was no longer just a feeling but an offshoot of every disaster I wielded.

Magic.

Black magic.

Dark magic.

A magic that would extract its payment in souls.

Drake's soul.

FURY.

His blood would flow.

His bones would snap.

His life squeezed to nothingness in my fist.

The man I'd been sank to the bottom of the ocean—useless to me now, a hindrance, a weakling who'd been afraid of his power.

A god who hadn't been able to protect his goddess.

I was no longer divine.

I was no longer human.

I was a vampire thirsting for blood.

I was hell.

I was death.

I. Am. Fury.

Chapter One

SULLY.

His fall into the ocean was on repeat inside my head.

Tripping out the door.

Plummeting down, down, down.

My heart squeezed each time his splash replayed.

A splash and then…nothing.

My thoughts weren't in my body, locked on Drake's lap, skimming over the sea, but *back there*. Back where Sully had fallen. Where he'd disappeared. Where we'd been separated against our will.

Sully…please.

Almost an hour had passed.

The longest, nightmarish hour since I'd last seen him.

Since I knew he was alive…

"Descending," the pilot yelled over the din. "Found it."

The pilot's voice brought me back; Drake's legs tensing beneath mine ripped me from my wonderings.

I glanced out the window, shuddering as Drake's hold on me tightened.

Monyet.

The island with a large laboratory hidden within its paradise, pumping out drugs that went above and beyond aphrodisiacs, creating who knew what else within its walls.

Sully…are you okay?

My mind split down the middle. It now had the ability to

focus on my plight while staying firmly on Sully's in my past.

It was like staring into two mirrors.

A mirror angled behind me—a portal to a man who I begged to rise from the sea. And another angled on my present—revealing unfolding events taking me farther and farther away from him.

"About fucking time," Drake muttered as the helicopter engines cut off mid-screech, the rotors slowing down the moment we touched land.

I shuddered again, overflowing with disgust as Drake pushed me off his lap and onto the seat beside him.

For fifty minutes or so, the pilots had skimmed over Sully's empire, peering at each island, trying to figure out which one housed a lab. Unfortunately, it'd become fairly obvious as darkness descended, and lights spangled below.

The smaller islands with no inhabitants were easy to discount, followed by those with smaller populations performing whatever tasks Sully had set for them to do. *Monyet* was at least twice the size of *Serigala,* and directly in the centre of a fortified encampment. Ringed with fences and palm trees, it sat in a well-lit facility reeking of scientific dealings.

"We're on the main helipad within the barbwire perimeter," the older pilot said. "They'll have heard us arrive. Better figure out your story, quick."

"I don't need a story," Drake said. "This is family owned, and I'm family. Therefore, it's mine, and everything inside is mine."

"Nothing is yours," I snapped. "You're a thief."

He chuckled, his eyes still tight with fatigue from his indulgence with elixir. "Thief? I prefer to be called an opportunist."

"Bastard suits you more."

He shrugged. "I don't mind that one." He looked out the window, eyeing up the lab he'd come to raid.

Drake had been bold and uncaring that he trespassed. He'd stolen so much from Sully already...and now, his thievery would continue on a different island.

Sully...

I hugged myself as goosebumps decorated me.

Please...please be okay.

"What's the plan?" the remaining mercenary asked.

I curled around my pain, turning my attention away from the mirror on my present and stared into the one showing that ever-repeating image of Sully being thrown out of the helicopter.

Falling.
Falling.
Splash.

"There's four of us," Drake muttered, rubbing his eyes as the exhaustion still consumed him from Euphoria. "They're just nerds. We'll knock, ask politely, and leave. They don't obey; they die. I want out of this stinking country the second we've got elixir on board."

"Fine." The mercenary nodded.

The pilots jumped from the cockpit, moving toward the door where Sully had tumbled.

Nausea lapped up my throat.

You better be alive, Sully.

The pilots—one young with brown hair, and the other old with grey—glanced at each other before the older one snipped, "You hired us to fly you around, Mr. Sinclair, not to shoot anybody."

Drake latched his fingers around my wrist, jerking me from the helicopter.

I tripped at the sudden inertia and fell to my knees as he yanked me from the machine. My skin scraped on the roughness of the helipad as he dragged me to the grass a few metres away and left me puddled at his feet.

I hissed at him.

He smirked.

Keeping his hand on my shoulder to prevent me from standing, he nodded at the mercenary to pass a spare handgun to each pilot. "Stand with me, gentlemen, and you won't have to shoot anyone. You're there for show, that's all."

The men accepted out of ingrained decorum, cringing against the arsenal. "What do you expect us to do?"

"Just have my back." Drake grinned, his fingers digging deeper into my shoulder. "They won't put up a fight. My brother hires pussies. Geeks who jerkoff into their test tubes. I promise."

"It'll be easy." The mercenary chuckled. "In and out. We'll be done in five minutes flat."

"Get off me." I struggled, shoving Drake's hand away and swooping to my feet. "Don't *touch* me."

Blood trickled from my grazed knees.

Sickness splashed up my throat.

Drake just laughed as if I was a silly gerbil caught in his paws.

Ignoring him, I locked eyes with the pilots, and snapped,

"Sullivan Sinclair will pay you an exorbitant fee if you use that gun you're holding and kill the man holding me prisoner. Take me back to Sully, and you'll be rewarded—"

"Stupid, *stupid* Eleanor." Drake slapped me around the head, sending me tumbling forward, my skull throbbing. "Don't listen to her, gentlemen." He cleared his throat. "I'll give you a bonus when we disembark in Jakarta. How about that? Help us gather this last item, and I'll pad your payday with another twenty grand each."

"Sully will give you a hundred," I hissed. "Kill Drake and—"

"Shut the fuck *up*, bitch." The mercenary tried to strike me, but he missed.

I ducked and ran.

A gunshot cracked in the night, kicking up grass and soil by my feet.

I froze.

Drake's footsteps padded lazily behind me.

My skin crawled as he moved in front of me and reached out like a considerate confidant, taking my hand in his. "First and final warning, Eleanor Grace. Move without my permission again, and the next bullet goes into your back. You'll either die or be disabled. Either way, I'm past caring."

He jerked me into him, his palm gluing itself to mine. "I'm getting old, you see. After fucking that goddess last night, my urge for sex has been well sated. I get hard at the thought of a billion dollars, not your pussy…even if my brother has become obsessed with it. When I've had some sleep, I'm sure your little outbursts will turn me the fuck on, and I will enjoy finding out why my baby brother couldn't keep his hands off you, but I will warn you, in my current mood, I honestly don't fucking care what state you're in when I *do* fuck you. Alive, bleeding, or quadriplegic, so I suggest…" Leaning putridly close, he ran his nose along my cheekbone before whispering in my ear. "…you listen to me and be a good girl if you want to stay alive."

Tearing myself away, I tried to unlock our hands, but he dug his fingernails into my knuckles.

I *despised* him.

I cursed him with a thousand hexes.

"That goddess you *slept* with was called Jess. You shot her. She's probably dead. Just like Sully is—"

"Dead. Yes, I truly hope so. A tad inconvenient seeing as I didn't get everything I needed, but…ah, well." Flicking his gaze to the pilots behind me, he asked, "Can a man survive a fall from that height?"

I looked over my shoulder, hope flaring, despair cloying.

The pilots threw each other a look before the older, greyer one shrugged. "We were over a hundred feet high."

"So…is that a *yes* or a *no*?"

"Depends." The younger pilot scowled. "Our velocity was still increasing, the tropics mean the ocean is warm not cold…the other man fell before him and broke the surface tension of the water."

"Yes or fucking no?" Drake growled.

The older pilot shrugged again. "Depends if luck was on his side. As far as preferred conditions went…yes, he could have survived. Water temperature, breaking surface tension, and velocity all play a part in the outcome. However, bones are brittle things. If he landed head first, his neck would've snapped, and—"

"And if he landed feet first?" I interrupted, unable to listen to his morbid conclusion.

The younger pilot pinned me with an apologetic stare. "His legs are most likely broken. Feet and ankles, too. He might have survived, but…he probably won't be able to swim and will drown as a secondary cause of impact."

I went arctic blizzard cold.

A pitiful moan escaped me as Drake chuckled. "Excellent. Let's hope the bastard chokes on his precious ocean." Dragging me toward the hulking lab in the distance, he added, "Let's get this over with."

The mercenary sandwiched me next to Drake while the pilots trailed us.

The older pilot said, "We'll walk with you, Sinclair, and we agree to carry a gun, but under no circumstances are we pulling a trigger."

Drake looked behind him. "You'll do as your fucking *told*." His cold bark was smoothed by a slithering smile. "But as I said, you won't have to shoot anyone if you play your part."

"And if you don't play, I'll happily give you a different type of bonus." The mercenary with his brown buzz cut snickered, enjoying his promotion to second-in-command.

I struggled as Drake carted me up the gravel path linking the helipad with the fortified door of the laboratory.

I winced as my tender feet bruised thanks to sharp pebbles instead of silky sand. My wardrobe of a simple yellow shirt left me exposed in all the wrong ways.

Hiding my pain, swallowing back my rage at Drake, I glanced at yet another diamond in Sully's crown of islands. The building was an oddity. The largest of Sully's villas—not that it could be called a villa with its sweeping white walls, barred windows, and keypad for entry outside. It looked clinical instead of tropical. Convinced on its purpose of housing drugs and specimens rather than fading into the scenery with thatched roofs and coconut wood.

A shadow of someone walking past a window appeared and disappeared, no doubt alerted by our presence thanks to the helicopter.

Had they heard the gunfire?

Did they see me as the damsel in distress?

Was Drake right when he said the men and women on this island were test tube geeks, or were there guards standing watch?

I peered into the pruned undergrowth, searching manicured bushes and pretty flowers, hoping to see men loyal to Sully and his enterprise.

Nothing.

Choking on my disappointment, I hissed again as Drake dug his fingernails into my wrist, breaking my skin. He dragged me the final way to the forfeited door. "No one speaks. I'll do the conversing."

"Sure." The pilots nodded.

Drake shook me. "Answer me, Eleanor. You'll keep that pretty little mouth shut, won't you?"

I bit the inside of my cheek and didn't reply. Once again, I would enlist silence to be my shield. If I spoke another syllable to this creep, I'd snap.

I'd *scream.*

I'd leap on him and beat him senseless. I wouldn't stop until someone shot me.

His threats of hurting me. His joy at his brother's death.

It all pushed me closer and closer to a ledge labelled mental breakdown.

Sully…you have to be okay.

I won't stay sane if you aren't.

His fall repeated again, my scream vibrating in my skull. Over and over.

You're coming after me.

I know you are.

You're alive.

I have to believe that's true.

"*Answer* me, Eleanor." Drake shook me, his watery blue stare malicious and cold.

I pressed my lips together and arched my chin.

Fuck.

You.

"Cat got your tongue again, huh?" Drake rolled his eyes. "Whatever. Your dramatics are tiresome." Dragging me up the three steps to the door, he tucked his gun into his waistband and knocked on the sparse white entrance as a sickly grin spread over his face.

I shivered, doing my best to sense if Sully was alive or not.

I wanted the taste of conviction like I'd felt when I'd raced crazily around Jakarta. Then, I'd known that he wasn't safe. I'd felt it in my bones...but at least I'd known he was alive.

Now all I felt was a blockage.

Almost as if the man I'd fallen in love with had vanished.

Please...Sully.

An intercom crackled above us, pouring a male's voice over our shoulders. "Who the hell are you? Get off this island. It's private property."

Drake lost his grin. His pompous businessman façade crumpled as quickly as he'd conjured it. "Open the fucking door."

"You expect me to open for you when I heard a gunshot moments ago? Hell no. *Leave.* Get back in your helicopter and—"

"Open the *fucking* door," Drake snarled. "I'm a Sinclair. Your boss is my brother." He cocked his head, doing his best to rein in his temper. "You have four hundred vials of elixir, and I'm here to collect."

A long pause before the intercom crackled again. "If you're Sullivan Sinclair's brother, why didn't he come with you?"

"Because Drake's a psychopath!" I yelled. Call the police—"

"Shut the fuck *up*." Drake growled beneath his breath and lost any hint of executing this burglary with calmness. "Just remember, you made me do this." Ripping out his gun, he drove the muzzle against my temple, forcing my head sideways.

My neck blazed with discomfort, the cold bite of the weapon sending my heartbeats wild.

"Open the door, please," Drake clipped. "Otherwise, you'll hear another gunshot...and see the consequences of a bullet."

"Don't hurt her!"

The intercom screeched.

A click of a lock.

The swish of a door being opened.

Drake grinned, his lips spreading with gloating triumph as a man with a widening waistline and white lab coat appeared. "Wise choice."

Giving up his attempt at being a chameleon and playing nice, Drake looked the man up and down.

With his dumpy frame and stained lab coat, the scientist looked like a peace-loving, petri dish enthusiast who played with Bunsen burners and beakers because he didn't like the messy mayhem of the outside world.

His gaze fell on me, panic blazing through a pair of yellow-lensed glasses perched on his nose. "Look, I don't want anyone to get hurt, and I don't want any trouble. Let her go."

Drake drove the gun deeper into my temple, making my entire body twist. "I'll let her go when you give me what I want."

"I can't." The man licked his lips, nervousness making him jumpy. "You're not on the list of approved visitors. I can't just give you—"

"Give him the vials, nerd." The mercenary swung his weapon upward, pointing it directly at the scientist's face.

Oh, shit.

The scientist blanched, his hands diving into his lab pockets. "If you are who you say you are, let me call Mr. Sinclair, and he can authorise—"

"Sullivan is dead." Drake grinned. "He died in an unfortunate helicopter accident. Just like this girl, who happens to be the love of his pathetic life, will die, and then *you* will die. Every fucking geek in that stinking lab will die unless you give me four hundred vials of elixir. Right. Now."

"We have other drugs. I can give you those—"

Drake let his head fall, sighing dramatically as if the man tested his already frayed patience. "I don't *want* any other drugs. I want *that* drug. Elixir. Lust in a tiny bottle. Liquid fucking orgasms." He smiled a crocodilian grin. "My brother is dead. I am now in charge of this lab, and you work for *me*. That means whatever you've cooked is *my* property. Just like this girl is *my* property. Just like I can shoot anyone I fucking want because you all belong to *me*."

The scientist gulped. "I'll trade you."

"Trade me?" Drake laughed coldly. "For what?"

"Elixir for the girl."

His temper flashed, driving the gun deeper into my skull. "Now, why did you have to try to be a hero, huh?" He twisted the muzzle, catching my delicate flesh with the coldness of metal. "No trades. No bargains. You have one last chance to get me what I want, or not only will I shoot you, but I'll also return with an army and blow up everything on this island."

Drake smiled icily. "You might have heard the explosion a few days ago? That was my handiwork. *Serigala* is no more. So many animals…it'd be sad to add scientists to that count. Especially seeing as you still have employment working for me now that my brother is gone."

"I refuse to work for men like you—"

"Men like me?" Drake yanked my hair back, exposing my throat and running his gun down toward my breasts. "Men who aren't afraid of power? Tell you what, I'll let you choose. My version of a trade. Thanks to your refusal, Jinx here is gonna die. Do you want me to shoot her in the heart or the head? I'm more of a skull shot kinda guy, but I can—"

"Stop!" The scientist's shoulders sagged. "Please stop."

My heart couldn't figure out a healthy beat.

I expected to drown with fear. Instead, everything shut down. Everything apart from my livid *hate* for this madman.

"Told you Sullivan hired pussies," Drake muttered to his mercenary.

The pilots stood well back, their willingness to be a part of murder waning.

There had to be other men and women in the lab. Were there enough to stop Drake? I might be a lost cause, but they didn't need to be. Where were Sully's guards? Surely, he'd protect this place with a trained militia?

"Run!" I blurted. "Get help—"

Pain.

Instant walloping pain on the back of my head as Drake cracked his weapon into me.

I groaned, tumbling forward in his embrace.

"Hush." Drake stabbed the gun into my head again. "You just keep pushing my limits, don't you, Jinx?" With me prone in his control, he snarled at the guard. "Right, I'm done negotiating." With disgusting aggression, he trailed his gun from my head, down my front and kept going. Lower and lower until he dipped under the hem of the man's shirt I wore and nudged the bare lips of my sex with the muzzle.

I jerked.

Snow settled on my skin.

Shock and stupor.

Hate and horror.

I wanted to attack him, but I daren't move.

The world swam.

Sickness drowned.

How could you fight a crazy person?

How could you win against someone who had no boundaries and followed no rules?

How the hell did Sully survive a childhood with this lunatic?

Drake drove the gun deeper into me, making me moan with disgust. "Vials. Now. Or I shoot her in the cunt right here, right now. She might not die, but it would be a horrific injury, don't you agree?"

"Fine! *Fine!*" The scientist vanished into the lab, yelling at max volume for elixir.

"Finally." Drake huffed, thrusting the gun into me one last time before removing it and wiping his forehead with his arm. "Was that so difficult?"

I swayed as Drake let me go.

I swallowed back a rush of loathing, doing my best not to run or attack him.

Nasty silence fell as we waited on the stoop, listening to the quick scurry of feet in the lab. Would help arrive? Was there anyone here with a damn weapon?

A minute later, a trolley with two large boxes shot from the lab, pushed at warp speed by the poor scientist. No one else. Just a terrified chemist with no background in warfare.

"About fucking time." Drake stepped aside, jerking me with him as the trolley came to a stop, the boxes clinking and clanging with glass vials inside. "The second you get back inside that little lab of yours, I expect you to make more of this stuff."

"But I can't. Not without—"

The mercenary angled his gun at him. "Get cooking, nerd. Your new boss expects a thousand more boxes of elixir."

Drake snickered, grabbing a box and shoving it into the older pilot's hands. "Carry this, please." He gave the younger pilot the second box. "And you."

Gripping the seemingly heavy boxes, the pilots turned and practically ran back to their helicopter as if they couldn't wait to be airborne.

Four hundred vials of a heart-crippling, body-hijacking drug.
And Drake has it.
Shit.

"See ya 'round." Drake waved at the scientist, then spun me around and dug the gun into the base of my skull. "Walk, Eleanor."

I had no choice.

I walked under his instruction and away from potential help.

The mercenary protected Drake's back as we marched, sweeping his gun at the lab.

Drake won again as we piled into the helicopter and took wing.

Sullivan

Chapter Two

I WATCHED MY LIFE instead of lived it.

I watched as a man who'd just sold his soul to fury broke the surface of his ocean.

I watched as a speedboat with five police pulled up beside him in a wash of wake and bubbles.

I watched as he was pulled from the sea and deposited dripping wet and clothing sodden on a bench.

I watched as the speedboat gathered inertia, carrying its drowned passenger toward the islands that'd become his hell.

I watched as that same man fell off the side of the boat when he went to stand and found that he couldn't.

That same man felt no pain as two policemen hauled him from the shallows and carried him up the beach. He felt no comfort when a green caique landed on his head, squawking in fear, cooing for comfort. And he felt nothing but cold-hearted fury as his body was dragged into Campbell's surgery and placed upon the very same bed where Eleanor and he had slept in each other's arms.

Eleanor.

Fuck…Eleanor.

My watching shattered.

I was no longer voyeur to a man who'd lost everything.

I *was* that man who'd lost everything.

I felt the pain.

I lived the misery.

Yet…everything was distant.

Muted.

Sound far away.

Sensation dulled by the cape of absolute *rage*.

Fury.

Motherfucking fury.

I didn't care about the pats of concern or worried questioning.

I didn't speak a goddamn word as police hovered like gnats and Campbell came bowling from other patient rooms.

His white coat held streaks of crimson.

Blood.

Jealousy's blood.

The metallic life force woke me up a little more, slicing through my fury-fugue. Not entirely. Not completely. Just enough to remember how to speak, how to function, how to be a man instead of a singular emotion.

"Is she alive?" I croaked.

The police began jabbering in Indonesian, one moving close to begin his interrogation. "Mr. Sinclair, we need to know—"

"Leave." I bared my teeth. "Leave this surgery. Leave my islands. You're too fucking late."

"We weren't too late. We saved your life."

"You let my life fly fucking *away*." I quaked on the bed, the frame creaking under my soaking, furious weight. Little plops of seawater splashed on the tile, ruining the sterile environment, unwilling to relinquish me just yet.

The ocean understood me.

It was liquid in its power. It filled my veins with briny fury.

"Go!" I snarled.

"But we really must insist—"

"GO! Your questions are worthless."

"There is a dead man with a gunshot to his abdomen and yourself who, according to requests for our help, have been dealing with a coup—"

"A coup that you're too late to stop." I dropped all my guards. I stopped pretending to be tame. I revealed the nastiness, the malice, the manslaughter I wanted to reap. "Get the fuck off my island! I won't ask again."

"But—"

"LEAVE!"

The men in their matching uniforms and polished buttons

scampered. An odd sight to see—law enforcement used to being in charge and prosecuting all the rules jumping at my savage command.

I couldn't see it from their point of view.

Couldn't know that to them, I was the worst kind of case.

I was a man who'd touched death and hadn't returned. A man who now waded in graveyards and welcomed power from ghosts. A beast who no longer had any morals or desire to obey the laws of man.

I was distant.

I was unreachable.

Dr Campbell was the one to show me, to dip into my fury-blackened numbness and reveal just how far I'd fallen. "Sullivan, snap out of it. You're scaring them. And scared police are dangerous police."

I snatched the finger he dared waggle in my face. "I will ask you again. Is Jess alive?"

He nodded, yanking his hand out of my icy fist. "Barely. I'm still working on her. I need help, Sinclair. I need another doctor."

"Contact the ruins on *Serigala*. They'll send the two vets who weren't killed."

"A vet won't—"

"A vet is all you'll get." Pushing off the bed, I snarled as if every predator and monster lived within me.

My legs buckled.

Pain.

Motherfucking mind-deadening *pain*.

"Sinclair!" Campbell caught me as I plummeted toward the salt-covered tile. He couldn't hold my bulk, doing his best to slow my trajectory until we both sprawled on the floor. Pika flew around the room, jumpy and unhappy, his chirps echoing off the walls.

"Fuck!" I blinked through the curtain of charred fury, pissed off at my useless body, cracking beneath the time I was losing not chasing Drake. *"Fuck!"*

"Your leg…" Campbell pushed me away, his hands running over the same thigh with its harpoon-stitched hole. He pushed a new bump, prodded at new heat. "Without an X-ray, I can't be sure, but I think you've fractured your tibia…wait…" He worked his way down my mangled appendage. "Your ankle." He circled the new swelling, moving his inspection to my foot when I cringed. "And your foot." He palpitated my toes, each exploration finding pain, pain, motherfucking pain!

"You're in pieces, Sinclair. Your ankle is fractured, and from what I can feel, at least three metatarsals. You can't walk. Not with the harpoon hole and—"

I snatched him around the throat, squeezing mercilessly. "Give me another dose of Tritec."

His eyes flared as his hands wrapped around my wrist, doing his best to get free. "No way." He gagged as I squeezed harder. "You'll...die."

I let him go, shoving him away from me. "Get me the syringe. Don't make me ask again."

He coughed and stood, his stare saying everything. "You're not asking now."

"You're right. Get it."

"You take it and you're a dead man."

"I'm a dead man if I don't." My fists tightened into boulders. "I'm not leaving her with him. I'm done."

"Send someone else. You're in no condition—"

"Tritec, Doctor. Otherwise, I *will* rip out your goddamn throat. I still owe you for what you caused. You're a traitor. Your denial is only cementing my need to punish you."

"Christ, Sinclair." He backed away. "I told you why I did what—"

"I don't have fucking time for this!" I tried to stand and howled like an enraged bear. "The needle. Now!"

He tripped and scurried away.

It wasn't just the police afraid of me.

He was afraid of me.

Everyone was afraid of what they'd salvaged from the sea. *Good.*

I no longer wanted to be a man, bound with weakness and feeble, breakable bones.

I wanted to be the creature in the dark, the fable no one uttered, the Grim Reaper swiping the sickle himself.

Fisting the steel frame of the bed, I gritted my teeth and hauled myself upright. Seemed at least one leg remained workable from my dismount out of a flying machine. The other...it would bow to my vengeance or I'd remove it. I was done with deadweight holding me back.

Pika descended on my shoulder, his tweets and panic sounding manic in my ear as he nibbled and head butted my throat.

Campbell took his fucking time raiding the cupboard.

Each minute was a minute that Eleanor was in Drake's possession.

Each minute he could touch her, hurt her, rape her.

"The syringe!" I held out my hand, sickly sweat pouring down my temples, mixing with sea and sins. "*Now.*"

He shook his head as his hands continued to rifle through the boxes. "Reconsider, Sinclair. You've already had a dose. You don't know when that will cease working. It might cause cardiac arrest, a stroke, a coma—"

"I'm aware of the risks." I hopped toward him, spying a pair of crutches resting against the wall. "The needle and a crutch, then you're free to tend to Jealousy."

"It goes against my Hippocratic Oath, Sullivan. If I give you another dose, you. Will. Die."

"And if you don't give me another dose, *you* will die." I cocked my head. "And as much as I want your blood to flow, I need you alive to keep Jess alive." Fury tried to suck me back, to delete the pain making my head swim, to pull me away from living and return to just watching.

It was calmer that way.

Distant and remote and focused.

I fought its pull.

I needed one last weapon before I allowed myself to succumb completely.

I snapped my fingers, jolting Campbell into action. "Last chance."

"Jesus Christ." Finding the right box, he pulled it free, ignoring the yellow and red warning sticker. A label coloured with dangerous pigments to alert the user of how risky its contents were. Warnings of death and serious complications.

The drug was another form of elixir with irreversible side effects. A tonic and stimulant—a brew that had the power to disable pain and enable the user to do what was necessary before they succumbed.

I didn't care about the price.

I didn't worry about the future.

All that mattered was *her.*

In Drake's hands.

Too far for me to protect her.

Facing a future of pain and horror and—

"Fucking *do it*, Jim."

"For God's sake." Campbell grabbed a crutch on his way past, handing it to me and placing the box of potentially lethal injections on the bed. Selecting one, he unwrapped it, uncapped it, tapped out any air, and tore open an alcohol swab from his pocket.

Pika fluttered to the bed, squeaking grimly, his beady black eyes intelligent enough to understand something dangerous was happening. Something he didn't like.

Campbell's jaw clenched. His hand lowered. "If I administer this, the percentage of you surviving are—"

"I know the math." I held out my arm. "Do it."

"What if it's not enough to get her back? To win?"

"It will be. I'll make sure of it."

"She won't be happy if you save her only to die a few hours later."

"She doesn't have a choice in the matter." I narrowed my eyes. "Once she's safe and Drake is dead, nothing else matters anymore."

"*Love* matters, Sullivan. Love can change you. It's already changed—"

"Love is dead if I delay any longer!" I hoisted my arm higher, ignoring my chugging heart and the quiet whisper of sanity. I could be buying Eleanor's life with my own.

And I would take that trade.

Because I refused to go back to the man I'd been.

I hated who I was.

No existence was possible for me unless Eleanor was in my world.

That was the point of a sacrifice. It wasn't noble. It wasn't heroic.

It was *selfish*.

Just like every other emotion a human being could conjure.

I would die because I was selfish and couldn't bear to live in a world without her.

Campbell sighed and swiped the swab over my bicep. With steady hands from a lifetime of being a doctor, he punctured my skin, pressed the plunger, and shot the golden contents into my bloodstream.

The second the needle had emptied, he tossed it into a biohazard bin and raked both hands through his hair. "I don't know what the hell I'm doing here anymore."

"Go back and keep Jess alive." Using the crutch, I hopped across his surgery to the phone resting on the wall. A landline.

Archaic in this day and age but technology I was grateful for.

Dialling a number I knew by heart, I waited until it connected with my hangar in Jakarta. The second Ametung answered, I growled, "Hire twenty mercenaries who aren't afraid of getting their hands dirty. Use Quietus—their details are still on file."

Pika tried to bite the cord, dangling upside down with his usual antics. I needed to console him. To offer some sort of commiseration that I was still his, even if every part of me was cloaked in rage.

But if I let empathy enter my soul in my current predicament…it wouldn't just be my broken bones destroying me.

Eleanor…

"Anything else?" Ametung asked.

"Prepare the jet. Get the crew ready. I'm on my way."

"Consider it done."

I hung up.

I marched outside even as Cal's voice followed me from his bed in the recovery ward. "Hey, *sir*. Sully!"

I didn't stop.

"Go to Skittles, Pika. You can't follow me where I'm going."

I once again leapt from my body.

I let fury be my master.

The bird studied me, cursed me, lost me. He squeaked, then gave up on me, flying away from a demon.

I inhaled hard.

Tritec iced through my veins, numbing me, freeing me.

Free to bathe in blood and turn into a nightmare.

I took my place above such mundane activities of men.

I played chess from my place of watching, cursing my physical weakness as I hobbled with a crutch, walking on a broken leg, fractured ankle, and foot, slowly standing taller as Tritec-87 kicked in.

Heartbeat by heartbeat, breath by breath, the pain receded, the panic deleted, and fury welcomed me back.

My pawn had become a knight.

I was ready for the final checkmate.

I'm coming, Eleanor.

I'm coming…

Chapter Three

THE HUMAN PSYCHE HAD always intrigued me.

From the dynamics in the school playground to the ethics within work environments, human nature was a fickle beast.

I'd seen the same theme while travelling.

Some people could accept rules with no complaint while others boycotted the mere whisper of boundaries. Those who were used to travel had the inherent ability to adapt to a new situation while those who'd never stepped out of their comfort zone panicked at the slightest unforeseen change.

I liked to think I was skilled at adaptation. I hadn't always been that way—I'd started off naïve and passive, my life unopen to challenge and change.

But now…I had no such qualms.

I gave up trying to predict or control.

There was no predicting or controlling when you were someone's prisoner.

Either by a man who bought your life and ended up stealing your heart, or by his brother who threatened your existence and wielded sadism as a personal skill.

I had no say in how I would be treated, no way to stop men from thinking they could own me, and even if I did, Drake wasn't predictable because he operated outside the usual parameters of human psyche. He had no switch inside to prevent him from doing terrible things, no empathy to stop him from hurting others, and no rationale to reason with.

He was just evil.

Simple and stupidly evil.

I stayed silent as he flew me away from Sully's archipelago and into the heart of Jakarta. He returned me to a city that'd done its best at blocking me from Sully. He dragged me from one winged machine to another one, stuffing me onboard a private plane where another two mercenaries waited on the tarmac to greet us.

The helicopter pilots didn't say goodbye, both their faces relieved to no longer be employed by a madman.

The boxes of elixir were stowed in the back of the plane, the engines kicked into life, the new captain and first officer prepared to fly us to who knew where, and Drake sat heavily in the luxurious cream seat across the aisle from me.

His outburst on *Monyet* and his success at stealing Sully's elixir had drained him of his reserves, and the moment the plane switched from taxiing to soaring into the star-dusted sky, he pressed a button on his chair, reclined to horizontal, draped a blanket over his body, and growled at his three mercenaries, "She moves, you shoot her."

The click of three safeties being flicked off echoed even louder than a Boeing engine.

I stiffened in my seat, my heart chugging, my mind skipping between past, present, and future, and Drake completely discounted me.

He fell asleep with a smug grin on his face, revealing yet another side to his nature.

This asshole needed to get his way in all things. He was a vindictive, nasty boy who'd never been disciplined, yet he could let down his guard and sleep beside a girl who couldn't stop plotting ways to kill him.

Of stabbing him with a fork.

Of strangling him with my seatbelt.

Of kicking him in the balls so hard they ruptured and bled out.

I *needed* him to die.

It was a visceral longing.

Something I chewed and choked on.

His every breath stole one from Sully. Two brothers genetically linked and bound—a symbolic bind that said one couldn't survive while the other existed. It was either Drake or Sully.

Yin and yang.

Light and dark.

And if I can just kill this bastard, Sully will be okay.

I still couldn't sense if Sully was alive or not.

And the farther I travelled from him, the more that panic grew.

Why can't I feel him?

Had I ever been able to sense him, or had I been romanticizing that in Jakarta when Sully had sent me away?

Sully…you better be okay.

I'm begging you.

My eyelids drooped as time ticked onward, and the monotonous sound of flying deadened the outside world.

I'd somehow stayed awake after suffering elixir through sheer willpower and then necessity. I'd fought my every need and walked beside Sully while he'd carried Jess to Dr Campbell's.

It'd been the *hardest* thing.

But I did it because I'd been such a hindrance to Sully when he'd tried to rescue me. I'd been dangerous and reckless, and my insides were still covered in slimy shame for what I'd made him do.

Having sex in front of those men.

Making him share me with strangers and their greedy gazes.

Ugh.

I wished I could delete my actions and get on my knees with atonement.

Walking beside him—staying awake despite elixir's toll—had been my apology to him. My oath that I would be strong for him after he'd been so damn strong for me.

And I would continue being strong because regardless if Sully was alive or not…I didn't have any other choice.

I wouldn't lay down and take this.

I wouldn't permit a man like Drake to steal my damn life.

It didn't matter that my heart still skipped unnervingly or sometimes tripped into ribs, keeping it trapped. It didn't matter that my dealings with Drake kept adrenaline coasting through my veins when I was wrung out, strung out, and afraid I wouldn't have the capacity to remain brave.

Elixir had left my body a wasteland of bruises and truant heartbeats, but I would never complain of my ills because…Sully.

Before he'd been pushed out of a damn helicopter, he'd already had more cuts, scars, contusions, and stitches than I'd ever endured in my entire life. He'd staggered beneath torture and marched against his enemies without ever bemoaning or giving in.

For all his faults, Sully had been stripped of every mask he'd ever donned and his soul had been revealed. A soul I'd known existed the moment I saw him kiss Pika. A soul that would do absolutely anything to protect those he loved.

If he was alive…I had no doubt he would come for me. I didn't have to second-guess or pretend our relationship didn't hold the same value to him. The only problem was…he would come for me no matter the personal cost. It wouldn't matter if he had one foot in this world and one in a coffin; if he still breathed…*he'll come.*

And that terrified me as well as mollified because if he *did* chase me. If he once again put me over his pain, he might be sentencing me to a future I wouldn't be able to survive.

Drake's touch could never break me.

Drake's rape, Drake's torment, Drake's ownership…they were just tremors in my life. Tiny earthquakes that had no strength to topple my inner towers or open giant fissures in my psyche.

But if Sully came…and if Sully lost…that would be an earthquake far too catastrophic to withstand.

But I need him *to come.*

I have to believe we'll both be okay.

Ugh, stop!

I rubbed at my stinging eyes.

Focus. Get through this. Worry when it's tomorrow.

Slouching in my seat, I once again fought the heavy weight on my eyelashes.

Sleep.

No!

Not with him next to me.

You have to sleep…you've run out of miracles.

My body knocked impatiently for rest, hammering on the door of my mind and slipping quietly past my worries to drag me closer to unconsciousness.

I *wanted* to sleep.

I *needed* to rest so my brain stopped being foggy and my body repaired. Sleep wasn't just a luxury but a necessity, but how the hell was I supposed to close my eyes in *his* presence?

The idea of sleeping next to Sully had taken me time to accept…I could never be that vulnerable next to Drake.

Never.

My visions bounced as I struggled to focus. My heart continued to trip and skip. My head ached from being hit, and my limbs weighed five times their usual mass.

Sleep, Ellie.

No!

I gritted my teeth, fighting off the sleepy smog.

I looked out the oval window at the endless carpet of sea, clouds, and stars. The moon turned an otherwise dark vista into a silvery masterpiece, etching clouds, highlighting the world in monochrome.

If I could just focus on that…*I can stay awake.*

"Would you like something to eat?"

I whipped my head from the outside and blinked at an airhostess. She swayed a little in my sleepy stare.

I blinked again, stifling a yawn.

Where had she come from?

She held a tray with a foil-covered plate and a bottle of apple juice. She passed it to me, pulling a table from my armrest. "Here. You look exhausted."

Everything was sluggish.

Scents of food wafted from the foil.

My stomach growled.

I might not be able to sleep, but I should nourish my body. I would do whatever it took to survive the turbulence that existed in my future.

I had no idea how long this flight would last or where Drake was taking me. I had some idea of what he'd do to me when we arrived, and I had a lot of fear over what state I'd be in once he'd had his fill, but all I could currently control was keeping my strength up, so I could fight when the time came.

Sully….

My appetite flickered as nausea returned.

The airhostess, with her carefully coiled blonde hair, murmured, "It's beef ragu, my favourite. Enjoy."

No…

My shoulders rolled.

I didn't bother peeling away the foil.

Padding away in high heels so impractical for long hours in the sky, the stewardess deposited food to the mercenaries behind me, filling the cabin with the scent of dinner. The stench of cow flesh and slaughter.

I already battled sickness not knowing Sully's fate. It

increased tenfold as I swallowed, my stomach gurgling with revulsion.

I couldn't sleep *or* eat.

What would I give to enjoy a spread of vegetarian fare from Sully's gardens? What would I trade to sit on Sully's deck overlooking Nirvana and share a simple, sweet veggie dinner with him?

Skittles would be there.

Pika, too.

Cal and Jealousy, goddesses and guests.

The world I'd tried to change suddenly no longer seemed so horrendous. I'd been so close to granting Sully's freedom, so close to freeing his goddesses, showing him a happier way of life, and claiming my forever.

The hot afternoons wallowing in the sea were gone. The belly-clenching desire of lust was trivial. The ark of hoofed and winged creatures that Sully conjured whenever he touched me had all died a violent death.

Sully…

Please be alive.

I sighed.

But if you're hurt…don't come after me.

Don't trade your life for mine.

Don't be a hero.

Please…

With tears distorting the sky, I returned to staring out the window.

* * * * *

I'd fallen asleep.

For all my convictions that I could never let down my guard and be so vulnerable in Drake's presence, the choice had been taken away from me.

My body didn't request it.

It just took it.

Knocking me out until I slumped in my chair, leaving me a jumbled doll just waiting to be snatched up and played with again.

I woke with a jolt as the false sense of stability was interrupted as tyres hit tarmac and the plane landed.

The mercenaries shifted behind me as I sat taller in my seat, rubbing away sleep and trying to focus outside. An airport with Arabic script welcomed us, the private plane taxiing to a private hangar away from the main hub.

Dubai.

As the engines cut off, the pilots came over the intercom. "Please stay in your seats. We're just refuelling and will continue our flight to Geneva."

Geneva?

What the hell is in Geneva?

Sullivan

Chapter Four

I ROLLED MY WRIST in the new dawn, sunlight streaming in through the airplane windows.

A Hawk diamond sparkled in my cufflink. My charcoal cashmere suit was pressed and perfect. My black shirt deliberately chosen to hide bloodstains.

To the twenty lethal mercenaries behind me, I looked like I always did. A magistrate of my empire, a man no one dared tango with, an untouchable scoundrel who'd left the public eye of pharmaceuticals and cloistered upon a hidden island.

Just as my islands hid what I truly was, my suit hid my wounds.

The skin around my wrist glistened in the sun. Parts of the bloody mess from struggling in Drake's handcuffs had scabbed and dried, and others continued to crack and ooze platelets. My body, with its myriad of injuries, had focused on different areas to repair.

The only difference was, I felt none of it.

I rolled my wrist again, marvelling at my deadened senses.

One dose of Tritec had helped mute the inconceivable agony of a harpoon hole and acid burns on my chest. It'd allowed my system to accept the never-ending burn in my chemically doused eyes, to hear past the chilli that'd been shoved into my eardrums, to function on a level that'd allowed me to kill men, rescue Jinx, and then fuck her away from deaths' greedy claws.

I'd thought the injection had been a godsend then.

But now…

After a second dose?

I didn't know if I'd created a compound even more valuable than elixir…or something a hundred times more devastating. A drug like this could create robots out of men. It could march wounded soldiers back into battle. It could cultivate a taskforce of terrifying, agony-immune individuals.

The second dose hadn't just numbed my every pain, it'd granted razor-sharp focus, whip-quick conclusions, and the ability to operate at a level most men only dreamed of.

I was in survival mode.

Every part of me that wasn't essential to survival had shut down. My appetite. My lethargy. My panic over Eleanor's fate. Those were things that would detract from my single-mindedness. From my triumph.

Eleanor would soon be mine again.

I was only an hour or so behind.

My private plane had taken off with my hired staff whose skills lay in knife play and gunshots, and my pilots had followed the jet stream of my brother.

It also helped I had someone from air traffic control on my payroll. Someone who fed me Drake's intended location and his flight manifest.

Geneva.

Out of the five estates our parents had left him, that was the most populated. A regal manor house built by one of the founding businessmen in 1814. It'd been the crown in my parents' portfolio for its connection to the first apothecary and subsequent base for the successful hub of pharmaceuticals within the Swiss country.

They'd likened themselves to pharmacists who'd tramped jungles and tested exotic plants to find cures no one had ever considered. They were pompous enough to claim ties to such prestige and purchased the house to be their second residence after their one in the States.

It was fitting that Drake had taken Eleanor there.

Fitting because, in that house, Drake had poured gallons of petrol into the private pond, killing every fish, frog, and swan. Why? Just because he could. He'd killed innocence there. He thought he could kill Eleanor.

He's wrong.

Dropping my arm, no longer intrigued by the empty sensation of a body that ought to pound with pain, I snatched up my phone.

It wasn't my usual one. That one I'd left on the sandy pathway while I'd carried an elixir-high Eleanor to the ocean to make our escape.

This one was a clone—complete with all my apps but empty of historical data.

I couldn't call Eleanor to tell her to hold on.

So…I called the only other person I trusted.

"Nice of you to fly off without me, you bastard," Cal muttered on the second ring.

"You're a hindrance in your current state."

"Campbell told me about your broken pieces. At this point, I'm guessing I'd be more helpful than you."

I smiled, enjoying the ice in my veins, embracing the coolness of my strangely anesthetized skin. "I'm operating at full capacity. Possibly even better."

"Because of the second dose of Tritec-87. Yes, I heard about that, too. Campbell is quite worried." His voice lowered with seriousness. "He said you need a defibrillator close by, Sinclair. You need a doctor shadowing your every move for when your heart gives out." He cleared his throat. "If they catch you when you go into cardiac arrest, they might be able to reset your system and stop you from dying—"

I scoffed, interrupting him. "Don't worry about me. Worry about yourself and those gunshots of yours."

"I'm being serious. If you die, I will…I'll…I'll fucking take Eleanor for my own and see if that doesn't drag you out of a grave. I'll marry her, Sinclair, just to spite you."

My heart gave one heavy pound. That was it. A tiny flicker. The drug that'd coated my nervous system had not only chloroformed my pain receptors but also my ability to rise to infectious emotions.

I'd always wanted to be completely apathetic.

I'd gotten my wish.

"See, a threat like that might've worked…if I hadn't been watching."

"Watching what?"

"I've seen you eyeing Jealousy lately."

"*What?*" He coughed. "What the fuck are you implying?"

"I'm saying I'm not the only one who's been tending to a goddess after serving in Euphoria."

"Who the hell told you?"

I shrugged. "Just observant. You've never provided aftercare for a goddess before."

"Neither had you."

"Until I fell in love."

"You're a sneaky son of a bitch."

"I'm sorry, Cal. I'm sorry Jess is—"

"She'll be fine. And if she isn't, my threat still stands. If she dies and you die…then Eleanor and I can just be miserable together."

Cricking my neck, I ceased unnecessary chatter.

If I died, I wanted Drake's cold heart in my fist beforehand.

And for Cal's sake, I hoped Jess would pull through. What he did on his downtime was not my business, but he did deserve to be happy. I'd half expected him to come and request for Jealousy to stop serving in Euphoria. If he was falling for her, watching her fuck other men would steadily drive him insane.

But…after today, he wouldn't have to worry about that.

If she survived, she'd never serve another guest again.

Not because I owed her the greatest debt for what she'd done with Drake but because I'd learned my lessons on exploitation.

"Enough gossip. This isn't a social call." I looked around, ignoring my crutch wedged against the emergency exit and the men of all shapes and skills sitting in expensive seats. The private plane was large enough for my army along with an arsenal. "We need to discuss business."

"What business? I'm stuck in a recovery ward with bloody parrots. I can't do shit—"

"First, an update on Campbell's patients. How *is* Jess doing? Skittles still healing?"

Cal's tone turned tight and full of strain. "He still isn't sure if she'll make it. He has the two vets from *Serigala* here helping him. And yes, your damn caiques are twittering away in the corner, preening each other."

I cricked my neck, keeping my fractured, sewn-together leg splayed out in front of me. "Tell him to give Jealousy a dose of Tritec…it's rather something. It's…helped."

"Of course, it's helped. It's a powerful blend of narcotics and—"

"What I'm feeling isn't fake."

"No, but it will extract the worst kind of toll."

I shrugged. I didn't care about that. As long as Drake was dead and Eleanor was safe, *fine*. I'd had this coming for most of my life. I didn't deserve a long existence. I wasn't owed peace and prosperity, love and longevity.

This was my karma, and I'd accepted that.

So long as Eleanor didn't pay on my behalf, I wouldn't begrudge the few days I had left to make amends for what I'd done.

"Are the police still there?"

"Yes." Cal sniffed. "Snooping. Asking questions."

"Call Arbi to keep the goddesses confined on *Lebah*. Don't let them back onto *Batari* before they're gone."

"Already called him and advised to stay hidden."

"And the guests?"

"I'll arrange private transfers to Jakarta. You can deal with refunds and threats when you're back."

I shook my head. "I'm not coming back, Cal."

"Like fuck you aren't, *sir*."

"You know my passwords. You've helped run Goddess Isles since conception." I pinched the bridge of my nose, saying goodbye to what I'd built. I wouldn't be there to make amends and dismantle my mistakes, but Cal could try to fix my wrongs. "If I'm right that you're developing feelings for Jess, I'm glad. Make sure Campbell keeps her breathing. I know I haven't shown my appreciation for your help over the years, but I am thankful. You're a good man, Calvin, and that's why I trust you to carry out my last request."

"Tritec is messing with you. Last request? You're not allowed to have a last request because you're coming back."

"Regardless, there are loose ends that need to be finished."

"What loose ends?"

"When the police have left, release the girls."

"What?"

"Let them go."

"*All* of them?"

"All of them."

"But—"

"Release them with the usual fee and warning. Shut down the dark web, revoke all future bookings, end it. End all of it."

"But Euphoria—"

"Burn it to the ground."

"Fuck no."

"When you're able, visit *Monyet* and stop the production of elixir. They won't be able to finish the next batch without me anyway, so the danger of it dies with me. Tell Peter Beck to use the rest of his ingredients and put it toward some other cure."

Cal's tone grew angry. "You expect me just to delete your life? Just like that."

"Call it a final decree from a dead man."

"If you play it smart and keep a defibrillator close—"

"Thanks for your service, Cal. And for your friendship."

"Sullivan, don't." His anger slipped into urgency. "She'll never forgive you. You die on her, and she'll—"

"Hate me, yes." I looked out the window at the snow-dusted rooftops of a city sprawled beneath us.

Geneva.

Switzerland.

The location of my end.

"It's better she hates me than loves me. Remember? Everything that loves me ends up dying. Everything that I love I end up killing. This way…I'll break the chain. She'll be free. I'll be free. My goddesses will be free. Jess and you will be free."

The landing gear whirred from the fuselage beneath my feet.

My heart picked up a quicker patter, still cushioned from spikes of stress thanks to Tritec.

Messy emotions would not get in the way of me eradicating Drake.

Fury would not make me sloppy.

Weakness would not make me fail.

Not this time.

This time, I would win.

I was ruthless.

Heartless.

Ready.

I'd said my farewells and given my blessings.

I'm coming, Eleanor.

"Goodbye, Cal. And thank you."

Chapter Five

I WAS GRATEFUL, EVEN in this nightmare.

Grateful for the sleep I'd gotten on the plane and the handful of grapes I'd stolen as we'd walked through a house full of Regency elegance. Grateful for the renewed vigour from rest and fructose. Grateful for the warmth of the residence after the bite of winter outside.

Drake led the way, strolling arrogantly through a house that'd been here long before the other suburbs. As we'd driven from the airport, behind blackened windows of a fortified SUV, I'd looked into the driveways of quaint houses and manicured lawns of cramped subdivisions, parcels of land getting smaller the larger the city became.

Not this house.

This house had a guard turret at the bottom of a long sweeping driveway. This house had frost-sprinkled oak trees lining the expansive snowy lawns and a large pond glittering with ice in the distance.

Drake hadn't said a word as he'd dragged me up the stone steps and over a double door threshold with carved angels in the wood.

Angels…*how ironic.*

Perhaps, it was Lucifer instead. The fallen one who'd turned his tricks to treachery instead of scripture.

The foyer held double-height ceilings with huge architraves

and heavy brocade on the walls. The parlour matched with equally impressive doorways and sweeping views over boxed hedgerows and military-precise cut lawn with snow pushed to the side in drifts. The kitchen held a fruit bowl overflowing with offerings—where I snagged my grapes—while cabinets glistened with a pearly veneer.

Each room held hints to its history but also buckled beneath modern styling.

"Set it up in here," Drake commanded as he hauled me into another lounge, this one deeper and darker than the rest. A tomb within a home. Navy wallpaper and black ceiling; spotlights highlighted a library on one wall and oppressive artwork of hunts and hounds on the other.

Watery sunlight did its best to illuminate the shadowy corners, but we were no longer in the tropics, and the sun had a weaker quality. It was grey light not golden. Sad light not hopeful.

It set my teeth on edge. My empty stomach snarled.

"Grab a curtain tieback," Drake snapped as his hired goons deposited the boxes of elixir onto the chaise by the pine-cone-filled fireplace. No flames licked at the stone façade or gave off cheery heat. But the house wasn't cold, so some form of heating had to be operational to keep the wintery chill at bay.

A mercenary arrived with a plaited rope of velvet matching the sapphire drapes.

The blue reminded me of Sully.

Of his eyes as they filled with ardent hunger.

Of his need as he undressed me.

Are you alive, Sully?

I swallowed hard, blocking out thoughts of him.

I needed to stay on guard, on edge.

The moment the mercenary dropped the tieback into Drake's hand, he came toward me and chuckled. "I was contemplating playing together tomorrow. After all, we've lived through a lot, you and me." Drake took my hand, kissing my knuckles as if he could convince me he was a gentleman of the manor courting me. "However, I've learned that waiting for what you want only leads to disappointment. I'm done waiting. So…I'm taking." He rose from his slight bow over my hand. "I'm taking you, and you'll be happy to know my libido has returned in full fervour thanks to the long rest on the plane."

Grabbing my wrist, he dragged me forward until he forced my palm against the erection in his crinkled trousers.

Shuddering, I tried to pull away.

"I'm hard at the very thought of what we're about to do, Eleanor. Gonna taste what's got my brother in such a tizzy." Dropping to one knee, he ran his hands down my hips, thighs, and calves until he reached my ankle.

I kept myself locked down. To not react to his heinous touch. To not ram my palm into his nose. We weren't alone. Men with guns patrolled. Until I had some chance of winning, I had to bide my time.

Wrapping the curtain tieback around my left leg, he pushed me backward until I bumped against a heavily embroidered aquamarine silk couch. Everything was so stuffy compared to the driftwood furniture and seagrass rugs of Sully's villas. The walls were too thick. The colours too dense.

The large room seemed to squeeze around me as Drake tied me to the couch leg, imprisoning me like some unwanted pet who wasn't allowed to jump on the décor.

Standing, he grinned. "Just so you don't get any ideas while we set up." His dark hair was as rumpled as his clothing. Shadows under his eyes, spite bracketing his mouth. A spoiled little asshole who needed to die.

"You know what? I'll tie your hands too. Just to be safe." Clicking his fingers at the younger mercenary, he barked, "Another tieback."

The request was brought.

Drake jerked me to my feet, the mercenary trapped my hands together, and Drake wrapped the velvet around and around until I was bound.

"Nice and snug?" Drake kissed the top of my shoulder, suffocating me with his conceited pride.

Had he noticed I hadn't spoken a word to him since *Monyet*?

Did he care that I'd slipped into silence for protection and mockery?

As long as I kept my tongue quiet, I would not give him extra ammunition against me.

He already has enough.

"Close the doors." Drake snapped his fingers as he opened another box that his goons brought in, rifling through the contents to fist sensors for Euphoria.

So he'd been coherent enough to take Sully's virtual reality equipment too.

Shit.

The sounds of three sets of doors closing sent my heart skyrocketing. I looked over my shoulder as locks were turned and any concept of escape was barred.

Drake scowled at the five men in the room. "Three of you get out. Two can stay." Arching his chin at the mercenary who'd been in the helicopter and *Monyet* with us and an older guy with a salt and pepper beard, he ordered, "You two, you stay. The rest leave. Stand guard outside." He chuckled, almost as an afterthought. "There are staff in this house, by the way. Don't shoot them. I need them to be at my beck and call."

The three unselected men nodded and slipped through the double doors back into the first living room we'd passed. The buzz-cut guy marched over and locked them, trapping me in hell with three men.

It wasn't the men who scared me.

It was a tiny mundane vial that held nightmares.

The same vial that Drake plucked from its four hundred bedfellows and stalked toward me. "You hungry, sexy goddess?"

I pursed my lips and didn't reply.

"I can have my chef cook you anything you want. I saw you snag a few of my grapes, so I know you are."

It's a trap. A trick.

And if it wasn't, I wouldn't allow him to take any other liberties with me. Raping me? Drugging me? That was one thing. *Feeding* me? Pretending to care if I stayed alive?

No. *No way.*

That was the worst kind of blasphemy.

He ran his hand through my hair, making hate flow in my blood.

"We have swans on the property. Rodents too if they haven't scurried away for winter. Or I can have the butcher cut up a lamb, a cow, a chicken…how about a turkey? Do you like turkey?" He cupped my chin, running his thumb over my bottom lip. "Ask me for anything and I'll give it to you. I'll feed you before I fuck you…on one condition." He leaned forward, pressing a dry, rancid kiss to my mouth.

I ripped my face away, glowering at him.

"Whatever you request, it has to have a heartbeat. No vegetables or vegan shit. Meat and only meat." He laughed as he deposited the sensors on the same couch I was tied to, opening each and pulling out their contents. "You'll be staying with me for a few weeks until I tire of you. You'll be using up a lot of energy in our…sexual perversions. You'll need to eat eventually." He grinned, eyeing me up and down. "Don't worry, you'll eat flesh to stay alive. Even Sully used to eat meat in his youth."

I didn't speak.

I balled my hands and stared past him to the drawn sapphire curtains. The older mercenary had pulled them over the watery sunlight, embalming us completely in the sarcophagus this house had become.

"Has he told you when his last bite of meat was?" Drake continued to arrange the sensors. "I was there, you know. I was the reason it was his last." His sickly smirk promised I wouldn't like this trip down memory lane.

"He somehow rescued a sheep. Don't ask me how. He was always bringing home beasts he wasn't supposed to. He thought he kept them hidden from me…silly brother. I watched him for a while with that sheep. I spied while he bottle-fed it. I rolled my eyes as he sourced hay in the city for a countryside creature. He was so fucking proud of that mangy woolly thing. So…it was only fitting I used it to teach him another lesson."

He straightened with importance. "After all, that's what big brothers do, don't they? We guide and teach our younger siblings. Our parents were too busy with the company to bother us most days. Who else would Sullivan have learned from?"

His hands landed on my yellow shirt.

The only thing covering me. The only protection I had.

I braced myself for him to pop the buttons and tear it off me. Instead, he slowly unbuttoned me, his knuckles grazing my nipples, his proximity making me sick.

The velvet rope around my ankle made me prickle with hate and horror. If I wasn't tied, I could try to run, but I wouldn't get far. Either Drake would catch me or a gun would kill me.

Just breathe.

It will be over soon…

Just…breathe.

Sucking in a harsh breath, I swallowed back my despair and glowered with every loathing as Drake continued to unbutton me. "I killed that sheep personally. Unlike Sullivan, I've never been squeamish about animal blood." He licked his lips as he finished with the buttons and spread open my shirt.

The lemon material gaped and clung to my shoulders, then skated traitorously down my arms and dangled off my elbows, unable to fall to the floor from my bound hands.

Drake didn't seem to care, gawking at my nakedness.

I hated him.

Fuck, I *hated* him.

The natural reaction to gag gave away just how repulsive I found him.

My nostrils flared.

Fear prickled.

My nipples peaked.

Panic built.

"You find my brother attractive…yet you act as if I'm an ogre." He licked his lips with undisguised lust, reaching out to fist my breast. "Don't worry, pretty Eleanor. You'll be begging me soon enough. Just like Sullivan learned to beg."

Pinching my nipple with cruel fingernails, he bared his teeth. "Back to my story. Where was I? Oh, yes. The lamb." He grinned. "I killed that lamb and dumped the carcass in the kitchen. I helped the family chef prepare it—said it was a special dinner for my baby brother. He came home from wherever the fuck he spent his days and tried to ignore me like he always did. However, both parents were at home that night, and they insisted on a family dinner."

He twisted my nipple, making me flinch, his touch as grotesque as his tale.

"Sullivan picked at his meal—he was always a fussy eater, even when he was fourteen. But our parents devoured that lamb. They sang its praises. Boasted how juicy and tender it was. And I had the perfect stage to clap my brother on the back and thank him for raising the best tasting lamb in our county."

He laughed blackly. "Should've seen him, Eleanor. He bolted from that table and ran all the way to the bottom of the garden where he thought he'd hidden his woolly friend. I'd left the carcass there for him. Rather nice of me, don't you think? Allowing him to say his goodbyes."

Letting my breast go, he ran his finger along his cheek where a silver scar of his own glittered in the lowlights of this crypt. "Can you believe, he grabbed a leg bone and struck me with it, the bastard. He attacked me quicker than I could defend myself. Drew blood and everything."

He smirked as he reached for the earbud box and pulled out both sensors. "That was the first time our parents blew up at Sullivan instead of me for violence. They grounded him. Took me to the hospital—I had to have ten stitches—and then they sat us down and made us promise we'd be better siblings. That we would stop our war over things they couldn't understand."

Drake's voice faded somewhat as he shoved the earbuds inside my ears. He'd learned how the sensors worked. He didn't ask permission to tether me to a virtual reality that would undoubtedly ruin me. He didn't stop talking about the past as he smeared the scent deceptor under my nose and rubbed oil into my nakedness. "You know…you're the first girlfriend he's ever had."

His fingers encroached in places I begged to wash with bleach.

He stroked me indecently.

He spun me around and kissed the back of my neck, nuzzling into my hair as he squeezed my ass with oily hands. "I can't wait to see what made you so special." He grabbed both my breasts from behind, making me jolt.

The two mercenaries watched from their posts by the doors.

Yet another experience where men watched me get fucked.

The only problem was…I would rather I put on any kind of show for them if only they'd kill Drake so he stopped touching me.

"Do you have any idea what it's like to have a brother who's such a fucking reject? A *vegetarian*. An animal lover. A cunt who didn't even like his own species enough to get laid."

Wiping his hands on his trousers, he grabbed the fingerprint sensors. Staring at the sheet of touch-deception stickers, he rolled his eyes. "We don't need this one, do we? When you touch me, I want you to know it's me you're touching and not him."

He chuckled again as he threw the sheet away and grabbed the eye lenses. Screwing open the small containers, he loomed over me.

The binds on my wrists bit into me as I struggled to protect myself.

It took everything I had not to bite him as he attempted to drop the lens into my eyes. I squeezed them closed, tilting my head away.

No way would I enable this.

"Bill, come here. You and whatever his name is finish putting those in her eyes."

The two mercenaries came forward.

There was no squirmish or battle. The older one grabbed me, smearing the oil on my skin as he dug painful fingers into my eye socket and ripped open my eyelid, while the buzz-cut one plopped the lens directly over my pupil in a choreographed move that left me completely at their mercy.

No!

I blinked as the world distorted.

I bit down on a scream as the other lens was inserted.

By the time they let me go and I could see through the haze, Drake stood before me naked. His cock still held redness from being with Jess so many times and his belly held muscles not nearly as defined as Sully's.

A few odd-shaped scars rested over his hip bones hinting that it wasn't just his face that'd received plastic surgery. Liposuction was also possible.

He caught me looking, his vain ego preening. "Like my cock, Jinx? It's the last one you'll have before you die."

I raised my bound hands.

Don't do it.

Don't.

I held up one finger.

I didn't speak but my message was clear.

Fuck.

You.

He just chuckled, quickly shoving earbuds in his own ears and lenses over his eyes. "Oh, I plan on fucking you right back, don't you worry about that." Dumping handfuls of oil over himself, he applied the nasal deceptor and swirled the mouthwash…wanting the full experience. However, he didn't bother with the fingerprint sensors…wanting to touch me instead of a fantasy.

"Right then." He smiled with his head cocked. "I think it's time we begin our little fuck session, don't you?" Palming the vial of elixir he'd left out of my reach, he clucked his tongue. "Oh, almost forgot." Ducking to pick up his trousers on the floor, he pulled free a cell phone.

A phone that was familiar.

Shit.

Sully…

He nodded, seeing where my thoughts had strayed. "I found it on the path when we came searching for my wayward brother. Imagine my surprise that the screen was still unlocked, the Euphoria app still open, and all ready to load another fantasy." He wriggled the screen in front of me, revealing lines of code and a load button.

The app that I'd seen Sully typing into each time before he'd sent me under was a travesty.

If he's figured out how to use that...

"I've been playing with it while you slept from Dubai to Geneva." He ran his thumb over the screen. "Pretty sure I just press this button and whoever is wearing the sensors is whisked away to play." He carefully placed the phone onto the couch, too far for me to stomp and smash it.

"One final thing before we leave, though." His actions slipped into fatal as he uncapped the tiny vial of elixir and stepped into me. "Drink up."

His thigh went between mine.

His erection wedged against my belly.

Our skin sucked together with oil.

I inhaled deeply, doing my best to fill my lungs with oxygen.

Not again.

Not again!

Dr Campbell said another dose of elixir and I might die.

No!

Drake cupped the back of my head, his fingers digging hard. "Don't fight. I'll just hurt you until you swallow." Yanking my hair, he jerked my spine into an unnatural bow.

Tears sprang to my eyes.

Pain ricocheted down my back.

The vial pressed between my lips.

"No. Don't. It will stop my heart." My first words in hours. A beg for my life from the devil.

He shrugged. "Don't care." Tipping the fragrant sugary nightmare, he splashed the entire contents onto my tongue.

I went to spit, to vomit, to expel it in any way possible, but he'd learned from Jealousy when she'd fed him elixir to save me. His mouth clamped over mine. Keeping the liquid inside me, his nose pushing hot air against my cheeks.

Elixir tingled. It burned a hole through my tongue. It promised to poison me even if I didn't swallow.

He groaned as he rubbed himself against me.

I choked.

His fingers pinched my nose.

I thrashed.

His cock pulsed against my belly.

I fought.

My lungs screamed for air.

His fingers granted no sip of oxygen.

I burned through valuable energy as I battled and squirmed

and tried to push away his kiss.

But in the end…I lost.

I always fucking lost.

Natural instinct overrode my stubbornness.

Reflex made me gulp.

Elixir tumbled down my throat.

Drake slipped his tongue into my mouth, ensuring every drop had been ingested.

Only then did he pull away, smile as if I was his every erotic wish, then bent to the side and grabbed Sully's cell phone.

"See you soon, Jinx."

He pressed the button…and everything went white.

Sullivan

Chapter Six

I WAS SICK TO fucking death of helicopters.

At least this one had its doors firmly shut and flew over a wintry city instead of a tropical sea. Larger than my own, it sat thirteen mercenaries plus me.

My one-hour handicap behind Drake had now been reduced to thirteen minutes. I'd bribed the tanker who refuelled us in Dubai and learned Drake had taken twenty-two minutes to fill his gas quota while I only took twelve.

Couple that with him driving to our parents' estate instead of flying, I was shaving time every minute, stealing it back, hoarding the seconds and getting closer to the end.

"The other team will meet us there. They're six minutes away."

"Did Jon-Paul secure what I requested?" I tore my attention from the rooftops beneath me and focused on the eager killer for hire. I had no opinion over his or his colleagues' career choice. No moral requirement not to use their services.

People were about to die, and I didn't give a shit.

It was convenient I could rent such a team.

"Yes." The blond guy nodded, his hands clenching between his legs. "Your phone call cleared the handover. All they had to do was land on the emergency helipad and a nurse was there with the package."

"Good." I turned back to the window, my mind still razor-sharp and shrewd. I hadn't slept a wink the entire eternal journey from Indonesia. I didn't need sleep. All fatigue, fury, and emotions had been stripped away.

I was clinical in all things, which allowed rationality to plot ahead.

If there was some chance of me surviving the inevitable death in my future, I owed it to Eleanor to at least attempt to reverse it.

It was Cal who dangled potential hope.

I wasn't afraid of dying. I never had been. But I *was* afraid to leave the one person who'd made my life infinitely better.

Therefore, I'd activated a resuscitation plan. One chance to kill the old Sully and let a new one be reborn. Thanks to my connections within big Pharma, and my regular donations and breakthroughs to modern medicine, I had acquaintances in Geneva only too happy to give me the two items on my list.

A travel defib and a strong sedative.

A simple phone call, a rendezvous on the top of the hospital's roof where mortally ill patients arrived by air, and a quick handover to the leader of the mercenaries following us, and it was done.

Whether or not it would work…*I guess, we'll find out.*

Either way, Eleanor couldn't be mad at me if I did die because at least I'd *tried* to stay with her. I did my best, and if I failed…that was fate's choice.

"Three minutes, Sinclair," an older mercenary muttered, touching his ear where an earpiece relayed information.

I nodded and pulled my cell phone free. Scrolling the copy of my contacts, I brought up the number for the head housekeeper of the Geneva estate. I hadn't visited this place in years, but our staff were loyal because we paid well.

If Mrs. Betha Bixel still ran the household, she might give me loyalty over Drake who visited more often. He'd never been her favourite person after she'd been the one to clean up swan feathers after he'd snared one and plucked it, *alive*, in his bedroom.

I wished there was some explanation for Drake's maliciousness—some excuse or cure for whatever psychosis he embraced. But the fact was, he was just born wrong. Rotten to his core and noxious in every way.

The phone rang as I pressed it to my ear and waited.

My heart didn't skip.

My palms didn't sweat.

I was so close to Eleanor, so near to finishing this, but my adrenaline didn't spike. Every ounce had already been employed into drowning out my injuries and operated entirely under Tritec's command.

"Hallo, we ist das?"

"Mrs. Bixel, it's Sullivan Sinclair. Rose and James' son."

"Of course! You do not need to remind me, Sullivan. I know who you are. My favourite son." Her Swiss-German accent filled my ear, half with comfort from our trips here and half with dread from what'd happened in that estate. "Your brother arrived ten minutes or so ago. He brought…friends."

"Can I assume you will not inform him of this conversation?"

She tutted. "You assume correctly. I do not like that man." Her voice lowered. "He brought a girl with him. Some poor thing dressed only in a man's shirt. It's early winter, Sullivan. A girl cannot be out in the snow in just a shirt." Her disapproval poured down the line as she opened her mouth to berate me some more. "Why can't he be caring…like you? You always were—"

"That girl. Is she hurt?" I cut her off. Already the helicopter had decreased its speed, flying closer to the sprawling acreage.

"No, but exhausted. She needs a bath and—"

"Where did he take her?"

"To the *Blau* lounge."

"How many men are with him?"

"I did not get a full count. Perhaps six? Seven?"

"How many staff are on-site?"

"Why?" Her voice turned wary. "What is going on, Sull—"

"Round up your staff, Mrs. Bixel. Confine them to your quarters away from harm. I cannot promise they won't get caught in the crossfires if they don't."

"Oh, my saints. Violence again? What is it with you two brothers—"

"Do what I say and do it now. I suggest you don't come out of your quarters until someone comes to get you. You won't like what you see if you do."

I hung up before she could question me further.

The Sinclair Manor House appeared below us, the oak trees dusted with snow, the gardens painstakingly swept from the light fall overnight. The pond had ice crystals glittering around the perimeter, and the sight of the stone mansion made my hair stand on end.

The pilots swooped low, scooping out the gardens and choosing a landing site not far from the sweeping deck that'd been added on before my parents bought the place. I'd eaten many a breakfast on that terrace and smuggled titbits from the kitchen for the birds and wildlife.

The second the skids hit earth, the closest mercenary to the door ripped open the fuselage and leaped to the grass. The rest of the men spilled out, waiting for me as I grabbed the cane one of the mercenaries had given me when we'd landed in Geneva.

A walking stick instead of a helpless crutch.

I'd loathed the thought of a crutch. Just the sight of it made sickness and weakness come to mind. I was neither of those things. I was deadly, determined.

Seemed a mercenary had felt the same way as he'd presented me with a simple black cane when we'd disembarked the plane. Where the fuck he got it from, I didn't know or care, but I'd accepted it and left the crutch behind.

With my hand wrapped around the smooth ball at the top, I commanded, "Sweep the house, shoot the men, leave the staff. If you can't tell the difference, shoot first then ask questions. I expect cold-bloodedness, gentlemen. My brother is out of lives. If he doesn't die today, you will. I fucking guarantee it."

They nodded, unholstering their weapons.

"Three of you, follow me." Sweeping my gaze over my black-clad audience, I added, "When the other team arrives, have them bring me the package."

The men fanned out—faster than me, more able-bodied than me, and that was why I'd hired them. They could do the dirty work. I only had one life to steal today.

As I climbed the steps to the deck, my cane slipped on ice. My leg bellowed, sneaking past Tritec's defences as I put more weight on my broken bones than I wanted. The bite of cold air was foreign after years in the tropics, but at least the colder weather matched the arctic chill inside me.

Sweat from pain just froze instead of rolled.

Flushes from agony had no place as I limped toward the many glass doors offering the weak winter sun to enter the family room and kitchen. The mercenaries had already run inside. Shots fired. Voices raised before being cut off quickly.

I was almost too late to witness the takeover as I stepped into the immaculate Regency home just in time to see the last man drop.

Three guards? That was all Drake had?

Bullshit.

Marching with a goddamn limp, I used my cane to point at

the locked doors to *blau* lounge. German for blue, it'd been decorated by my father who had a love of dark spaces after working in bright labs. He and Drake had spent many a summer holed up in gloominess while I'd run wild in the sunny gardens.

"Shoot the lock," I snarled.

The mercenary closest did as I requested, blowing apart the intricately carved door. Wood shards flew like shrapnel, and the doors swung inward thanks to his powerful kick.

A gun fired from within, lodging a bullet right into his forehead.

He fell to the floor just as my team let fire, shooting at the enemy who'd killed one of my men, completely eradicating the remaining guards inside the lounge protecting my brother.

"Don't hurt the girl!" I yelled.

Two heavy thuds of corpses.

No returning fire.

Another few bullet volleys from my eager men.

"Enough!" The click of my cane on the grey flagstones echoed as I limped into the lounge, stepping over carcasses as if they were nothing more than roadkill.

And there.

In the centre of the room, tied to a couch and deep in the grips of Euphoria was Eleanor.

Eleanor.

Her hands were bound, the yellow shirt I'd dressed her in from a guest villa dangling off her elbows. Her skin glistened from oil and her eyes were wide, seeing things I couldn't.

Fuck.

My hand curled around my cane. My teeth clenched. And my heart managed a painful thrum before Tritec took control again.

I allowed the iciness to drag me back.

Cricking my neck, I peered at Drake.

Equally as naked as Eleanor, they were both no longer in Geneva but whatever fantasy he'd shoved them into.

Which one?

What hallucination would become my brother's casket?

Everything seemed to slow. I stayed cold and unscrupulous.

I limped toward them, taking in the scene, noticing the fatigue shadowing Eleanor and the whiteness of her skin.

A small moan escaped her parted lips as Drake reached for her. Tethered to the couch, she had nowhere to go. She fought him off with bound hands even as her skin flushed and lust made her shudder.

I shoved him away.

He crashed over the coffee table, an empty vial rolling from where he stepped on it. He grunted in pain but even flipping over a piece of furniture couldn't stop his attention from locking entirely on Eleanor, his eyes glazed with a different reality, his mind somewhere I couldn't touch.

The vial crashed against my shoe.

I swallowed a growl, unable to control the flush of raw fury. Fucking *bastard*.

He'd given her elixir.

Again.

She'll die.

How ill-fated our love story had turned out to be. We both might die today. We might be buried side by side before we'd even lived.

I'm ending this.

Now.

A mercenary on my payroll sidled up to me as I snatched my cell phone lying on the floor. The same phone Drake had stolen.

"Want me to shoot him?" He raised his gun, aiming it at Drake's head.

It would be so easy.

So fucking tempting.

But they shared the same fantasy.

Kill Drake and kill Eleanor.

I can't.

"He's mine to deal with," I growled. "Sweep the house. Kill any other intruders. I wish to be alone with my brother."

The man nodded without question. "Call if you need us. We'll station ourselves by the door."

A helicopter screech cut off outside, signalling the other team had arrived. "Go collect the package."

"Sure thing." He nodded and jogged from the room.

Drake scrambled over the coffee table, doing his best to return to Eleanor.

Urgency tried to undermine my precision. I wanted nothing more than to rip his fucking throat out, but they were linked. Their minds were threaded with hallucinations that were so real, so tangible, it became real.

I need her free from the fantasy.

Eleanor's moans, as she continued to fight elixir, did their best to distract me.

Fire blazed in my blood for instant and brutal retribution.

The old Sully—the one impassioned and ruled by his love for this girl—would've carried her from the room and punched a hole in his fucking brother's chest. He would've tried to skirt the very rules he'd coded for Euphoria and lost Eleanor in the process.

That man kept losing because he kept being controlled by his mistakes.

I wasn't that man anymore.

Thanks to Tritec, I was clearheaded and methodical. It gave me the willpower to stand before my goddess and my brother all while he made his way back to her and reached to grab her.

I swallowed down my hatred. I quaked with my fury. And I permitted him to paw at her because I needed to do this right. I needed to not only kill him but fucking *obliterate* him.

And I know just how to do it.

Eleanor cried out, her tone full of disgust but also rapidly building need.

Elixir was winning.

Hold on, Jinx…hold on.

I couldn't help her overcome elixir's insidious consummation the same way I had on my island. She needed to be fucked so her overstimulated system didn't kill her. It wasn't about pleasure anymore, but survival. She needed orgasm after orgasm, and…I couldn't give her that.

I'd put her through enough.

I'd hurt her past forgivable.

I had another plan.

A *better* plan.

One that I didn't know for certain would work, but I had to try because nothing else was possible. I had no stamina to fuck her to the levels she needed, and I wouldn't lay a hand on her while my motherfucking brother still breathed.

This is the only way.

A man ran into the room, holding out a medic bag complete with the travel defib and syringe in sterile packaging.

I accepted it.

He left immediately, leaving me alone with the woman I loved and the brother I cursed.

Placing the defib on the couch, I shoved Drake away again and untied Eleanor's hands and ankle from the curtain tiebacks holding her prisoner.

The yellow shirt fell to the floor. My fingers sparked with electricity. My hands shook as I forced myself not to caress her, not to tangle her mind any more than it already was.

She shivered and groaned at my proximity, her breasts heavy, and lust trickling down her inner thigh. She had no idea I'd been the one to touch her, yet her skin flushed for me, her invitation heavy with her scent in the air.

Drake's cock thickened at her cries, once again trying to get to her.

I braced, ready to keep him at bay. However, Eleanor was no longer tethered and she bolted.

She left Drake clutching at air and his hard-on bouncing in his haste to chase.

It took fucking *everything* to stand still while Eleanor tripped over a rug and fell to her knees, scurrying like a mouse, bumping into a bookcase in her hurry.

All instincts told me to protect her. *Go after her.* The primal need to kill Drake almost overrode my discipline.

You snap, she dies.

You kill Drake, she dies.

You do anything wrong, she dies.

So get it fucking right.

My teeth almost turned to dust as I ripped my gaze off the hunt in front of me and locked onto my cell phone.

In this world, I was a cripple.

But in that world…I was god.

I was the creator and architect. I could bend the rules to suit me. I could use Drake's mind to break him, instead of his body.

If I couldn't stop the fantasy, then…I would join in.

My desire for bloodshed unfolded with morbid magic.

It would be the worst thing I'd ever done.

I would step over every boundary and humanity I had left, embrace every shred of darkness in my soul.

And I would relish every fucking minute of it.

My thumbs flew over the screen as I typed new lines of code. I added a cypher, changed a character, conjured a new kind of nightmare. Every edit I made, Drake and Eleanor would witness each revision, their illusion morphing around them. As I snuffed out the sun and drenched them in darkness, they'd see all manner of changes.

Amendments that shouldn't be possible.

Tricks that couldn't be true.

My fingers flew faster, twisting the code past all realms of comprehensible.

This was to be Drake's crypt. It was only fitting that I spared no expense to his demise.

Currently, Drake and Eleanor were in a campsite set in an American forest on the dawn of the Revolutionary War. A meagre camp where the guest who'd asked me to cypher such a fantasy wanted a bearskin tent, an avatar skilled at combat, and a native Indian girl who happened to be gathering water at a river. A girl who would be overpowered, overcome—a goddess high on elixir who would spread her legs for the illusion of forced conquering.

It'd proven to be a success.

The guest had left entirely satisfied.

Yet Drake would find death instead of pleasure.

My lips thinned as I typed faster and faster. New lines of text slipped into the old, distorting a fantasy within a fantasy, a world within a world.

A world unlike any explorer in the 18th century would've found.

Only once I'd completed the amended falsity did I prepare to join them.

Grabbing a few boxes of my Euphoria supplies where Drake had left them scattered, I inserted eye lenses and earbuds. I didn't bother with anything else, only requiring the bare essentials for my insertion.

Ensuring the lounge doors were closed, I grasped the sedative tight in my fist and hovered my thumb over the screen.

I pressed the button to load a third person into their delusion.

The world went white.

Geneva vanished.

And Sully…was no more.

Chapter Seven

STRANGE THINGS WERE HAPPENING.

An odd thing to think—considering how strange my life had become—but strange things occurred nevertheless.

Things that shouldn't be possible.

I was no longer in Switzerland but in a forest filled with towering pines. Autumn leaves crackled beneath my moccasin covered feet. Soft beaded leather clothed me, feathers bounced in my hair, tattoos glowed on my arms hidden beneath ivory bangles.

My skin was darker, my hair black instead of brown.

I felt wilder, more in tune with the forest, knowing the breeze swept from the north and the sun signalled late afternoon. I was as native to these woods as the chipmunk watching us and the herd of deer running past in the distance.

Unlike the man doing his best to bed me.

He was an outlander.

A ruffian who stood like a tree trunk with flaming red hair, matching copper beard, and hands the size of dinner plates.

I'd been dodging him since he'd tried to pounce on me by the river's edge. I'd darted out of his grasp, nimble and swift while he was lumbering and slow.

The only problem was with every second that ticked past, my swiftness drowned beneath sex. Elixir crept faster and crueller through my blood, ensuring I buckled beneath its horror, all while I did my best to ignore it.

I ran from its lust as surely as I ran from the man who no longer looked like Drake but *was* Drake.

A man who grinned and offered to ease my burning, needy desire. A man with an appendage perfectly created to grant me release after release so I didn't sink into the quagmire from before—the sticky agony of not being able to come after doing my best to fight it when Sully tried to rescue us.

I'd fought it for far longer than I'd thought possible that night.

Could I do that again?

Could I lock down my system and prevent an orgasm? And if I did, would I be sentencing myself to death by a heart ready to self-implode?

There was no middle ground.

No right and wrong.

If I didn't bow to my needs, I might not be breathing if Sully arrived.

But if I did give in…*how can I ever live with myself?*

My heart galloped, hiccupping as I parried out of the way of the man running toward me. "You know you want my cock, girl. Just let me give it to you."

He was right.

I wanted him.

I wanted his tanned, scarred hands on my symbol-tattooed flesh. I wanted his red beard to scratch my inner thighs as he ate me. I wanted to attack the drawstring holding his tweed trousers around his hips and have him sink inside me.

But it wasn't *me* who wanted him.

It was a lie, a drug—the worst kind of trick.

That man wasn't Sully or the owner of my soul.

He was my enemy.

A troll.

I would rather my heart kick its last beat before I permitted him to fuck me.

"Leave me *alone!*"

"You'll be begging me in a few more seconds." He smirked, scratching his beard. "I'll just wait here for you to come to your senses."

"I'll cut off your balls and throw them into the river if you come near me."

He laughed hard, his baritone scattering pigeons from the pines.

My skin prickled.

Heat clenched my core.

Wetness dribbled down my leg.

Shit!

Turning away from him, I breathed hard through my nose.

Ignore it.

Ignore it.

Please, God, ignore it.

I wedged my hands into my belly, only to have the insane urge to drop them between my legs.

My leg...

I shivered as a breeze but not a breeze licked around my ankle.

A phantom touch. The sensation of a man's fingers on my skin before it was gone.

The tease came again, this time around my wrists, a simple brush and then no more.

Drake ran at me, his brawny frame ploughing through fallen leaves and making orange foliage dance around the campsite.

I ran.

Until a few minutes ago, every time I'd tried to run, the boundary of my cage included just a few steps. I could race from the river where my weaved and waterproofed flax pot waited in the grasses. I could reach the bearskin tent and vault over the crackling fire. I could kick his pottery bowls and throw dirt at his face, but I couldn't gallop into the trees.

I couldn't chase the deer as they ran.

An invisible blockade prevented me, keeping me within the confines of my hell.

But now...I had no such parameters.

I leaped into the thicket, relishing in the release running gave me. I bumped into invisible things, sharp corners, and hard barriers. I couldn't see the obstructions, my path clear within the fantasy, but who knew what my body ran into in the outside world.

How had I been freed from where Drake had tied me?

Who untied me?

I ran faster, uncaring I collided and crunched into obstacles. That was why Sully insisted on the harness in Euphoria. Why a goddess was tethered because it prevented bruises and pain by running in one world and crashing in another.

He also said it was to prevent the illusion from breaking apart.

Could I smash this hallucination to pieces if I just kept running into things I couldn't see? If I forced my body to jerk my mind back into its control, could I be free?

Can I escape Euphoria?

Even if I escape, I'll still need sex.

Elixir bubbled and grumbled in my blood, doing its best to make me submit but unable to take centre stage while I ran for my life.

My heart couldn't double beat when it was needed to feed depleted muscles.

Is that the key?

Could I stay alive by pushing myself to the brink of exhaustion in exercise?

"Fuck, come back here!" Drake's snarl chased me from the campsite.

I looked over my shoulder and tripped over a stupid tree root.

The moment I rolled in the bracken, any thoughts of running were over. Leaves against my skin, moss against my breasts. Everything was erotic. Everything made me *need*.

My hips shot skyward. My fingers rubbed my clit.

God, please!

I need. I *need!*

My system stopped asking me and stole all my control. An internal seizure rippled from my shoulders to my toes, bringing with it lust and longing and the undeniable build-up of a release.

No.

No.

Shit!

My lips spread wide as I contorted on the forest floor. My first orgasm bowled through me without permission. Sharp and savage, intense and instant.

My inner muscles clenched, rippling with heaven.

Oh!

Elixir bypassed my mental refusals, hijacking my sight, my breath, my *everything*.

I came apart, humping my hand like a wild animal all while Drake caught up to me. If he landed beside me. If he touched me in my current position, I wouldn't survive what would happen.

I wouldn't be able to sleep with him and stay mentally intact.

I wouldn't be able to stay *me*.

No!

Launching to my feet, the echoes of my release still clenching my belly, I tripped and scurried deeper into the forest.

"Hey, get your ass back here!" Drake yelled.

I ran toward the tree-studded horizon.

My breasts bounced with tingles and desire.

My naked skin kissed by breezes and flower petals.

I kept running even as the world became a sinful playground to indulge in.

Elixir turned my vision red with lusty haze.

I gasped for a different type of exercise.

Sex.

God, sex.

Yes.

No!

I ran faster.

I focused on the horizon.

So close.

So near.

Too far.

A crack and a whir. A gust of power and oddness.

And the horizon vanished, spitting me out at the campsite, its fire still crackling as if I'd never left.

A reboot.

A portal that offered a sweeping vista but ended so suddenly and transported me back to the heart of the fantasy.

No!

NO!

Drake suddenly appeared beside me, his shock matching mine as we stood panting by the fire.

How?

How did this labyrinth work?

How could you escape somewhere that didn't exist?

How did you find an exit when all exits led back to the beginning?

No…this can't be happening.

I hugged myself.

My skin rejoiced.

The urge to drop my touch lower crippled me.

I hated this.

Hated it!

There has to be a way out.

There has to be!

But there wasn't. No way to run out of this nightmare. No

way to swim or climb or bolt. No way to stop my descent into a horny, helpless hologram.

Tears stung and slipped down my cheeks.

I'd hoped...

Please.

"Oh, God." I jack-knifed forward as elixir turned vicious in its hunger. One release was not enough. It was just the start.

Come.

Do it.

Finger yourself.

Fuck him.

Do it!

I balled my fists into my belly, pleading with my nasty thirst not to *do* this. Not to hurt me like this. Not to kill me like this.

"Stop it!" I screeched. I wanted to slap myself. Drown myself. Throw myself into the fire if it would stop the curse in my blood.

"I'll help." Drake put his hands on me. "I'll fuck you like you need."

I crumpled.

I shivered.

Fire and need.

Ice and dread.

He manhandled me until his arms locked tight, his body pressed close, and his lips tried to kiss me.

I was two people in one.

A nightmare and a dream.

Heaven and hell.

I ducked his kiss.

I embraced coherency and slapped him. "Get *off* me."

"Fuck, you're—"

"Stop!" I kneed him in the balls; my strike only grazed him, but he dropped me instantly.

I ran.

His hand caught my wrist, yanking me back.

Another wave of hot, horrid elixir made me keel over. I fought myself all while trying to fight him.

"Stop trying to run. You're supposed to want this." He tried to kiss me again.

I raked my nails down his cheek.

"Come here," he grunted, keeping his hips away from mine in case I kneed him again. "Why isn't elixir working?"

We grappled and fought, grotesque lust swarming, his paws

tearing at my calfskin clothing, his pants coming undone in our struggles.

"Beg me," he barked. "Beg me to fuck you."

Yes.

"NEVER!"

We fell to the ground, still fighting.

He pinned me on my back, still battling.

"Gotcha." He dragged his tongue up my neck.

Elixir was a heinous master.

I almost came.

"Fuck you!" I tried kneeing him in the balls again as he slithered on top of me, his hands shoving my hand-crafted trousers down, his hips angling to mount.

For a mortifying second, I contemplated giving in.

Sully was most likely dead.

I would be too if I didn't buckle beneath elixir.

Drake would kill me—I had no doubt about that—but perhaps not today, not now, not here.

If I allowed him to use me, wasn't that *me* using *him*? Wasn't I the one high? The one who *needed* this?

But as his mouth clamped onto mine and the tip of his cock found my entrance, I couldn't do it.

I chose death by cardiac arrest.

I choose Sully!

I went wild.

I scratched and clawed.

I squirmed and kicked.

I twisted every bone and contorted every muscle, making him curse and growl above me.

Dirt coated us, scents of earth and fallen leaves, the heat of the fire beside us.

We fought for a minute or maybe a second, but for all my pride and ferocity, he managed to slam my hands above my head, managed to splay my legs with his, managed to grind his cock against my pussy.

Tears spilled faster.

Rage knotted with need, and lust tangled with terror.

I squeezed my eyes shut.

This was it.

The death of Eleanor as I knew her.

I waited for him to plunge inside me.

I braced myself to die.

Only…strangeness wasn't done with me today.

Yet another bizarre twist in my godforsaken fate.

The sun suddenly snuffed out.

Gone.

Vanished.

No more.

Only the glow of the fire illuminated a suddenly haunting forest.

Daytime to night-time, just like that.

Chills decorated my skin as Drake stilled above me. "What the—" He looked around, his eyes peering in the sudden blackness, sensing the dangerous change. The perilous whispers in the trees. The slithering serpents in the dark.

The campsite, equipped for erotic couplings between guest and goddess, switched.

It morphed and cracked from one cocoon to another, shedding a chrysalis of daylight for shadows drenched in menacing peril.

Trees sloughed their leaves and stood like mighty stakes. Fissures opened up in the ground, glowing with crimson lava, revealing the stomach of the underworld. Crows flocked through the sky, their caws grim and condemning.

The world switched from normal parameters to a wasteland of trickery.

A deeper level of fear attacked me.

A fear born from a human steadfastness in seasons and the fact that the sun couldn't just…*disappear.*

A forest couldn't become hell, bleeding normalcy into fiction. Spiders the size of cats weren't supposed to crawl by, nor wolves the size of polar bears to slink in the shadows.

I swallowed a scream as more and more predators arrived from nowhere.

Sabre tooth cats with canines still holding carrion from prior meals. Bears as tall as houses, their shaggy fur dreadlocked with gore. Vultures fell from the sky, ringing us in our fire circle. A stampede of furious wildebeest snorted in the gloom. A howl and snarl of more wolves sent elixir second-best beneath my desire to flee.

This…wasn't possible.

This threatened to break my mind, to prove my imagination had limits and I'd reached the threshold of what I could accept.

It's not possible!

Wait…

It's not possible unless the man who made *all of this possible is here.*

Hope sprang.

Wishes spilled faster than my tears.

Sully!

I fought harder, knocking Drake sideways in his stupor of what'd happened to his fantasy. "Did I load it wrong?" He scowled, crawling back over me and pinning my wrists deeper into the dirt the more I struggled. "Quit it."

A wolf snapped at his head.

Drake didn't react, almost as if he believed it was just a mirage. A program glitching that couldn't hurt him.

But I smelled the wolf's rancid breath. I felt the breeze of its jaws. I heard the thunder of its paws.

"Let me *go!*" I fought again. I fought to wake up before something far more dangerous than Drake decided to have me. This might not be real. This might be entirely in our minds.

But our minds *made* it real.

Our brains told our skin what to feel and how to react. Our nervous system was the only reason we felt the world we lived in.

This was now the world we lived in—regardless if it was true or not. This world could kill us as surely as our old one.

"Get *off* me!"

God, I need.

Need!

My hips rocked as instinct suffocated beneath elixir.

Stop it!

It wasn't the animals I had to be afraid of, it was me.

I was my own worst enemy.

Please!

"Shut the fuck up." His red beard shuddered as he spoke. "Let me think." He rocked his hips into mine, his cock still unnervingly close to taking me.

I hated that I shuddered in horror but also hunger. I contemplated riding him just so I could be free of the constricting, clutching mayhem of my heart.

I needed to come again.

The palpitations and skipping, tripping beats made me sick and lightheaded.

"You've been in these illusions plenty of times, how do you reset it?" Drake stared at me, his gaze orange from the flickering fire.

Elixir bowled through me, no longer willing to play nice, dragging me deeper into sex-crazed.

My back arched. My core begged. I let out a pitiful scream.

I need.

I can't.

Stop it!

Drake pressed his hips into mine, scattering me in all directions, leaving only hate and shame behind. "Finally want me, huh?" He rubbed his cock against my clit, driving me headfirst into the beginnings of the most diabolical release. "I'll fuck you, girl, but not until I figure out what the fuck is going *on* around here."

"Allow me to show you."

That voice.

My head whipped to the side.

The release taunting me erupted from the sinful snarl.

I convulsed with carnal clenches.

It wasn't Drake who granted me pleasure. It was the owner of that magnificent growl. A grumble full of hellfire and brimstone fury. Darker than night, blacker than sin, as deadly and as lethal as venom.

Sully?

Disgusted tears drenched my cheeks as echoes of my climax made me feeble, unable to fight Drake off me. I had a small window to get away before I lost myself entirely. A few precious seconds to stay loyal to Sully and myself.

"Let her go."

Drake twisted to look behind him as the night shimmered and parted like a veil, delivering not a man but a monster.

We both froze.

My heart tangled and tore, quadruple beating with rapidly encroaching death.

The new arrival wasn't just a monster. He was a beast so much scarier than all the predators currently stalking. A beast standing on two legs with fangs like a vampire, eyes like a snake, and scales like a dragon.

Shaped like a man but taller than any I'd ever seen, he had no hair, no softness, no vulnerabilities. He had goat horns and bat wings and talons stolen straight from a devil.

Drake gulped as the nightmare stepped toward us. No, not stepped. *Flew.* An effortless swoop of membrane wings and snap of power.

Drake was lifted in one hand.

Thrown with one toss.

Eradicated with a single thought.

He cried out as he landed on the other side of the fire.

And the demon fell to one knee beside me. He held out his scaly hand, his glowing reptile eyes raking over me, and *I knew.*

My heart knew.

My soul knew.

My body instantly wanted him.

It wanted this monster because it knew who puppeteered such a thing.

It wasn't biologically possible. He wasn't my species anymore.

But he was male.

He was mine.

He's...Sully.

With tears pouring, I placed my tiny breakable hand into his claw-frosted paw.

Electricity crackled. Chemistry ignited. That all-knowing, all-consuming, all-binding bond between a god and a goddess who no longer played in the human world but had strayed directly into myth *ignited.*

It gushed between us.

It branded us, burned us, broke us into pieces that belonged entirely to the other.

This was what Sully was.

He wasn't just a man.

He wasn't just a monster.

He was *everything.*

He was every creature and element.

He was fury and faith and utterly blinding loyalty.

Elixir refused to be thwarted any longer.

I'd found the man I loved and lusted.

He was here.

I could be given redemption and releases.

I could feel him beneath the fantasy. Not wearing fingerprint sensors meant I touched his skin beneath the scales.

I *burned.*

Scooting to my knees, I crawled into him. "You're alive. You came for me."

I twined myself over his scaly skin, my body with its oil sensed the otherworldly armour he wore but my fingers stroked the contours of human muscles. I kissed the ice-cold angles of his cheekbones.

I wanted him.

I *needed* him.

Now!

A savage growl echoed in his throat. The wolves surrounding us answered back, a symphony of snarls and yips.

Goosebumps prickled me, activating my lust a thousandfold. My thirst for him was maddening, terrifying. "*Sully.*"

Holding me in his massive paws, cords of power etching his reptilian skin, his features remained vicious but a soft glow appeared in the snake-slit eyes. "I found you."

My stomach clenched as he brought my hand to his icy lips.

"I love you, Eleanor. I'm sorry I'm late. I'm sorry for what you've endured. But this is the last time you'll ever be hurt this way. I give you my word."

His voice wasn't just a voice. It wasn't a bear's growl or wolf's howl, it was a blend of all of them. A thick thunder of gravel and hurricanes.

Another orgasm threatened to split me in two.

I was turned on by his sheer potency. The fact that he could kill me with a single misplaced touch. He was so dangerous in this new form. It made every feminine, female part of me spread her legs and *beg*.

I wanted to be ridden and claimed.

I wanted him to take me for his own, and if he killed me while doing so, I would gladly give him my life forever.

"*Sully…*" More tears fell. "Thank God, you survived."

"I did."

"You came after me."

"I'll always come after you." He nuzzled my nose with his. "You're mine and I'm yours and I have so much to atone for."

My heart smashed against my ribs, triple beating, failing. "I need you."

He pulled away, his slitted eyes flashing with regret. "I can't fuck you, Eleanor. Not like last time." His voice rumbled, stroking me with fiery licks.

His denial hurt me worse than anything. "*Please*…it hurts. My heart…I need. Please, don't refuse me."

"I can't feel you almost die in my arms again." His talon-tipped thumb stroked my knuckles, his massive paw skating higher up my arm. "I can't be the reason you suffer."

My limb looked like a twig in his grasp. A silly little twig that he could snap at any moment. I gasped as my heart fisted and suffocated, making me breathless. "But I won't be able to—"

"I'll help you, Jinx..." With his strange eyes locked on mine, he hurt me. "I'm sorry." His claw punctured my skin, driving the sharp tip into my vein, poisoning me with whatever venom he carried. "I love you, Eleanor. Please...please forgive me."

"Forgive you...?" My eyelashes fluttered.

My heart heaved a final lurch.

Tiredness.

Heaviness.

Nothingness.

Sullivan

Chapter Eight

I MIGHT WEAR THE FLESH of a beast, but my heart was still that of a man. A heart that stuttered and howled as Eleanor turned limp and lifeless in my hold.

She hadn't been able to see the syringe. The illusion keeping her firmly in the spell of my new conjuring. I hadn't been able to see the injection either, but I could feel it in my unsensored hands. I uncapped the needle and punctured her arm, plunging the sedative into her veins.

In the fantasy, my claw was what pierced her.

Her shock at my causing her yet more pain made my stomach seize. Her rapid unconsciousness did its best to cleave me out of Tritec's icy control.

I'd taken a gamble.

I'd used a sedative that I'd thought would be used for my failing heart and shielded hers instead. Sleep was the only gift I could give her.

It has to work...please.

She turned into a ragdoll.

No longer haunted by elixir. No longer at my brother's mercy or mine.

She's free.

It was the only solution I could think of to protect her.

Take her mind out of the fantasy and that solved one deadly consequence. Put her to sleep, and elixir could no longer play havoc with her heart.

But my theory hadn't been tested…

Yet again, I'd put her in grave danger just like I had since we'd first met.

I'm so sorry, Eleanor…for everything.

Cradling her gently, I placed her on the forest floor. Her gorgeous hair swept over her face as she sprawled at my feet. Her lips parted, her features utterly serene, her eyelashes thick stencils on her cheeks.

Was her mind free?

Was her heart calm?

Had I saved her or killed her?

I wanted to stand vigil. I needed to ensure I'd done the right thing by knocking her out. But I didn't have the luxury to stand guard.

I'd entered this hallucination for two reasons.

One, to save Eleanor from being raped by my sibling.

And two…to kill that sibling motherfucking dead.

Sweeping her hair away from her face with savage gleaming claws, I stood. The bat wings spread from my spine, heavy and pulling on muscles already fatigued. The sensation of being ten feet tall and controlling a frankensteined creation of reptile, carnivore, and chimera made my body throb within its new skin.

My eyes remained on Eleanor, flinching as she suddenly disappeared.

Her mental awareness of the fantasy completely shut off in sleep, extracting her from all the lies I'd coded. She was gone simply because her mind was no longer reachable.

I stared at the empty dirt, missing her. I would give fucking anything to be beside her in the lounge of my parents' estate. To collect her from the floor and carry her to a soft bed. To lie down beside her and keep her safe.

But…for now, I was locked in this mirage until it ended.

Time to play.

Balling my fists, feeling the sharpness of my talons embedding into my palms, I cricked my neck and turned away from Eleanor and love, and focused on my brother and hate.

He stood on the opposite side of the fire, his face illuminated by flickering flames, darkness thick behind him, a ring of wolves penning him in a trap made of teeth.

So *that* was why he hadn't approached me. Why he hadn't been a nuisance after I'd thrown him off Eleanor.

He can't move.

My lips spread over fangs as sharp as scalpels. "Seems I have allies holding you at bay."

Drake straightened, his hastily tied pants hanging low on his hips, his avatar of a burly redheaded lumberjack not fooling me. Drake had always been sick in his proclivities of hurting those more vulnerable than himself, but when the tables were turned on him…his fear stunk in an instant.

His armpits released an aroma reeking of sour stress. His muslin shirt soaked with sweat, and moisture glistened in the dip of his throat. "Who the fuck are you?"

I laughed, awed at the hastily created creature I'd typed. The creature I now lived within. When I'd altered the text and coding, I'd thrown everything into the mix. Every predator, pain, and poison I could think of. I'd followed no boundaries or common-sense.

I'd embraced the nonsensical and whatever beast I'd conjured now chuckled with dread and death, its chest purring with feral blood thirst. "Don't pretend you don't know me, brother. You and I are well acquainted."

Drake blanched, the redheaded complexion flushing grey. "Sullivan…?"

"Unless we have another relation I am unaware of."

"I thought you were dead."

"Assumptions will get you killed." I cocked my head, complete with gilded horns. "And I'll happily deliver."

He gulped. "What the fuck did you do?" His pompous arrogance returned, dragged around him like tatty armour. "Sick of being the fool so fashioned a monster?" He sneered. "It's just fake. Just like this whole piece of shit fantasy is fake. Do you honestly think you can scare me? That I'd cower before you?" He stepped toward me, earning the terrifying snarls of timber wolves. He stopped but continued sneering, "You're just the same old cocksucker as before. A laughing stock. A nerd who somehow convinced himself he's powerful. Newsflash, you cunt, you're not powerful. You and your computer games can take a flying leap, Sullivan, because unlike you, I don't wet my fucking pants over something that can't hurt me—"

A wolf lunged, snapping at his wrist.

Drake backpedalled.

Jaws bit down, missing by a hair.

He thought that wasn't real?

That that bite couldn't *hurt* him?

This is gonna be fun.

Yes, this was virtual. And yes, in the outside world, his body would remain unscathed. But in here…thanks to my careful immersion and the tweaks I'd made along the way, myth had the unnerving ability to become real.

Brain damage had been an unsightly side effect because my mirages were…entrancing. Hypnotic. A mesmeric tool to trick the mind into accepting fiction over fact.

While being used as a stage for sex, that realness wasn't a problem.

But use it in warfare? Turn its salacious nature into treacherous?

Well, there was a reason the Pentagon had contacted me a few months after a high-placed politician came to get his kicks. Why I received offers with unlimited zeros for their exclusive use of my Euphoria.

Use my VR for anything other than its intended purpose and it became the most dangerous thing on the planet. Not Tritec, not elixir, not all the other scrapped and trialled drugs combined.

This…this was *true* power because Euphoria could take war into the mind. Battles could be won without troops being stationed overseas. International squadrons could be patched into a battleground where no loss of physical life occurred, only the liquefying of a brain.

Drake would not die…not physically.

But holy fuck how his mind would snap.

It would crack like bone and dribble out like marrow.

I could trap him here forever, keep him awake so he couldn't escape, flay him from sanity, one body part at a time.

A slow, sadistic smile spread my lips. "Allow me to give you your first lesson, brother of mine."

"I don't need a lesson from a bastard like you. Give me back my goddess, fuck the hell off, and—"

"Ah, Drake. How sweet this is going to be." I sucked in a sulphur laced breath. Scales hissed down my spine and thighs. Inky black, soaking up the fire flames, natural shielding for sensitive flesh within.

"Bite me, asshole." He bared his teeth. His stupid, useless human teeth.

I grinned, my monster teeth stabbing into my lower lip, making me bleed and staining my mouth red. "Oh, it will be my fucking pleasure."

He backed up as two wolves stalked him, their snouts low to the ground, their coarse fur quivering around their scruffs. Drool dripped from black gums, yellowed fangs glistening for his jugular.

"Not yet," I murmured, mostly to myself, partly asking a wild animal I'd encrypted to back the hell off because Drake's proverbial death was mine.

I didn't expect the wolves to freeze. For their moon-yellow eyes to lock onto me. For their heads to duck in obedience.

Huh…that's interesting.

I flexed my shoulders, feeling the colossal weight of bone scaffolding and fibrous membrane that formed the wings behind me.

When I'd hastily written this deception, I hadn't typed anything about animals listening to a master. They were there just as background threats. An atmosphere to turn forest into boneyard.

But…

Wasn't that poetic? Fatalistic even.

Drake had not only tried to kill me, he'd killed so many other beasts.

It was only fair his death would be shared.

"Tear off his left hand," I whispered, the grumbling of my creature sounding part earthquake.

There was no pause.

No signal the wolf couldn't understand.

In a single heartbeat, the wolf on Drake's left side launched, snatched, and bit.

Drake howled.

Fuck, he howled.

The crunch of bone, the tear of tendons, and the slap of something heavy landing in the fire.

Instantly, the sizzle of skin and pop of blood scented the sky with charred meat.

Drake fell to his knees, cradling the stump where his hand used to be. Blood poured down his forearm, pooling in the dirt.

The wolves sat back on their haunches and joined in his howl. An orchestra of worship and agony.

Drake's avatar met my gaze. The redheaded man crumpled in on himself, cuddling his arm into his impressive belly. "What the fuck! Tell them to back the fuck off!" His face twisted into livid hate, and the same haughty arrogance he used whenever he'd beaten me and killed my strays appeared.

He tried to see past my disguise of fang and claw and berate the boy he'd tortured from the crib. A kid he'd always won against.

A brother who'd been too weak to stop him in his human form.

Pity.

Such a fucking pity that his own ego had ensured the slowest, most sickening death possible. I would spare him nothing. I would grant no leniency.

I wanted him in motherfucking pieces.

Not wanting to walk, aware that my thrice broken leg outside the fantasy would not tolerate exertion, I spread my heavy bat wings and flew.

A conscious instruction. A whim delivered by virtual reality. A simple tilt forward and swoop...and I soared through the fire.

Drake blanched as I landed before him, right in the midst of timber wolves.

"Sullivan...break the illusion. Get us out of here and we'll talk...alright? We'll have a beer in the *blau* lounge, even smoke one of Dad's old cigars. We'll—"

"His ear," I murmured.

A wolf on his right side pounced and sank its incisors into Drake's gristle. With a fierce yank, it tore Drake's ear straight from his head.

"FUCK!" Drake bellowed, his remaining hand slapping over the hole where his ear used to be. *"Sully!"*

With a toss of its muzzle, the wolf shot the bleeding body part straight down its gullet and swallowed.

I laughed.

The noise in my chest sounded like asteroids colliding with mountain tops. A pummelling of rock and unmovable stone.

Drake rocked on his knees, blood drenching his clothing. "Fuck you, Sullivan. Fuck!"

I wished it was the brother I recognised and not an avatar before me, but...it wouldn't ruin my enjoyment of his destruction.

"A hand for touching what wasn't yours to touch. An ear for believing I'd listen to your lies. And a..." I cupped my chin, stroking the scales running down my throat. "His foot, if you'd be so kind."

A wolf behind him nodded its giant canine head and snatched at Drake's foot. It yanked him clean off his knees, biting down hard, the crunch of his jaw heard even over Drake's bloodcurdling scream.

It took a few gnaws, a death shake or two, before Drake's ankle shattered, his Achilles tendon severed, and the mangled meat of his foot was removed from his borrowed body.

The pack squabbled over it, tearing at toes, eating Drake all while he watched.

"And a foot for ever stepping onto my islands."

He screamed again, his face glazed with agony.

How did the pain feel?

Was it just mental or had his mind taken full ownership of this form? Could he feel the throbbing wrongness of no longer having complete limbs? What did his body look like in the outside world? Did his nose bleed as his brain scrambled? Did sweat coat his nakedness?

I hope it's the worst thing he's ever felt.

I truly fucking hope so.

I hoped he felt every tear, felt every droplet of blood, heard every snarl from the wolves.

A spider the size of a small dog scuttled past.

"Wait."

Its eight legs paused, its many eyes locking onto me.

"Gag him, his screams are tiresome."

It happened faster than Drake could suck in a breath to beg. A web of silky strands shot from the spider's funnel and slapped over his mouth with sticky, silvery strands. It covered his nose too, making his chest heave for a proper breath.

His intact hand rose to scratch it off, achieving a small tear to breathe.

"Another snack?" I smiled at the timbers. "His right hand, if you please."

Two wolves leaped on him this time, both biting down on his forearm, tearing more than just his hand but everything below his elbow.

The pack lost its hierarchy, pouncing onto Drake as dirt flew. My brother was stampeded by starving canines, and his hand and forearm were devoured.

His screams were muffled, his eyes flowing with disbelieving tears. He shook his head, holding up the stumps he now had, blood spurting from ripped arteries.

The spiderweb still hushed him.

"Muuuuuummyyy."

"I'm sorry, what was that?" I bowed over him, my wings cocooning us in a morbid cape where earth scattered, and wolves continued to squabble over his tissue, fighting each other in a tumbling mass of fur. "Are you saying Mummy or Sully? Because neither of those can save you."

"Mweeeassee."

"Please?" I stabbed a claw beneath his chin, tilting his head up until our eyes met. "You're begging me now?"

He nodded so fiercely that he punctured his own chin on my talon. *"Mweeeassse!"*

I clucked my tongue, sounding like a snake hissing over its prey. "Ah, brother. When did you ever show me mercy? Do you remember me begging when it was me you hurt?" I cupped his cheek, shaking my head. "No, you can't remember because I never begged for my own salvation. I only begged for those I tried to protect. But you don't have any idea what that feels like, do you, Drake? No loyalty to an animal, a lover, a friend. No loyalty to a brother who was your only kin."

"Memanor."

"Eleanor?" I squeezed his jaw in my fist. "You *dare* try to say her name. Why? You think by reminding me of her that I'll take *mercy* on you? That I'll stop before I go too far?"

He nodded, his nostrils flaring over the web gagging him. *"Mont."*

"Don't?" I chuckled right in his face. "Oh, there's no going back now, Drake. I couldn't stop myself, even if I wanted to. Even if you showed some meagre redemption at this late hour, I wouldn't be able to prevent myself from extracting every droplet of pain I can." I let his face go, swooping to my feet. "Not because I need revenge for myself, but because you owe it to *Serigala*, to my otters, pigs, dogs, rabbits, apes, and everything in between. Your screams are for them, Drake. Your howls are for Eleanor. Your agony is theirs because it's justified...but your death..." I grinned, once again revealing blood-stained fangs. "Your death is mine, and frankly, I'm having far too much fun to rush to that finish line, aren't you?"

He thrashed in the lava-racked earth. He mumbled and moaned, turning dirt rusty with his blood.

The wolves took off, sated with what they'd eaten, no longer bound by my control. They were free, just as all creatures should be.

Another carnivore arrived.

A sabre tooth tiger that only existed in history books and fiction. Its sable coat gleamed in the fire as it prowled around

Drake, sniffing the remaining pieces.

I crossed my arms, flaring my wings and flying back a little. "Fancy a taste?"

The tiger growled, licking its chops.

"By all means, please shred my brother of his clothing."

The cat didn't wait. With unsheathed claws and a paw bigger than Drake's chest, he sliced ribbons into my brother's skin.

Drake's pain reached levels that threatened to pop eye vessels and cause cardiac arrest. He writhed and tried to crawl away, but the cat rolled him onto his stomach and slashed at his shirt from behind. Furrows of blood erupted down his back as the sabre grabbed the sliced muslin and threw it to the side.

"Good, now his trousers."

The tiger snarled and swiped at Drake's ass. Claws cut through dense material, sinking into his flesh and dragging him across the ground until the cat shook his paw to remove him.

Drake's caterwauls mingled with sobs as the tiger repeated the shredding, dragging its sharpness down Drake's legs, catching on the stump of his missing foot.

Taking the trousers in his teeth, the cat shook until Drake fell out of them. A naked, bloody, still-breathing corpse who could never die.

Not here, at least.

I could tear out his organs, one by one, and he would remain breathing.

He was a true condemned immortal.

He was sentenced to watch himself be eaten by creatures he'd never dined on but taught an agonising lesson what it felt like to be an unwilling meal.

The tiger dragged its sandpaper tongue along Drake's footless leg. It grumbled in delight, suckling at the wound.

Drake sobbed harder. His chest heaving, his nose flaring over the web, his eyes popping out of his head.

"One bite. You can choose," I whispered, never taking my eyes off the graphic smorgasbord before me.

The cat roared before pinning Drake onto his belly and sinking its fangs into his shoulder. With an effortless tug, he shredded a steak of flesh from Drake's back, revealing the whiteness of his shoulder blade, the beads of his spine, the innermost workings of a man who was full of evil.

I stayed silent as the cat gulped back his delicacy before slinking into the dark forest.

For a moment, we were alone, and I flew back to Drake. Rolling him onto his flayed back with my cloven hoof, I murmured, "I actually pity you, Drake. I pity the man I am *because* of you. I wonder if we're as bad as each other, and if I should die beside you tonight."

My wings stabbed into the ground with their hooked barbs as I braced myself. Drake tried to claw at my leg with his handless stubs. *"Mweeasssseeeeeeeee!"*

"I have a secret, brother." I looked down at what I'd done. I took responsibility that he was evil but…so was I. I'd just chosen different victims. I'd used humans. I'd purchased souls. I should be beside him having my sins ripped from equally rancid flesh.

"I'm on borrowed time." I hissed in the fiery gloom. "My heart is close to its final beat, and I have one chance of staying alive…if I choose to use it."

I ducked to my haunches, cupping my perspiring, pained brother's cheek. "But…if I can do this to you and feel no regret or want to stop…I don't think I deserve that chance, do you? It proves exactly what I feared. That I'm unredeemable, just like you. That I deserve to die. I should end our line…eradicate the last two Sinclairs from this earth because really, it's a better place without us."

Drake's gaze caught mine, amber pupils instead of our inherited blue. He was drawn and haggard, white-fleshed and small.

An echo of the man who'd locked me in a cage and tortured me.

I'd never seen him so petrified or so defeated.

It was a look I'd craved to see my entire life.

I'd finally earned it.

Finally taken vengeance on so many things.

And all I felt was empty.

Empty because it didn't bring *Serigala* back. It didn't stop him from laying his hands on Eleanor. It didn't make me a better person. If anything, it showed me just how fucking similar we were because I *liked* seeing him this way. I liked destroying him in every depraved and despicable way possible.

We're as bad as each other.

I'd come here knowing my intentions weren't heroic. Accepting my selfishness of keeping Eleanor for myself and removing my brother so he couldn't ruin our future but…what sort of future did a man like me deserve?

By doing this, I'd just condemned myself because how could I ever claim a happily ever after now? How could I sleep beside Eleanor and believe myself to be worthy of her after I enjoyed the sick pleasure of watching my brother bleed out?

Fuck.

I'd been kidding myself.

Sighing heavily, I stood to my full height and scanned the hungry beasts waiting their turn. Interspersed with bears and hyenas were shadows of so many other animals.

The darkness came alive with four-legged and feathered.

Ants and beetles, crows and vultures, deer and badgers. Rabbits from labs and apes from cages. Mice and beagles, guinea pigs and rats.

And they all had their eyes locked on Drake.

Drool dripped from jaws and cackles of hunger sent a shiver down my scale-covered spine.

Seemed I'd created an illusion that'd taken on a life of its own.

An ending I couldn't stop.

I smiled at my brethren, bowing respectfully. "Our task is not yet complete."

A growl from a bear; a wing ruffle from a vulture; a bark from a dog.

"Each take a piece. You have my blessing."

"Mwat?" Drake shook his head furiously, rubbing his bloody stumps over his mouth to try to rid himself of the spider's webbing. *"Mooooo!"*

"Goodbye, Drake." I unfurled my wings and swooped backward, avoiding gore splatters—relinquishing my sibling to them.

Only once I nodded again did the creatures move in mass. They were a part of me. Figments of my psyche, every painful memory, every doomed stray. Each of them made up Drake's destiny, ready to tear him into *nothing*.

I clenched my hands together, almost as if I worshipped at the church of carnage as a bear lumbered into Drake and knocked him onto his back. With a bared snout, he buried his teeth into Drake's belly.

My brother did more than howl.

He howled with his entire body. His soul screamed in clamour, tears spilled down his cheeks, and he wailed as he endured the cracking of his ribs and the wet mastication of his kidney as the bear burrowed deep and tore out one of the iron-rich organs.

Once the bear had swallowed, he moved away, granting a smaller animal to take his place.

A swarm of ants covered Drake, fire stinging and swift.

Drake shrieked as they poured into his abdominal cavity, reappearing a few seconds later with pieces too small to recognise. They marched into the eerie forest, each holding aloft micro pieces of what I assumed were Drake's intestines.

Gritting my teeth and feeling my fangs dig into my chin, I never took my eyes off Drake as he slowly turned from man to misery.

A deer nuzzled next, pulling out Drake's liver before tossing it to a hyena to eat. A chimpanzee hopped close, wrapping its dexterous fingers around Drake's cock and yanking it clean off his body. Balls and all.

Drake screamed louder, his throat shredding with ear-splitting screeches.

I winced as the demolished manhood vanished into the monkey's mouth.

Both herbivore and carnivore systemically broke him apart, representing so many dishes he'd chosen. So many lab tests he'd approved.

Time lost all meaning as Drake's internal organs slowly vanished into the mouths of beasts. Shreds of his flesh were torn off, revealing his skeleton beneath.

His heart pumped with terror in an open hole within him.

His screams turned to wails and finally fell into whimpers.

His body jerked as each creature approached, chose, and chewed.

A spurt of lava erupted from the encrusted ground, rumbling with warning that a volcano bubbled beneath our feet, ready to wipe this fantasy clean once Drake had been consumed. Once his evil had been spilled. Once he was no longer capable of surviving.

I stayed and watched it all.

My wings kept me propped up when my heart stuttered and buckled beneath Tritec, warning I'd reached critical consumption. The stacking effect, keeping me strong and functioning, had reached its fatal toll. I was at the pinnacle of my power. The crest of my strength. The only way forward from here was the inevitable shutting down of my body that could no longer survive on lies.

Tritec-87 was designed to give high strength and whip-quick

intelligence in bad accidents requiring self-evacuation. It did precisely what it'd been designed to do—stealing health and vitality from other parts of my body, conning the brain into believing all systems worked perfectly.

But the brain was too smart to be lied to by adrenaline for long. Eventually, the neural network kicked back in, revealing the extent of injuries and exhaustion, prompting a rapid contingency plan to stay alive.

It was that contingency plan that killed the host. A cannibalistic side effect of the brain taking back control. The chemicals it released, the attempts at self-repair, all rapidly increasing the pressure of a system that already operated at max voltage.

The result?

A fried circuit—a stroke or heart attack caused by the very same body you'd been trying to save.

I could feel the distancing already, the strangeness of acknowledging I would soon be free of this form. Not just freed of this fanged monster I'd created, but the shell I'd been born into.

I sighed as the wolves returned, awaiting their final snack once the furred and feathered crowd had had their fill.

Not much of Drake was left.

His inner organs removed. His eyes pecked out by vultures. His tongue chomped on by a beagle. His torso the only thing left with no arms or legs.

"Wait," I whispered, splaying my membrane wings and swooping to stand over Drake.

The wolves paused, sitting on their haunches as I did the same and cupped Drake's cheek.

Sticky with blood and ice, ice cold, Drake mumbled with a tongueless mouth something I couldn't understand.

His empty eye sockets couldn't relay a message.

His missing lungs couldn't draw breath.

He was well and truly my prisoner, unable to run, beg, or strike. For a man who'd been spoiled and privileged his entire life, being reduced to nothing but a pile of viscera and bones was a savage and fitting end.

"I'm leaving you now. I'm leaving you within this nightmare where you can never die. That is your true punishment, Drake. Not being mauled and devoured but never being whole again. You took so many pieces of my happiness. You never let me be who I could've become because you took so much of my trust.

This…this is my attempt at showing you how it feels to exist with parts of you missing. Parts you need to be a functional individual. Parts that are integral to being human."

I scanned the animals, their peace granting me peace. Their satisfaction doing its best to fill the emptiness within me. I'd done my best at plugging up my holes by caring for those far more innocent than me. I'd fought my love for Eleanor because it showed me just how much I'd failed at life.

This was the burnout I'd been running from. The absolute acknowledgment that I couldn't be saved. That I didn't *want* to be because I hadn't done enough to be absolved. My lack of trust had been exhausting. My life of loneliness had been miserable.

If this was the end…at least I would be free of such things.

Eleanor would be free of me making further mistakes.

The world would be free of my entitlement and black and white rules.

Looking down at my bleeding brother, I accepted our joint end.

I chose a fate far more fitting for a man like me and let the burnout wash over me. I was tired. So, so fucking tired. It was almost a relief to stop trying. And besides, thanks to Tritec, I was most likely dead anyway—whether I chose such a finale or not.

"I've made my choice, Drake. Just like you stole pieces from me, I refuse to keep on living with them gone. I was kidding myself to think I could heal. That Eleanor was the cure I needed. A devil cannot change his colours…not after he's embraced such a calling—not when we are true brothers and share the same sickness and sadism."

I ran my hands through his bloody hair. "But don't worry, brother. My time is short so you won't suffer too long. When I feel my heart failing, I'll come back for you. We can die together…just like we were raised together."

Standing, I bowed at the creatures who'd formed a semi-circle around Drake and the fire. "Guard him. Nibble some more if you get hungry."

A lone wolf howl made Drake's eyeless sockets weep.

I looked one last time at the most horrific thing I'd done.

I waited for regret, for shame, for some barometer of right and wrong to tell me I'd gone too far.

But just like I was empty, I was grateful too.

Grateful that Drake was dealt with.

Soon, *I* would be dealt with.

And the circle of life for two monsters would be complete.

But before that happened…

Before I took my last inhale and accepted my encroaching death, I had a goddess I wanted to make love to one last time. A woman to adore and a queen who wore a priceless crown.

A crown that needed one last jewel to be complete.

It needed my heart because she was the one and only owner of it.

She could cut it from my chest and chisel it into a diamond because only in her care could it be redeemed.

Tucking up my wings, I inhaled a sharp breath.

I didn't have another sedative to knock me out of this fantasy.

But I did have a thrice broken leg just waiting to black me out if I put full pressure on it.

Gritting my fangs, I stepped forward.

I walked in the illusion.

I tripped in real life.

My bones fractured further.

My ankle shattered.

My toes cracked.

I passed out and left the realm of myth.

Chapter Nine

I LOST HIM.

In the inky blackness of fake slumber, I felt a severing of our bond.

A decision I couldn't undo.

A finality I couldn't stop.

I sat at the bottom of a pit. A pit with no walls to climb and no air to breathe. Dark and dismal, it kept me far away from the light of consciousness.

I couldn't wake up.

Couldn't move.

I screamed.

No one heard me.

I tried to climb.

I fell back down.

I begged Sully not to leave me.

Only darkness replied.

Sullivan

Chapter Ten

DARKNESS HAD DESCENDED BEFORE I gained consciousness.

I woke on the Oriental silk rug that my father had bought in Taiwan after buying the copyrights to an anti-aging serum made of rhino horn—one I obliterated from my pharmaceuticals the moment I took power.

Lights had come on automatically and snow fell softly outside—worlds away from my crystal sand and swaying palms.

No birds flew, making my heart pang for two parrots that'd been a part of my life for so many years.

That hurt.

So fucking much.

I wouldn't be able to say goodbye to Pika or Skittles. I wouldn't be able to explain to them why I never came home.

Home.

I had no heirs. No one to bequeath my islands and fortunes to.

I struggled into a slouched sitting position, careful not to twinge my leg.

My gaze fell on Eleanor. She lay across the room in a foetal pose. Her arms wrapped tight around her knees as if she dreamed of horrors. Her hair covered her shoulders like a coffee blanket, tendrils hiding her nipples and cleavage.

Her.

She was my heir.

She and Cal would inherit it all because they were the purest people I knew.

My to-do list before death had just increased.

Time is running out.

If you want her one last time…you better hurry.

Looking past Eleanor to Drake, I curled my fists. Still locked in the illusion, he sat stiff on the couch he'd tied Eleanor too. Sweat ran in rivulets off him, staining the embroidered settee with wetness. His skin was so white, his veins stood out like the wiring of a machine, criss-crossing blue veins and red arteries.

He panted short, tight breaths as if he fully believed he had no lungs to inflate.

He moaned and thrashed, his eyes tightly closed.

Blood trickled from his nose and ears, symptoms of his brain suffering aneurysms from what I'd done to him inside our shared hallucination.

Seeing him whole after watching his avatar be devoured made my need to hurt him billow again. I might have torn apart his mind. I might have turned him into a vegetable that he'd always mocked and reduced him to something I could uproot from my gardens in *Lebah,* but his body was still whole.

No bones had been broken; no physical punishment delivered.

Had I done enough? Or should I hurt his body as well as his soul?

A knock sounded, wrenching my head to the closed double doors. "Mr. Sinclair…Sullivan, not Drake. You alive?"

"Ye—" I choked and coughed, my voice returning to that of a mortal man instead of a fanged monster. "Yes, I'm alive. It's done. I require your services."

The door cracked open, and the leader of the mercenaries, hired from a firm I'd used in the past, entered. His black hair was slicked back, his goatee trim and precise, just like his aim. "What can we do?"

Two men trailed after him, staying back for commands.

Still on the floor, not willing to risk passing out again, I pointed past the Euphoria boxes to the defib on the couch beside Drake. "Do you know how to use one of those?"

The leader stepped closer, holstering his weapon when he saw Drake weaving and moaning, another trickle of blood seeping from his ears.

His lips twisted in disgust, a quick flicker of wariness at me for what I'd done, before he glanced at the medical bag and nodded. "The travel defibrillator. Yes, I was in the Army as a medic. I'm aware of how they work."

"Good." Holding out my hand, I barked, "Help me up."

The leader marched to me, gritting his teeth against my proximity as he hauled me up onto one leg and passed me the cane from the floor. He shot a look at naked Eleanor sleeping on the carpet and back to nude Drake drooling with the occasional hiccupping sob. "What happened?"

"Nothing that didn't need to happen." Curling my hand around the smooth ball of the cane, I ordered, "Hook him up to the defib. Have one of your men sit beside him. The moment he shows signs of falling asleep, zap him. I want him to stay awake until I say so, got it?"

The leader nodded respectfully with a fair dose of wariness. "Consider it done."

With the help of my cane, I limped toward Eleanor. Her skin puckered with goosebumps, and even in a drugged sleep, she shivered.

Unlike her nakedness, I still wore my clothing, fully aware that we weren't in the tropics and even a heated house was not warm enough for long stints of nudity.

She needs a bed and covers.

Now.

Drake let out a guttural groan.

I narrowed my gaze, looking his way as he swayed and jerked as if something gnawed his bones. The mercenaries swallowed hard as more blood gushed from his ears, staining the sides of his face with crimson.

For hardened criminals with the taste of delivering death, they seemed unsettled with Drake's condition. Afraid of a man who seemed intact, yet his brain dribbled over his shoulders like treacle.

"I do expect him to stay awake." My voice resembled a drill, slow and merciless, puncturing their concerned fascination. "If you allow him to sleep, I will not be kind with my displeasure."

Radcliffe, the leader of this merry band of murderers, nodded. "He will be kept awake. You have my word."

"Good." Pointing at the ancient armoire tucked against the wall, I ordered, "Inside you'll find a blanket. Bring it to me."

One of the men shot into action, ripping open the cupboard and pulling free a thick silver blanket. Carrying it to me, he waited while I did my best to duck and drape it over Eleanor.

I struggled with pain threatening to send me under again and the agonising need to protect her. I couldn't bend. Couldn't crouch. Couldn't do a goddamn fucking thing.

Cursing my broken leg, hating my limited mobility, I eyed the men.

Goddammit.

I wanted to be the one to carry her to bed. I *needed* to be that man. To still show strength even in the shadow of my death. To hold her weight and cradle her while she slept. But...carrying her up the flight of marble stairs was an impossibility. Even climbing them myself wasn't going to be doable.

Sighing hard, I pinched the bridge of my nose, doing my best to squeeze out the poisonous weakness inside me. "Someone will need to carry her."

"I'll do it." Radcliffe volunteered, striding quickly as if understanding how fucking gut-wrenching this was for me. How much I wished I wasn't a goddamn cripple.

Without a word, he tucked the blanket around her and scooped her naked form from the carpet. I ensured no part of her skin touched his and the blanket protected her decency before nodding stiffly. "A guest room is on this floor, toward the back of the house. Follow me."

He nodded, waiting for me to hobble back to Drake and scoop up the abandoned cell phone beside him.

Drake mumbled something incoherent as another gush of blood dribbled out of his nose. He jerked as if something mauled him, followed by a thin scream. He trembled and hyperventilated, looking every bit a pitiful prey.

Enjoy your evening, brother.

Turning my back on him, I led the leader with Eleanor in his arms through the maze of wide artwork-adorned corridors. My pace was slow and laborious. My nervous system no longer able to ignore the shards of agony in my leg, ankle, and foot. The flesh wound from the harpoon had been demoted in terms of pain, and the consuming ache from broken bones made me snappish with fresh fury.

I wanted to be there when Eleanor woke.

I wanted to kiss her and love her and say goodbye without sweating with pain. I needed her one last time, and I'd be fucked if I let her remember sleeping with a broken man instead of the monster she'd fallen for.

"Tell one of your men to bring all the painkillers available in the house. Mrs. Bixel will show you where they are."

"Of course," the leader murmured, following me into the large guest suite decorated in muted blues and greys. The large king bed with its carved white headboard, looked out to the snow-dusted gardens. A sculpture of swans caught the moonlight. Snowflakes glittered like fallen stars from the heavens, catching in the deck lights.

"Place her on the bed."

The mercenary did as I asked, lowering her carefully in the bundled blanket. Only once her weight had been completely transferred to the mattress did he let go and back away. "I'll bring the painkillers as requested and keep Drake Sinclair awake. Is there anything else?"

I wobbled, clutching my cane for support. "No. Mrs. Bixel will arrange breakfast. For the rest of the night, I wish to be undisturbed with Ms. Grace." I swallowed back another wash of pain. "I appreciate your meticulous work, Radcliffe."

He bowed. "Appreciate the business, Sinclair." Heading to the exit, he wrapped his hand around the doorknob. He looked over his shoulder, adding, "If you require protection for…" His gaze skittered to Eleanor before settling on back on mine. "You can set up a contract with us for a lifetime of cover, whether or not you are around."

I hid my sneer. "That obvious, huh?" If the mercenary could taste my death, it meant I didn't have much longer.

He shrugged. "Been in this business long enough to recognise the end."

Hopping toward the bed, I nodded. "Keep her safe and do what she asks. Her word is your new law."

"We'll do whatever she asks and protect her at all costs."

I hadn't intended on gifting Eleanor an entire team of hired killers, but who better to keep her safe after I died? They would return her safely to Goddess Isles. They would do what I could not and ensure she went home.

Home.

Christ, I missed my sand, my sea, my sunshine.

The only way I'd be going home was in a body bag.

Shaking off my stinking self-pity, I caught his shrewd stare and cocked my chin at the door. "Thank you for your loyalty. My lawyer will be in touch."

"Sleep well, Sinclair." He left and closed the door.

The moment he was gone, I collapsed onto the mattress and

pinched the bridge of my nose again. This time I added nails, driving into the cartilage, causing more pain because I had no way of bleeding out the agony.

Fuck!

Drake was dealt with.

Eleanor was safe.

My animals were safe.

Our future could've been…happy.

Rubbing my eyes, I removed my lenses and earbuds from Euphoria then repeated the process and freed Eleanor from hers. Looking at her, so vulnerable and worn out, I fought the indescribable urge to crawl under the blanket and hold her.

Happy.

I'd wanted that.

I'd wanted her to teach me how to embrace joy instead of justice.

But after what I'd done to Drake. And what I'd done to purchased women and rented souls… I doubted I'd ever see her again.

Certainly not in heaven and definitely not in reincarnation—if such realms existed. She was destined for wings. Either as an angel or as a bird—free to soar the skies.

Me?

I was destined for hellfire or the life of a creature that had to creep and crawl.

Stroking the delicate contour of her cheek, I sighed. *I wish I deserved you.*

Shadows crept over my vision, whispering of sleep and rest. My fingers tingled from touching her, the never-ending hum of our bond.

It would be so easy to slip. To sleep and gather my strength beside her, so I could say my physical goodbye, but…I still had one last thing to do before I could allow myself any final indulgences.

Pulling my phone from my pocket, I pulled up a new email and typed:

To: MurphyandCockran@law.com
From: S.Sinclair@goddessisles.com
Subject: New Will and Testament.

To Elliot,

It seems I have need of updating my Will and Testament. Please amend the bulk of my fortune to be gifted between Ms. Eleanor Grace and Mr. Calvin Moor. My islands are to be bequeathed to Ms. Eleanor Grace. Sinclair and Sinclair Group to Mr. Calvin Moor. The animal charities I have already donated to will receive fifteen percent of everything with the remaining stocks, shares, and savings to be split equally between the two individuals mentioned.

Ownership of my two caiques, Skittles and Pika, are hereby transferred to Ms. Eleanor Grace.

Please also include amendments to ensure Mr. Calvin Moor makes a two-million-dollar donation to Jessica Townsend, if she survives.

Please accept these new conditions as they are made while I am of sound body and mind.

Thank you for your services throughout the years.

Yours sincerely,

Sullivan Sinclair.

I pressed send.

Standing, I stripped my clothing, keeping my grunts of agony as quiet as I could.

Only once I was naked did I let down my guards and allow exhaustion to find me.

With the heaviest sigh of a man saying goodbye to everything he'd hoped to be worthy of, I slipped under the blanket and pulled Eleanor close.

I kissed her hair.

I inhaled her orchid and island scent.

I loved her.

I missed her.

I slept.

Chapter Eleven

I OPENED MY EYES.

No villa rafters or Skittles.

No muggy heat or soft waves.

Where am I?

I blinked and looked around the room. A large space with wraparound doors leading to an expansive deck. Light grey walls, whitewash blue drapes, and a pressed steel ceiling glittering silver in the moonlight.

Snow fell.

As it blanketed the world, it reminded me we weren't in the tropics one icy flake at a time.

I shivered as a breeze slipped over my skin.

So that was what woke me.

A chill.

No, not just a chill…the removal of a large comforting presence who'd held me while I'd slept.

Sully.

My heart stuttered and rejoiced. Energy gathered to throw myself across the mattress and hug him.

But…I stilled.

My heart hiccupped and mourned. I lay in the shadows and drank in the man who'd bought me, broke me, and set me free. A man I would love for eternity…through thick or thin, rich or poor, sickness or health. A man who looked as if he was about to test that last promise and see if was strong enough to hold on to him.

Instincts had been given to all creatures, wild and domestic, to keep them alive. A sixth sense that whispered all wasn't well, even if your eyes and ears told you otherwise.

Those instincts yelled too loudly now.

Sully was alive. My eyes told me so.

But…something had happened.

Something he couldn't undo, and I couldn't stop.

A new enemy neither of us could fight.

He sat on the edge of the bed in the snow-cast moonlight, his nakedness revealing so many mottled and marred bruises. His spine bowed, his torso a patchwork of cuts, scrapes, and punishments at the hands of Drake.

I gasped at what he'd lived through.

I wept for every talisman of pain he wore and the utter defeat of his rolled, sculptured shoulders. This wasn't the same man who'd stood high on his sandy throne and couldn't take his eyes off me as I'd arrived on his islands. This wasn't the same mogul who'd yanked me from a bath and kissed me as if he'd die from not taking me.

This wasn't Sullivan Sinclair—the perfect puzzle piece to my soul—who'd made love to me in Nirvana and sat beside me while two parrots completed our chosen family.

He's a hologram.

A living, breathing man quickly fading into a flickering, disappearing mirage.

No.

I won't let it.

I refuse.

Pushing onto my hands and knees, I went to him. I crawled across the bed with the large blanket still draped over me and kneeled beside him. "Sully…"

He shuddered as his head tilted to face me. His blue eyes rose. Our gazes locked. He gave me a heartbreakingly tender smile. "I didn't mean to wake you."

I didn't answer.

I *couldn't.*

Words formed a plug in my throat. Apologies and affirmations, violence and vows. I wanted to thank him for saving me, ask how he'd entered Euphoria, how he'd freed me and stopped elixir from killing me, and just how it'd come to pass that he was here, sitting on a bed with me in Switzerland when the last time I'd seen him, he'd been plummeting to the unforgiving sea below.

I wanted to demand to know what he'd done to make him so despairing.

I needed to scream at him.

I needed to love him.

So many things.

Too many things.

So…I ignored it all.

I focused on the only important part…*us*…and snuggled close to put my head on his shoulder.

He sighed heavily, his chin tilting to kiss the top of my hair. His body shuddered and his voice held a thousand daggers. "Fuck, I love you, Eleanor…the greatest jinx of my life."

Fresh tears mixed with old. I nuzzled into his throat and kissed him.

His skin was cooler than I was used to, thanks to the missing heat of his Goddess Isles. He tasted salty and stale, as if he hadn't had a shower since being plucked from the ocean and flying to find me.

I wanted to suggest a warm bath. To soak away the many bruises painting him and wash away his harsh misery, but my attention fell to his leg, and my insides clenched in a vice.

His stitched thigh looked angry and once again infected. His flesh was swollen and so much redder than the rest of him. Bumps and new contusions hinted he'd been hurt in his fall to the sea. Hurt enough to drain him of his final brutal reserves.

He inhaled, spreading his chest, revealing his tanned torso and powerful muscles slipping beneath pained skin. He looked pinched and at max exertion—an athlete who'd kept racing, even if it meant consuming his own body mass to convert fuel into energy.

"You need to eat," I murmured, lifting my head off his shoulder. "And you need to see a doctor."

He chuckled quietly, opening his palm that sat between his spread thighs. "I'm my own doctor tonight."

I sucked in a breath.

A handful of pills had jumbled together. Some with white casings, some with blue. Round and oval, gel capsules and dissoluble. My gaze skittered to the bedside table and the numerous empty bottles of painkillers scattered there.

"I didn't mean to disturb you," he whispered as he ran his thumb over the small apothecary he'd formed in his palm. "I'd hoped I could consume these and have them kick in before you did."

"You can't take that many, Sully. Your system won't handle it."

"My system?" He laughed under his breath. "My system can't handle much these days." Wiping his mouth with the back of his other hand, he continued staring at the drugs, a deliberation weighing on him.

I tried to claim them, to scoop them from his palm. "Let's call a doctor. They'll give you antibiotics for your wounds; they'll give you a stronger painkiller than those you can find in a bottle."

He jerked his hand away, shaking his head slightly. "Don't have the time for that, my darling Jinx."

Icy dread skated down my spine. "What do you mean?"

"I mean…" His vibrant sapphire gaze met mine. "I'm in pain, and I want that pain to go away."

Flickering images of the monster he'd been in Euphoria came and went. His pupils had been snake slits then. His handsome face fanged and scaled.

He'd been invincible.

And I had absolutely no doubt he'd won against Drake. He'd faced his brother in a realm of his own making and he'd come out an only child.

I didn't need him to confirm that he was the victor. I *felt* it. I felt it in the peace he held and also the emptiness. I saw it in his eyes—the acceptance of finally ending a lifelong feud and the hollow aftermath.

He might've been a hellion within that nightmare, but now…now he was just a man.

A man I was desperately in love with, and one I couldn't help because I didn't have the skills necessary to heal him.

I stroked his cheek, forcing myself to touch him and feel his realness.

He's alive.

And he'll stay that way.

You'll see.

His eyes snapped closed, his entire body quaking at my touch. "I'm sorry." His cock hung heavy and thick between his legs, swelling rapidly with need. "I'm sorry that he took you. That he hurt you. That I was almost too late—"

"Stop." I kissed him softly. "No apologies. It's over. It's just us now."

He trembled, a husky groan falling from his lips. "I must've done something right amongst all the shit I did wrong…to have deserved you…just for a little while."

My heart forgot how to beat. "You have me forever, not just for a little while."

He didn't reply.

His large, strong hand cupped my breast. His gaze locked on my nipple as if awed he had permission to touch me. The sinew of his fingers. The pronounced veins roping his impressive forearm. Such masculine attributes did their best to convince me that Sully was undefeatable, all while he spoke as if he'd lost.

His touch dropped from my breast over the curve of my waist to the swell of my hip. His eyes devoured my nakedness, the blue of his pupils flashing as if he took photograph after photograph of my nudity, creating a collage of memories…as if he might never see me this way again.

His intensity made me shiver, but I made no move to cover up. His cock kept hardening, a proud mast with desire glistening at the tip.

No clothes were required.

No lies.

No embellishments.

It was everything he didn't say that made me cry and every way he touched me that made me moan.

His cashmere suits and silken ties had deceived me into thinking he was more than just human. Yet his stripped back viciousness and vulnerability made him otherworldly. The severity of his stare. The graveness of his voice and the grimness of his touch made everything between us lethal to my heart.

"I love you, Sully." I snuggled into him, smashing the tension and hugging him close. "I love you with everything that I am."

His arms snapped around me. Shackles and sonnets. Chains and confessions. He squeezed me as if I could become a part of him. He shuddered as I hugged him back, inhaling his scent, imprinting him, not just on my heart, but on my forever.

The hum that never failed to spark between us struck a smouldering match. Our linked souls sank deeper into their connection. We were joined, knotted and tangled.

For always.

"Sully…" I kissed the shell of his ear, struggling to breathe because he held me so tight. "Whatever you're afraid of…tell me."

He quivered in my embrace, a tumbling growl echoing in his

chest. "I'm not afraid."

"Then why—"

"I'm grateful. So fucking grateful that I found you."

"I'm grateful too. I'm so thankful that you survived, and that you came, and that we can go home now, and—"

He kissed me, deeply, thoroughly.

The flat of his tongue massaged mine. His teeth scraped my bottom lip. His lust swept down my throat with a different taste of before. It wasn't just lust he kissed with…it was sharper than that, scarier than that.

It's goodbye.

Ripping away from him, I struggled in his arms. "What's going on?" Narrowing my gaze at the painkillers still clenched in his fist, I added, "If you're in such pain, let me get help. Let me—"

"I hope you can forgive me…one day."

"Forgive you? Why would I have to forgive you?"

He cupped my breast again, pinching my nipple and activating the faded thirst of elixir. My thoughts scattered; my worry evaporated.

"I need you, Eleanor." His grunt set fire to the liquid between my legs, ensuring I needed him just as much. *No, I need him more.* I needed him because he was scaring me, because he was hiding something.

He wasn't allowed to do that.

There was no space for fibs or fakery.

Not after everything we'd fought to overcome.

"Sully…please, tell me what you're hiding. How do I fix this?"

"By letting me have you." His mouth once again claimed mine. Swift kisses and violent hunger. Snatching me from the bed, he dragged me from the blanket and onto his lap.

He groaned, and I moaned as our skin slid against each other, his chilly from sitting with no protection and mine toasty from the blanket. His erection nudged my belly as he gathered me close and spread my legs, wedging them on either side of him.

He kissed me harder, all while the pings and bouncing chaos of pills as they fell to the floor became background noise. Both his hands swept through my hair, cradling the back of my head as he deepened our kiss.

He kissed me until my mind swam and my heart curtsied, and I was a melted, molten puddle in his lap.

He grunted as I rocked my hips, the natural need to mate

overshadowing the skill of conversation. The heat of his stitched thigh pressed against my ass, and I froze. "I'm sorry."

He gritted his teeth as I tried to slip off his lap. "Don't."

"But I'm hurting you."

"You'll hurt me more if you deny me." Grabbing my thighs, he spread them wider. Running his powerful hands down my legs, he locked them into position behind him, linking my ankles together as if binding us together. "You're not going anywhere."

"But you're hurt—"

His mouth plundered mine.

His hands grabbed fistfuls of my hair, and he kissed me as if he'd been kissing me his whole life. Savage and smooth, sinful and sensual. His tongue licked me and made love to me and fucked me with every debased, divine way possible.

I met his invasion with my own tongue, lapping at him, dancing, knotting everything that we were.

The chill coating his skin vanished, leaving his body unbearably hot. I held onto his shoulders and let him kiss me. Sweat broke through his pores as another grunt of sheer agony rumbled in his chest.

I tried to pull away, to get off him and go for help, but he wrapped his arms around me, keeping me prisoner, ignoring my denial.

Our mouths slipped free as he buried his face into my cleavage, panting hard, steam almost rising from him in a mix of pain and need. "Let me have you, Eleanor. I'm begging you."

His hands spasms around me. Another low growl of discomfort made me mad. "But I'm *hurting* you—"

"You could never hurt me."

"My weight on your leg—"

"This is the only position I can have you."

"You're in pain from the helicopter—"

"I don't care."

"*I* care." I tried to push him away, my hands colliding with the brick wall of his very male chest. "I refuse to hurt you when—"

"You're hurting me more than I can stand by saying no."

"I'm not saying no. I'm saying you can have me in a few days...when you're feeling—"

"I need you now. I can't wait."

"Why? *Why* can't you wait?" I ran my hands through his damp hair. "You need to rest."

"Rest?" He snorted. "I can rest later." He shoved my hands away. His temper appeared, fierce and flashing over his gorgeous face. "And I'll tell you why I can't wait. I watched my brother fly away with you. I arrived to you fighting him off. I came face to face with almost losing you, and it made me realise so many fucking things." His nostrils flared. "I love you more than anything, and I've caused you the worst kind of pain. Multiple times over. I look at you, and I can't stop seeing everything that I've done. Every hurt I've caused. Every drop of blood I've spilled. And I—"

I kissed him.

I shut him up as his chest seized and the thunder of his heart stuttered strangely.

I kissed him because I didn't want to hear the aggressive torture in his tone, but his heart once again thrashed behind his ribcage and jolted his whole body.

I went to pull away, pressing my fingertips to the out-of-sync drumming of his pulse, but he dragged me close. So close. Too close.

He inhaled me, devoured me.

He dropped his hand between my legs and rubbed my clit with every electrical fire we shared. "Is elixir still in your blood?"

I moaned as he pinched my clit, activating a million sparks. Didn't he know *he* was my elixir? I didn't need a vial of lust when he was the creator. "Faint...if any."

"The sedative kept your heart from giving out." He tested my wetness, dipping the tip of his finger inside me, making me clench and shudder. "I'm glad it worked."

"You knocked me out?"

"I wasn't in the position to fuck you at the time." One long finger dipped inside me, frustrating and provoking. "I couldn't allow you to be in such pain. After last time...Christ, Eleanor, I would've done whatever it took to protect you."

His heart continued to thrum oddly, distracting me. "Sully...please talk to me. What's going on—"

"Stop." His forehead pressed to mine. His glowing gaze so close, his face twisted with ardent need. "Don't question me. Don't stop me. Just...let me have you before..."

I frowned, hearing a phantom sentence that wasn't verbalized.

Let me have you before ...*before we go home?* ...*while it's still dark?*

Horror made me shiver.

Let me have you before ...*I can't.*

My eyes flared.

Pain cracked my ribs.

Fear made me snappish. "Sully, stop this. Right now. Whatever you're not telling me—"

"Hush." He ducked his head again, breaking eye contact to deliberately keep his secrets. His mouth found my nipple, sucking my breast deep into his mouth. "Be mine...just for a little longer."

His voice vibrated along my sensitive skin. His plea doused the terror in my blood. All while his heart continued to pound, strong if not regular, possessive if not normal.

He came for you.

He's asking for one thing.

Give it to him.

His teeth teased my nipple. His nose pressed against my soft flesh. His fingers found my pussy again, driving two deep inside me.

I wasn't immune to him, no matter my worries. He'd always had the power to command my body without elixir deleting my proprieties. We had undying magic, a potion and alchemy that switched rationality into insanity.

"Eleanor...give in." He licked and nipped at my cleavage, inhaling hard before capturing my other nipple.

I gave up.

I gave in.

I crumpled in his arms, totally at his mercy.

He felt my acquiescence straight away, gathering me tight and suckling hard on my breast. He laved and bit, tugging on invisible strings connected to my heart and core.

He'd been given my permission.

But he remembered he wasn't a gentleman who needed submission but a monster who took what he wanted, and he switched from sensual to primal, pulling deeper on my nipple, sucking blood to the tip, making my pussy clench with hunger.

I bowed in his arms.

He was killing me.

Killing *us.*

"I love you so much, Eleanor, so fucking much. I need you to remember that. Remember me."

I stayed quiet.

I choked on my tears.

I allowed my awful suspicions to sweep me into pain all while he granted me pleasure.

He didn't have the strength for this.

I wouldn't survive whatever waited for us at the end.

But I wouldn't stop him.

He wanted me.

He would have me.

Always.

Three of his fingers speared inside me.

"Oh, *God.*" I clung to his head, all while his teeth sank into my shoulder and his chest thudded with peculiar beats. He held me as if he used up every remaining bit of strength to stay with me. His fingers bruised me. His lust scorched me. He drove his fingers deeper, stretching me, corrupting me, making me ready to fuck.

His thumb pressed against my clit, conjuring an unwilling release, proving once again he was the maestro and I was his silly conquest, a sheep bowing to the wolf.

I didn't let the orgasm shatter me. Not yet. I was afraid of it. Afraid of what it represented and the end it promised to deliver.

"Sit on me." His fingers withdrew, and his cock replaced them. His hands clamped onto my hips, pushing me down, down, down his impressive girth.

My lips parted on a silent scream.

His groan echoed in the silent room.

Our bodies rejected the pressure, overwhelmed with the suddenness, the sweetness, the savageness.

I shuddered as he plunged inside me, filling every space, spreading me to take more. No one else had ever made me feel this consumed, this taken, this owned.

He *owned* me.

And it hurt because I didn't think I had that same right. Whatever ownership I'd had over him was fading, and I couldn't stop it.

Couldn't stop missing him even as he filled me. Couldn't stop worrying that this was all I'd ever have.

I clung to him as we sank into each other. Only once we were sheathed tight and together did he look up.

And my heart fucking *shattered.*

His blue eyes sparkled with wetness.

A wetness that glittered with diamonds as he pushed me up and pulled me back down. Smearing my lubrication over him, reacquainting my body with his hard possession.

His jaw clenched as he felt my every ridge and ripple.

His hips drove upward, followed by a full-body spasm and heavy groan. His heart went haywire, shaking his body with peculiar pulses.

"Sully!" I tried to climb off him.

His lips pulled back in a snarl. "*Don't.* You're mine. I'm having you." He shook his head as if struggling to stay coherent. Pain chiselled his face until each stark angle looked like blades. He coughed, his voice less violent than before. "Move for me...please."

Such a profound perforating request.

"Move. Fuck me, Jinx." He kissed me, our eyes wide open and so close. Understanding rife between us but words too afraid to make it true.

It's not my heart in trouble this time...it's his.

No...

His hips rose again, making him tremble and almost black out.

"Stop." Suffocating on silent sobs, I placed my hands on his scorching shoulders and pushed away. "Please, stop."

"I can't." He gathered me closer and sighed heavily, his messy bronze-tipped hair sticking to his sweaty forehead. His head tipped as he looked at where we joined. He bit his bottom lip as he watched the graphic impalement of his flesh within mine. "Make love to me, Eleanor."

Tears rained down my cheeks as I followed his stare and looked at where we were linked.

I witnessed the raw and fundamentally basic connection between lovers.

The glisten of me and the steel of him.

And I did what he requested.

I moved.

I didn't have the strength not to.

We never looked away from our joining. Of the heavy veins of his erection as I slid up, and the spreading of my folds as I sank low.

It was hypnotic, entrancing—doing its best to trick us that this was ordinary sex between ordinary people when really...it was rife with unsaid, unmentionable things.

His hands caressed my breasts as I settled on a rhythm.

Deep and drawing, a rocking that confirmed ownership over each other.

We lost ourselves to the beat. Our lips sought each other's, and we kissed and fucked and made love and promised and vowed and fought every farewell and miserable goodbye.

The bed creaked as my pace grew faster.

His breath scalded my cheek as his nostrils flared, kissing me deeper.

Our tongues tangled and our hands touched and worshipped, memorizing every scar and imperfection, cataloguing it all because we *were* perfection.

Together, we were exactly what we were meant to be. Precisely who we were meant to find.

I sank deep, hitting the top of him with the top of me.

He quaked and tore his mouth from mine. "Jesus *Christ*." His arms wrapped tight around me, holding on or holding me close—I couldn't distinguish anymore.

I rode him and climbed the mountain of a climax that promised suffering instead of ecstasy.

He rocked me faster.

I fucked him quicker.

We clawed and thrust, gasping and begging for reprieve.

I closed my eyes and memorized what it felt like to have his body inside mine. The hardness, the heat. I savoured every touch and tingle. I swooped up and sank down, over and over, taking him, riding him.

I loved his mind, his soul, and his body. I loved the feeling of tenderness and threats in his arms. I treasured the sensation of his thirst for me and the swelling of his pleasure.

But most of all, I loved the way his love was a tangible, touchable thing. It glowed in his eyes, it scalded his skin, it set fire to the room with commitment and calamity.

I rode him harder, punishing both of us.

His entire body trembled, his heart continued to flounder, and his groans of need welded with his grunts of misery, finally punctured with a howl that made my tears turn inward and flood me.

Sullivan Sinclair reached his pinnacle and let go. His cock spurted inside me. Wave after wave as if his body knew it only had one last chance to come. His back rolled, his arms spasmed around me, and his teeth found my throat as I chased him.

My release focused more in my heart than in my core—a transmuted, diseased orgasm that offered no release, only a series of rapid clenching and palpitations.

It was the worst release of my life because it wasn't a release…it was a cruel incarceration into whatever was about to happen next.

We clung to each other as the pulses of our shared climax faded.

Only once we could breathe again did I pull away from Sully, slip my leg over his lap, and disconnect us.

He winced as I disengaged and sat beside him.

I did my best to keep my stare off his mottled injuries, the black stitches in his leg or the new bumps that he refused to acknowledge.

This wasn't the time to bring up my fears.

It wasn't my place to get angry with him when he had no energy to fight back.

But…

We *had* no more time.

And it was my right to worry.

I'd done what he'd asked…*now it's my turn.*

With his seed trickling out of me, I wrapped the blanket and my temper around my shoulders and prepared for war. I allowed my suspicions to whisper truth in my ears. I stopped being blind. I let logic reveal everything he'd hidden.

He thought I wouldn't guess? That I wouldn't remember?

Stupid man.

Stupid, *idiotic* man.

"You're on borrowed time because of that injection Dr Campbell gave you…in the cage back on your island, aren't you? Your heart is beating abnormally. You're struggling to catch a proper breath. You wanted me, not because you needed affirmation that I'm okay after what Drake did, but because you're afraid you're about to pay for whatever you injected."

For the longest moment, he didn't reply.

Silence turned thick and tormenting.

"Answer me, Sully." I crossed my arms, unable to stop shaking. "I'm right, aren't I?"

His shoulders tensed, and he dropped his head into one hand. And then the faintest laughter shook him. "And that's what I get for falling in love with someone vastly more intelligent than myself." He looked up, dropping his hand and wincing again as he tried to shift his weight. "Your quick thinking would scare me if I had the chance to marry you as I'd hoped. I would never get away with anything."

"You can still marry me."

"You're smarter than lies, Eleanor." He smiled sadly. "And yes, you're right…it's Tritec that's killing me."

Killing…?

I winced. "But…he said it would kill you in a few days if it was going to. It's been more than a few…" I stopped myself, cursing him for the shadows filling his face. "Goddamn you, Sullivan."

He flinched and looked away.

"What aren't you telling me? What did you do? Please tell me you didn't take more. Please tell me you weren't that stupid!"

Raking both hands through his hair, he groaned and made eye contact. "You're right again, I had another dose. I was lucky the first time…I'm not so lucky now—"

"You took it because of me."

"I took it so I could come after you."

Rage exploded through me. Anger and pain and every fury on the planet. "How *could* you?"

"I didn't have a choice." He flinched and rubbed his chest, a greyness creeping over his sex-glowing skin. "I couldn't let you die, not because of me—"

"And by taking more of that awful drug, you took away all *my* choices. Don't I get a say in this?"

He shook his head. "I'm sorry, you don't."

I grabbed his arm, hating the ice chilling him already. "That's why you want me to forgive you? You think I can forgive you for killing yourself for me? I love you, you son of a bitch, and you've just taken everything we had and burned it to the ground. How am I supposed to survive without you—"

"At least I know you're safe—"A grunt of pain shut him up. Internal pain I couldn't see or stop.

Tears splashed down my cheeks. My chest cracked open. "Safe? I'm the opposite of safe. I'm *heartbroken.*"

"Don't. Please, don't—" His eyes flared as if internal twinges grew worse.

"We have to get you help. Get you to a doctor." I flew off the bed, racing with my blanket dragging behind me. *Hurry, hurry.* "If we hurry, we can—"

"Eleanor." His hand clutched his chest over his heart. "Ah, fuck."

"No!" I bolted back to him. I dug my nails into his shoulders. "Sully, don't you dare. Don't you even fucking dare—"

His eyes met mine again, wild and full of regrets. "Jinx…I—"
He tipped forward, crashing off the bed.

Sullivan

Chapter Twelve

SO THIS IS WHAT it feels like to die.

Not at the hands of someone else.

Not through torture or torment, elixir or old age.

This was how it felt when your very body shut up shop and shooed you out the fucking door.

Christ!

I lay on the floor, vaguely aware that my broken leg had crunched in my fall. Who the hell knew if I'd broken another bone or at what angle it rested. I'd lost all sensation in my extremities.

"SULLY!" The floor shuddered beside me as Eleanor crashed to her knees and clutched me close. Her touch was ruthless and unforgiving, rolling me from my crumpled pile and lying me flat on my back.

I blinked, doing my best to focus on her.

I thought I'd have more warning.

I stupidly believed a clock would start, counting down my remaining heartbeats, giving me a heads-up to kill Drake, kiss Eleanor, and somehow make peace with my passing.

But no…the wall that I'd been running headfirst toward had appeared, smashed me to pieces, and left me for dead.

"Goddammit, Sully, don't you *dare* do this to me!" Eleanor shook me. "*Breathe.*"

I couldn't feel her.

I couldn't feel her heat or her worry.

All I felt was the strangeness of having to fight with everything I had for another breath. A breath that refused to come because my heart no longer operated.

"Someone! HELP!" she screamed. "*Anybody!*"

It sounded as if she existed down a long black tunnel. A tunnel I could no longer travel through.

I choked.

My heart turned into a fiery pyre.

"Sully, God. *Please!*"

My back bowed in her hold, muscles overriding my nervous system in their quest to function.

I'd watched people die before.

I was even the reason for a few of those endings.

I'd read studies on death and was an expert on all manner of demises—thanks to my position in pharmaceuticals. However, this was new.

No one mentioned in the medical journals how a life was systemically snuffed out.

Two things happened.

One, your body went into preservation mode, shutting off sensitivity to all areas apart from the one thing killing you. It was like a suction. A numbing, erasing suction that forced all my attention to lock onto the scrambled thud of a breaking heart.

Two, your soul—if that was what we housed inside our mortal shells—detached. It no longer took ownership of a body it'd been birthed into but hovered free, unwilling to be associated with a rapidly failing machine.

"Sully. Fuck, don't do this. Please, *please* don't do this! Fight it! Stay with me." She hugged my head on her knees and rocked over me. I couldn't console her. I couldn't apologise or tell her how much I fucking loved her.

I couldn't feel the fierceness of her hands or the wetness of her tears.

All I could feel was the fading.

The pain and the coldness.

The inevitability of goodbye.

"HELP! For God's sake, **help**!"

Her screams were muted now. My ears failing.

Her manic strength was feeble now. My body no longer reacting.

Her attempts to keep me with her useless now as my heart chased its last beat.

My hectic, harrowed pulse grew quieter, slower…gone.

"No!" Shoving my head off her lap, she bent over me and pressed her mouth to mine.

Breath poured into my lungs.

Bracing over me, she pumped my chest with two fists, performing CPR on a body that had already died.

She screamed words again, but I no longer comprehended such a tongue.

Her mouth on mine. Her fingers pinching my nose. Her breath filling my chest.

Her pummels on my heart grew fiercer, driving my spine into the floor.

Eleanor…stop.

She screamed and yelled and shouted incomprehensible things.

I loved her.

Please don't be sad. It's better this way.

She breathed into me again, delivering oxygen that my body no longer knew how to convert into life.

I had no way of begging for absolution. No words to beg for a second chance. No way to tell her how grateful I was for her. How I'd *always* be hers…even if we now had to exist apart.

I would wait for her.

I'd claim her again…if she ever fell to hell.

I'd wait for her forever.

My muscles seized in their death dance.

I jerked on the floor, sending another gush of screams from Eleanor.

My eyes popped wide as the final lance of pain stabbed clean through me. A lance directly into my heart and the useless non-thumping chambers.

Eleanor…

She faded.

Darkness gathered at my edges, spilling into my corners and descending over me.

It took my vision.

It took my soul-mate.

It took me.

Goodbye…

Chapter Thirteen

I WON'T LET HIM die.
I won't.
You can't die, Sully.
I forbid it.
Forbid it!

I alternated between forcing every drop of oxygen I had into his mouth and pounding his chest with furious CPR. Digging the heels of my fists over his heart, I wanted to crack apart his ribs and bury my hands inside him. I wanted to massage his heart and force it to restart.

Stay alive!
Please!

He felt wrong.

He felt...gone.

His mouth lax. His body prone. His life force and essence, his mercurial, wonderful spirit had abandoned me.

He can't!

"God, *please*." Feeding air into him, I sucked in another breath for me, driving my weight against his ribs. "SOMEBODY HELP ME!"

I ducked again, pinching his nose and breathing before returning to my war against his stopped heart.

"Sully!"

His head bobbed each time I dug into his chest. His lips

parted and glistened from where I breathed into him. His skin was icy, the colour already receding from his tanned skin. His legs lay sprawled in painful directions, his arms useless beside him.

There was no vitality left.

No sinful smirk or savage power.

Just an empty puppet with no one to pull its strings.

"Sully, don't. Come back. Please, *please* come back." I breathed and pounded, breathed and pounded.

I *screamed.*

Tears began, breaking through my panic holding them at bay.

I breathed into his mouth, leaving his lips painted with wet disbelief.

I depressed his chest, leaving splashes of grief on his nakedness.

"Anybody…somebody…*please*!"

Every second he travelled further and further from my reach.

Every useless attempt at keeping him with me sent him deeper into a realm I could not follow.

"Sully!"

I punched his heart.

I kissed him instead of breathed for him.

I lost myself.

I hit him and begged him and did things I never thought I'd do.

I kicked his wounded leg, hoping the pain would bring him back.

I slapped his scruff-shadowed cheek, pleading shock to wake him up.

I bit his lip as I exhaled deep into his lungs.

"SOMEONE HELP ME!"

He's dying…

He's leaving.

He's gone.

"No!"

This was hell. This was utmost purgatory, and I was alone.

I threw myself on him, renewing my efforts with heart presses and oxygen pouring.

And finally, the universe decided to send aid.

The door to the bedroom swung wide in the night.

Not just one person to help me but four.

Three men bolted forward while an older woman wearing a fluttering white nightgown ran in.

A man with slicked-back dark hair and a goatee shoved me aside without apology, pressing his fingers to Sully's throat.

His eyes met mine. "No pulse."

I choked on sobs as I wrapped my arms around my bleeding, brutalising insides.

Moving to Sully's other side, he linked his hands together, placing them over the bruise I'd caused while palpitating Sully's unbeating heart. "You breathe, I'll pump."

Nodding manically, I swiped away my tears and did my best to swallow my sobs. Taking position by Sully's head, I pinched his nose and breathed into his mouth.

The man set a punishing pace, swift and deep with his compressions. "Brent, go get the defib. Andrew, call an ambulance."

Both men vanished.

I continued breathing for Sully, keeping air in his cells and hope in his blood.

The woman wrung her hands. "If he can be moved, there is a fully equipped surgery within the east wing. The previous owners needed in-home specialist care." Her voice was pinched but calming. "There is oxygen and adrenaline and—"

"We'll move him if he breathes again." The man kept driving his full weight onto Sully's sternum while I continued breathing for him. No one cared that Sully was naked. No one eyed up my lack of clothing either. No self-consciousness or pity could be spared while we all focused on denying death its chosen soul.

The slap of shoes on flagstones sounded as both men reappeared. "Ambulance is on its way."

A medical bag with its ominous red plus sign slid against the floor as a blond man tripped beside Sully. Ripping open the zipper, he pulled out a travel-size defibrillator.

Use it quickly!

I breathed everything I had into Sully.

Come on. **Come on!**

The leader swapped places with his underling. He grabbed the guy's hands and placed them over Sully's heart. "Keep performing CPR. Don't stop until I say."

The man nodded and set into the rhythm of a strong and purposeful pulse.

With confident fingers, the leader unfurled the cables and slapped electrical pads onto Sully's chest.

Fiddling with the machine, he pressed a button, and a high-pitched whine sounded.

"Clear!"

I sat away from Sully, and the man stopped depressing.

The leader punched the button, and Sully's form jerked off the floor. He collapsed again, his head lolling sideways.

The leader paused, pressing his fingers once again to Sully's throat. "Still nothing."

Resetting the machine, he yelled, "Keep your hands off him until I say otherwise." He electrocuted Sully again.

He jerked up and flopped down.

Nothing.

My own heart threatened to go into cardiac arrest. Still tender from elixir and foggy from a sedative, it couldn't cope with the possibility of finding Sully and then losing him forever.

Tears tracked silently.

The urge to touch him became excruciating.

The machine whined again before another bolt of power shot into Sully's useless heart.

"Fuck." The leader searched for a pulse again. His gaze met mine. "Breathe for him." Pressing his hands together, he shoved the other man away and drove the heels of his palms into Sully's chest.

A rib cracked.

He grunted as he pressed harder.

I did as he asked, blowing as much air and love as I could down Sully's throat.

Come back to me.

Please, please come back.

He kept pumping.

I kept breathing.

Come on, Sully.

This isn't the end.

I know it isn't.

It can't be.

Panting hard, the man pushed me away and picked up the small machine again. Activating the charge, he gritted his teeth and pressed the button. "Clear."

Sully jack-knifed off the floor.

He fell back a second later, sprawled and lifeless and...

Dead.

He's...dead.

The finality of such a thing.

The totality of the word.

"NO!" I threw myself on him. I slapped his righteous cheek. "Wake up, you bastard. Wake up!"

The woman grabbed me from behind, murmuring sweet nothings in my ear, making the urge to break down unavoidable.

"The battery is getting low," the man mumbled. "One last attempt." Raking his hand over his sweaty face, he barked, "Clear!"

And pressed the button.

Sully shot upright.

He fell backward.

Still nothing.

I broke.

A keening sound escaped me. A high-pitched wail that I couldn't control. I hugged myself and rocked. I bowed over my knees. I fell to the side, hugging the explosions annihilating me.

The bomb in my soul. The shrapnel in my belly. The extermination in my core.

He can't be dead.

He can't.

No!

The faint howl of sirens announced the paramedics had arrived. The woman bustled to the door. "I'll bring them here straight away."

The men lingered, not knowing how to help me or Sully.

"I'm sorry, Ms. Grace." One of them tried to pat my shoulder.

I lashed out with claws. "Don't touch me! *Don't touch me!*"

The leader slowly removed the sticky pads from Sully's chest. His head bowed, and regret bracketed his mouth. His hand trailed over Sully's throat, his fingers searching one last time for a pulse.

He froze.

My sobs silenced.

Sick, *vicious* hope exploded.

I would die from this hope.

I would perish beside Sully because hope was the only thing keeping me alive.

Please…

If this turned out to be fake…

If he's dead…

The urge to vomit burned my throat.

Nausea and vertigo, hot flashes and icy sweats.

Please!

The man closed his eyes, his entire focus on the faintest flutter of life.

One second.

Two seconds.

Three.

Four.

Five *nightmarish* moments.

His eyes soared wide just as the paramedics spilled into the room. "Shit, he's alive." His attention shot from me to the uniformed men falling to their knees around Sully.

The man I loved more than fucking life itself became the centrepiece of calm professionals and panicked mercenaries.

"Heart attack?" one of the ambulance workers asked, opening his bag of tricks to create a miracle.

"I think so." The leader nodded. "Shocked five times. CPR administered since cardiac failure. Pulse has restarted. Faint...but it's there."

"Good work, we'll take it from here."

I tried to breathe and couldn't.

I tried to move closer...I fainted.

Sullivan

Chapter Fourteen

I WASN'T HERE NOR there.

I wasn't alive nor dead.

I didn't know what I was or who.

I sucked in a breath, only to find I had no such ability.

No lungs, no heart, no physical presence to control.

Darkness all around me. Coral spires and sand caverns, jewelled anemones and sleek oily sharks.

Was this reincarnation?

Had I traded a form that walked on land for one that swam in the depths?

And if I had…why couldn't I see my new shape?

Why did no fingers or fins appear when I tried to move my extremities? Why did no bubbles explode from my mouth when I tried to exhale?

Why couldn't I remember what I was before this?

I had a name; I was sure of it.

I had a life…I was convinced.

Yet the more I tried to remember, the faster it dissolved until I was just a speck.

An unnamed, unclaimed speck lost in the global vastness, adrift and unwanted.

Darkness thickened.

My speck vanished.

I was nothing.

Chapter Fifteen

"HE'S CRASHING AGAIN!"

I stood by the door, pressed against the wall so I wouldn't be kicked out. The doctors had tried to keep me out of surgery while they worked on Sully, but…well, I fucking refused to obey.

Thanks to the housekeeper, I'd been dressed in a loose-fitting pair of track pants and a grey hoodie while I'd been unconscious. My useless body had been carried by one of the mercenaries as Sully was placed on a stretcher and wheeled into the ambulance.

I'd been given a ride too, my brief stint of weakness snapping me awake the moment the ambulance started.

The second time I'd ever fainted, and both were caused by Sully.

He owed me.

He owed me so much for the panic he'd put me through and the fear that even with his pulse flickering, he might not pull through.

I'm sorry for cursing at you.

My guilt weighed more than I could bear.

I'd yelled at him as he'd died.

The last things I'd said were awful and mean and…

God.

I choked on tears, fresh tears, old tears, forever tears.

"Charge to three hundred joules."

"Clear!"

I hugged myself. I screamed silently. I watched as electricity that'd infected us with passion was now used to keep him alive.

His form absorbed the voltage.

His body jerked under its surge.

Nothing.

The doctors rushed and muttered, and I tuned them out.

All I focused on was Sully…once again dead and not caring just how much that killed me.

Come on! Wake up. You can't keep doing this to me! I promise I won't yell at you again. I won't call you a son of a bitch. I won't ever swear.

I swallowed curses.

I locked myself against the wall, so I didn't leap onto the table and pummel his pathetic heart. Ever since we'd screeched into the ambulance bay and Sully had been whisked away, I'd fought a never-ending battle to let experts keep him alive instead of relying on our bond to drag him back.

Could he feel me there?

Could he sense my claws digging into his soul?

I wasn't going to let go.

He could try to die, but he'd only half succeed because I was the owner of his heart now, and I fucking *refused* to give it back.

Come on, Sully. Fight!

A doctor threw me a dirty look over his mask.

Maybe I yelled that aloud or shouted in my mind. I didn't care. I no longer knew reality from fable and hope from despair. I'd already proved to be a nuisance after I'd refused a wheelchair when we arrived at the hospital and glowered at anyone who tried to direct me to a waiting area and prevent me from staying with Sully.

I didn't want to get kicked out…but didn't they get it?

I *couldn't* leave him.

I refused to leave his icy, sheet-shrouded side.

Not until he either woke or died.

And even in death…I didn't know if I'd ever be able to walk away.

"Try again. Three hundred and sixty joules."

I gritted my teeth. My fingernails dug into my palms.

Please.

Please, please, Sully.

I love you.

Don't do this.

Please!

I was alone, shivering in shock and woozy against the wall as Sully was once again electrocuted.

No one else had come to the hospital.

I was in a city I'd never travelled to before and surrounded by strangers who I didn't trust. Doctors who didn't know that Sully was the most important patient of their career because if he died…

God!

I doubled over.

My cheeks stung with fresh salty tears.

"Got a pulse."

I choked on air. My eyes swooped to Sully and his team of lifesavers.

"Administer lidocaine. Let's keep him with us this time," a woman doctor clipped, her face covered by a mask, her hair pulled back in a hairnet. Her group of emergency staff jumped at her commands, inserting needles and focusing on tasks to keep Sully breathing.

My legs gave out, slithering me down the wall as the heart rate monitor registered frail beats.

Stay with me this time.

You owe me that much.

I couldn't keep doing this.

The highs, the lows.

The hope, the misery.

I'm not letting go, Sully, so stop trying to leave me and breathe!

I gulped my own advice, swallowing down gasps of air and praying my woozy head wouldn't pass out again.

Satisfied that her colleagues had Sully's life in their capable hands, the doctor turned her attention to Sully's leg. Her gloved hands trailed from the infected wound in his thigh, down his kneecap, calf, ankle, and foot. Her forehead furrowed as she slowed over certain areas before repeating the exploration on the other side.

Finally, she sighed heavily and turned to look at me crunched at the bottom of a ventricular diagram of a heart.

The urge to be sick had never left, and it was a constant battle to keep stomach acid where it should be and not contaminate the sterile room where Sully's existence hung in the balance.

Snapping off her gloves, she came toward me. Pushing open the swing door, she arched her eyebrow, cocking her chin for me to go through.

I threw Sully a look.

The swarm of doctors still hovered over him.

He resembled a ghost. His hair shockingly dark against pallid skin. His lips blue. His eyelashes black spiders on his cheeks.

I shook my head.

She cupped my elbow, yanked me to my feet, and ushered me through anyway.

Only once the door swung shut and she stood in front of it to prevent me from slipping back inside did she remove her mask and study me.

She was younger than I'd expected. Brisk and all business, the fine lines of early aging caused by a high-stress job didn't detract from her auburn, freckled prettiness.

"You must be his wife?" Her Swiss-German accent reminded me all over again of the foreignness of this place and the lostness of being alone.

I gulped. The time for labels and titles was obsolete.

I might not lawfully be his wife, but by God, I was in spirit. "I am." Balling my hands, I did my best to keep my voice from wobbling. "Will he be okay?"

She pursed her lips, weighing her words before slipping into a doctor's spiel. "We've achieved a successful resuscitation. The administration of lidocaine will help stabilise his rhythm. The aim is to keep his pulse steady and prevent another arrest." She paused before asking gently, "I believe his heart was also restarted prior to arriving here, is that correct?"

I nodded.

She sighed again. "That could create complications down the line, but we won't focus on those just yet. He's alive, that's all that matters." She smiled. "Look, I'm aware you don't want to leave him, and I'm sympathetic to the worry you must feel, but—"

"I'm not going anywhere." Bracing myself for news I wouldn't be strong enough to hear, I asked, "The complications…please tell me what they are. And anything else he's suffering. I…I need to know."

Pinning me with a brutal stare, she said, "Fine. His heart could have potential scarring from the prolonged use of high-voltage defibrillations. He might suffer a stroke if there are blood clots that have formed while his pulse has been intermittent. He might wake up in a few hours, or it might be a few weeks. This sort of trauma doesn't come with a textbook, and his system might remain on shutdown for the foreseeable future."

"He'll be in a coma?"

"Possibly. It's too soon to tell if he has brain damage from lack of oxygen. Even with the CPR administered, he may suffer neurological defects or lose cognitive ability. He might suffer amnesia and potential lifelong conditions that will require careful assistance."

My mouth went dry.

The idea that he might not remember me.

That he could steal my heart and then not recognise me…

I moaned with pain.

I bit my lip until rusty blood filled my mouth.

I would pay any price to have him stay alive…even if it meant losing him in entirely different ways.

Blinking back my blinding grief, I forced myself not to break down. "Anything else?" My voice cracked, but I held it together.

The doctor gave me a sympathetic wince. "He has a few cracked ribs—most likely from the CPR. A fractured tibia, shattered ankle, four broken metatarsals, not including the prior wound that's already received medical treatment. And his other leg also has a contusion on his kneecap and a possible crack in his femur. Those are just injuries obvious enough from a physical exam. To ensure there are no more, I'll need to arrange for X-rays." She crossed her arms. "Can you enlighten me why his legs are in such poor condition?"

I dropped my gaze to the grey and white linoleum. "He fell out of a helicopter into the sea." I waited for some inhale, some sign of shock. Instead, all I received was professionalism, and for that, I was grateful.

"Well, he seems to have survived that catastrophe, so I have hopes he'll survive this."

A pause filled in the gaps between us before she asked, "What was he doing prior to cardiac arrest?"

My cheeks pinked. "We'd just finished having sex."

"Sex? In his condition?" Her eyebrows flew up. "His pain threshold must be immense."

"I know it wasn't advisable, but— Eh, he…" I lowered my voice, fighting awful tears. "He was determined, almost as if he knew he was going to die."

"Why would he assume that?"

"Because he…" I chewed my cheek. I had no choice but to tell her about Tritec, but I wasn't an expert. I had no idea the ingredients flowing in his veins or the possible fatal reactions to other drugs they might have to administer. "You'll need to call his main doctor. Jim Campbell is aware of his history. He took a drug called Tritec...I'm unsure how it works, but it overloads the system and can cause stroke, heart attack, and coma."

"And he willingly took such a drug, knowing the side effects?" Her voice pitched with concern.

"He didn't have a choice."

Because I was in danger, and he put me first.

Because he sacrificed himself for me.

Because he took away my choice to keep him healthy instead of dead.

I gasped as black, bleeding pain crashed through me. Tears spilled, and the urge to be sick and faint and scream attacked me all at once. I was itchy and snappy, lost and tired.

And I was afraid.

Absolutely *terrified.*

"Please...can you...will he be okay?"

Her gentle hand squeezed my shoulder. "You need to rest."

"I need to be with him."

"He'll be okay. I won't let him crash again."

"You can do that? You can stop a man from dying?"

"I can try, and my track record is pretty good." She let me go. "In all honesty, if he's hung on this long, he has something to fight for. He's in good physical condition. His heart is responding to treatment, but..."

When she didn't continue, I flinched and asked, "But...?"

"Logically, we should wait seventy-two hours before attempting to set his legs and explore any further injuries. Administering anaesthesia so soon after cardiac failure can cause increased risk of perioperative mortality. However, his bones need setting, so we might cast and assess when he's awake. If you are his family, you need to give us permission to continue with this course of care."

"I give consent, but only if I can stay with him."

"Does he have any other family?"

I flinched again.

Drake...

He killed him.

His parents?

He killed them too.

I shivered.

I was in love with a murderer.

But he was also my friend and future...my forever.

"No, just me."

She nodded with a small smile. "In that case, stay by the wall, don't be a nuisance, and we'll do our best to piece your husband back together again."

* * * * *

It took three days.

Three days for the doctors to be confident in Sully's strengthening pulse to attempt surgery on his ankle. I wasn't allowed to follow as they wheeled him into the theatre to remove shattered bones and implant steel rods to repair the damage falling into the sea had done.

Sully hadn't woken in seventy-two hours.

And I hadn't slept.

My eyes saw double. My tongue slurred. And I paced and paced until the shiny linoleum was dull from my borrowed sneakers.

They took Sully to surgery in the early afternoon and returned him to me by early evening.

His bed was wheeled back into his private room where I'd been given permission to sleep on a cot beside him. Mrs. Bixel, Sully's housekeeper in the Geneva manor, had brought me a few extra overly big clothes and a toothbrush. The hospital delivered my meals, and the longer Sully refused to wake up, the more I suspected their leniency toward my presence wasn't because of my obvious distress but because Sully's notoriety had paved the way.

That night, while he remained still as a corpse and white as a poltergeist, I padded from our shared room. I needed to walk. To exhaust myself. To find some way to turn off my terror and sleep.

Every time my mind blanked out from exhaustion, I woke a second later, screaming. A repeat of Sully falling off the bed. Of Sully grabbing his chest. Of Sully dying.

I relived that awful, *awful* moment.

I drowned beneath fear and failure.

I'd fallen in love with him while he'd played the role of god and monster. He'd captured my heart and stolen my trust, making me believe a fantasy that he could never be hurt because he was untouchable.

Those lies had now unravelled, and he was just a man.

A man still dancing on the border of life and death.

A man who might never wake up...

A man who might not remember me.

My eyes ached from three days of sadness as I patrolled the empty corridors and nodded at the night nurses. I found evidence of Sully's sway in the hospital thanks to the cardiology wing and the patronage sign naming it Sinclair's Triage.

Was it serendipitous his donations had been used to benefit the cardio ward?

Or fate playing a sick joke?

The sudden panic that he'd died after being in surgery urged my legs into a run. I bolted back the way I'd come and shot into his room.

A nurse nodded and passed me by, a regular visitor with her hourly rounds.

The interruptions, the tests.

I was grateful but also possessive.

She closed the door behind her, and my eyes soared to the heart rate monitor. My ears begged for the steady *beep, beep, beep* of a healthy heart.

The faint beep.

The comforting vision of Sully still lying in bed. Both legs had some version of a cast. One leg was almost fully encased, leaving just his thigh where the harpoon had shredded his muscle. That had been tended to and rebandaged, and antibiotics once again administered intravenously. His ankle and foot stayed above the bedding in a low sling while a white bandage wrapped around his torso to protect his cracked ribs.

His bruises and cuts from Drake's fun and games stood out starkly against his sickly pallor. His cheekbones were sharper. His five o'clock shadow grown thicker with a short beard.

Dragging the yellow comfy chair from the window—sunshine yellow for hope and patient morale, I supposed—I sat beside Sully and took his cold hand in mine.

"Can you hear me?" I murmured. "Can you feel me touch you?"

I squeezed his fingers.

No response.

His eyelids didn't flutter. His lips didn't part. The heart rate monitor continued its *beep, beep, beep.*

I sighed and rested my forehead on the back of his hand, careful not to bump the IV. "I miss you, Sully." I swallowed back tears, sick to death of crying. "I'm so afraid." My mind raced with so many things to say.

Threats to force him to wake up and know me.

Pleas for him to stay alive, even if he never knew my name.

"I'm sorry for being so mad. I'm sorry for losing you. I'm

sorry that you had to come save me. But please…you have to wake up. Give me the chance to save you back." I kissed his knuckles. "Don't you miss your islands? Don't you want to go home? If you open your eyes, we can go. We can return to Pika and Skittles, and you can get better on the beach."

I sucked in a shaky breath. "I don't like it here, Sully. It's cold, and it's snowing, and the sun is all wrong." I glanced out the window where silver snow gleamed beneath the moon. The hospital grounds were expansive. Large gardens for patients to rehab and quaint flowerbeds to bring joy, but the air was dense with population, the scents of society strong, and the overall hum of humans in a congested city put me on edge.

I missed Goddess Isles.

I missed Skittles and Pika.

I missed Jealousy and sand and sun and—

A shrill ring broke apart my self-pity.

I jerked upright, glaring at the cell phone Mrs. Bixel had brought from the manor. Sully's phone that he'd left on the bedside table. A phone I'd tried to unlock but had no success.

It rang again, flashing with an international number.

Swiping it from the small cabinet, I accepted the call before the person hung up. "Hello?"

"Eh, hi…Jinx? I mean…Eleanor?"

I slouched over Sully's arm, wedging my elbows into the bed. "Dr Campbell." Tears sprang anew. Damn blasted unwanted fucking tears.

I sniffed, doing my best to stay in control.

"What's happened? Where's Sinclair?"

I glanced at the man in question. I studied his slack mouth and the oxygen tubes stuck beneath his nose. I tried to convince myself that he was just sleeping. That at any moment he'd wake, and the brilliance of his blue gaze would sparkle with seduction, and everything would be better.

But the vision of Sully opening his eyes didn't feel possible. Not here. Not while we were stuck in this snowy city with prodding nurses. Not while we were alone with no friends or familiarity.

He needs to go home.

He needs his islands.

He needs peace.

Sitting straight, I swiped at my tears and spoke with renewed vigour. I had a purpose now. A goal. I could *do* something.

Something that might benefit Sully and reverse the horror that he might have brain damage or be gone. "Sully had a heart attack. He's currently in a hospital in Geneva. I don't know the name or the address. All I know is, he needs to go home. I need your help, Dr Campbell. Can you arrange medical transport to get him back to his islands? Can you speak to the doctors in charge here and find out if it's safe to move him?"

A long pause before he asked, "Travel over that distance is not advised for patients who have suffered such traumatic events. I did warn him that Tritec-87 would demand pain in the end." He cleared his throat. "But you said hospital not morgue, so he's still alive?"

"Yes, but he's—"

"Put him on the phone. I'll discuss the pros and cons—"

"He's not awake." I buried my hand in my unwashed hair. "He hasn't moved since he collapsed three days ago." My voice wavered, and once again, I had a terrible premonition. A foreboding worriment that filled my heart with truth.

He won't heal here.

He'll die here.

"You need to do whatever it takes to get him back home. I'm not asking."

Dr Campbell cleared his throat again. "If we move him while he's unstable, you run the risk of losing him."

"I know."

"He's in good hands in Geneva. I know the head of paediatrics. The hospital is well funded and not afraid of progress."

"I agree they've been great, and they brought Sully back when he crashed the second time, but…this isn't his home, Dr Campbell. Call me stupid and that a hunch is lunacy when faced with logistics of such a request, but I'm *telling* you…he needs to be back on his island. He needs to hear Nirvana. He needs Pika." I rubbed my eyes, doing my best not to sound crazy or strung out. "He needs a reason to fight. He needs to remember who he is, before it's too late."

He stayed silent for so long, I feared the call had dropped out.

Finally, he muttered, "I won't say he deserves this as he's paid for his crimes, but this is the last favour I can do. After this, I'm officially retiring."

"You'll need to care for him if he goes home."

"You trust me to do that? After what I caused?"

"I know your intentions were in the right place." I sucked in a breath. "I…I already forgive you, because without you, Sully would've died days ago. You saved his life, more than once, and I will always be grateful, but I'm asking you to save him one last time."

"Your forgiveness means a lot to me, Eleanor. I won't lie that I'll carry the guilt over *Serigala* for the rest of my life." He cleared his throat. "But can I ask you a question? It will help with my decision."

I clutched Sully's hand. "Fine. What is it?"

"You know what he's done and what he's capable of. You've changed him, there is no doubt about that, and what Drake did…well, no one—no matter what they've done—should have to endure such things. But…do you think the world would be a better place without—"

"Stop." I swallowed back my temper, speaking from my heart. "I give you my word, Dr Campbell, that the man you've served is no longer the same tyrant. He cares, Doctor…about *all* life now, not just his creatures."

"In that case, leave it with me." He sucked in a breath, preparing to fight for a man he'd almost destroyed. "I'll call the team caring for him. I'll be in touch."

He hung up.

Shaking slightly, I placed the cell phone back on the small cabinet beside Sully's pillow. I squeezed his fingers, treating him as if he could hear every word instead of being utterly unreachable. "We're going home, Sully. You'll feel the humidity again and be away from people, and everything will be okay, you'll see."

Bowing my head over his hand, I did something I'd never done.

I prayed to a higher power because if Sully had somehow tapped into such a magic with his prior perversions, then perhaps I could use it to bring him back.

And maybe, just maybe, he would keep me an honest woman and prove to Dr Campbell that he *had* changed. That he would rethink his business of using the girls' lust for his gain. He might even dabble with what I'd asked before *Serigala* blew up.

He might let them go.

The door swung open just as I scrambled for a prayer.

I looked up, expecting to see another nurse checking Sully's vitals and nodding encouragingly, even while her eyes swam with uncertainty. Instead, the mercenary who'd helped me administer

CPR and brought Sully back to life stood on the threshold.

He didn't enter.

His slicked-back hair shone from the harsh overhead lights, revealing deeper-set wrinkles of a man inching through his fifties. He bowed slightly in my direction, his attention skipping from Sully to me.

He sighed and scratched his goatee. "Still no improvement then?"

I sat taller, extracting my hand from Sully's, doing my best to be resilient and strong. "Not yet but the doctors are hopeful."

When they aren't side-eyeing each other with concerns they refuse to verbalize.

"Shit." He stepped into the room, throwing a look behind him. He looked sketchy and on edge. For a man who'd made a career out of killing for a pay packet, it made sense for him to look at everyone as his enemy, but there was something else too…

I stood, my knees locking me in place. "Is something wrong?"

He licked his lips, a wry smile tilting them. "Well, my employer is currently playing roulette with death so that's enough but…" He lowered his voice, stepping closer to me.

I met him in the middle of the room, goosebumps covering me under my baggy hoodie. "What is it?"

"We have a…situation. Back at the manor house. Sinclair gave me strict instructions before he, eh, passed out, but I can't keep doing what he requested. I'm unsure of how to deal with the situation going forward."

"What sort of situation?"

He scoffed almost with disbelief. "Something I've never dealt with before, and one that has become rather pressing." He glanced at Sully again. "Is he aware of any stimulus? If I asked him a question, could he respond and give direction?"

I shook my head. "You can try, but so far, he's shown no reaction when I talk or touch him."

He nodded with frustration. "In that case…" His eyes scanned me, growing darker with decision. "You. You'll have to help me. You have to come back to the manor with me. There's something you need to see."

"Me?" I stepped back. "What are you talking about?"

The mercenary closed the distance between us, lowering his tone once again until only a murmur sounded. "You are his voice now. It's your decision. Whatever you decide, I will take as his command, and I'll have served out our agreement." He took my hand, tugging me toward the door. "It can't wait anymore."

I struggled to get free. "I can't leave him. What if he wakes up or…"

Dies.

What if he crashes when I'm not here?

"I give you my word that I'll have you back within an hour."

"Tell me what's going on."

Pulling me harder, he gritted his teeth. "You'll see."

Sullivan

Chapter Sixteen

I WAS AWARE OF being…aware.
Past that, I had no idea.
I knew I was a sentient being.
I hadn't quite died, yet I hadn't figured out how to live.
I was in limbo.
Suspension.
In bondage.
I had no way to shout.
No way to wake.
No way to force my fate to go one way or the other.
All I had was a tether.
A glowing, fragile string binding me to someone I couldn't

see.

A string that hummed with a voice I fell instantly in love with.
A thread that filled me with warmth and want.
While that thread connected me to my destiny, I was content.
I could rest, heal, accept.
But when the string snuffed out.
When there was no touch, no hum, no light.
I floundered.
I was lonely.
I was afraid.
I missed her.

Chapter Seventeen

"OH GOD, I'M GOING to be sick."

I clamped both hands over my mouth.

The *stench* in the room.

Sewer and decay. Sourness and sweat.

All laced with the rancidness of rot—emitting from a man who'd almost raped me, tortured his brother, and did his best to steal everything I ever cared for.

Drake.

Not that the mumbling, bumbling mess before me could be Drake.

Can it?

I gagged as I studied him.

In three days, his body had sunken to a frail skeleton, his flesh almost mummified on his bones. He lay on his side on the same couch he'd tied my ankle to. Putrid tracks of shit and urine stained the embroidered silk and dripped upon the floor. A huge puddle of spit glued his cheek to the material while his eyes alternated between being wide open and in horrendous agony before squeezing shut and scrunching up his entire face in excruciation.

This wasn't a man to be afraid of but a creature who yanked utmost pity from my heart.

Sully's temper had finally overflowed. The volcano I'd sensed inside him—the rivers of unforgivable lava—had let loose, and I stood looking at the aftermath. The hardened magma, the cracked destruction, the decimation of cities and minds.

Drake's mind.

Gagging again, I tore my gaze away from what was left of Drake and looked at the grim mercenary beside me.

He hadn't forewarned or forearmed me. We hadn't spoken a word since he'd escorted me from the hospital and driven me here in the resident BMW. He'd nodded to his colleagues as he led me through the house and bowed respectfully at Mrs. Bixel as she baked apple and spice in the kitchen.

And then he'd balled his hands and waited for the man posted outside the living room doors to step aside and let us enter.

The moment I'd entered, the smell hit me, followed by the diabolical scene of a demented, mind-broken individual whose nose had a steady trickle of blood along with his ears.

Blood covered him in various stages of congealed.

Crimson and maroon, dried and wet.

Pinching my nose, I asked, "What happened? What caused him to be like this?"

The mercenary shrugged, sipping breath through his lips so he didn't have to smell the reek. "Sinclair happened. He did something to him within his virtual reality program. He commanded us not to let his brother fall asleep. We've been keeping him awake ever since."

He grimaced. "I pride myself on following orders to the letter and have never shied away from any method of extermination my clients' request, but this…" He flinched when he looked at Drake again. "His brain is slush. He's wearing most of it from it trickling out of his ears. His screams have kept us awake for days. I'm running out of excuses to keep the housekeeper out of here, and the smell is starting to escape this room and infect the manor."

He turned to face me, his body braced. "I'm done keeping this madman alive. Whatever Sinclair did to him was justified and deserved, I have no doubt about that, but…keeping him alive any longer goes past cruel. It's fucking evil."

Shutting down my natural instincts to gag again, I forced myself to step toward Drake.

He thrashed on the couch as if Euphoria had become unbearably brutal.

Was he still locked within a fantasy?

Without sleep, I didn't think there was an escape. Had he been forced to spend the past interminable hours enduring whatever nightmare Sully had coded? No food, no water…nothing but horror.

What sort of punishment had Sully delivered once he'd knocked me out? What had he done to his brother to leave his body resembling a voodoo-hexed corpse?

Drake was a zombie.

A real-life, breathing zombie. No mind anymore, just a bag of flesh and bones, steadily cannibalizing itself the longer it was forced to stay alive.

For a moment, I cursed Sully for what he'd done.

My stomach roiled with a different sickness, wondering all over again if my love-coloured glasses had hidden far worse traits than I wanted to see. If Sully was capable of not only delivering pain but also trapping his victim in a perpetual cycle of reliving it...what did that say about him?

Just how far was he capable of going when vengeance gave him the freedom to be the worst kind of monster?

But I'm sure he didn't mean to keep him alive this long, right?

He hadn't planned on dying the same night.

He probably only wanted to prolong Drake's torture for a few hours, and then would've released him from his misery.

"I need your permission to kill him."

I whipped to face the mercenary. "But Sully should be the one—"

"Sinclair might never wake up."

I winced. A flush of horror and pure hate toward the mercenary for even *suggesting* such a thing, followed swiftly by painful acceptance.

That was true.

He might never wake up.

And Drake was not allowed to fall asleep.

Two brothers trapped in a hell of different makings.

I sighed, instantly regretting my inhale as I breathed in Drake's stench. "I agree that Drake needs to be free of whatever—"

Drake suddenly screamed. A high-pitched shriek that sent nails down my spine. He jerked as if something bit him. He sobbed as if the worst pain imaginable devoured him bone by bone.

"See what I mean? Those screams are getting on all our nerves." The mercenary shuddered. "We did what Sinclair asked but, enough is enough."

Drake had done unspeakable things.

He'd been the reason Sully fell from a helicopter, why he was now in a coma, and why so many innocent animals were dead.

I cursed Drake's every existence, but the mercenary was right.

Enough was enough.

Sully might not wake up for days…or he might not wake up at all.

Either way, Drake had paid his karma, and it was done.

Eyeing up the Euphoria boxes strewn on the floor, spying the abandoned sensors that enabled a user to step foot into a world that didn't exist, I was tempted to step into Drake's illusion to see what Sully had done.

What sort of power did Sully wield with VR to ensure Drake jerked and defecated himself, moaning and pleading in a voice that'd long since stopped making sense?

Was it smart to know the darkest parts of the man I'd given my soul to?

Or was it a decision that would break us apart?

If I entered Euphoria and saw exactly what Sully had conjured, I honestly didn't know if I'd be able to forgive or forget.

It wasn't the smell or the sorrow of the room. It wasn't Drake's patheticness or his plight. It was self-preservation. *Selfishness* to continue loving a man who had never lied about who he was. Who lived in black and white, who dabbled in both dark and light with no apology.

I'd always known Euphoria was the most dangerous thing Sully could create. Any drugs cooked by his lab could *never* compete with the terrifying potential of a virtual reality that could turn a man into a vegetable.

Ironic, perhaps?

Serendipitous that mankind was ultimately just a mindless organism if the brain could be broken.

"Miss?" the mercenary murmured. "Your decision. Are you willing to speak on Mr. Sinclair's behalf and give me the order to kill this man?"

My nausea faded.

My exhaustion of the past few days vanished.

And I accepted that I'd just transcended from a goddess Sully had bought and fallen for into his irreproachable equal.

I hadn't requested to share his power. I had no intention of ruling his empire with his ruthless fist, but I had been given ultimate control.

Strangers who didn't know how Sully and I had met had accepted something I still had yet to believe.

I'm not just his anymore.

He's mine.

And what was his belonged to me, too.

Until the moment Sully opened his eyes, I was in charge, and that was a heady, heavy crown to wear.

The mercenary never looked away from me, waiting for my decree. He watched me for my leadership, and I struggled to step into Sully's shoes.

I had no intention of dethroning him…merely supporting him.

He'd given me his trust and his heart, and when he woke up, the decisions I made on his behalf would have to be acceptable.

I have to keep him safe.

Straightening my spine, I nodded once. "On behalf of Sullivan Sinclair, I request you kill Drake Sinclair. I believe that that was Sully's intention all along before circumstances prevented him from doing so."

The mercenary nodded in relief. "Thank you." Marching to a gun resting innocuously on an ancient sideboard, he screwed on a silencer attachment and pointed at the door. "Leave, please. I'll drive you back to the hospital once I'm done."

I shivered and looked at the exit.

It would be wise to leave.

Smart not to have a graphic murder blatant in my mind.

But I needed to know for sure that Drake was no longer breathing. I needed it for my own peace of mind, and to be able to look Sully in the eyes when he woke.

I needed to be able to vow that Drake could never hurt us again. That I'd witnessed his extermination.

Sully needed that.

He needed to claim his trust back from the brother who had stolen it.

Shaking my head, I crossed my arms and locked my gaze on Drake.

He twitched and gasped, more drool covering his cheek. The astringent whiff of urine tainted the air as he wet himself.

"I'll watch."

"No. I must insist—"

"I'll. Watch." I didn't take my eyes off Drake. "Do it."

The mercenary huffed and paused for a moment. "Seeing death can affect people in different ways."

"If Sully doesn't wake up from death, I am already well

acquainted with it." I narrowed my gaze at him. "I'll be fine. Do it."

He shrugged and marched toward Drake. Glancing at the closed doors leading to the rest of the house, he pressed the muzzle of the silencer against Drake's temple.

Drake keened, sounding exactly like something stuck in a slaughter chute.

Locking gazes with me, the mercenary pulled the trigger.

The soft pop made me jolt.

The sudden silence of a wretched moan.

The coldness of a life being ended.

He was right.

Watching a merciless murder *did* change me.

It hardened my heart.

It dried up my tears.

It made me older, wiser, and far more accepting of my new given power.

I'd just killed a man.

I might not have blood on my hands, but I did on my voice. I'd commanded, and it had happened.

I swallowed hard.

Striding forward, I avoided the gruesome puddles of human waste and looked into Drake's blank stare.

No breath. No blink. Nothing.

I waited for regret. I froze for self-hatred and panic over what I'd done.

But I only felt relief.

I'd killed him to protect the man I loved, but I'd also killed out of mercy.

It's done.

Perhaps now that one brother had been freed from purgatory, the other one could be too.

A trap that worked both ways...freeing both at the same time.

Sully...

Urgency filled me and I ran to the door. "We need to get back to the hospital. Now."

* * * * *

Sully was still trapped.

Still too far for me to reach him.

If anything, he seemed further away—his skin icy, his breath slower, his heartbeat not nearly as strong.

Sully…please.
Wake up.

I sat by his bedside.

I'd sat beside him since I'd killed Drake and returned to the hospital.

Another night and I hadn't slept.

A new dawn and still Sully didn't wake.

I'd stayed vigil beside him, but I hadn't reached out to touch his hand.

Something held me back.

Anger perhaps?

Confusion?

Fear?

I was angry because he'd proven to be even more coldblooded than I thought.

I was confused that I could ignore such things because I loved him.

And I was afraid he would die, regardless of me taking his brother's life on his behalf.

And I'm lonely.

So, so lonely.

I missed him.

I was lost without him.

I was tired of having to be strong, and knew the chance of any peaceful rest was far, far away.

I couldn't rest until he was awake.

I couldn't trust that he would still be here while I slept, almost as if we were tethered by a string that kept him from falling deeper into a soundless abyss.

I promised I would do whatever it took to keep him safe and alive, even if it meant sitting in a hospital chair in a snowy city for the rest of my life.

Closing my eyes, I flinched as images of him suffering a heart attack found me again.

His grunt of agony.

The thud when he fell.

His final gasp.

No!

I tore them open, focusing on his slack, handsome face.

I needed a distraction.

Or a sedative.

The phone ringing sliced through the heavy dawn silence.

I snatched the phone gratefully. "Dr Campbell?"

"Yes, hi. How're you holding up, Eleanor?"

I cleared my throat, keeping myself cool and brave. "I'm fine. Sully is still asleep. The doctor popped in an hour ago to assure me it's perfectly natural for a body to shut down after such an event and told me I just need to be patient." I balled my hand in my lap. "The thing is…he's fading. Don't ask me how I know…I just do. I feel it. He's not got anything to fight for here."

"He's got you."

"It's not enough."

"You're more than enough."

"He needs to go home."

He paused before saying, "It so happens that I agree with you."

I sat taller. "You do? Is it possible?"

"Sinclair's bank balance is going to take a serious hit with the exorbitant cost of such medical repatriation, but yes…it's possible. I've arranged a special charter and purchased the time of his current doctors to make the journey with him."

"When?"

"Tonight. If he remains stable for another twelve hours, they're satisfied to take the risk transporting him."

My heart pounded.

Home.

Islands and sunshine and Skittles.

"It will help. I know it will."

"It might." His voice turned sceptical but honest. "You have to prepare yourself, though, Eleanor. He might not survive the journey. He might go into cardiac arrest again and not return."

"He might do that here."

"That's true. I've informed the doctors of the ingredients and side effects of Tritec-87. Hopefully, they'll be able to adjust his treatment accordingly until he lands on home soil…or sand, as the case may be."

I closed my eyes, bowing my head. "Thank you, Doctor."

"Don't thank me yet. This might be a suicide mission."

Needing a distraction before my mind raced with all the things that could go wrong, I asked, "How's Jess? Skittles? Cal?"

Dr Campbell sighed. "Cal is operational, Skittles is healing, and Jess…she's holding on. I hope for both our sakes that Sinclair handles his upcoming journey and Jess wakes soon. I'll call you again when it's time to leave. For now, rest and get ready for the longest trip of your life."

Sullivan

Chapter Eighteen

IT WAS LIKE BEING trapped inside a monochrome kaleidoscope.

A tumbling, refracting kaleidoscope that was all blacks, greys, and shadows with no escape.

But instead of the chaos being visual, it was auditory with the occasional scent and the quick comings and goings of heat.

The longer I remained trapped, the more I strained to understand my new world.

For the first part of my prison sentence, I'd felt nothing.

I was just an inconsequential speck floating around, adrift and unwanted. A speck of no substance or history. No knowledge of who I was—just a vessel of lost memories.

I'd struggled to stay alive as that speck.

I had no reserves to stay clinging to the strange kaleidoscope my world had become. No power to endure the flickering in and out of lucidity.

But...

As time ticked onward, I grew stronger.

My speck grew to a seed and the seed into a vine. A vine that somehow latched onto the glowing string that occasionally lit up my dark world.

Her.

Whenever she touched me, she managed to tug me back a little more.

I had no comprehension of time and space, but as long as she touched me, I could *stay* with her instead of fading away.

Even though I didn't know her name or recall her face, I knew she was special. I knew she was the reason I had to clutch to whatever scraps of aliveness I could.

And she had to keep holding on to me.

Otherwise, I would lose everything.

I'd…go.

To where, I didn't know.

But it was a destination with a one-way ticket, and I wasn't finished yet.

I needed to tell her something. Words I couldn't remember, and apologies I didn't know how to say.

But then, something changed.

The routine of my shadowy, silent world switched.

She stopped touching me.

The stability of whatever form I hid within became inherently unstable.

I sloshed up the sides of whatever container I was trapped in. I couldn't brace myself against the motion that rocked me from side to side. I couldn't tense against the sudden swoop of flight.

All I could do was remain gagged and blindfolded, too weak to move, too broken to cry out.

* * * * *

The string was back, warm and comforting around me.

I sighed and settled, the calamity in my blackened mind hushed.

I'd vanished for a while.

My consciousness clocking out as if I'd slept, even within this dark dimension.

But thanks to her, I was awake.

And I had more pieces to fit into the puzzle I couldn't figure out.

I'm alive.

But I was also…not.

I'm a monster.

But I was also…human.

And if I was human, that meant I had legs and arms, fingers and toes. I should be able to move such things, to alert the girl keeping me bound that I could feel her. I might not be able to hear or see but I *felt* her.

She was the only reason the darkness hadn't claimed me. It couldn't because *she'd* claimed me. She was the only glow of hope in my otherwise pitch-black limbo.

But then, she let go again.

The string unravelled.

And I fell.

* * * * *

I blinked within my kaleidoscope world.

I *blinked*.

I had form again. Or at least…the knowledge of form.

I couldn't see my body or signal responses of ownership, but phantom parts obeyed me. I blinked past the alternating shadows and contorting colours of chaos. I searched the blackness for signs of the glowing, humming string.

Nothing.

All progress I'd made reverted.

I forgot…

I forgot what blinking was.

I felt ice lap around the existence I fought for.

I couldn't fight it, couldn't stop it.

No.

I want to stay.

I want her to touch me.

Please, touch me!

But no string, no bind, no hope.

I slipped under again.

* * * * *

I gasped this time.

Aware that I once had lungs and those lungs still functioned, even if I couldn't feel them.

I blinked in the blackness, and thankfulness swept through me.

The string.

It was back.

She was back.

I floated or flew, or maybe I crawled. Whatever method of movement I had, I made my way to her and wrapped a non-existent hand through the tether she offered.

I held on with strength I hadn't had in a while.

I needed her to feel my answer.

She had to know I couldn't exist in this darkness without her.

She couldn't let go again.

She was the only thing I had left.

Chapter Nineteen

I'D LEARNED SOMETHING ABOUT myself in the thirty-one-hour journey from Geneva back to Goddess Isles.

More than one thing, actually.

One, I could discuss the disposal of Drake's body as if he was a discarded banana peel. Agreeing with the mercenary to dismember and bury his pieces in undisclosed locations before he vowed his allegiance to me and tried to travel with me back to Goddess Isles.

I'd refused his escort, even though he'd pledged to Sully that he'd protect me. I already had far too much company: our flying convoy with doctors, machines, and potential death stalking our every move was enough. And besides, with Drake gone, Sully's greatest enemy couldn't hurt us anymore.

Two, I could fake bravery and somehow look into the eyes of the three doctors and smile when they smiled and make sense of the regular updates of his condition as he worsened and improved. I learned how to ignore exhaustion and somehow shut down my feelings so they didn't get in the way of caring for Sully while in the sky.

Three, every time I believed I'd reached my capacity for tragedy, I found a deeper well of strength in which to tap. A well that was bound to dry up eventually, but thankfully had kept me breathing while Sully did his best to crash.

Three times he'd almost died again.

Three times his pulse faded, and three times the doctors

prepared the defib and drugs to kick-start him.

And each time, I'd swallowed my tears until my throat was raw and clung fiercely to his hand. I'd pressed my forehead to his. I'd murmured things. Nonsense things. I'd kneeled on the aircraft floor and bowed over his stretcher, plastering myself to his unresponsive body.

The doctors had withdrawn after doing what medical attempts they could provide. They patted my shoulder in consolation as if *this* time was *the* time.

The moment when Sully gave up.

But…with my hand in his and my breath skating over his cheek, his pulse hiccupped and restarted with a stronger beat. I'd drift into delirious sleep while draped over him, rocked by the plane and high above the clouds, and as long as we stayed linked, he breathed.

Dr Campbell had been right.

That journey was the longest damn journey of my life.

I *never* wanted to repeat the panic of hearing the heart monitor growing quieter, slower, silent. I never wanted to see sympathy in anyone's eyes again. I never wanted to fall in love again if Sully left me.

This was pure agony.

An agony that had whittled me into nothing and left me scarred and hollow.

I'd reached a plateau as we landed in Jakarta, and Sully's obscene wealth and contacts once again purchased him the swiftest, safest transport possible.

He was transferred outside the same hangar where I'd been given his credit card and told I could never return. I grimaced at the irony that I *had* returned, and somehow, I'd inherited Sully's kingdom just by being by his side when he died.

I was too tired to walk between the private plane and helicopter.

Giving up my battle to seem invincible, I kept my hand on Sully's arm as a crutch. I used his wheeling stretcher as a walking frame and did my best to keep my eyes open as he was placed into the helicopter and a friendly doctor helped me inside.

Sully's pulse once again slipped down a slippery slope.

I didn't know if it was ego or truth, but he seemed to fade each time I stopped touching him.

The doctor with auburn hair who'd questioned me when we'd first arrived at the Geneva hospital sat beside me as the helicopter whirred into rotor-spinning violence.

"Touch him." She took my wrist and placed my palm on his shoulder. Her gaze remained locked on the monitor, watching intently as I touched Sully and winced against his chill.

It took a few breaths, but sure enough, as I kneaded his rigid shoulder, his heartbeat steadied out and found a healthier rhythm. A sudden spike of his pulse, the sudden choice not to die.

The doctor pulled away as the helicopter shot into the sky. She eyed me warily, looking between my link with Sully and my exhaustion aging me by decades. Placing a headset over my ears so she could speak to me, she said quietly, "A few years ago, I was on a team that wanted to prove souls truly existed. We requested the help of terminally-ill patients and asked if they would share their moment of death with us."

I blinked, her words turning to scrambled eggs in my fatigue-fuddled brain. I shook my head and blinked, then nodded for her to carry on, wanting to understand her point.

"They were placed on a weighing scale and hooked up to monitors. At the precise moment of their passing, all data was processed. We recorded the shift from an alive individual into a cadaver." She pinned me with a stare. "Know what we found?"

I shrugged weakly. "That there is no such thing as a soul?"

She smiled gently. "The opposite."

I sat straighter. "You mean…you have scientific proof that something other than blood and bone make up a living thing?"

"It's still early days, but yes. We have proven that the electrical impulses of the body are caused by two things. The brain and nervous system…and something we can't explain. Something that weighs the smallest amount but registered on our scales as missing at the exact moment of death. An indisputable finding that something left the body when it was no longer viable."

I dug my fingernails into Sully's shoulder without thinking. I transmitted my shock because I wanted to tell him that I'd been wrong when I said it was biology as we'd strolled around *Lebah*, discussing our unfortunate desires.

I'd made him accept our connection by delivering it in terms he was comfortable with: biology between compatible mates. The instinct of herds and harems that paired up individuals to ensure survival and procreation.

But if what this doctor said was true, then I'd lied.

It wasn't biology at all.

It was kismet all along and his soul—the very thing doing its best to jump ship—was intangibly linked to mine and always would be.

The doctor smiled at where I touched Sully, adding, "I'm a woman of facts and medicine. I'm a sceptic until undeniable evidence is provided, and what I'm witnessing between you two just solidifies the study of souls. Your touch works better than any adrenaline or drug we could give him to keep his system stabilised. Whatever bond you guys share is worthy of further investigation because I see it in action before my eyes."

Shifting on the seat, looking out the window to a new dawn blanketing Indonesia in creams, golds, and crimsons, she said, "He'll have other things to fight for the moment he senses he's home, but my suggestion for the duration of his coma…don't let go."

Sullivan

Chapter Twenty

ELEANOR.

That was her name.

It exploded through the darkness. A neon word full of narrative of our forgotten beginning…and our unknown end. A flash of togetherness and the undeniable acceptance that I loved her more than *anything*.

I looked for the soft glow of the string I'd grown accustomed to—the only light in my darkness.

It was there, pulsing with a golden shimmer, warm and comforting when I reached out to grasp it. I shuddered as a familiar sizzle of electricity infected my fingers.

This wasn't just a string.

It was a rope.

A rope made of affection, one we both held on to, and hopefully a path back to her if I could figure out how the hell to wake up.

Eleanor.

Jinx.

I'd named her Jinx.

And for the first time since we'd met, she was no longer a curse.

She was my saviour.

* * * * *

Weightlessness could even upset someone deep within their mind.

A sway of unnatural flight.

A screech that sounded mechanical.

My mind recognised certain things but couldn't grant me pictures as to what they were.

It was frustrating. Worrying. Compounding my growing strength and feeding me toxic anxiety to be free.

I didn't know how to escape this prison.

There were no locks or doors or keys.

I was alone with just a string for company.

The weightlessness ended.

The screech cut off.

A different kind of motion manipulated a body I couldn't see or operate.

Outside sensations became stronger.

The bumping journey of whatever I lay upon.

The whisper of heat upon my skin.

Relief filled me.

I didn't know how or why, but the darkness stopped being my enemy and paused.

I hovered in nothingness, trying to figure out what'd changed.

And something was put into my hand.

I *felt* it.

The ambient heat. The spillage of softness. The stress of *knowing* what it was yet unable to name it.

And then the sensation was gone.

I panicked.

The darkness drew ranks and closed with thick curtains.

But the glowing string between Eleanor and me brightened, and for the second time, I felt touch and knew where it originated.

My cheek.

Lips on my cheek and breath by my ear.

I could feel my body, systemically regaining ownership…even if my mind was still faraway.

And my ears obeyed me, accepting her voice and unscrambling the words I hadn't been able to understand while I'd been a speck.

But I was more than just a speck now.

I was stronger.

I'm aware.

I'm hers.

"You're home, Sully. Keep fighting and wake up because you're home."

Chapter Twenty-One

SAND SPILLED THROUGH SULLY'S fingers as I once again scooped up a handful and placed it into his palm.

He hadn't twitched or showed any sign that he recognised his home or his islands.

But I wouldn't give up on him.

I refused to believe he'd vanished, leaving only his body behind.

His mind was in there, somewhere...*it has to be.*

"Feel that, Sully? That's your beach. No more people or cities. No more Drake or wars. It's over, and we're home."

I kicked off my sneakers as the doctors struggled to push Sully's stretcher through the heavy sand.

After what the doctor had told me, I was careful not to take my touch off him for too long. I remained close. I spoke often. Now that he was home, I would be his constant shadow until he opened his eyes and gave me permission to collapse in exhaustion.

I would not rest until he came back to me.

I will fight for you, Sully...even if you can't hear or feel me.

A squawk sounded as the doctors pushed Sully toward the pathways leading toward goddess villas and an island that'd been touched by death and decay.

The palm trees still swayed in the glittering sunshine. The sand still twinkled gold and silver like micro-diamonds scattered on the shore. The sea glowed with turquoise, and the occasional flitter of jewelled fish darted in the spangles of sunlight.

Hibiscus lived on the muggy air along with lush greenery and island sweetness. Sully's wonderland seemed both apologetic and welcoming, as if it needed to erase the pain and demise that'd happened here and promised the power to reverse the anarchy that Drake had brought.

I tripped as my body urged me once again to sleep.

This fatigue was different to the catatonic urge to shut down after enduring elixir. This wasn't just mind fatigue but physical, emotional, soulful.

I'd done what I could for Sully.

I'd killed his brother on his behalf.

I'd spent his money via Dr Campbell to fly him home.

And I'd stupidly, *stupidly* hoped that the moment Sully smelled his tropical jungle and heard the licking waves, he'd remember. He'd wake up. He'd be healthy and mine again.

I couldn't lie and say I wasn't disappointed.

And I couldn't stop my heart from breaking all over again as Pika shot from the glossy bushes and zipped straight to Sully, lying like a warrior who'd been carried from battle to be buried amongst family.

If anything could snap Sully out of the unwakeable sleep, it was the winged comedian with such attitude.

The tiny green, white, and apricot parrot landed on Sully's chest. He squeaked and puffed up, his black eyes glistening with pure joy.

The doctors stopped wheeling Sully, all watching Pika as he rolled onto his wings and waved his scaly legs in the air. He chattered and chirped, slithering around on Sully's chest, nuzzling into him, showing every possible affection.

When Sully didn't react, Pika squawked with annoyance and flipped back to his feet. Marching up Sully's chest, he pecked at his chin. He fluttered and landed on his nose.

I did my best not to get my hopes up.

I tried to prevent my mind from tormenting me with images of Sully sitting upright and laughing. Of him kissing the tiny bird and proving that he'd been faking his unresponsiveness all along.

However, the heart rate monitor didn't register a pulse-kick. His skin didn't flush. His lips didn't twitch.

Nothing.

Oh, God.

I wedged a hand against my stomach as Pika switched from

happy little tyrant into melancholy mope. His wings sagged, his puffed-up feathers fell, and his tiny questioning squeak made me cry all over again.

"Pika…" I scooped him from Sully's face and kissed his sagging head. "It's okay. He'll be okay." The tiny bird struggled to get out of my hand.

I let him go, only for him to fly back to Sully and sit on his forehead, pecking at Sully's eyebrows, a string of chirps, cackles, twirls, and tweets falling from his beak.

You didn't need to be an animal whisperer to see his absolute pain. His rejection. His panic that Sully wasn't okay.

I stroked his tiny head, brushing aside my tears. "He's just sleeping, little Pika. He'll wake up soon. You'll see."

Pika suddenly hopped onto my finger and let out a heart-stabbing screech. He whipped his stare from me to Sully and cocked his head until horizontal.

And then, he exploded off my finger in a burst of green.

He zoomed into the jungle and vanished.

"Everything okay?" the female doctor, who I'd learned was named Louise Maldon, asked. Her colleagues began wheeling Sully down the pathway leading toward my villa.

I swallowed back the pain that'd lodged tight in my throat. "Pika just doesn't understand. Sully is his soul-mate. I guess he's a little heartbroken that Sully didn't respond."

So am I.

Louise nodded, sweat breaking out on her brow as they continued to battle against sand and heavy stretchers. "If he means a lot to Mr. Sinclair, you need to keep him close. I suggest you gather everything that means a lot and surround him with as much familiarity as possible."

I made eye contact. "In that case…I was going to suggest going to my villa as its closer and not as far to push, but…we should take him to Nirvana."

"Nirvana?"

"His waterfall." I trailed my fingers over Sully's forearm resting over the white sheet covering him. IV lines still punctured his body and oxygen tubes still stuck beneath his nose, but for once, his skin wasn't icy.

It'd warmed thanks to the island sun.

Please, please wake up.

"He needs to hear the falls. He needs to feel the water." I looped my fingers with his. "I'll do whatever it takes to make him come back—to me and to Pika."

* * * * *

I sat on the bed with my hand on Sully's chest and blurrily watched the commotion as the doctors set up an in-home triage. Dr Maldon was a good leader, precise and kind, traipsing with her colleagues to gather the medical supplies and equipment they'd brought from Geneva with them to monitor Sully.

I'd thought they'd leave the moment they'd shifted Sully from the travel stretcher onto his mosquito-netted bed, but she'd pulled me aside and asked if I would object to them sleeping in cots in the lounge for a few nights to monitor Sully's condition after such a long journey.

I'd nodded and plopped heavily beside Sully. Him lying with tubes and sensors tracking his heart and me swaying by his side, linked by our hands...even if only one of us was aware of the contact.

The setup was like a dance. A choreography of wheeled machines and medical equipment that slowly transformed Sully's bedroom into a hospital.

The sugar glider who lived in Sully's rafters blinked nocturnal grumpy eyes and did its best to go back to sleep. The beetles and geckoes kept their distance but were too reluctant to leave, and the heron and kingfisher on the balcony watched with intelligent eyes, weighing up the likelihood that the monitor wires were eels to snatch.

"Have a shower. I'll keep an eye on him." Louise arched her chin at the bathroom.

I blanched.

How could I have a shower alone when the last time I'd stood in his open-air bathroom and listened to Nirvana splashing, I'd just enjoyed the best day of my life? Sully had stripped down his masks, told me he loved me, and spent the day with me naked in the natural pool.

We'd reached a level of sweet domestication, even if our blood was full of deviant desires. If I showered on my own, I was effectively erasing the best day of my life with one of my worst.

"Go." She patted my shoulder as I blinked away my haze. "You'll feel better. Once you've washed the flights off, you can sleep beside him. He'll sense you're there, and you can rest."

I nodded blankly, allowing her to pluck me from the bed and shoo me into Sully's bathroom.

* * * * *

I slipped into one of Sully's business shirts and tied a bronze tie around my waist as a belt. Clean body and clean clothes helped me perk up a bit.

Yes, I'd hoped Sully would have a miraculous event and wake up the moment he felt he was home. But just because we weren't in a storybook where the villain fell asleep and the hero was reborn didn't mean he wouldn't open his eyes soon.

Tomorrow maybe…or the day after.

The point was, I had to stay positive.

With my head held high, I strode back into Sully's bedroom and jerked to a stop.

Five policemen stood at the foot of Sully's bed all muttering in Indonesian and waving at Sully's prone form as if he was an obstruction of justice and deserved to be arrested.

Louise and her doctors faded into the background, running diagnostics and settling their patient into a new routine.

"Can…can I help you?" I crossed my arms over Sully's black shirt and narrowed my eyes.

"We have questions, ma'am." One of the uniformed men stepped toward me. "We are not permitted to leave these shores until our questions have been answered."

I braced my shoulders. "You've been staying here?"

"Our superior's orders." The man who seemed in charge wore a badge stating his name was Susilo and had a bigger array of emblems and insignias on his uniform than the rest of his decorated team. "When will Mr. Sinclair be awake for questioning?"

"Like I told you before," Louise muttered, "he's in a coma. That means his brain is operating at the lowest levels of alertness with minimal recognition and abilities."

The policeman looked her up and down. "How long will the coma last? We are busy men. We have other things to investigate."

"I *told* you." Louise threw me an exasperated look before brushing aside her sweaty auburn hair. "Mr. Sinclair cannot initiate voluntary actions in his current state. That means he will not respond to any stimuli, such as light, sound, or pain." She finished pressing a few buttons on the heart rate monitor before adding, "We have no timeframe for when he'll wake from the coma. This is not medically induced. Mr. Sinclair suffered a highly traumatic event with multiple heart failure episodes, and we are unsure if he will wake naturally. He might slip into a vegetative state where the chances of him being a fully functional individual diminishes to approximately eleven percent. Even if he woke today, there's no saying his cognitive abilities won't be damaged or he won't suffer from amnesia. So, gentlemen..."

She walked toward the police. "I must request you stop harassing my patient because he is too unwell to assist you and will continue to be for the foreseeable future."

I wanted to high five her. Instead, I took the baton and joined her fight. "I'll help." I stiffened as all five men peered at me. "You? You're aware of Mr. Sinclair's dealings and—"

"I'm aware."

"In that case." Dismissing his entourage, the leader, Susilo, waved his arm toward the deck outside Sully's bedroom. "We talk outside, yes?"

I glanced at Sully.

His pallor had paled again, his pulse not as steady.

I shook my head. "In here." Moving toward the bed, I sat beside him and linked my fingers with his. Like in the helicopter, it took a few moments for the monitor to register a stronger heartbeat, but it did. The rhythm steadied and vitality returned to his cheeks.

Damn you, Sully.

I didn't know if I should be honoured that my touch had such an effect on him or terrified. I didn't want power over his life or death. I didn't want to go to the bathroom and return to find him in heart failure because I'd left.

I squeezed his hand as the police grabbed chairs from around Sully's lounge and brought them into his bedroom. They arranged them as if I was the suspect and they were the jury.

Keeping my back ramrod straight, I asked, "What questions do you need answering?"

Susilo pulled out an electronic device from his front blazer pocket and pulled a stylus from the side. Turning on the screen, he brought up a document before looking at me with a suspicious stare. "Almost one week ago, Sullivan Sinclair—the man lying unconsciousness beside you—fell from a helicopter along with another man who'd been shot in the stomach."

I stiffened. "That man was a mercenary hired by Drake Sinclair to kill Sullivan and everything he cared about."

He scribbled something on his e-pad. "That is the reason for the three phone calls we received asking for our help?"

"Three?" My eyebrows rose.

He referred to his notes. "We received a call from Mr. Ross

Grace via the American embassy in Jakarta. He said his daughter was in grave danger and gave coordinates to this group of private islands."

Goosebumps washed over me.

Dad.

Oh, my God, he'd called. My hastily formed and frankly feeble plan had actually worked.

I need to call him. He needs to know I'm okay.

"The second call was from a local fisherman who spoke of bribes and bad karma. He mentioned he dropped a woman off on the request of the man you just mentioned...Drake Sinclair."

"That's right." I nodded. "That was me. I hitched a ride back here after a misunderstanding meant I'd been flown away." Not giving them time to ask more questions, I asked one of my own. "And the third?"

"The third was from a Mr. Arbi Pambudi who claims he is in the employ of Mr. Sinclair but is nowhere to be found on this island." He pinned me with his black stare, his equally dark hair glistening in the sun. "Dr Campbell and Mr. Calvin Moor have been obtuse with their answers. They informed us that Drake Sinclair tried to take over this island and bombed another in the private cluster called *Serigala*." His gaze returned to his notes, skimming other interviews no doubt extracted from Campbell and Cal while we'd been in Geneva. "They state that Drake Sinclair flew off with an Eleanor Grace, and that's the last of their knowledge."

"If you're aware of the unwanted invasion and the illegal attempts at theft by Sullivan's older brother, why are you still here? We did nothing wrong. Sullivan was protecting his shores and me. He was tortured at the hands of his brother." I pointed at Sully's still bruised and healing body. "See for yourself. He blinded him, drugged him, and inflicted as much misery as he could, all because Sully refused to give him what he asked for. We are not the criminals here, sir. Drake is."

"I agree that Mr. Sinclair seems to be the victim, as are you. However, we need to account for the body we scooped out of the sea. We also need to verify why Mr. Sinclair refused questioning and left with multiple broken bones before he'd been cleared of any wrongdoing. The fact that he ran away from law enforcement after we were summoned here by three separate calls for help is...suspicious."

"Not suspicious. He was chasing after me. I was in danger."

"And how did he end up in heart failure and a coma?"

"His brother."

"How?" He scribbled my answers down, poised for the next one. "I am unaware of a weapon that would cause cardiac arrest. Why not use a more common method of violence?"

Common?

I bit the inside of my cheek, swallowing any mention of Euphoria and the virtual reality weapon that'd broken a brother's mind. No longer a human but a creature left on the couch, drooling and defecating, a vegetable beyond repair...*until I had him killed.*

Doing my best not to seem guilty of murder—even if it was justified and merciful—I said, "Sully's system shut down due to overexertion. The stress of protecting me, of seeking vengeance for all the animals and human lives that Drake stole when he bombed *Serigala*, of doing his best to fix what his brother had ruined—it all took a toll." I squeezed his fingers, my temper brushing aside my tiredness and making me snap. "The only enemy here is Drake. He would've raped and killed me if Sully hadn't arrived in time. Sully gave up his life so he could save mine. Therefore, I would *appreciate* you close whatever report you need to and allow him to recuperate in peace."

Susilo frowned. "Where is Drake Sinclair? Allegations of murder, rape, and kidnapping are serious, indeed, and he should be brought to justice."

He's in a million pieces buried around Geneva.

I stiffened. "I have no idea where he is."

"None?" He studied me far too closely. "Where did he take you when you were kidnapped?"

Louise flicked me a glance. I ignored her and answered honestly. "Geneva."

"So he's in Switzerland?"

"No idea."

"If you know something that you're not telling me, ma'am—"

"I don't know anything more." I stood, breaking contact with Sully and crossing my arms. "You really need to leave."

Almost on cue, the heart rate monitor spluttered with a flickering pulse. Dr Maldon might have told these policemen that Sully had no reaction to stimuli, but he reacted to me, and my lack of touch sent him into a free-fall.

The doctors leaped into action, ripping aside the mosquito net that'd fallen around the bed to check hastily on their patient.

The police officer never took his gaze off me, almost as if he could taste my dance around the truth and didn't know how to rip the real story from my lips.

If they took me to Jakarta for questioning.

If they take me away from Sully…

Swallowing back my temper, I allowed my exhaustion to smother me, to etch my eyes and thicken my voice. I wasn't above using weakness for sympathy. "Look, we're happy to answer anything you need when Sullivan recovers. Leave your card and we'll be in touch the moment he wakes…*if* he wakes." I dropped my gaze to the floor, embracing every bit the grieving widow. "But please…if he doesn't, he is not the one you need to hunt."

Four of the policemen picked up their chairs and left the bedroom while Susilo stayed, his stare too shrewd. "It is not my intention to cause more distress after your ordeal, ma'am. However, I am also not an idiot." He moved toward me. "Sullivan Sinclair is well-known to law enforcement in America. He has a file the size of encyclopaedia on vigilante behaviour, bribes, and even murder. I'm aware he has never been officially convicted, but where there are rumours, there is truth."

Running his hands down his decorated blazer, he nodded brusquely. "We shall return…with a search warrant. There are secrets on this island that require deeper investigation. Until then, please do not travel. This is an on-going case, and your freedom has been restricted until we learn the full story." Turning on his heel, he strode from Sully's bedroom and out of the villa.

Shit.

Shit!

Sully was innocent in this mess…but he wasn't in others.

He had purchased goddesses who were hiding on another island. Women who would gladly blab that he'd drugged them with elixir and rented them out to guests.

I doubted the police would be as lenient if they knew he traded in the black market and dabbled in trafficking.

If they find his goddesses…

It wouldn't matter if he woke up, he'd die an old man in prison.

I need to see Dr Campbell…Cal.

I need to figure out a way to protect him.

He might have committed those crimes but…he's different now.

He's changed.

He has to.

"Eleanor." A tap on my shoulder. "Eleanor."

My panic broke, dropping me back into my current stress. "Yes?"

"Go back to him, please. His pulse is unsteady."

Sucking in a breath, I nodded and returned to Sully's side.

I sat beside the man I loved.

I slipped my hand into his and gave him something to fight for.

All while my mind raced with ways to fight on his behalf.

The old Sullivan had to disappear.

And to do that...I had to rip apart the very dynasty he'd created.

Sullivan

Chapter Twenty-Two

THIS FADING IN AND out bullshit had to stop.

One moment, I was nothing.

The next, I was something.

One second, I was strong and able to sense movement around me, hushed voices, and glowing strings.

The next, I was weak and washed away to some blackened wasteland.

But now I was back.

I was 'awake' even if my exterior form still registered no aliveness.

I'd returned from wherever I'd been, and panic filled me as I searched the shadows for my string.

There.

A faint glimmering of gold, undulating like kelp beneath the sea, beckoning me to grab and take hold.

The moment I wrapped a non-existent hand around the rope Eleanor had braided for me, I felt better.

I shoved off the remaining cloak of darkness and *remembered.*

Shit, I remembered parts I hadn't before.

I remember…me.

I am Sully Sinclair. I'm thirty-three, and I'm in love with a woman named Eleanor Grace. She's trustworthy and kind and whenever she touches me, she grants me power to keep fighting.

The strain of recalling even that much threatened to pull me under again.

I refused, chanting my name and the woman I loved like an incantation to stay.

I'm Sully Sinclair, and I love Eleanor Grace.

I'm Sully and Eleanor is mine.

Why she loved me or how we met I couldn't recall, but I pictured her perfectly—her chocolate hair that fell to her ass. Her smoky grey gaze that never let me hide or lie.

And I remembered that I was *happy* with her.

She could be trusted.

And for some reason, trust was my most fundamental law.

I paused, straining for more pieces.

I work for…

Nothing.

I am a…labourer? Accountant? Builder?

Shit.

I live in…New York? Hong Kong? Manchester?

Blank emptiness.

Why can't I remember those things?

Why did I have holes where instinctive facts had fallen free, leaving small pockets that'd stored just a few basic knowings.

My name is Sully, and I love Eleanor.

Jinx.

Why did I call her Jinx?

Why did I ever think she was a curse?

My head throbbed as I tried to push the gathering blackness away and *remember.*

However, something outside my realm of internal entrapment happened.

Voices.

Eleanor's wonderful lyrical tone followed by a man I did not recognise. A man I was obscenely jealous of as he was with Eleanor and I was not.

"How are you holding up?" he asked, his voice sympathetic and soft.

"As well as to be expected," Eleanor replied. "How are you, Dr Campbell? How are Cal and Jess doing?"

"To steal your words…as well as to be expected," the man answered with a slight chuckle, pushing his glasses up his nose. "Better. Calvin has cabin fever and wishes to resume his duties. He doesn't accept bullets were inside him, scrambling his organs, only ten days ago. And Jess has chosen the same method of healing as

Sinclair. Her vitals are steady, but she's yet to wake up."

I flinched.

This man knew me?

Who the fuck were Calvin and Jess?

"I hope Jess wakes soon." Eleanor sighed.

Her hand squeezed mine.

I tried fucking everything to squeeze her back, but nothing.

"Just like I hope Sully wakes up too," she murmured.

"You did the right thing by bringing him home, Eleanor."

She sniffed as if tears had escaped.

Don't cry.

Fuck, please don't cry.

"I'm not so sure. He's no better here than he was there. I'd hoped…" She inhaled hard. "I'd hoped he'd snap out of it the moment he smelled the beach and heard Pika but…"

Pika?

What the hell was a Pika?

"These things take time." The man's presence moved closer.

I snarled in my mental cage.

"At least the police are gone. I don't know what you said to them, but I'm grateful. They've been a pebble in my shoe for days. Getting underfoot while I tried to keep my patients alive."

"They're coming back, though," Eleanor said. "With a search warrant. They suspect we're keeping things from them."

"Ah." The man clucked his tongue. "That is not good news…not for Sinclair at any rate."

"I need to release the goddesses," Eleanor said. "Now. Today."

Goddesses?

What the fuck was she on about? Was I in purgatory after all, and touched an angel instead of a human girl?

"You need to talk to Calvin. He will help arrange it."

"Will he, though? He's not exactly been glad of my existence. Why would he help me destroy everything he helped Sully create?"

"Because he knows it's time too. Enough is enough."

"He'll still hate me."

"Does it matter?" the man said. "Come, I'll sit with you. I'll offer moral support while you tell him what needs to happen."

"Can he come here? I can't leave Sully."

"Cal can't travel, especially over the sand. He's not strong enough yet. It's best if you go to him. He'll help you with the logistics of freeing the goddesses and show you what documentation and evidence to destroy before the police return with their warrants."

"Why are you helping me keep Sully out of jail?"

Jail?

What the fuck?

Jail?

What the hell had I done to deserve jail?

My willingness to remain awake faltered. No wonder I couldn't snap out of this limbo. Self-preservation had kicked in if my fate included being locked up like a beast.

"He's paid enough. And I don't want you to suffer any more than you already have. You love him, and I'd be an idiot not to see that he's head over heels for you too. If anyone can change the king of these islands, it's you." The man moved closer still.

I growled, wanting to rip him apart for being so close to what I loved.

I couldn't protect her in my current state.

I had no way of keeping her safe.

Get away from her!

"And the honest to God truth, Eleanor? It made me fucking sick to my stomach for what I caused. Instead of going behind Sinclair's back, I should've served up my warnings directly. Actually, I *did* tell him—after what he did to Jupiter, Neptune, and Calico—that I'd had enough. That he'd overstepped too many rules. I'd hoped we had enough mutual respect that he'd at least *think* about what he was doing with those goddesses' lives. But…anyway, that's in the past, and I cannot change what I've done—just like he cannot change what he's done before you came along."

Eleanor sighed softly as if he'd touched her.

Don't lay one finger on her!

Don't go near her!

The man continued, "I'm at your service, Goddess Jinx. I will help you free those girls. I will do whatever it takes to give them back their happiness, and I will do it without sending Sinclair to jail because that would mean I'd break *your* happiness, and that is a price I cannot afford."

My brain bled with information.

Facts I couldn't compute. Words that held no meaning.

Goddesses?

Goddess Jinx?

So…she was immortal, after all?

Why else was she named after a deity?

And who the fuck were Jupiter and Neptune? Were we in a different galaxy where such planets were touchable? Unlike on Earth where they were so, so far away?

I choked as the darkness thickened.

I clutched harder to the glowing string. My only light and constant.

"Come, I'll take you to Calvin. We can begin dismantling Goddess Isles immediately."

A pause before Eleanor murmured, "I can't leave him."

"Of course, you can. He's in good hands with the three doctors in the other room. They'll keep watch."

"No, you don't understand. Each time I stop touching him, he crashes."

The man scoffed. "I'm sure you're reading into things. The long journey will have made him weak, but he's home now and has a stable environment. Come…the sooner we do this, the safer he will be."

The longest pause in my sorry excuse of a life.

"Eh…" Eleanor's fingers feathered around mine. "Sully…I'm not leaving, okay? I'll only be half an hour or so. I'm not leaving, you hear me? Just…hold on and I'll be back as soon as I can."

No.

You can't.

I was weakened from the nonsense they'd spoken.

I was riddled with confusion and exhausted from my lack of memories.

I was afraid.

Fucking terrified of what I was and what I'd done and why this man spoke of me as if I was a demon.

Don't go!

"I love you. I'll be back as soon as I can." A soft kiss on my cheek. "I love you so much."

And then…nothing.

The glowing string vanished.

Darkness plummeted.

Nightmares closed in.

Sharp teeth gnashed in the black.

No!

Eleanor.

I fell backward, free-falling with nothing to hold on to.

No anchor, no grip, nothing to stop me from vanishing.

Eleanor!

I spiralled.

I forgot everything I'd just reclaimed.

I fell in perpetuity, never hitting the bottom, tumbling and tangling.

Fading and dissolving…pain.

Pain spooning out my insides. Pain crushing my skull.

Stop

Come back.

Fuck, please come—

"Sully!"

The string reappeared, glowing silver and crimson instead of just gold.

I grasped it, bleeding and panting, weaker than I had been in a while.

I dangled from her bond.

I didn't even have the strength to lift my head and focus on their conversation again.

All I could do was sway there like bait on fishing line just waiting to be swallowed by something far more vicious than me.

From far, far away, Eleanor said, "See? I can't leave him. He gives up if I do. I…I'm sorry."

I couldn't hear the man. I no longer had ears that worked, but I felt Eleanor curling into me.

Her heat warmed my icicle-riddled soul.

Her love once again had a flavour.

When I'd fallen for her while taking her in Nirvana, love had tasted sweet and sour. It'd smelled of fresh rain and new beginnings.

Now it tasted of comfort and longing. A scent of commitment and orchids.

I love you.

I'm sorry.

I blanked out.

Chapter Twenty-Three

I HAD A DILEMMA.

I needed to free Sully's goddesses before the police returned. I had documents to shred and emails to hack into and delete. But…how could I do a damn thing if Sully kept trying to die the minute I couldn't touch him?

Going to the bathroom had to be done in short bursts. Eating had to be done curled up by his side. Whenever Louise and her team changed his catheter or inserted a new IV with sustenance to keep him alive, I clung extra hard to his hand, just in case he felt the discomfort. In case he confused one touch from another and slipped.

For two days, I'd tried to figure out how to protect Sully from future complications all while doing my best to keep him safe from the current one. I wished Calvin wasn't injured, and Jess wasn't in a coma. Why were the only people I knew all in different stages of maladies and utterly useless in a mass freeing exercise?

Come on, Sully…please wake up. This would be easier with your help. Hopefully you understand why I need to do it.

I continued stroking my fingers through Sully's hair. The bronze-tipped dark strands were longer as was his beard. His cheekbones starker. His lips cracked and dry.

Each day, he looked more unkempt. A little wilder and unreachable.

I should shave him…wash him.
Make him feel better.

With the decision to do something for him, even if I couldn't do what was immediately pressing, I sat up and looked for Louise. She'd have to run the warm water and bring scissors, razors, and towels. However, the doctors were deep in discussion in the living room, and I didn't want to disturb them.

Damn.

"You know, Sully...you've got me trapped better than you ever did, even when you first bought me." I bent and kissed the tip of his nose. "Who would've thought love was a bigger trap than trafficking."

His pulse kicked, ripping my gaze to the heart rate monitor.

"Wait...can you hear me?"

What if he could?

My God...

"Do you remember when we first saw each other? You standing on that sandy ledge and me being delivered to you by helicopter? When our eyes met...you felt it, too. I know you did. That first trip into our destiny."

The monitor remained steady, showing no hint I'd affected him.

I tried again.

Lowering my voice, I shared our story in the hopes that he'd wake, ready to relive it, eager to write more pages and give us a happily ever after ending. "God, I hated you for what you'd done. I was prepared to find any and all ways to either kill you or escape you. But..." I sighed, reliving the smash of connection and the flash of incomparable lightning the moment I'd seen him. "I knew, even then. When you first spoke to me, your voice reached past my ribs and claimed my heart. I told myself it was loathing. I mean...how could I ever fall in love from just a stare? But...I had. I'd found you. I was home."

A tiny flicker on the monitor.

I rushed with more of our tale. "You might've asked traffickers to find me, Sully. You might've purchased other women and turned them into your goddesses, but without that criminal habit, we might have never met, and that...that's inconceivable. How could I ever have thought I was whole without you? How did I ever think I could be happy somewhere that wasn't by your side?"

Another kick, a quickening of his pulse.

I nuzzled into him, shivering with hope. "I'll always be grateful that you found me. So glad that you gave me your trust.

So honoured that you put your life before my own. But I need you to come back now, Sully. I miss you *so much*. It's killing me not being able to talk to you. Not seeing your eyes or hearing your voice. I know you're in there. Your heart reacts to mine because we're linked in every possible way. So why won't you wake?"

Tears squeezed from my eyes as I murmured, "What's trapping you? What can I do to bring you back?"

The monitor recorded a skip of nonsense. A flurry of half-beats and speed.

I sat up, my own heart pattering with growing worry. "You know…if you can hear me, I'll tell you anything you want to know." I switched to happier subjects as his pulse continued to scatter across the screen.

I never took my eyes off the irregular hills and valleys. Was this development a good thing or bad?

Keeping my hand on his, I murmured, "Are you hungry? Do you miss your chef's delicacies?" I kissed his cheek and lay alongside him. "If you wake, I'll gladly make whatever you want. How about some of those mushroom stuffed aubergines? Or that tempeh satay? Your food is one of the first things I fell in love with. And *Lebah*? Seeing where you grow all your fruit and vegetables…it made me fall in love with *you* because you have so many pieces to fall in love with. So many facets to discover."

His pulse kicked again, making my brow pucker in concern. "Sully…"

Goosebumps sprang over me as I put my hand in his. "Sully…if you can hear me…please squeeze my fingers."

I stared and stared.

I waited and waited

I begged and hoped and prayed.

And nothing.

"Am I interrupting?" Dr Campbell smiled and waved from the threshold of Sully's bedroom. The critters that shared his home had grown used to the influx of guests, staying on their perches and chosen rafters.

Dr Campbell looked around as a butterfly fluttered past followed by a hungry kingfisher. One of the Komodo dragons that Sully promised wouldn't eat my toes lumbered out of the bathroom where he'd been sunning himself while Nirvana splashed musically in the background.

I winced as a dragonfly flew too close to a gecko who'd positioned himself by Sully's pillow; his tongue snatched the iridescent jewel from the sky and munched on folded wings.

Glancing at the heart monitor, my concern faded a little.

The peaks and blips were back to a steady line, perhaps a little faster than normal but strong and sure.

Dr Campbell cleared his throat. "Is this a zoo or a bedroom?"

"It's both…a symbiotic existence." I forced a smile and sat up, pushing aside my long hair that I hadn't bothered to wash or brush in days. "Everything okay? Is Jess alright? What about Skittles?"

That was another thing I found exceedingly hard.

I wanted to go see Skittles so, *so* badly.

I missed her.

I would've given anything to run to the infirmary and tell her I loved her and missed her, but I was under villa arrest, and as much as my body itched for a swim in the sea and my heart begged to see Skittles, I would never leave Sully…under any circumstances.

My patience would be rewarded. My steadfastness would bring him back.

You'll see.

"Yes, fine. Everyone is healing. In fact…" Dr Campbell disappeared for a moment, returning with a tray and a tiny perch that'd been sticky taped in place. "I have someone who wants to see you."

"*Skittles!*"

I leaped off the bed, only to freeze.

The tiny caique went crazy. Her twirls and chirps broke my heart as I backed up and rested my fingertips on Sully's arm.

I was unbelievably happy to see her but absolutely terrified of losing Sully.

I can't let go.

Dr Campbell saw my pain. Marching toward me, he held out Skittles on her tray. Her little green wing still held a splint and bandage but that didn't stop her from trying to flap and fly to my finger.

I shivered in pure delight as I held out my hand and Skittles immediately hopped onto me, her talons wrapping tight around me almost like an avian version of a hug.

"Hey, tiny bird." I brought her to my lips, kissing the top of her feathered head. "You're looking better."

She puffed up and launched into a happy song complete with squawks and cackles, a serenade interrupted with scolding.

I laughed and looked at Dr Campbell. "Thanks for bringing her. Can she stay here? I'll look after her."

"Of course. I figured you missed her and aren't exactly in the position to leave your needy patient." He looked at Sully. He seemed whiter than usual. His island tan had faded a few days ago, but now his skin was almost translucent.

Icy worry dripped down my spine.

He frowned. "Is he well?"

I licked my lips, panic a common sensation in my chest, billowing out of control. "I…I don't know. His heart has been spiking. I thought he might be waking up so I was talking to him."

"What did you say?"

"Just about how we met and that I love him and can't wait to share life with him again."

"Huh." Dr Campbell sat down on the edge of the bed just as Pika swooped in.

My shoulders slouched in relief as the crazed parrot tore around the room at warp speed, his squeaks and caws so at odds with Skittles's scolding song. He sounded positively pissed off. His wings snapped with annoyance. His black eyes gleamed with rage.

"Where have you been?" I asked as the parrot tucked in his wings and dive-bombed Sully. He jerked them out at the last second, halting his arrow and plopping onto Sully's chest.

He hadn't visited Sully once.

I hadn't seen him since the beach when we first arrived, and I'd been at a loss as to how to bring him home. Sully needed his feathered friend. He needed something else to cling to, besides me.

But I couldn't explain to a bird that Sully wasn't ignoring him intentionally. That he didn't want to be this silent and still.

"Pika…" I went to Sully's head while Dr Campbell took Sully's wrist and counted his pulse. Worry clouded his elderly face.

Unable to fret about yet more things I couldn't control, I focused on helping Pika first. "He still loves you, Pika. He…just can't wake up right now."

"Lazy! Lazy! LAZY!" Pika stomped around, his little legs soaring up and slapping down on Sully's chest. "Sully. Pika. Hungry. Tired. Now, now. Lazy!"

The spew of English made no sense. The poor bird chaotic with confusion.

Skittles slouched on my finger, eyeing up her broken-hearted brother. She squeaked softly, ripping Pika's beady-eyed attention to her. He let out a cry so full of hurt he even made Dr Campbell suck in a breath.

And then his tyranny began anew, hopping onto Sully's cheek and scratching at the thick beard that hid his face. "Lazy!"

"Pika…it's okay." I tried to grab him, but he skipped to Sully's left eye and pecked at his eyelashes. "Hey, don't do that."

Pika took wing, fluttering like a mad Ping-Pong ball around the rafters. He continued to squeak and chatter, his speed turning him into a blur.

"Slow down. You're going to hurt yourself!" I cringed each time he went too close to the wall. The sugar glider scurried from its snoozing spot, swatting at Pika as he rudely interrupted his nap.

Skittles made no move to flap after him, either aware her wing hurt or smart just to let her brother have his temper tantrum.

Finally, Pika once again dive-bombed Sully, landed on his head, and buried himself in Sully's hair before squeaking with grief. His little feathered chest flurried from exertion, and his eyes closed, rubbing his beak through Sully's strands, preening him with the softest chatter of sadness.

Oh, God.

How could a tiny parrot symbolise everything I was feeling?

The chaos for a cure? The impatience for this to be over? The ever-constant panic that he might never wake up? And the all-powering need to be close, to ensure he kept breathing even if it meant I had to force that breath into his lungs myself?

"Eleanor." Dr Campbell looked up, catching my stare.

Everything inside me froze. One giant blizzard frosting everything. "What…what is it?"

"Call the other doctors. I think we have a problem."

"What? *What problem?*" My screech sounded like Pika's, manic and desperate. "What's happened?" Launching onto the bed, I smothered myself alongside Sully.

His skin was on fire.

Sweat drenching him.

No!

Skittles joined Pika in Sully's hair as I hugged him and kissed him and cursed, *cursed* myself.

I hadn't been touching him.

I'd forgotten while welcoming Skittles.

This is all my fault!

"Don't do this, Sully. I'm here. See? Feel me? I'm here." I clutched his fingers. I kissed his palm. "Wake up."

The heart rate monitor let out a tattered screeching *beep,* bringing the Geneva doctors running from the living room. Louise took one look at Dr Campbell's concern and my mania beside him and leaped into action.

Checking Sully's vitals, she stayed calm even as the monitor screamed with a slew of irregular thrums.

Sully's heart wasn't crashing like normal.

His pulse wasn't dropping or growing weak.

It was skyrocketing.

"He's at two hundred and thirty beats per minute." Louise snapped her fingers and pointed at one of her colleagues. "Get the defib ready. If he flat lines again, be ready."

"God!" I pressed my head into Sully's neck, inhaling the wrongness of him. The sickness, the staleness. "Come on. What are you doing? Stop it, Sullivan. Just wake up and *stop this*!"

His heart rate climbed again.

"Two forty. Shit!" Louise shoved Dr Campbell aside as she wheeled a machine toward the bed.

"Do something. Stop it!" I cried.

"We can't stop it," Louise barked. "This isn't treatable, not in his current condition. We have to deal with the aftermath once his system reboots."

"He'll die."

"He's moments away from cardiac arrest. His heartbeat is too fast. The only thing to do is to shock him when he reaches the end."

"What about a beta blocker?" Dr Campbell asked. "Elixir has a habit of causing arrhythmia. Beta blockers—"

"No. All drugs are risky in his current weakness." She crossed her arms. "Beta blockers might crash him."

"Two-sixty!" one of the other doctors yelped. "He's not going to make it."

"No! NO!"

Pika screeched as I swooped to my knees.

Skittles hopped out of my way as I cupped Sully's head and pressed my lips to his.

I kissed him.

Properly kissed him.

I drove my tongue down his throat, and I tasted the death that Sully had ingested. I blew air past his tongue and drove my hands against his mayhem-mangled heart. And I snarled with every temper and fury I ever felt.

I embraced the heat.

I swallowed the fire.

If he wanted to die…so be it, but he would do it with my words chasing him to the grave and my broken heart scattered at his feet.

"Sully Sinclair, you listen to me. Whatever you're doing. Whatever you see or hear or feel…*stop it*! I love you. That's all you need to focus on. *I. love. You.* I love you, and I'm not leaving, but if you leave me, you son of a bitch, I will *never* think about you again. I will erase all memory of you. I will sell myself to the nearest bastard and let him hurt me until the day I die because *no one* could ever hurt me as much as you are right now."

I slapped him. "So *fight*. Fight for me, you bastard. Otherwise, you kill both of us. Do you hear me? You die, I die. Is that what you want? Because if it is, keep going. Die for all I fucking care. Give up after everything we've done for you. Go on. Take my fucking heart and—"

"He's in a tachyarrhythmia. Three fifty BPM." Louise lost her calm bedside manner.

Pika took wing.

Skittles scurried away.

And I went fucking wild.

Sullivan

Chapter Twenty-Four

SOMETHING STRUCK ME.

Over and over.

Pain on top of pain.

But the external pain was nothing, *fucking nothing,* to the hellfire I now existed in.

I *remembered.*

All of it.

Thanks to Eleanor, she'd unlocked my broken mind.

Her stories of our beginning.

Her murmurings of love at first sight and belonging.

Fuck!

It unlocked the gates.

It granted back my sins.

It poured them down a chute until I drowned beneath them.

Memory after memory.

Realisation after realisation.

Of what I was.

Of what I *am.*

I couldn't escape.

It wouldn't stop.

I thought my love was pure. I believed I was a simple man who loved a simple girl. That we'd found each other through simple measures and lived a simple life.

Fuck!

I was the antichrist.

Diabolus.

A demon's brother, devil's protégé, and Prince of Fucking Darkness.

That was why I couldn't wake up.

Why the blackness refused to let me go.

This was where I belonged.

In the shadows and the inky shade where only filth survived.

Every despicable thing I'd done.

Every girl I'd purchased.

Every guest I'd indulged.

Every vial of elixir.

Every program of Euphoria.

Every bite of Drake's torture.

FUCK!

Flames of absolute damnation obliterated the darkness I'd been living in.

A fire struck into full catastrophe, ready to burn me alive.

Truth became my pyre.

This was my cremation.

My systematic incineration.

Every disgusting act.

Every murder.

Every life.

I'd skinned a woman for her refusal to leave the fur trade.

Bludgeoned a man for his role in slaughterhouses.

Poisoned and watched my parents drown.

Trapped my brother in a VR world and had animals tear him limb from limb.

I'd used people for my own gains and failed all the creatures I'd tried to save.

I was worthless.

Less than worthless…I was scum.

Who the hell could love me?

Who the fuck could even look at me after what I'd done?

Flames licked around my non-existent legs.

My legs might not exist, but the pain did.

Pain was my punishment.

It chewed through me until my bones turned to char. Flames snarled over my skin, turning my corpse into dust.

My organs popped and sizzled.

My heart shrivelled up and vanished in an inferno.

And I recalled why I couldn't trust.

Why I couldn't get close.

Why I couldn't be happy.

Because it was all my fucking fault.

I was the product of my end.

I'd chosen my path.

I'd stolen every drop of happiness from others because I would never experience such joy.

Until her.

Until the dream turned nightmare.

Until I purchased a figment of my imagination.

A speck of fucking hope.

That was how I'd come to know Eleanor.

I'd bought her.

I'd requested men to grab her, steal her, and send her to my shores.

What a fucking monster.

I'd torn her from her friends and family.

I'd trapped her and molested her.

I'd stolen her heart and left her for vengeance and now…

Now, I wanted to fucking die.

I intended to keep my promise.

I didn't deserve to live.

Two brothers who were the epitome of evil would be gone, and the world would be a safer place.

My body seized.

I gasped as the flames crept higher, burning my cock, my stomach, my lungs.

It took everything.

It scorched me, blackened me, destroyed me.

Something sharp struck my face.

A parrot squawk ripped through my ears.

Pika.

Even the parrot that I'd loved for half of my life couldn't absolve me.

I'd killed on his behalf.

I'd arranged for the deaths of so many men who still used animals as their test subjects.

Blood suddenly poured into my prison.

A tsunami of crimson life force, hissing with hate as it met the flames of my cremation.

It painted my flame-riddled corpse.

It clung to me.

The blood of my past.
The blood of my truth.
It poured down my throat.
It struck a match on my soul.
Fire howled.
Pain exploded.
And I burned out.
My invisible form collapsed into a pile of bone charcoal.
Traffickers.
Purchases.
Girls.
Goddesses.
Teeth.
How fucking wrong I'd been.
How stupid I was to believe I could be redeemed.
This was burnout.
Not mental. Not symbolic.
Real.
Literal and legitimate, it didn't just wipe out my power or my
pain.
It burned me alive.
It sacrificed me.
Removed me.
It chewed through everything I had left, flames and fire, pain
and promises.
It burned me until there was nothing left to burn.
Until there was nothing left of
Lust.
Love.
Life.
Me…

Chapter Twenty-Five

HE DIED.

He died while I pounded on his heart and begged into his ears.

He died as his pulse blazed past survivable.

He died as the monitor switched from chaotic chirps into flat line screaming.

And I lost a piece of myself.

He died to hurt me, to spite me.

He died *because* of me.

And I lost another piece.

He died because he'd come after me.

Because he'd saved me.

Because he'd loved me.

And I lost another piece.

His islands weren't enough to bring him back.

Pika wasn't enough.

Skittles wasn't enough.

I wasn't enough.

And I lost another piece.

Grief came swift.

Tears brewed heavy.

Terror was absolute.

And I lost another piece.

The flat line screech of his dead heart broke me.

The slack lips and closed eyes broke me.

The loss of such perfect possibilities *broke me*.
And I lost a final piece.
I spiralled.
I sobbed.
My grief mutated from pathetic to furious.
Vicious violence bled past my tears.
I crawled on top of him and struck his beautiful face.
I struck again.
He left me?
He abandoned me?
Well, he would arrive at his reckoning bearing my sorrow-inflicted scars.
My sobs overflowed.
I lost all my pieces.
And I snapped.

Chapter Twenty-Six

....
....
....
....
....
....
....
....
..
.

Chapter Twenty-Seven

DARKNESS HAD FALLEN.

A skip into the future, transforming sunlight to midnight.

I groaned as I tried to sit up. Muscles didn't obey me. Limbs didn't bend right, and the world didn't stay still. Nausea spun me upside down, and I lay sprawled where I'd woken.

Where am I?

I blinked, gritting my teeth against the swirl and sickness of the world.

Sully.

Oh, God.

The memory.

The awful, awful reality.

Dead.

Gone.

He's dead!

A keening, screaming pressure fissured my chest.

He's dead.

I lay on my back.

Sobs erupted and wracked my weak frame.

He can't be dead.

Please.

It can't end this way!

It can't.

"Sully! God, please."

Noises sounded behind me.

Someone came to offer condolences, their presence unwanted and cruel. "Hey. It's okay, Eleanor. I'm here." Louise Maldon appeared beside me, ducking to her haunches and taking my frigid hand. "You're okay."

I tore my hand from hers, needing to roll over, to curl into a ball so my grief couldn't dig its blade deeper into my belly.

Sully...

My sobs came faster, harder, *crippling* me.

She wiped at my tears, unable to stem the gush. "I'm so sorry that I had to do that. Let it pass. The nausea will fade."

In my suffocating sorrow, I didn't understand.

All I knew was I couldn't live in this horror.

Let it be Euphoria.

Let it be a nightmare.

Anything but real.

He's dead.

No!

I cried harder than I'd ever cried before.

She hugged my head and brushed my tear-wet hair aside. "Listen to me, you're fine. I had to administer a sedative because you were out of your mind. You were hindering our efforts. We couldn't have you striking him while we tried to save him."

Her words did their best to wriggle into my misery. The grief pressed harder, stabbing its blade, cutting up my entrails.

Sully...

Louise stood and grabbed me by the shoulders. Dragging me into a sitting position, I dry retched as nausea pushed acid up my gullet. She moved to the side, pre-empting my attempt at vomiting but continuing to brush aside my hair. "I need you to listen now, okay? He's alive."

Liar.

Deceiver.

Trickster!

I swiped at her, mad in my misery. "I watched him die!"

"You did." She grabbed my chin, fixing my dizzy-drunken eyes on hers. "He flat lined. You lost yourself to grief. I tried to remove you from the room so we could work on him, but you were uncooperative." Her fingers dug into my cheeks. "I injected you with a sedative for your own sake...and for his."

I blinked, tears still rivering down my face. "How could you tear me away from him? He died!"

"He died, but he didn't stay that way."

I stilled.

Everything stilled.

Sanity did its best to tiptoe through my lost willpower and comprehension. "You're lying."

She dropped her hand from my chin, taking both my hands in hers. She stayed bent over before me, imploring me to trust. Her usual medical scrubs had been replaced with a cream dress more suited for the island humidity and her freckles had grown into a thicker scattering thanks to the sun. However, her clear green eyes were still those of a professional.

A doctor who spoke with truth, even if some truths hurt.

"I need some sign from you that you're listening. That you're not checking out on me. Shock can create so many complications, Eleanor, and I need you to listen to me." She squeezed my hands. "Can you do that?"

I shook my head, grateful that the sickness dispersed this time.

I no longer felt nauseous, only confused and heart sore and bruised in every bone. "I...I don't understand."

"Come with me. It will be easier to show you." Pulling me from the couch where I'd woken, she escorted me through Sully's living room where a pair of macaws had made themselves at home on a dining chair and past a bushy-tailed squirrel raiding the fruit bowl.

My knees wobbled. I tripped as my body buckled beneath mourning, but she never let me go or stopped dragging me back into the bedroom that'd become a grave.

No, wait.

I didn't have the strength to go in there.

I would shatter beneath her lies and her truths.

I clenched my jaw as she pulled me over the threshold, and instantly Pika and Skittles chirped from the corner. They sat squished together in a rattan bowl holding smooth sea glass pieces. Bottle green and sapphire blue—refracting memories of Sully's turbulent eyes.

My heart bled all over again, filling my bruised bones with horrendous pain. "I don't. I can't—" I tugged on her hand.

"Come." With fierce strength, she yanked me to the bed.

A bed holding a sheet-shrouded man who I loved more than everything combined.

I couldn't stop shivering.

My teeth rattled.

Tears burned as I looked at Sully.

Lying regally beneath the white sheet, he was sublime unblemished perfection. No more sweat or fever. No glistening skin or broken heartbeats. He was serene and as solemn as any artfully prepared cadaver.

My keening began anew.

I couldn't see this.

I couldn't *remember* him like this.

I wanted to recall his sexy smirk and violent passion. I wanted to hear his husky laughter and stony commands. I needed life. I needed him.

But...*he's gone.*

His face was slack. His lips slightly parted and mostly blue. His skin had turned to snow, showing tracks of veins twining up his sinew-etched throat. His powerful frame and gorgeously toned muscles were fading; reducing in mass and strength the longer he remained buried beneath a sleeping curse.

He'd left me, discarding his earthly remains, ready to be scattered with roses and goodbyes while displayed on a funeral parlour podium.

My legs buckled.

Louise tried to keep me standing, but I puddled to the floor at the foot of his bed. Tears flushed out my bleeding soul. I was surprised I cried salt instead of crimson.

Skittles squawked and tried to come to me, her splint preventing her from flying. Pika fluttered for her, perching on my lap as my tears dribbled over him. He cooed and nudged my numbed fingers, then flew to my shoulder and nuzzled into the crook of my neck.

I broke.

I buried my face into my hands and sobbed.

Fingers pried at my wrists, pulling my hands away. "If you won't believe what I'm telling you. Look." She nudged my chin up, angling my head at the heart rate monitor hooked permanently to Sully's sculpted chest.

It shimmered in my tears.

Faint squiggly lines. Muted blips and beeps.

"See? His heart is still beating. Your shock is making it hard to believe me, but it's true."

Pika left my shoulder and flew to his master. He didn't unleash his rambunctious terror upon Sully but twittered softly and fluffed up his feathers before nesting on Sully's chest.

His slightly *breathing* chest.

I moved.

It was as if I'd been struck by lightning, infected by electricity, and enduring a bolt through my heart.

Crawling like a madwoman, I closed the distance and kneeled by Sully's side. I snatched his hand and pressed two fingers against his wrist. I closed my eyes and sniffed back my agony-laced hope and waited.

Thud-thud.

Thud-thud.

Thud-thud.

And then, I did the most embarrassing thing of all.

I convulsed with sobs of relief.

Snotty and wet.

Wild and loud.

I wept.

I wailed.

I cried harder for hope than I had for an ending.

I cried until a migraine attacked me, dehydration made me weave, and Louise plucked me from the floor and guided me to my place beside Sully.

The moment I felt the softness of his bed and smelled his sea and coconut scent, I plastered myself alongside his unconscious form.

I shivered.

I sighed.

I slept.

* * * * *

The second time I woke, sunlight had replaced midnight, leaving my world topsy-turvy. Stealing days I hadn't known and scrambling the calendar of how long Sully had been asleep.

Unlike all the other days of waking after a fitful night, snatched seconds, and repeating nightmares, I felt rested.

Heavy and hurting but rested.

Sitting up, I groaned as my head pounded and my eyes felt twice their usual size. I needed to wash my face from the stickiness of grief. To rinse my mouth out from my sobs.

The thought of a shower made me glance at the bathroom.

The fear of Sully crashing again made me crush closer and rest my hand on the strong pulse in his throat. To run my fingers through his thick hair and bask in utter gratefulness that he was still alive.

Breathing and sleeping and *alive*.

"Don't scare me like that again, okay?" I bent and kissed the tip of his nose. "No more, Sully. The next time you want to do anything shocking…just wake up."

"Ah, you're awake." Louise padded into Sully's bedroom, her hands scooping up her auburn tresses and securing them into a bun at her nape. "How are you feeling?"

"Better." I wiped under my eyes, then placed my hand back on Sully's arm. Always touching him. Forever there. I would never leave his side again.

Louise frowned slightly at my touch on him before moving to grab a deck chair from outside and placing it in front of me.

I prickled with unease as she sat and sighed, brushing away the fine tendrils that'd escaped her bun. "You slept for fifteen hours. I'll call for some food, and you need to drink, but before we get to that…are you coherent enough to talk?"

I swallowed hard.

Fifteen hours?

I'd never slept that long in my life.

"Can we have a conversation, or would you rather wait?" she asked again, peering at Sully's silent form before settling back on me.

I raked hands through my knotty hair and nodded. Surprisingly, my brain was no longer stuffed with tears, not sluggish and full of smog. "We can talk."

"Good." Leaning forward, she slipped into doctor's clipped tones and authority. "You are not to do that again."

"Do what?"

"Allow your system to deplete so drastically. You hadn't slept in god knows how long. I barely see you eat. You aren't useful to him if you're not looking after yourself."

"I think sacrificing a bit of sleep is—"

"Over a week of no sleep is medically dangerous, Eleanor, which is why your shock yesterday didn't let you register that he was alive. Why your emotions are on a knife's edge. Why you snapped when he had an episode. Why you're mentally and physically exhausted. And I get it. Of course, I do. You're under a lot of strain. You keep watching the man you love try to die. It's understandable that it became too much."

She made me sound weak.

I didn't like it.

I looked away and looped my fingers with Sully's. Nothing

happened. He didn't twitch. The monitor didn't react. It was as if I didn't exist.

I shook my head, hating the coldness of his unresponsive hand. Ice. Stiff. A stranger.

"How is he still alive?" I forced out nasty questions. "I watched him die."

"Once he flat lined, it interrupted the tachyarrhythmia. We were able to stabilise him. His pulse resumed with the defib, and we injected him with anticoagulant to reduce the likelihood of a stroke."

"And he stays stable without me touching him?"

"He does."

I squeezed his fingers.

No spike. No flutter.

Just the steady pump, pump, pump of a heart I no longer trusted.

Would it keep Sully alive this time, or would it throw him to the wolves again?

It was my enemy.

I *hated* that heart. I wanted to scoop it out and give him a new one.

Give him mine...at least mine was strong—I could feel it hammering at my ribs with dismay.

Louise gave me a moment to accept that whatever link we shared no longer factored in his desire to stay alive. He didn't need my help anymore. I was unneeded.

That hurt.

It made me flounder and second-guess. What did I do wrong? This had to have been my fault because he'd crashed when I'd talked to him. When I'd reminded him of *us*. Perhaps it was true, and he couldn't remember me. Maybe he didn't want to cling to a goddess who'd only meant to be his employee. Maybe he saw me as he did Calico and Jupiter—a girl trying to steal his heart to win her freedom.

Sully...

I wanted to dive into his head and find him. I wanted to shake him until his eyes snapped open.

"This is the part where you need to listen to me carefully, okay?" Louise murmured. "It's important."

I tensed.

Pika flew to me, and Skittles squawked in frustration from her spot on the side table. Her tiny wing flapped awkwardly in her splint. Going to her, leaving Sully without my touch, I held out my finger and shuddered with friendship as she hopped onto my perch and rubbed her beak along my jaw as I kissed her.

Tears pressed all over again, but I swallowed them back.

Placing Skittles onto my shoulder, I returned to Sully's bed and sat on the edge facing Louise. Pika landed beside Skittles, digging their claws into my muscles as I tensed. "Go on."

She winced. "There are things we need to discuss…going forward."

I'd woken with fresh optimism, but her words punctured me until all faith and belief escaped. I sank again, deeper into the darkness. Unable to live in this roller-coaster world anymore.

Soar and fall.

Climb and dip.

Hope and failure.

He's alive…but for how long this time?

"I'm…" The room swam and my empty stomach clenched. "I'm suddenly not feeling very well."

"I know. It's the shock still. Your symptoms will come and go until you accept certain things. I know you're still holding on to the hope that he'll wake and everything will go back to normal. I want that too. And I will do whatever I can to ensure it happens, but…you also need to accept the facts. It's important to be informed so your body doesn't suffer."

I couldn't reply.

I appreciated her advice, and I agreed. I'd always been one for as much knowledge as I could get, but…I didn't want to hear this. I didn't want to be slapped with reality.

Not yet.

Not while Sully had only been stable for a little while.

He'll wake up…you'll see.

"You've been so diligent staying by his side. I believed, like you, that as long as you touched him, he might pull through this but…"

Shaking my head, I buried my face in my hands. "Stop. I don't—"

"He no longer responds to your touch. He's alive. His vitals are stable, and he's breathing unassisted, but no other sensory perception is operational. We did tests on his reactions, and each one reveals the systematic shutting down of a human nervous system."

That explained the nasty sensation of touching a stranger.

Why he no longer needed my closeness.

Why there didn't seem to be a tether between us anymore.

If Louise was to weigh him, like her prior patient studies, would she find his soul missing? Were the electric impulses that were gone from his body mechanical or mystical?

I sucked in a breath, my skin turning icy.

He'd shut me off. He'd let me go.

It was his choice and only his, and I couldn't do a damn thing about it.

My hands fell from my face as an eerie calm smothered my panic.

I didn't know if it was shock or I'd finally reached the bottom of my well and I had no more strength to siphon. Either way, I would listen. I would register. And then I would survive whatever future I'd been given. "Continue."

Louise sighed heavily. "I'm sorry that I have to hurt you further."

"It's the truth. I need to hear it."

She stood and put her hands into the pockets of her sundress. Her face smoothed out from the friendship we'd formed and settled into the mask of a death deliverer—a doctor who'd had this conversation so many times before with the families left behind.

I stood too.

I hugged myself and waited for her to ruin my world.

Inhaling a deep breath, she said, "Sullivan Sinclair is now in a realm where medicine can't make a shred of difference to the outcome. The longer he remains in a coma, the less likely his chances are of waking up. The negative outcome of the tests today shows he may be slipping and will continue to slip until all neurological activity is inactive. If that happens, he will enter a vegetative state and may require a ventilator and the ultimately hard decision of keeping him on life support or letting him go."

I gritted my teeth as acid burned up my chest and splashed into my toes. "Anything else?" I swayed on the spot, keeping myself locked down so I didn't explode with violence or sorrow.

"My team and I are happy to stay on until such a decision has to be made or another outcome is presented. You have my word that we will ensure his body remains in the best possible care...but it's his mind that we cannot help." She came toward me, glancing at the parrots on my shoulder before locking eyes with me. "I still believe he can feel you. He might not react to your touch, but my advice still stands. Regardless of his disappearance, it would help him if you stayed present. Love has proven to be a stronger drug than any the modern world has created, but even that has its limits. I wish I had better advice, but all I have is the truth. Love him…until the end. Don't say goodbye…until it's truly over. But most of all…don't lose yourself. Be prepared for the day when that monitor goes quiet for the last time. Forearm yourself for the likelihood of his death because that will help ease the pain if it happens."

I swallowed hard and nodded.

I stumbled as things cracked and crumbled inside me.

The pillars holding up my legs. The bricks keeping my spine straight.

They all started to tumble.

I thought I'd reached rock bottom yesterday.

I was wrong.

My internal strength was collapsing.

I couldn't be here when it fell.

"If that's everything…" I tripped toward the exit. "I think…I might go for a walk."

Sully didn't need me.

My touch was no longer my shackle.

I needed fresh air. Aloneness. Somewhere to shatter.

"Of course. I'll look after him." Louise's sympathy chased me from Sully's bedroom.

I didn't look at the man I loved, frozen in time on his bed.

I didn't think about Skittles with her splint or Pika with his grief.

I fell out the front door, and I ran.

I ran beneath sunshine and through thick, golden sand.

I ran until I couldn't run anymore.

Chapter Twenty-Eight

FOR FIVE DAYS, I cycled through all stages of grief.

Hourly, minutely, I ran the gauntlet of denial, anger, bargaining, depression, and acceptance.

It was exhausting.

It was cathartic.

It was a never-ending crushing wheel.

Denial would come as I sat cross-legged on Sully's bed, guarding over his still and silent form, refusing to accept his unconsciousness. I'd roll my eyes. *This can't be true.* I'd fist my hands with rage. *How dare you leave me!* I'd sit and bargain with an imaginary devil and promise everything I had and everything that I didn't. *Please, please just let him open his eyes.*

I'd sit and stare at the man I loved, never taking my gaze off his handsome face, *willing* him to gasp with alertness and smile with possession, only to suffer incurable stress and rage.

Depression began when the stars rose and the moon twinkled.

I'd trip from the villa and run.

Pika would flit beside me, and Skittles would hold on for dear life, and I'd push myself until I fell to my knees in the sand.

And there, surrounded by manicured jungle and cicada song, I'd scream.

I'd scream until every ounce of sorrow stopped infecting me. I'd cry until that eerie calm fell over me and I had the strength to return to his villa with acceptance of this tragedy and fall asleep beside him.

For five days, it'd been a repeat of the one before.

Louise allowed me to lose myself in emotions, and Dr Campbell kept his distance. Pika guarded Sully when I couldn't, and Skittles guarded me when I needed her sweet presence.

But by day six, I'd had enough.

I couldn't keep killing myself this way.

Keep *living* this way.

I needed to *do* something. Anything. And saving Sully from police search warrants and saving girls from ownership was a worthy pastime.

Sully didn't need me anymore.

He didn't even know I was there.

I was superfluous.

I was free.

Free to destroy his dynasty one goddess at a time.

* * * * *

I left Sully's villa early and padded barefoot to my old home on the beach.

I entered the space where Sully had fucked me in the shower and over the sink, violence still hovering in the air from his lies at sending me away.

I embraced that violence and passion as I placed Skittles in the cotton balls on the vanity, and Pika chose a perch on the tap.

As I turned on the shower, it felt like Sully was still here, and I kept my eyes closed as water sluiced over me, remembering his aggressive touch, his possessive kiss, the hunger in his every stare.

I *missed* him.

I lusted for him.

But most of all…I wanted him back.

Even if his memory was wiped clean and he no longer loved me. Even if he sent me away all over again—I could exist in a world where Sully survived even if we weren't together.

I finished my shower—the first in a while—and dressed in clothing made for a woman instead of shirts crafted for a man. I brushed my hair from lugs and knots that'd steadily been forming dreadlocks while I'd mourned Sully's stillness, donning a grey dress with a black hem and neckline, and applied kohl to my eyes.

Only once I no longer looked like a creature dragged from the bottom of the sea did I place Skittles back on my shoulder and welcome Pika to fly beside me all the way to Dr Campbell's surgery.

Stepping inside, sniffing antiseptic and medicine, I braced myself to go to war with Calvin Moor.

It was no secret that we weren't best-friends. The truce he'd given me, when we'd last been in Dr Campbell's surgery before Drake marched Sully and me away, had been given in genuine generosity.

Would that stand when he learned what I wanted to do?

The interconnecting door to patient rooms suddenly swung open, revealing the very man I'd come to see. Lying in a bed, scowling in annoyance, Calvin glowed with health—the exact state I wished Sully could be.

The man wheeling him, a local to Indonesia with long black hair tied in a topknot and intelligent eyes froze. "Ah, you must be Ms. Grace."

Calvin stiffened on his bed, propped up with pillows and frustration wafting off him. "Jinx…what the fuck are you doing here?"

"I…" I looked between the two men. What had I interrupted? "I was coming to see you actually."

"Wish you'd waited until tomorrow, then you wouldn't see my fucking embarrassment at being wheeled around like an invalid."

"You are not an invalid, sir. You are recovering from multiple gunshots—"

"I was ready to leave this place a week ago. It was you and Campbell forming a conspiracy against me and locking the doors that kept me here against my will."

"Etti was only following my orders," Dr Campbell muttered as he followed them through the door. "Ah, Eleanor. What a pleasure." His face fell. "Is Sinclair okay? Have the Geneva doctors got it under control?"

Cal never took his gaze off me as I flinched. I couldn't help it. Sully's name was a trigger to me. A fatal shot to my heart. "He's steady."

"No improvement then?" Campbell asked gently.

"No." I sniffed and braced myself all over again. "I came to talk to Cal. It can't wait."

Cal smirked. "They're finally taking me to my villa. I'm free of this place full of bleach and beeping bloody machines."

I could understand his loathing toward the beeps. I was forming my own love-hate relationship to the one announcing Sully's faulty heart.

The Indonesian man held out his hand. "I'm Etti. I'm a vet, but my patients have been two-legged of late."

I shook his hand. "You were on *Serigala*..."

He winced. "I was. But I was one of the lucky few and very grateful when Jim requested my help."

I looked at Dr Campbell. "How is Jealousy?"

Cal stiffened. A barely noticeable inhale.

Dr Campbell nodded with professional calm. "Same as Sully. Stable and sleeping."

"Is she showing any signs of waking?"

"Not yet."

Seemed everyone was trapped on this island.

I was trapped in a never-ending circle.

Sully was trapped in a prison of his mind.

Jealousy was trapped in a never-ending sleep.

And Cal was trapped in a bed until he healed.

But there were lives in the balance that didn't need to be trapped.

Girls who'd been purchased for sin and who'd been living in secret for the past two weeks on *Lebah*. Goddesses who had to be freed before the police returned with a warrant, regardless if Sully woke to his crimes or not.

"Look, you guys can discuss happy topics, but I'm leaving. I need to be outside, right now." Cal swiped the sheet off his body and swung his legs to the edge of the bed. "I can walk."

Dr Campbell groaned as if he was over having this fight with Calvin. "As I said so many damn times before, yes, you are feeling better, and yes, your system is healing, but if you overdo it, you'll only set yourself back."

"I'm not going to run a triathlon, Doc. I just want to walk on the beach and sit in the sun for a while." His voice was strained. "I...I can't be here anymore."

"The fact that I'm letting you even return to your villa and away from urgent care is pushing my limits, Cal. You shouldn't be walking anywhere. Your lungs suffered—"

"One was punctured, I know. I'm aware." Cal threw me a look. "Jinx here will dob me in if I overdo it. Won't you, Jinx?"

I gulped, pinned in place by three men. "Eh, sure?"

"Good." Cal shoved off the bed and almost fell to his knees.

"For God's sake, Moor." Dr Campbell reached out to catch him, but Cal shoved him away. "I'm fine. Let me get strong again, Doc. Just...leave me be. Look after Jess and keep her alive. If I need you, Jinx will come running." He scowled in my direction. "Now, let's go."

I stayed silent as Cal shuffled toward the main exit.

Dr Campbell rolled his eyes behind smudged glasses, and Etti huffed. Both men gave up on their stubborn patient, placing him into my care. "If he passes out, come find us."

"Oh, no. No way." My heartbeat turned nasty. "I can't be responsible for yet another man's existence. If you believe he should stay, then he should—"

"I'm not fucking staying. I need fresh air," Cal barked, reaching the door and yanking it open. "Come or not, the choice is yours, Jinx."

Dr Campbell squeezed my bicep. "He's strong, Eleanor. He won't die on you, I promise you that. He might get tired and fall asleep from exerting himself too soon, but he's too much of an asshole to die." He smirked. "Takes after his boss, I'm afraid."

I smiled weakly. "Then why hasn't his boss woken up?"

"He will." He dropped his hand. Smiling at Pika and Skittles who'd been my constant shadows, he added, "Now, I'd follow that stubborn man before he disappears into the island somewhere."

I took his advice, slipping from the sterile surgery rooms and breaking into a faster pace to catch up. However, Cal hadn't gotten far.

His lumbering steps were punctured with heavy breathing as he navigated the steps from the second-story tree-top walkway and sank his bare feet into the sun-warmed sand.

He groaned.

His head tipped forward, and his simple outfit of a white t-shirt and grey track pants shivered as he shook himself free from medicine. "Finally."

I stayed quiet as he hauled his healing bulk forward and set a slow pace to the beach.

Pika zipped between us, cawing with impatience and almost goading Cal into ambling faster. Skittles showed more decorum, just eyeing up Sully's friend and employee as if she knew how he felt being hindered by a body that hadn't quite healed.

Half an hour passed as we walked in silence.

When the sea finally came into view and Cal fell to his ass on the sand, his face shone with sweat and his t-shirt turned see-through with his strain.

Sitting beside him, I let him get his breath back before I asked quietly, "Are you okay?"

He gritted his teeth and reclined to his elbows, digging them into the sand to prop himself up. "You can ask me that once and only once. I'm fine. I'm out of breath, and I'm pissed at my lack of endurance, but I'm fine."

"Okay." I dug my hand into the soft granules, trying to figure out how to begin. He might be tired from a long walk before his body had healed, but I was mentally and spiritually exhausted from Sully's tightrope of life and death.

I didn't have the energy for a fight.

I wished Jess was awake. She was strong and seemed to have a bond with Cal. She could've fought on my behalf and prevented any more animosity between us.

"So...did he kill him?" he asked.

"Excuse me?"

"Did Sullivan kill his brother?"

I winced, remembering the slobbering, brain-dead creature in Geneva, but then morbid pride twitched my lips. "Would you believe me if I said we *both* killed Drake?"

His eyebrow rose, his gaze shimmering with respect. "And that's a story for another day." He winced and repositioned himself. "I want a beer in my hand and both of you to regale me with every gruesome detail."

My smile faded.

I slouched.

I wanted that too.

I would give *anything* for Sully to wake and share a beer with his friend.

"How is Sinclair?" Cal asked quietly, turning his green gaze to the mirror-perfect tide. Sun spangled the top, reflecting gold on turquoise and promising a refreshing rinse from the humidity that'd slipped down my spine and cleavage.

Sighing heavily, I cursed the sudden press of tears.

No.

Don't you dare.

I dug my fingers into my eyes, stemming such weakness. I would not cry. Not in front of him. I would show no weakness because if I showed a single sliver of vulnerability, Cal would never help me.

Pika landed before us, pecking at a pretty pink shell.

"It's okay, you know. I won't hurt you. We're friends, remember?" He threw me a quick smile. "If you don't want to talk about Sullivan, then why seek me out?"

I gulped back the wetness in my throat and straightened my back. "Allow me to speak without you jumping in first."

He frowned. "Why?"

"Just…let me speak, and then you can yell at me, okay?"

He clenched his jaw. "Fine." Looking back to sea, he added, "I won't open my mouth until you're finished."

"Thank you." Raking both hands through my sun-dried hair, I sucked in a breath and rushed, "I'm sure you're aware the police were here. You most likely know a lot more about their visit than I do, seeing as they were here for days before we returned."

He threw me a look but didn't interrupt.

"When they came to see Sully, they mentioned they were suspicious of his dealings here and were going to return with a search warrant. I'm…" I looked down at the beach and stroked Skittles's green feathers as she climbed down my arm and perched on my knee. "Sully might wake up tomorrow or he might never open his eyes again. Either way, his business and records can't be here when the police come back. And…the goddesses? Well, they need to be freed. They have to go home and all guest access revoked. Drake stole the last of the elixir so at least that's gone, but Euphoria shouldn't be used anymore against unwilling participants. Those girls—"

"Should be free." Cal licked his lips, his stare still locked on the sea.

I let silence colour in the space between us for a bit before I finally asked, "Will you help me or hinder me?"

He sat up, sand cascading off his elbows. Rubbing his chest, he winced from his wounds. "It so happens that you're not the first to ask me to release them."

"*What?*" I sat up so fast that Skittles fell off my knee and plopped onto the sand. She twittered in complaint, waddling away to investigate the shell Pika still nosed around. "What do you mean?"

"I mean, when Sinclair left to bring you back, he called me. Said he didn't think he'd make it, and as a dying man's last wish, he wanted me to free the girls, burn Euphoria to the ground, and destroy every aspect of his Goddess Empire."

I froze.

So many things filled me at once.

Adoration.

Condemnation.

Pain.

"He…he didn't think he'd survive? Yet he came after me…knowing that?"

"He's a man in love." Cal sniffed. "And men in love do stupid things."

I shivered. "Do you hate me? For being responsible for him hovering in death?"

His head whipped to mine. "What? I don't hate you, Jinx. Far from it. Fuck."

My heart stuttered at the honesty on his face. "But…you've been so cold to me. You seemed to despise my presence and did whatever you could to stop Sully—"

"Only because he asked me to."

This was a day of punches.

I felt hammered. As if his voice were fists, delivering blow after blow. "He *asked* you to keep me away from him?"

"He made me promise I would never let him fall in love with anyone. That he wouldn't be able to survive it. That he'd do things he'd regret and would probably either end up killing the person he'd fallen for or killing himself." He sighed. "Seems like he was right."

A headache formed along with deepest heartache. "When…when did he ask you this?"

"He was twenty-something. Just killed his parents. His trust was at an all-time low. He'd waged war on test animals being released and drowned himself in work. One day, he rescued a cage of cats that'd been used for testing laxatives of all things. The poor things couldn't stop vomiting or shitting their guts out. He stabilised them. Got attached. They relapsed, and the vets told him that it was their choice to live or die. He didn't buy it and administered one of his own drugs that'd showed promise in rapid rejuvenation."

"What happened?"

"They haemorrhaged, dying a messy, miserable death, and I guess he just snapped. He came back that night covered in blood. Whose blood I don't know, but it was the start of his new crusade of fighting wars, not just in courtrooms with lawyers, but in vicious, violent revenge. He got drunk and made me vow never to let him get close to anything." He shrugged. "I promised. And I've done my utmost ever since."

Glancing at me, he half-smiled. "The thing is…I know him, and I know you affected him the moment you arrived. His shields shattered. He was hurting. I didn't want him to suffer, so I did what he'd asked, even if he cursed me for getting in the way. But..." He sighed, rubbing his chest again. "You have to understand, it was never personal. I like you. When he told me to call the guest that afternoon...that you were willing to serve in Euphoria, I knew he was bluffing. There was no fucking way he could hurt you that badly. Not after he'd fallen so hard for you. I figured it was more about hurting himself, so I gave him space. I kept the goddesses in their villas, and the guests far away so you guys could figure shit out."

He coughed and winced. "You're welcome by the way."

I couldn't move.

Or blink.

Or speak.

Cal wasn't my enemy.

He was just a friend.

A loyal, helpful friend who would always have Sully's back.

He would do anything for him because Cal was the only family Sully had ever truly had. The only person he could trust...until me.

Something slotted into place inside me.

Affection sprang from wariness, and I turned to Cal with deep respect but also a healthy dose of suspicion. A slightly crazed laugh fell from my lips. "Now that your secret is out and you're not such a prick, after all. Let me guess...you've already freed the goddesses? Here I am, ready to go to war with you, and you've already done what Sully requested."

He smirked. "Think you've figured me out, huh?"

"I think you love him and would honour a man's dying wish."

He raised his hand, mock horror on his face. "I'm not in love with the bastard if that's what you're implying." He sighed dramatically, almost as if theatrics could hide the truth. "I'm interested in someone else entirely. You and I have a lot in common currently, Jinx."

I froze.

Who...

His eyes glittered. "In fact, I know exactly how you feel. The anger at them just lying there. The helplessness that you can't wake them." He blinked as if he hadn't meant to say such things.

Oh, my God.

Jealousy.

He's in love with Jess.

Images of them walking together. His arm slung over her

shoulder. Her feverish need to stay past four years. Her loyalty to this island and desire to make everyone happy.

How long?

How did I not see?

"Jess…"

He cleared his throat. "Yes, well. Early days but…fuck."

I reached for his hand, my grief swelling to encompass his.

We did have things in common.

So many painful things.

"She'll wake up. You'll see."

He pulled his hand from mine, glowering at the ocean. "That cunt shot her in the womb. Campbell had to give her a complete hysterectomy. He doesn't even know if she can have sex without pain."

"I'm so sorry—"

"We hadn't even gotten to that part. Christ, forget I said anything." His face settled into stone. "And to answer your question, no I haven't freed them. Not yet. I've tried for the past week to get out of that hellhole of a hospital, but Campbell and his minions locked me in."

Waving at his chest where a wheeze rattled and his vitality faded, he added, "I'm not at full speed. In order to free five girls…I need help."

I shifted to my knees in a sudden sand spray. "I'll help you. I'll do whatever you need. I'll burn all Sully's files. I'll wipe all his hard drives. I'll murder any future guests who step foot on this island expecting a goddess to serve them. And then, I'll help you wake Jess up."

He nodded, his energy flagging rapidly. "Got the taste for killing now, huh?"

I rolled my eyes. "You know what I mean."

"Poor guests no longer able to indulge in their fantasies."

"They're not my concern. Sully, Jess, and the goddesses are."

"Is he showing any signs of waking up?"

I shut down my pain. "Not yet, but I'm sure both he and Jess will randomly open their eyes very soon. If they don't, I'll make them…just see if I don't."

His shoulders fell. "I'm not sure you can create miracles, Jinx."

"I made Sully happier, didn't I?"

He eyed me, chuckling once. "You did. But…it hasn't made you very happy has it?"

"It will…when he's awake."

"And you want to keep busy while you're waiting." He squeezed the back of his neck. "I get that." Rolling his shoulders as if summoning energy he didn't have, he muttered, "Fine." Holding out his hand, he added, "Help me stand, and we'll clean up this mess. Maybe they'll both wake if we change the world they'll return to."

Clasping his dry grip, I hauled his heaviness upright. Pika fluttered to my shoulder, and Skittles squeaked for me to pick her up.

Cal lumbered toward Sully's office.

And I followed him with two caiques.

Purpose gave me hope.

Action gave me strength.

And together, we might, *possibly, hopefully, maybe* save more than five lives.

We might bring back two people we adored.

We might turn Goddess Isles—a place of debauchery and domination—into a magical second chance.

Sullivan

Chapter Twenty-Nine

.
..
...

DEEP WITHIN, SOMETHING STIRRED.
A stubborn nucleus who refused to die.
Covered in soot.
Buried by ash.
Burned to dust and forgotten.
I was nothing.
But I wanted everything.
I deserved nothing.
But I needed something...
Her.
...
..
.

Chapter Thirty

LIFE SETTLED INTO A new rhythm.

Not moving forward in terms of Sully's progress but spring cleaning the present for when he woke. Two weeks where I systematically destroyed his business, brothel, and broke apart every whisper of his crimes.

Week one started off tentative and new; Cal and I still wary of each other and what our tasks would be. It soon slipped into an easy partnership with a shared end goal of fixing every wrong.

Leaving Skittles and Pika with Sully, I entered his office and almost keeled over with pain. Everywhere I looked, a memory flashed with heat and passion—Sully drugging me when I first arrived, him drinking the spiked-elixir liquor, the way he looked at me as if I was his sun and sea.

Cal moved slowly but determinedly as he sat at Sully's desk and logged in to his laptop. I swallowed down my worry and focused on deleting such a big part of Sully's life.

Cal called Arbi and told him to bring the goddesses back from *Lebah*. He rang some guy on their payroll to update passports and documentation required for the five girls who would be going home. And contacted Sully's bank manager to have two million dollars in cash delivered to his private hangar in Jakarta.

Four hundred thousand per girl.

He wrote down Sully's passwords while we waited for the boat to arrive from *Lebah* and gave me access to the curtain I'd tried to see behind for so long. He popped a few painkillers and hung up on Dr Campbell when he called to ensure Cal was taking it slow, and we fell into a comfortable allegiance.

An hour or so later, the grumble of a motorboat echoed from the bay.

"You go. I'll catch up." He waved me out the door, and I jogged down sandy pathways, beneath sun-stencilling palms, and into bright skies as Sully's Euphoria harem arrived.

I stood with braced shoulders as they climbed from the boat and padded barefoot up the main beach of Sully's empire.

Five girls.

A few I'd seen around but not officially met and one who'd begged to be released by a guest who'd known my name. Jewel with her red hair bowed her head in respect as they lined up before me.

What did they think of me? Standing as Sully's overseer instead of beside them? Did they hate me? Pity me? Not care in the slightest?

Cal arrived out of breath and fighting a body unwilling to walk through soft sand after being wounded by bullets. The girls stiffened as his green gaze swept over them. Only I heard the strain in his voice and the wheeze in his chest as he nodded at each and recited their names.

"Sailor, Trinity, Jewel, Diamond, and Blossom. Welcome back to *Batari*."

Sully had said there were seven goddesses on his island, including me.

That left six to free but only five were ready to leave. Jess and I would stay, but none of us were possessions any longer.

The girls fidgeted in matching wardrobes of the gardener's uniform on *Lebah*. Either they'd been put to work tending the produce while they'd stayed in staff quarters or they'd run out of clothes and had to borrow from the employees. Regardless, they all looked healthy and well-kept, if not bored and sullen.

Cal clasped his hands in front of him. "You're to return to your villas. Rest, bathe, and pack whatever belongings you wish to take with you. Whatever trinkets guests have given you, you may keep. Whatever memories you have from this place, you may remember. However, from this day forward, you are no longer a goddess and you will no longer be trapped here."

Five pairs of eyes swooped to his. Hope sprang, suspicion glowed, and a flurry of energy trickled through the girls.

"Tomorrow, you will be escorted to a main airport where you

will advise where you wish to fly to. You will be provided with the necessary documentation to get home. You will be compensated for your service here. And..." Cal's eyes turned lethal. "You will be threatened with the typical warnings to protect our anonymity. You speak of this to no one. You will be watched to ensure you do not break this final rule. You will slip back into the lives you left, and we shall all go our separate ways amicably."

He stepped forward, glowering at each goddess. "If you stay silent, you are free. If you spill our secrets, you will be hunted, eradicated, and all those you told will suffer the same fate. Is that clear?"

Slowly, the girls nodded.

"Good." Cal rubbed his chest and stepped to the side with his arm spread. "Go on then. Relax on your final day here. Swim, sunbathe, and order whatever you want from the kitchens. Be prepared to leave at noon tomorrow."

* * * * *

11:52 a.m.

I stood on the beach, squinting in the bright noonday sun at the sleek silver helicopter, ready and waiting to escort Sully's goddesses back home.

Yesterday, Cal had returned to his villa to rest. I'd returned to Sully to whisper in his ear and run my hands through his hair. We'd all spent the night doing whatever we desired and now...now five girls slowly appeared from the treeline. They no longer wore slinky, sexy bikinis or kimonos. Each wore an outfit appropriate for travel. Each carried a large duffel with whatever mementoes they wished to take with them. And each gave me a relieved smile as they headed toward their glossy transportation.

Cal appeared, keeping his distance and lurking in the trees for shade.

I stood in direct sunlight, dressed in a cream maxi that fluttered softly around my ankles. I wanted to wave goodbye to them. We might not know each other, but we'd share things that linked us forever.

The helicopter blades fired on, whining and thundering with building power as the girls climbed onboard.

Jewel was the last goddess to arrive. Her red hair bounced, and her freckles reminded me of Louise who stayed protectively by Sully's side while he remained unreachable.

I expected her to run to the helicopter and leap inside with the other goddesses but she beelined for me and wrapped her arms tight around my waist. "Come with us."

I squeezed her back. "I belong here."

"You belong with your loved ones."

Pulling away, I stared into her pixy face. "Exactly."

She frowned and dropped her arms. "You were telling the truth that day…on the path with the guest. You truly don't want to leave."

"I truly don't want to leave."

"Love makes people do stupid things." She hoisted her bag higher up her shoulder. "I hope you're making the right decision."

"Safe journey home, Jewel."

She smiled, shielding her gaze from the bright sun. "My real name is Baylee." Striding toward the bamboo jetty, she paused and added, "Goodbye, Eleanor Grace."

I watched her join her fellow goddesses, and the helicopter took off.

I didn't look away from the horizon until they'd vanished into the hazy humidity.

* * * * *

"He told me to burn it to the ground," Cal muttered.

"We can't." I spun in place, opening my arms and incorporating the cathedral-size space of Euphoria's entrance. "It would be a waste."

"It's not going to be used again." He moved toward the playroom where a harness dangled from the ceiling and cupboards ringed the space with props. Last time I'd been in here, Jess had sacrificed herself, I'd broken beneath elixir, and Sully had killed Drake's guards.

There were no bloodstains or corpses. No signs of rape or violence.

The mess had been cleaned and deleted.

It was just a room.

A villa that could be repurposed.

Cal kept moving, leaving me to follow him as he entered rooms I hadn't been in before. More playrooms with more harnesses. More outdoor bathrooms and lush gardens. "I'll get the gasoline."

"No!" I darted in front of him. "I…I have a suggestion."

The goddesses had left two days ago.

Pika and Skittles were with me today after staying by Sully's side for the past few days, and Pika darted through the rafters, making Skittles grumble in frustration on my shoulder that she couldn't join him.

Cal scowled.

Yesterday, I'd gone to see Jess in Dr Campbell's surgery. I'd left Sully in his coma and joined Jess in hers, holding her hand and telling her how we were the last girls on this island—barring the invisible staff who made this place run.

Etti, the vet helping Dr Campbell, had found me. Sharing a quiet moment with me and Jess, discussing the animals who'd survived the bombing and all the others who'd been en-route to arrive for rehabilitation.

Serigala couldn't be a sanctuary again until it was rebuilt, but Euphoria was no longer unwanted.

He'd put a seed into my head, and it'd grown into something I couldn't uproot.

"What suggestion?" Cal crossed his arms, wincing at his healing chest.

"Euphoria can become *Serigala*."

"Say what now?"

"Let it be home to creatures in need. Etti could be in charge of setting it up. The animals that survived need care and many more besides—"

"Sinclair won't go for it. After what happened, he'll swear off helping anything again. He blames himself for their deaths."

"Their deaths were Drake's fault."

"He doesn't see it that way."

"Drake is dead. He can't hurt Sully or anyone he loves ever again."

Cal strolled around me, eyeing up the space as if planning where to drop explosives and do what Sully had requested.

I couldn't let him burn it.

No way.

Pika barrelled through the air, chirping and playing. He wasn't his usual happy bossy self, thanks to Sully's unbreakable sleep, but he was a bird and needed to stretch his wings.

Catching up to Cal, I said with a firmness I was starting to embrace, "Euphoria stays. I'll tell Etti to begin transporting the animals that survived here."

Cal stopped, turned to me, and looked me up and down. His nostrils flared as if he'd fight me. "Flexing your power, I see."

"Learning to fight for things that are right."

He rolled his eyes. "You're the one who'll be at the mercy of his temper when he wakes and finds out what you've done."

I hugged myself at the thought. "He can yell at me all he wants because it will mean he's awake and healthy."

Cal chuckled, breaking our tension. "Christ, you've got it bad."

"And I accept it wholeheartedly."

"Meh, it's your funeral."

"As long as it's not Sully's, I'm okay with that."

His shoulders slouched. "You and me both. Fine, you win."

I did my best to smile, but all I could remember was Sully telling me I'd won the night on the path after we'd been to *Lebah* together.

'You win, Jinx.'

He'd told me I'd won, and he'd send Calico, Neptune, and Jupiter home. I'd saved three lives that day, but I hadn't had an inkling of the death swooping toward us.

Sully...please, wake up.

It's lonely and wrong without you here.

I ignored the arrow of worry that Sully might never wake up. That everything I was doing was worthless. A black cloud crept over my thoughts, but I did my best to disperse it.

If I stayed busy, I could keep my pessimism at bay.

Cal strolled ahead and I stayed in Euphoria, plotting design, planning new pens, new veterinary equipment...a new start for Sully and his rescues.

Wake up, Sully.

Please.

* * * * *

Week two brought more paperwork than I could read without going cross-eyed.

Cal spent a few days staying by Jess's side after she suffered an episode similar to Sully's, which set her prognosis back.

His attention was on her...as it should be, and mine swung back to focus entirely on Sully. I didn't want to leave him, so instead of sitting in his office and studiously deleting any file or email that might be incriminating, I took his laptop to him and used the passwords Cal had given me to hack into his online life.

One of my first tasks was messaging my father. I thanked him profusely, apologised for the long delay and stress in not getting in touch, and advised that I would call him soon to tell him what happened. I would need the time to come up with a fictional tale rather than divulge the real one.

He responded almost immediately in typical 'worried father'

style, demanding answers and to speak to the man I'd put my life at risk for. I'd typed back with a promise he would meet him soon…

And then, I'd logged off Facebook because my heart hurt too much at the thought that Sully might never meet my father or that I would never see the man I loved smile again.

The melancholy was never far away. The heartache and the strain of sitting beside him while he lay unmoving almost drove me to madness.

Work was my salvation, and I threw myself into it.

"I'm rifling through your emails, Sully. If you wake up now, you can stop me." I glanced at the silent, stunning man beside me.

I stared so hard, my eyes strained seeking the slightest shiver. Nothing.

Sighing, I stroked his arm and clicked into his online domain. "I won't delete anything important, you have my word…just the stuff that could ruin your freedom."

I earned a new appreciation for Sully's intelligence and the lengthy text-heavy emails he received from his scientists about new drugs, successful trials, and strategic focus groups. Those I kept, placing them into a file labelled Sinclair and Sinclair Group.

Searching his folders, I kept my heart guarded against trafficking emails and correspondence, not really wanting to learn his acquiring methods or the payment amounts he'd given for the girls' lives. However, after two days of snooping, I found nothing even hinting at his unlawful predilections.

Not a single deleted spam link or saved internet cookie that might lead back to sites and men that the police could never know about.

He'd either used an encrypted server or he'd already cleaned his inboxes personally.

Biting my cheek, I looked at Sully.

He lay as still as always, like a knight entombed in marble. His arms neatly by his sides, the sheet hiding the constellations of healing bruises, cuts, and scars. The cast on his ankle and the bandages on his thigh remained blocked by the bedding while his cheeks grew hollow and his muscles sharpened from lack of solid food.

Needles vanished into the back of his hands and a pillow cradled his handsome head, sensors stuck to his chest, and his eyes remained stubbornly shut.

"Can you hear me, Sully?" I ran my hand over his forehead.

Cool to touch. Empty. "Every day is harder…every day is scarier."

No response.

"I love you, even if you are putting me through hell…again."

I tried to laugh, but it just sounded pathetic. Sighing, I returned to rifling through his life and stumbled upon a reply email from his lawyers.

From: MurphyandCockran@law.com
To: S.Sinclair@goddessisles.com
Subject: Re: New Will and Testament.

To Sullivan,

We have received your request and updated as per your instructions.

- *Sinclair and Sinclair Group will be bequeathed to Calvin Moor upon your death.*
- *Jessica Townsend will receive two million in cash.*
- *Eleanor Grace will inherit Goddess Isles along with two caiques, Pika and Skittles.*
- *Your prior donations and preferred charities have also been updated along with your current assets that will be equally split between Calvin Moor and Eleanor Grace.*

Anything else, please don't hesitate to email.

As always, we appreciate your business and wish you good health.

Elliot Cockran.

Tears that I'd managed to keep locked inside overflowed.

All my worst fears compounded.

He'd come after me even at the detriment of his own health.

He'd known he was going to die and put me before his own life.

He'd ensured everything he'd controlled and created had been divided.

Cal deserved it after a lifetime of friendship.

But me?

I'd already taken the most expensive thing from him.

I'd taken his life.

I'd captured his heart.

And now…? Now he'd given me an end instead of forever.

Chapter Thirty-One

...
..
.

OUT OF THE DARK came a choice.

A single question that hovered on my fading periphery.

Live or die?

The time had come.

Fight or give in?

I hovered in absolute darkness with no answer.

I wanted her.

The girl I couldn't see or hear or touch.

I wanted happiness with her, the world with her, forever with her.

But I couldn't have her without having all my misdeeds and trespasses.

The fact still remained that I'd done things that couldn't be undone.

Things that couldn't be forgiven.

Things that would prevent me from happiness because I didn't deserve such absolution.

Live or die?

Make the choice.

Decide.

Now.

The blackness thickened.

Something crushed my phantom chest.
And I made a choice.
I gritted my non-existent teeth as my misery selected for me.
My answer was non-verbal.
The response silent but suffocating.
Things started changing, morphing, preparing.
I waited for the end.

...

..

.

Chapter Thirty-Two

THE COMA BROKE ON the third week.

And I wasn't there.

The phone call came at four in the morning, ripping me from sleep and racing me in my night shorts and pink singlet all the way to Dr Campbell's surgery.

Cal was already there.

His eyes stuck on Jess as if she was the only woman alive, his hand wrapped around her small one, his body slouched in a chair beside her bed.

I crashed into the room, unable to stop my speed, ripping both their attentions to me.

Sully had written a new Will and Testament to include the three of us. He'd gone after me knowing he wouldn't survive, and it didn't matter that for the past week I'd done my best to erase the fate that he'd written and scribble completely different things, I couldn't seem to stop his choice.

I hadn't told Cal that he was the new CEO of the largest pharmaceutical company in the world. I couldn't wait to tell Jess that she was a wealthy woman—earned by sacrifice and tenacity.

That part was happy.

The fact that she was awake was *happy*!

Yet as Jess licked her cracked lips, blinked her hazel eyes, and beamed a great big smile, I burst into noisy tears.

I couldn't stop the ache for Sully. The guilt at his suffering.

The pain of our separation.

Why won't you wake up!

My tears exploded harder as Jess murmured, "Come here."

Sniffing with no grace, I stumbled to her bedside and kissed her warm cheek. "You're back."

"I am," she said softly. "Are you okay?"

"I'm just so glad you're alive." I forced a watery smile. "I missed you."

"I missed you too. I was just asking Cal where you were." Her voice was different. Husky and hazy, the slight shadows of wherever she'd been still slinking through the syllables. "He told me that you freed the other goddesses. That we're the only ones left."

This was conversation.

This was a life raft from my sudden drowning in misery missing Sully.

I clung to it and ripped my thoughts from death to life. "We are. The island feels empty."

Cal grinned up at me, his skin flushed and green eyes glowing. "I haven't told her what you did with Euphoria yet. That there's already a menagerie installed, and the tile is covered in hay and god knows what."

I squeezed his shoulder, shaking with relief that at least one of us had gotten our happily ever after. My knees threatened to buckle with relief and envy.

As grateful as I was and as happy as I was that Jess had survived...I couldn't ignore the hooks and splinters that Sully was still unresponsive. No matter how much I whispered to him by night or kissed his cheek by day, I couldn't wake him. I couldn't entice him to twitch or reveal any sign that he still existed.

Jess had woken, but Sully...

God, I couldn't breathe around the fact that we'd already ended.

We'd ended with a broken heart.

In some cracked place inside me, a piece of depressed psyche began the process of acceptance. Grief was a sneaky, slithery thing—self-preservation beginning the task of erecting a wall around my soul for the inevitable. It did what Louise had told me to do and prepared for the day when the heart monitor no longer beeped cheerfully like Jess's did but slipped into a single monotone.

I didn't want it.

I'd *never* accept that Sully was gone.

He's not gone.

Not yet!

"Ah, Jinx…I'm sorry." Jess's eyes filled with matching tears. "Cal told me about Sullivan."

I slashed at the wetness on my cheeks and ducked to kiss her again. "Don't. Now that you're awake, I'm sure he'll follow. You'll pave the way back for him."

She held my stare and so much was said. Our strange sisterhood. Our unlikely bond. It was all there, familiar and steadfast, and I was so, *so* grateful that I had her because she would hold me up when I fell.

Because I would fall.

I would plummet if Sully chose death and not me.

Dr Campbell came bustling in, his elderly face etched with sleepiness but thrilled at the same time. "Don't you two tire her out."

"I've been sleeping for weeks, Dr Campbell. I won't get tired." Jess smiled. "Don't make them go. Not yet."

"I'm not going anywhere." Cal squeezed her hand. "You sure know how to run from a guy. If you didn't want to chase whatever this is, you didn't have to try to die on me."

Her cheeks pinked. "So…you still want to see where this goes?"

I shouldn't be here for this.

I was the third wheel. The unwanted watcher.

Swallowing past the ball in my throat, I backed away only for Jess to snap, "Don't you think about leaving, Jinx." She untangled her gaze from Cal's and looked at me. "I've been dying to share, and I'm annoyed that Cal told you instead of me."

Her face spoke of flirty, fanciful things, but her gaze was sympathetic and understanding. This wasn't an overshare when she'd literally just woken from a coma, but her attempt at distraction.

Fine.

I needed a distraction.

I needed her to help me stay sane when that sanity had frayed to the point where I could no longer hold on.

I glanced at Calvin. He sat stiff and chilly, but a smirk teased his lips. He was in on the attempt, both of them pitying me, pitying Sully, pitying us.

Bracing my shoulders, I met their courage with my own.

"Okay, tell me everything."

He nodded, accepting my agreement to be distracted and looked from me and back to Jess, speaking to her. "Sinclair guessed. He gave me hell."

Her eyebrows vanished into her blonde hair. "He guessed? How?"

"Said I'd never provided aftercare before."

"Ah, yes well. That wasn't exactly planned." She blushed again. "But I'm glad you finally opened your eyes and saw me." Her gaze sought mine, and her face glowed as if she'd woken full of vitality and gossip instead of a body weak from sleep and drained from haemorrhaging from Drake's bullet. "I've been kind of in love with him since I arrived. Men, huh? Blind as bats."

I hugged myself, attempting normal conversation when this was anything but a normal topic. "But…serving in Euphoria with different men and—"

"I'd rather not be reminded, thanks," Cal muttered.

"When?" I asked. "How?"

"The night I slept with Markus Grammer as you," Jess said. "Cal came to check on me after he helped Sully put you to bed."

It was my turn to blush.

The caveman fantasy.

The first time Sully took me, wearing his masks and telling his lies.

I'd fallen that night and never gotten off my knees.

Sully, goddamn you, wake up!

"Elixir hadn't quite finished with me." She laughed, only to stop suddenly, wincing at the pain no doubt in her lower belly. In her womb that no longer existed thanks to fucking Drake.

"Hey, it's okay, you can tell me later," I rushed. "Focus on yourself instead of—"

"I kissed him when he tried to tuck me into bed." Her eyes glowed with pure affection as she glanced at Cal. "He didn't kiss me back, but…it got him thinking."

"You were high," Cal muttered.

"I wanted you."

"Elixir wanted me."

"No…I did." She looked at their joined hands. "Every guest. Every Euphoria session…I was with you. When you didn't notice me, I figured I might as well make everyone else happy because that way…maybe *I* could make *you* happy. Maybe we could *all* be happy." She flicked me a glance. "Maybe I could make Sullivan happy so he'd give me the opportunity to sleep with the one guy who I actually wanted and to be his equal."

Her motivation.

Her hidden agenda.

So much simpler than her sinister plots that I feared. The age-old fatalistic hope of matchmaking in order to find her own freedom.

"You're a brave, brave woman, Jess." I smiled.

She blushed. "Just stubborn."

I pushed away tears that still leaked, attempting a joke. "And to think I ever suspected your motives."

"Well, I was rather persuasive." She grinned but then turned serious. "I knew how you were feeling when you first arrived because I was feeling it too. You wanted Sully, but he kept refusing you. I wanted Cal, but he didn't see me. I figured...if I could help, then someone might help me."

Cal stood and bent over her.

He kissed her hard.

Hard enough to make the heart monitor spike and Dr Campbell to growl from the next room. "Get your tongue out of her mouth, Moor."

Cal pulled away, his nose nudging hers in sweet affection. "I see you now, woman. And I'm not going anywhere."

Once again, the intimacy in the room was a dagger to my heart.

It took a mallet to my legs and swept them from under me.

I tripped and rubbed at my chest.

The craving to be next to Sully cracked my bones with need.

I needed to touch him, kiss him, murmur to him, even if he couldn't reciprocate.

"I...I—" I choked on a sob and swallowed hard. "I'm unbelievably happy for you guys, but...I have to go."

Jess looked tired, her body no longer willing to ignore her injuries. "I'm so sorry, Eleanor. He'll wake up...you'll see."

"Uh-huh." Blind with tears, I backed toward the door.

Cal stood as if to help me, but I held up my hand. If anyone touched me right now, I'd scream. The urge to bolt fizzled down my legs, but a single question drilled into my head. Loud enough to stop my tears and freeze my heart.

I halted.

I locked Jess in a stare. "Can I ask you something?"

She shivered but nodded. "Of course."

"When you were sleeping…what was it like?"

Cal turned to face me, his features stern and tight.

Jess took her time answering, knowing why I asked and deliberating on any help she could give me. "It was like…a long dream. I wasn't aware of the outside world, but I knew I was dreaming. For a while I was on the beach, just standing there. The sun rose and the sun set, but I couldn't move. My skin burned from exposure, and a magnifying glass concentrated the rays onto my belly where it burned a hole right through me. I remember looking down and seeing the ocean turning red with my blood." Her face clouded over. "Dark things happened after that. Things I don't really want to discuss and will work on forgetting, but it wasn't a nice place. I was back with my parents and the uncle who…anyway." She shook herself and clutched the sheet. "I'm sure each person is different. Some might be in a dream. Some might be in heaven for a time. Some might be in limbo and not remember a thing. Don't take my experience as something Sullivan might be enduring."

I shivered, saving what she said to comb over and dissect later. For now, I needed to know another important thing. More important than all the rest. "And how did you wake up? Was it a choice? What sent you back?"

She waited for a moment, her thoughts flittering over her pretty face before she said softly, "The dream ended, and whiteness wrapped around me. And I just knew. Go left and I'd travel to whatever came next. Go right and…I'd be given a second chance."

"So, you made the choice to wake up?"

She nodded but then backpedalled when she saw my face crumple. "But, Jinx…it might not be that way for everybody. He might not have a choice. He might not be aware he's even alive—"

I bolted.

I ran all the way back to Nirvana and bowled through Sully's villa not caring that I woke Louise on her cot by the deck.

I didn't stop until I slammed my hands on either side of Sully's head and pressed my fists into his pillow. Rage poured through me. Injustice and fatigue and thwarted tangled love.

With my lips hovering over his, I growled, "Make the choice, Sully. Make the damn choice and return to me."

His eyes didn't open.

My anger boomeranged into me, making me bleed. "Please, Sully. Come back to me. I'm *begging* you."

My plea fell into a void.

Tumbling like a copper penny to plink into an empty well.

A spent wish that would never come true.

I fell to my knees and cried.

* * * * *

Sully didn't wake.

Not that night or the next night or the week after.

By week four of his excruciating silence, I couldn't take it anymore.

I needed off the island. I needed some space to scream or sob. I needed to be free from the twitchy hope that he might wake up followed by the dismal darkness when he didn't.

As the sun broke through the rainclouds that'd drenched the island in a thunderstorm last night, I summoned Pika to stop harassing the sparrows on the bird table outside Sully's bedroom and plucked Skittles from her place on my pillow.

Today, two things were going to happen.

One, my special friend would fly again, and two, I was leaving this mausoleum and embracing life.

Carrying Skittles into the bathroom, I glanced at Nirvana as it spilled its crystal droplets into the clear pool. My skin often craved the coolness of its waters, but I hadn't had a swim. Yet another thing I couldn't do because I'd done it with Sully, and I didn't want to colour over our memories together with ones only of me.

"Sit still," I commanded as I turned on the vanity lights and cast Skittles in illumination. Her green feathers fluffed, and her apricot and black head cocked. But she didn't move as I carefully grabbed a pair of sharp scissors for personal grooming and concentrated on snipping away her splint.

Dr Campbell told me her wing should be healed two days ago when I visited Jess on my daily rounds. I'd been afraid to remove the brace in case he was wrong, but I couldn't deny her flight anymore.

The second the splint fell away, she chirped and hopped to the sink. Pika shot into the bathroom, landing beside her and skidding from his speed. He nipped at her, his eyes cheeky and goading her to chase. He took off again, doing his best to instigate a game of cat and mouse.

Skittles watched him flap around like a green tornado before looking at me and squeaking.

"It's okay. Give it a try."

For a moment, I thought she would. I wanted her to soar into the sky and swoop around the island because that would mean another invalid of Drake's evil had healed. Cal was better, Jess was better, everyone was better apart from Sully.

But Skittles hopped to my hand and scrambled her way up my arm using her talons and beak.

I sighed as she settled into her place on my shoulder and chattered nonsense into my ear.

"Not today, huh?"

She squeaked again, and I balled my hands.

The anger I felt toward Sully hadn't left. The fear I felt had become a mutant, polluting my entire body with a crawling, cloying madness.

I didn't want to be angry.

This wasn't his fault.

None of this was his fault.

But I couldn't stop the taunting voice inside my mind.

He *didn't choose you.*

He's *not going to wake up.*

He's *gone.*

My rage turned into a dagger.

I was either going to destroy this bathroom or destroy myself.

Dropping the scissors, I backed away from the mirror showing an unhinged, heartbroken girl with wild eyes.

I need to go.

I need to breathe…just for a little while.

* * * * *

Skittles sat on the throttle of *Singa Laut.*

I'd told Cal I was borrowing Sully's speedboat, Sea Lion, and he'd followed me to the wharf to show me how to operate the craft. After his lesson and stern warnings not to be too long or go too far, I glowered at him until he'd left.

I was hanging on by a thread, and company would only cut me loose and not in a good way.

I was so black inside I didn't even appreciate the colossal differences in my life since arriving in Goddess Isles. Previously, this had been my prison cell. Now, I'd inherited every parrot and property. I was free to go where I wanted. Free to use Sully's toys and call them my own.

However, I'd gladly go back to being imprisoned if it meant Sully would open his damn eyes.

Stop thinking.

Just go.

Pika flew beside me as I added speed and learned how to navigate a rudder instead of a car. Not that I'd driven in a long time, what with travelling and then kidnapping, but it was nice to be in control of something, even if I couldn't be in control of Sully's decision to wake up.

It took longer to cut across the turquoise sea and skim over peach coral reefs than when Sully had captained us, but I found some resemblance of peace.

Another banded sea snake slithered through the wake. A pod of dolphins out to sea sprayed water, transforming droplets into blinking rainbows. Jewelled fish darted beneath the hull, and the sun massaged my tense shoulders with thermal fingers.

This was still utopia…even if the devil in its midst was dying.

Damn you, Sully.

I love you dammit! You can't die!

The urge to turn the boat around and hammer on his chest until he woke up was crippling.

Breathe, Ellie.

Just…breathe.

Pika did an air roll, and Skittles twittered in a sweet song. They kept me grounded. They helped commandeer my worry, and I did my best to appreciate everything I had. There was so much to be grateful for. So much to live for.

I forced myself to inhale properly and not the ragged sips of the past few weeks. I drank in air and leaned my head back, letting the sun colour me and soothe some of my heartaches.

Can you feel me, Sully?

I'm still here.

I'll wait for however long you need.

Pika landed beside Skittles just as I pulled into the small bay of *Lebah*.

I tied the boat like Cal showed me, adding an extra knot to be sure it stayed secured, then stepped onto Sully's garden grove.

The atmosphere was different here.

His main island no longer held prisoners or greedy guests and had turned into a reflective, peaceful paradise, but this island…it burst at the seams with life.

Determination from freshly planted seeds to break through the soil. Aspiration from seedlings to sweep as high as they could toward the sky. And the bounty of fruits and vegetables as they transformed sunlight into nutrition that kept so many things breathing.

This was what I needed.

To see life in progress.

To witness the stubbornness of existence and inhale fresh oxygen from their leaves.

I strolled through the orchards and helped myself to sun-warmed berries. I collapsed beneath a hazelnut tree and watched Pika attack a nut while Skittles practiced flapping her newly knitted wing.

I stayed on *Lebah* until the enraged helplessness loosened its net of despair and dismay around my heart, just a little.

Skittles took her first flight from the almond grove to the berry greenhouse, and I once again focused on being grateful instead of fixating on what I'd lost.

Sully...

Please, I need you.

I'm not ready to say goodbye.

Drawing my knees to my chin, I buried my face into my hands and wept.

At least, these tears were cathartic. I was able to purge instead of suffocating beneath torment.

I cried for Sully and for me.

I cried until a gentle hand touched my shoulder and ripped my head up.

Self-consciousness made me swipe at my tears, and propriety made me stand in a rush. My navy dress fluttered around me as I made eye contact with someone I never expected. "You."

"You not dead." The girl who'd been on the boat with her grandfather and brother, who'd brought me back at Drake's command, eyed me in the dying sunlight. Her pinched disapproval had faded, and an openness in her dark eyes hinted she felt pity for my tears.

Ignoring her curiousness of my state of existence, I rubbed dirt from my dress and glanced around the orchard. "Sorry, I didn't mean to be in the—"

"Is fine. You not in the way. No worry."

I let my shoulders drop and wiped away my final tear. "Are you harvesting?"

"Harvest all time. Crop rotation mean always ready." She eyed me, her body language hinting that she didn't know how to address our past and preferred to just focus on the now.

There was history between us, but it seemed as if we both wished to forget how we first met. I wanted to ask how her grandmother was. Did she have enough for the medicine she needed? But instead of dredging up painful things, I merely asked something simple. "Do you enjoy working here?"

"Yes." She smoothed her olive uniform with its logo of a banana leaf over the breast pocket with the initials SSG. "It...eh, English word? Relax."

I nodded, glancing at the edible greenery all around us. The splashes of colour where fruits hung and the glossiness of vegetables waiting to be collected. "It is relaxing, I agree."

"Why alone?" She smiled as Pika and Skittles darted over her head and descended onto my shoulders. "I change my question. Why you not with him? My boss?"

Pika chattered and chirped, and Skittles puffed from exertion, her endurance weakened from healing. I flinched and looked away. I'd come here to escape pain, and instead, I'd run straight into another version of it. "He's not well."

"No?" Her forehead furrowed. "He should eat more fruits. Make better."

I smiled sadly. "He's not capable of eating much at the moment."

"Need make him eat." She put her hands on her hips, reminding me of the fierce girl who'd told me I would die if I jumped overboard and fell into Drake's hands.

I hadn't died, but Sully...

Please, Sully!

Make the choice to stay.

Moving away, the girl plucked a blackberry off a vine that'd crept across the ground in the nut orchard. "Feed him this. Big vitamin. Good for body." She placed the oozing berry into my palm. Pika promptly fluttered down and smeared the black sweetness all over his beak. Skittles joined him, squabbling over the dessert.

I sighed with a worn-out smile. "He can't eat."

"Then drink?" She mimicked squishing the berry and making wine. "Liquid many vitamin."

"He can't swallow. He—"

I froze as ideas unravelled.

Plans concocted.

Fate once again intervened.

Senses.

Flavours.

Reasons to live and indulge.

I'd forgotten the most important thing.

The rules of Sully's Euphoria were based on changing perception with sensory deception. Sound, taste, smell, touch, and sight.

Sully was locked in a Euphoria of his mind's making. It'd blocked him from sensation. It'd muted and deafened his world.

But what if I could break that?

What if I could slip past the deadening of his mind and give him a final taste of what he was giving up?

He couldn't drink or eat or move.

But…there were ways.

There has to be.

I have to try.

My fist closed around the sticky berry.

Pika and Skittles took wing with a squawk.

And I ran.

I didn't say thank you.

I didn't pick holes in my flimsy plan.

I ran and sailed and flew back to Sully's side.

But on my way, I made a detour to the kitchens.

I grabbed blenders and berries, ice and tropical delights.

I was a witch making a potion.

A witch with one last trick to try.

Chapter Thirty-Three

SOMETHING WRENCHED ME FROM the infernal darkness.

I thrashed toward the grey, desperate for light after so much *black*.

I'd made the choice.

I'd vowed to never make the same mistakes and find some way to atone.

I'd chosen to *live*.

To return to her.

To fight for happiness even if I might never earn such a thing.

But instead of granting me a second chance, something had grabbed my ankles and sucked me deeper. An entity, an evilness—something monstrous was inside this blackness with me, and it'd dragged me down, down, down until I'd been shackled inside a dungeon where no light, sound, or air could reach.

That cruel presence was still here, slinking in the shadows, gliding through my mind, but there was something else.

Something refreshing as rain and as life-giving as the sun.

Something that was the opposite of the evil within me and it smashed the shackles and hoisted me higher into consciousness.

It made me *aware*.

More aware and alive than I had been in weeks.

Eleanor!

I fought harder. I swam in muck and molasses. I kicked and crawled.

I opened my mouth and bellowed.

Eleanor!

Could she hear me?

Could she feel me fighting?

Could she see how much I wished to keep her?

I was trapped.

Trapped in this cranial cage with no fucking way out.

And I wanted out.

Fuck, I wanted out.

I wanted to make amends. To free those girls. To banish those guests.

I froze as sensation broke through the stifling silence of nothing.

Temperature.

I groaned.

I never thought I'd almost cry at the ability to differentiate between hot and cold. To know I had skin. To feel the body that hadn't forsaken me. A body that I couldn't manipulate or return to the helm, but a body that still fed me senses.

I gasped as it came again.

Coldness.

On my lips.

I groaned at the sheer delight.

Not just cold.

Ice.

Freezing snow upon my lips being pushed into the hot cavern of my mouth.

Stripped of every extremity and faculty, denied every pleasure receptor and passion within this vacuum of blankness, that single taste of sleet undid me.

I shivered with need.

I grew hard for a single sensitivity.

Hunger slammed into me with another sensation.

I had a stomach. I had muscles. I had an appetite that'd been denied for so fucking long.

The ice vanished on my tongue, melting into a non-distinguishable temperature.

I mourned it instantly.

I had nothing to break the monotony. Nothing to rip off my blindfold or pull out my gag or unplug my ears. I was empty without noise and sight and *her*. Empty and cornered, being pulled down into the blackness.

Things hissed and slithered. Nightmares rolled in. Numbness resettled over my awareness.

No!

Christ, no.

I wouldn't survive if I slipped again.

That dungeon was my coffin. A coffin that would slam shut with a padlock that would never reopen. If I let the evil have me, I would never see Eleanor again, never talk to her, kiss her, look at her.

NO!

I went berserk.

I did my best.

I enlisted every weak skill and broken power to wake up.

Wake up.

WAKE UP!

Something cackled in my mind. The blackness thickened. And I—

Ice on my lip.

Oh, thank God.

It interrupted the suction; it gave me vividness to cling to. A violent tear in the never-ending ether.

I crawled toward the lighter grey.

More ice melted on my tongue.

More.

Please, more.

It came again, this time the frost didn't just coat my lips but dribbled down my chin.

I felt that.

I tracked the slow-moving trickle. I relished in the intensity— in the sheer magnitude of survival.

I want to survive.

I want to wake.

I searched every crevice that I'd already searched before. I scratched at the blackened corners. I reached for the endless ceiling.

I lost myself to fighting and almost missed the gift that switched grey into red, granting the first blaze of colour in so long.

Colour!

I blinked at the blinding pigment.

Violent crimson and bittersweet scarlet.

Sanguine and vermillion.

Words spilled from my mind that'd forgotten speech and intellect.

A colour wasn't just a colour. Colour was what painted the world with dimension and depth. It was what gave life purpose and precision—the honour of being alive to witness such saturation of self.

I inhaled with lungs I couldn't see and bathed in the colour of red.

It felt warmer than black.

It promised to keep me awake, all while another sensation thunderstruck my anesthetized world.

Taste.

Sweet.

Sharp and fresh and perfect.

Berries.

I closed my eyes and allowed the third gift to wash through me. To grant another tear in my paralysis, to slowly bring me more aware.

So long since I'd tasted.

Just like colour, flavour gave meaning to the world. It made eating more than perfunctory but pleasurable. Flavour was a goal, driving us to cultivate and experiment, to create recipes and source new ingredients.

Flavour was another rung on my ladder, allowing me to creep higher from the darkness. To cling to the scaffolding. To have something tangible when the claws of darkness wrapped around my ankle and tried to claim me again.

I'd been reduced to nothing but three things.

Temperature, colour, and taste.

Three things that I'd always taken for granted but now were the three most important things to me.

My senses shook off their atrophy and craved more stimulation.

More!

Please, more.

I basked in the treasures.

I was grateful and in awe, but I was also greedy.

Greedy for sight and sound and touch.

For her.

Eleanor...please.

Slowly, the berry taste faded, the ice melted, and the redness around me snuffed out. The ladder I'd formed vanished from beneath me, sending me hurtling back into the starkness.

NO!

I couldn't go back.

I couldn't die down there.

I couldn't detach myself from every precious gift that a body could give me.

I needed to touch again, laugh again, swim again.

I needed to marry the goddess I was fated to meet and get on my knees before her and offer her everything.

I owed her everything because I knew these flashes of awareness were thanks to her.

She was the one interrupting the midnight.

The one throwing me lifelines and trying to pull me free.

I didn't want to let her down. I didn't want to leave her alone.

Give it to me again!

The blackness thickened.

I slipped.

A diving belt lassoed around my middle, complete with weights and anchors, yanking me into the deep.

. . .

. . .

. . .

Blue lit up my world, drenching me in periwinkle, teal, and cobalt.

I was ready this time.

I charged toward the pigment. I harnessed a body I could not see and used colour as my instrument to feel it.

To slip into fingers and toes.

To focus on the softness along my back and the faint throbbing in my legs.

I gave up on swimming toward a surface that didn't exist and instead fought to regain ownership of something that would have the power to keep me from the black's grasp.

Ice returned…smeared gently along my lower lip before inserting just a little onto my tongue.

Flavour smashed through me, vicious and all-consuming.

It tasted like summer and sunshine.

Blueberries.

Ambrosial medicine making me want more and more and *more*.

I moaned with greed.

I tried to stick out my tongue for a bigger serving.

Nothing moved.

Why can't I goddamn move?

I couldn't do this anymore.

I couldn't be trapped here any longer.

I wanted to open my eyes.

Open my eyes!

Open my eyes!

My furious heart pumped hard, filling the void with rapid drumbeats.

I lost it.

My heart had killed me, yet it was the only part of me still alive. It'd deleted me as its host and now existed in an empty chest, keeping an empty body the prison for a broken mind.

I couldn't accept that.

I won't!

It's mine.

I went wild.

I sank into violence and beat up nothing and everything.

…

…

…

Another taste of ice.

Along with a fourth gift.

A gift that I'd had at the start of my incarceration but had lost along the way.

Hearing.

"…so hard, seeing you like this."

That voice.

Like stardust and sand, like raindrops and satin.

Eleanor.

I stopped my endless war.

I hung in the darkness to listen.

"I've tried everything, Sully. I've argued with Louise about what I'm doing. She tells me I could kill you. That I might choke you by giving you a taste. But…the first night I ran my finger with berry smoothie along your bottom lip, your heart spiked. Did you feel it? Did it mean anything at all? Can you hear me, or are you fading, just like she warned?"

Silence slipped between us.

Speak again.

Please, for the love of everything fucking holy, speak to me.

"Three nights I've repeated myself. Three nights, I've made you a smoothie and fed you just the essence of it, knowing how dangerous it is to put something in your mouth when you can't swallow. By trying to save you, I might just kill you, and you know what...I'm beginning to think you might want that."

Her voice cracked, but she heard my plea and kept talking. "Jess is awake, by the way. She woke up over a week ago. Dr Campbell let her move into Cal's villa yesterday. Her wounds are healing. She'll never have children, but she's alive, and I've never seen her so happy. She said you're aware Cal had finally seen how she felt about him. Well, they're taking things slow...obviously with them both wounded, but they're together."

A quick slash of blueberry on my tongue before her voice dropped with painful secrets. "I can't be around them for long. Does that make me a terrible person? I'm happy for them, of course I am, but seeing them laughing together, touching...it breaks my heart, Sully." Her voice was as tragic as I felt, heavy and hitched with grief. "I just wish...I wish you were here. I mean, you are here, but you're not. I have your body, but without your soul...there's nothing."

I'm so fucking sorry, Eleanor.

"Almost six weeks you've been hiding. Six weeks of sleepless nights and endless hoping. I hate myself that I'm complaining when you're the one trapped in there, but...it's so, so hard. So hard not knowing how I can help. So hard thinking I'm not helping enough. So hard just letting time either cure you or kill you."

I'm here.
I'm not going to die.
I give you my word.
I'll find some way to get back to you.

"Louise said if you stay under much longer, your body will start shutting down. She keeps trying to talk to me about the end. Whether or not I'm prepared to sign documents that allow you to fade peacefully, or if she needs to have life support ready to drag out your catatonic existence forever."

A sliver of ice danced over my lower lip as she ran her thumb with blueberry smoothie.

"I told her that it's your choice. It's *always* been your choice, and I have no power to make you choose, but...if you can hear me, I need to say something. I need you to know. After all, you can only make a choice on informed facts. You don't know what

I've done. You think the world you left is still the one you'll wake up in, but…it's not."

What do you mean?

What did you do?

"Before I tell you, you have to promise me you'll forgive me. Then again, if you wake and hate me, I can accept that. Wake and send me away and I'll go. I'll leave and I won't come back because I'd rather live in a world where you're alive and not with me, than a world where you don't survive."

You're scaring me, Jinx.

What did you do?

"I keep wondering if I've gone too far, but…I did it because it was the right thing to do. And something tells me…you were ready to do the right thing."

Tell me.

She paused and darkness crept from the shadows. Cloying and deleting, blackness came for me.

Speak, Eleanor!

Keep me with you.

"I went through your emails." She stopped for a moment before continuing, "I cleared out anything that could be read as suspicious and saved correspondence from your company. Cal has been in contact with Peter Beck and your scientists are working as normal. And as far as your corporate life is concerned, your requests to your lawyer were wise. Cal is aware you've left Sinclair and Sinclair Group to him—not that he's accepted that you're gone, of course—but he is looking after your investments."

She saw.

She knows I bequeathed—

"You gave me Goddess Isles." Her voice cracked with tears. "You gave me Pika and Skittles." Something thumped against my chest. A feminine fist. A bite of pain. "You chased after me all while knowing you wouldn't come home, and I *hate* you for that. I curse you for putting me first because it was never meant to be that way. We were equals, Sully. You are not my master with the obligation to keep me safe. You are not my husband with vows to protect me in sickness and in health. You were meant to stay alive so we could be happy!"

Christ, Eleanor.

My beating heart splintered down the middle. Her sadness kept me shackled, not allowing the blackness to claim me.

"Anyway." She sniffed back tears and kept going, "The police came back two days ago with a search warrant."

What?

"Cal and I gave them free access to your databases, your laptop, and your office. They swarmed the island from the guest villas to the goddess villas and every pool and restaurant in between."

Holy shit.

I would wake—*if* I could wake—in handcuffs.

What was the fucking point in leaving one jail for another—

"They left with a profuse apology. They wished you a speedy recovery and are satisfied that Goddess Isles is a simple respite for married couples who come for some sexual counselling and relationship advice. That was my idea, by the way."

Her soft laughter undid me.

"I could wipe your emails clean and destroy any files that might have hinted at purchased goddesses, but I couldn't hide the abundance of accommodation and the aura of paradise and perversions."

Her lips pressed against my ear. "I stayed with the police as they did their tour. I grew wet as I led them through my villa and looked at the sink where you took me. I wanted to touch myself as we walked on the beach where you fucked me on all fours in the shallows. I answered their questions as we stood in the same place I watched you appear from the sea and strode half-naked toward goddesses who wanted you. I escorted them around the restaurant and onto the terrace and recalled every vicious thing I said to you after you made me sit on your fingers. So many places you've corrupted me, Sully, and now, all those sins are washed away. They found nothing incriminating because there *is* nothing. Not anymore. A fresh start."

How?

How did she hide the goddesses? Were they still on *Lebah*? What about the girls' files and their real names and—

"Cal burned almost every piece of paperwork in your office, and together, we sent the goddesses home. I memorised the files before they went up in smoke. Sailor, Trinity, Jewel, Diamond, and Blossom, also known as Danielle Scott, Selena Narce, Baylee Sharp, Alana Black, and Ashlee Colt. All five girls are free. They're being watched, don't worry, and they were paid their usual fee, but they are no longer prisoners, and you no longer have the curse of being a procurer of women."

I hung in the darkness.

I couldn't process.

I couldn't reply.

I was blind to the ever-lightening grey around me.

"So you see, Sully? You can wake up because you're no longer that man. You might have done things, you might have hurt people, but…I know in my heart that you aren't that person anymore. You honour *all* life, not just wildlife. You love me, and by loving me, you can't hurt humans because *we* are human. I have to believe that, and if *you* believe that too, then…you don't need to be afraid of waking up anymore."

I was dizzy.

Drowning.

Things swirled and collided, bouncing me around in the grey.

"While I'm confessing, I might as well tell you everything."

Another slice of sleety blueberry on my bottom lip.

"You told Cal to burn the Euphoria villa, but I stopped him. The animals that survived on *Serigala* have been relocated here. They're currently housed in Euphoria's villa and being tended to by the two vets you'd sent for—one large animal and one small— along with Etti and Johan, who survived the bombing. The shipment of cows and donkeys that you agreed to take on is due to dock next week. I've contacted your usual feed suppliers and took the liberty of asking Peter Beck to replace the medical equipment and drugs that were lost in the bombing of *Serigala*. A clinic is due to be built when locals can source building materials."

I couldn't breathe anymore.

I couldn't cling to one thing because she'd given me *everything.*

The greyness kept swirling, pinpricks of light spearing through the shadows.

Something warm spread along my side as if she'd lay down beside me. Another lash of blueberry before her sweet, liberating voice murmured, "Oh, one last thing."

She yawned as if her confessions had drained her into slumber.

"I gave the order to kill Drake. He lasted three days in his illusion before a bullet was lodged into his brain. He's gone. I watched it with my own eyes because I wanted to be able to tell you, with all the conviction in my heart, that he can no longer touch you, touch me, touch your animals, touch anyone or anything you care about. Everything you've been fighting, everything you wish you could undo is undone. His body is in pieces and buried…just like I buried you…Sullivan Sinclair. The man you used to be is dead."

I faded.

The greyness blended with darkness, threading with splashes of reds and blues.

"If you do wake up, Sully...you won't wake up as you." Her soft lips pressed against my cheek, her voice slipping into sleep. "You'll wake up as no one. You don't have to be who you were. If you choose to come back to me...you can choose to be whoever you want to be because... *you're free.*"

Chapter Thirty-Four

EXHAUSTION FROM BLIND HOPE and bedside devotion finally knocked me out.

Three days since I'd been on *Lebah*.

Three days since I'd left Sully's side.

With his goddesses gone, emails dealt with, animals tended, police mollified, Cal and Jess healing, and Pika and Skittles healthy, I had nothing else to occupy my torment.

I found no enjoyment on the island. I had no desire to go swimming in the warm tide or dive into refreshing Nirvana. Walks beneath palm trees and sitting in crystal sand held no appeal. I wanted nothing to do with paradise—even if that paradise had been bequeathed to me.

It was a forgery—just like Sully had said when I'd first arrived. Every perfect thing was fake because nothing had the power to bring him back.

I didn't even have the willpower to cry anymore. With each hour that Sully continued to lie beside me, vacant and still, I withdrew into myself. I lost my spark, my faith. I sank into aching acceptance that perhaps love was a lie and our blistering electrical connection was the biggest con of all.

He's made his choice.

And…I have to honour that.

I have to let him go…

Louise had pulled me aside this morning and told me my shock had most likely slipped into depression.

She'd offered me a few pills to take the edge off.

She'd told me to stop tracing Sully's lips with berry smoothies because it could cause asphyxiation, pneumonia, and so many other complications.

She'd said I needed a break and suggested I sleep at my villa on the beach for a night.

I'd snapped.

I'd crawled out of my sloth-like sadness and thrown her and her two colleagues out. I'd told her to sleep in my villa instead. That I needed some time alone with Sully, even if our conversation and affection was completely one-sided.

I needed privacy to say a proper goodbye and tell him everything that'd happened without an audience. I wanted him to myself after having to share him with needles and monitors and oxygen tubes.

As exhaustion pulled me deeper, tears broke free.

I didn't know if I cried in my sleep or if I was still awake, but fragmented images played across my mind.

"Drink." Sully forced elixir down my throat and stripped away my clothing. "Let me see what I've bought."

I trembled and stood before him naked. His cruel collected visage crumpled as he drank me in. "Fuck…I've finally found you."

He dropped to his knees and brought my clit to his mouth. "I've been waiting for you my entire life."

The dream swirled and dumped me into another splintered fable.

"Are you ready, Jinx?" He grinned, naked and proud, his gorgeous ruthlessness taking my breath away.

"Ready for what?"

Strapping me into the Euphoria harness, he ducked to kiss me. "For the rest of our lives together."

The dream popped and exploded into a new scene.

"Feel me inside you?" Sully's teeth clamped on the back of my neck. A love bite from a mate. My perfect other half, hilt-deep inside me, mounting me from behind as I braced on all fours.

I moaned and rocked back, pushing him deeper. "I feel you."

"It's not just my body that's inside yours, Eleanor. My soul is. My heart is. Every thought and fear, every hope and dream are now inside you because you're inside me."

Another switch, this one breaking my heart with longing.

"Do you, Eleanor, greatest Jinx of my life, Grace, take me, Sullivan Sinclair, as your lawfully wedded husband until death do us part?"

"I do. I do with everything that I am."

"You've made me the happiest—" He clutched his chest. He fisted his heart. His eyes caught mine, widening with worry and pain. "El—"

I caught him as he fell.

I cradled him as he died.

I rocked over his body and SCREAMED.

Sullivan

Chapter Thirty-Five

WAKING UP WAS A mundane habit.

An inconvenience if you were a light sleeper, and a nightmare if you were an insomniac. Waking up happened automatically and spontaneously, so much so that most people took it for granted— just like they took breathing for granted, and blinking and swallowing and all the other mechanical parts of a body that didn't require conscious thought.

Waking up for me wasn't like that.

I didn't slip from sleep to immediate comprehension. My eyes didn't snap open and energy didn't shockwave through my body.

Waking up happened gradually, slowly, so painstakingly frustratingly I wanted to slash at my face and pry open the heaviness of my eyelids.

But my arms wouldn't move.

My legs wouldn't move.

Nothing would fucking move.

All I could do was grit my teeth and blink.

I traded the horrendous blackness for a world I no longer recognised and winced against the brightness even though night kept everything muted.

The lamp in the corner.

The moon casting Nirvana in silver.

It *hurt*.

I slipped again.

Just below the surface of awareness, I gathered strength that

I'd lost while lying on my back for so long.

I clawed my way back through the grey and clung to everything Eleanor had given me. Every word was a stepping stone. Every sentence she'd delivered a life raft to sail free from my mental entrapment.

I blinked.

My eyes burned at the exposure to air and humidity. I glanced around my villa and reacquainted myself with the geckos above me, the thatched roof, the exposed beams, the driftwood furniture that was functional and unobtrusive.

How?

How was I here when I'd flown to Geneva?

Tiredness swept over me, unavoidable and thick.

I slipped again.

The next time I opened my eyes, it was a little easier. They only burned a little. They weren't as fuzzy or as reluctant to stay open.

The triumph over such a tiny victory made my heart pump harder, finally working with me and rushing through my veins to wake up withered muscles and knock against weary bones.

My waking up happened in stages.

A systematic checklist where things came back online the more I settled firmly into my body. The urge to slip under didn't hold as much sway. The fear that if I closed my eyes I'd vanish into the wasteland of nothingness was deleted by the rapidly growing feeling of home.

I was *home*.

Not just on my island but in the body I'd been born into.

Limbs refused my commands to move, but I forced myself to be patient. My body was familiar and comforting, unlike the horror of being detached and forgotten.

Blinking taxed me.

Exhaustion tiptoed back over me.

But I forced it away and swallowed.

I swallowed for the first time in weeks and tasted the faint flavour of sweet berries on my tongue.

That one action alerted my organs to resume their duties. My stomach growled with hunger. My lungs demanded a bigger breath. It was as intimate as slipping into Eleanor the first time. As humbling and enlightening as having sex with her because I was relearning my own form.

Tears of gratefulness stung my eyes, but I didn't feel weak for wanting to cry. I was overwhelmed. I was ash-covered and fire-charred, hauling myself from the dust of my ruined remains.

Thanks to Eleanor, I'd been reborn.

She'd erased my prior life. She'd given me the opportunity to be reincarnated into whatever man or monster I wanted to be.

Eleanor.

I felt her.

I wanted to kiss her. I wanted to thank her every fucking day for the rest of my life for what she'd done. She'd not only cursed me when she first arrived but broken a different type of curse that could've separated us. A hex that would've killed me if she hadn't figured out a way to remind my senses of the vibrancy of love and life.

I had no concept of time anymore, but the moon slowly crept over the horizon as I wrangled muscles that'd atrophied and commanded nerve endings to twist my neck, so I could look at the most stunning, incredible woman sleeping beside me.

It took everything I had to look down.

It took every willpower not to break into pieces at the tears glistening like starlight on her cheeks and the twisted stress of her face. She'd lost weight. Her cheekbones were sharp in the night, her chin dainty, her eyelashes dark, and her entire beauty dauntless and devoted.

She twitched in her dream as if she fought against demons. She curled deeper into my side as sadness made her tremble.

Fuck.

My useless, decrepit body jolted as a bolt of pure love electrocuted me.

I loved this woman.

I loved her more than myself, my wealth, my animals, *anything.*

I'd loved her before, but now? Now, I couldn't comprehend the depth that'd carved me out and filled me with eternal, ever after, and every unconditional love imaginable.

I love her.

Fuck, I love her.

I couldn't stop staring.

I ignored the heaviness of my eyelids.

I shoved away the need to fall into a healing sleep instead of a caged coma.

I couldn't leave her again...not until I thanked her.

Turned out, her strength was a savage thing. Her courage was so strong, it'd been fed into me with every drip of the IV and every whispered promise in my ear. She'd loaned me her fortitude, and I could never repay her.

She'd been the only reason I'd woken. The only purpose I had left on this planet that didn't make me sink in sin.

"Ele—" My voice was a switchblade cutting into my unused throat.

I wanted to cough, to swallow and lubricate but those muscles didn't work either. Water trickled from my eyes from exertion.

I clung to awareness but struggled to stay with her.

No! I have to talk to her. Please!

A flutter of feathers made me blink away the haze and focus on Eleanor's gorgeously long chocolate hair. Most of it had strewn above her on the pillow, but tendrils tangled on her shoulders where she lay tucked on her side against me. Her fists had locked under her chin and her forehead nuzzled against my ribcage.

My mosquito net had been tucked back to make room for the wires creeping over me and needles puncturing within me, allowing two tiny parrots to nest wherever the hell they wanted.

And they'd chosen Eleanor's hair as their bed.

Pika popped up first, his head cocking and tiny body bristling as if unbelieving that he'd heard my scratched whisper. Skittles appeared next, her delicate head with its sprigs of black feathers smaller than Pika's tangerine brightness.

The muscles in my face remembered how to work, and I smiled.

I smiled so fucking hard it threatened to send me back under again.

"Pik—" I winced and swallowed. "Pika. Skit...tles."

It happened faster than I could comprehend.

One second, the two caiques assessed me with sleepy, suspicious stares, and the next, the room filled with squawks and squeaks, blurs of emerald feathers, and the scratch of their talons against my face.

Pika couldn't control himself.

He rolled down my cheek only to fly onto my head and somersault down my forehead and bite my nose. He trilled and cooed; he sang and muttered. Skittles sat by my ear and bumped her head against my cheek, giving gentle feather kisses with the occasional happy chatter and nip.

But Pika...he was a ball of zesty zeal. Bursting with happiness and unable to ignore the need to fly.

He swooped around the room, screeching his head off. He bashed into the lamp and made it rock on its stand. He looped in the air and spun to the bed. The spew of cackles and calls made my ears ache with noise.

Eleanor suddenly bolted up beside me. She scrambled to her knees, brushing glossy hair from her face and gawking at Pika as he performed cartwheels and caterwauls.

"Oh, God. He's lost it. He's cracked." She stood on the mattress, her bare feet sinking into the white sheets as she tried to grab the chaotic caique from the sky. "Pika, it's fine. You're okay. You just had a dream or nightmare or…I don't know what's going on with you. But please, come here." Her voice cracked as if she feared his mental capacity had broken. "Pika, stop. It's okay. You're not alone. I promised I'd take care of you and Skittles. Even if Sully—"

"Sully. Sully. SULLY!" Pika screamed and dive-bombed her hair. "Lazy, Sully. Hungry, Sully. Now, now, now!"

If I could laugh, I would have.

My heart had never felt so warm or so content.

Eleanor suddenly froze.

The bed rocked as she spun in place.

Her hair flung out behind her, cloaking her shoulders just as her gorgeous grey gaze locked on mine.

She gasped.

She choked.

She plummeted to her knees beside me.

And for an endless second, she just stared. Her hands clamped over her mouth and tears gushed from her eyes. But she didn't reach for me. She didn't leap onto my unmovable form or tackle me with a kiss.

Goosebumps covered me as fear did its best to make me doubt.

Had she said goodbye to me? Had she accepted that I'd never wake and now had to figure out how to accept I was alive?

She shook her head, a moan slipping through her gagging fingers.

"He…llo." I grimaced, wishing I could sit up and grab her. That I could delete the distance between us and sink inside her to remind her, in every certain way, that I was alive. That I had the endurance to make love to her, to kiss her, to laugh with her.

Instead, I was locked in a different type of prison. This one I'd been given my life back, but I still couldn't operate within it. I was still a voyeur, forced to lay prone on my back and wait for her to come to me.

"Elea…nor." I swallowed twice. A third time. I tried again. "It's o…kay, Eleanor."

She shattered.

Crumpling into a little ball, she hugged herself as a wracking sob rocked her body.

She successfully ripped out my traitorous heart that'd started this mess and made me swallow down my own tears. I wanted so fucking much to touch her. To hold her.

"Come…here. Please, please…come here." I arched my chin, triumphant at that small achievement all while cursing the rest of my unresponsive form.

Pika continued his loud celebration, and Skittles flew to her soul-mate, cooing in Eleanor's ear, pecking at her hair so she could press into the crook of her shoulder and neck in sympathy.

Eleanor reached for the little parrot, and with her fingers on Skittles's feathers, she looked up again. "Is this really happening? I'm not dreaming? I just dreamed you married me. We promised each other until death do us part, and then…you died. Two seconds after our vows, Sully. You—" She pinched herself, making Skittles squeak at the fast movement. She pinched hard enough to leave crescent marks of her nails in her forearm.

"You're not…dreaming." I coughed.

My muscles gathered enough energy to cough.

I grinned, not caring if it was sloppy or resembled a grimace instead of gratefulness. Every moment I stayed awake, my body slipped back under my command.

Just like she would.

Just like I was at her command. I would do whatever she asked and be whoever she wanted if only she would fucking come close.

"Jinx…"

One second, she was on her knees, and the next, she launched at me. Her cheek pressed against my heart. Her arms lashed around my chest. Her body on top of my body in a full-welcome, relief-filled hug. "*Sully*. Oh, my God." Her lips danced over my cheeks, my eyes, my forehead, my chin.

Kiss after kiss.

Fast and furious, I couldn't keep track of sensation, and the kisses all blended into one. I gasped as my nervous system struggled, threatening to short-circuit and send me under again.

"Eleanor…stop."

"Shit." Immediately, she slipped off me, resting on her knees, her chest rising and falling. "I'm sorry. I shouldn't have done that. Did I hurt you? I'll go get the doctors." She went to slip off the bed. "Damn! I sent them away for the night. The *one* night I send them away, and you wake up." Her panic bled through her swift syntax. "I'll run. I won't be long. I'll get help, and they can give you whatever you need." She stood, raking her hands through her hair, one of my charcoal business shirts buttoned and hanging loose on her stunning frame. "You'll need food and painkillers and—" She looked back at me, her hair once again flying every which way in her hurry. "Are you hurting? What do you need? Tell me and I'll—"

"Eleanor…quiet."

I winced at the crashing consonants in my head. Too much, too soon. Her panic bled into me, reminding me that I *was* in pain. That every little achievement in speech and motion cost me dearly, but she was so full of life, so fierce, so tenacious that I fed off her.

I stole more of her energy because her will for me to survive was contagious.

"Just…sit with me." I swallowed again, wishing I could pat the bed so she'd join me, begging to stand and grab her in a hug. How long before I could do that? How many more weeks would I be bedridden and useless? "Please?"

Instantly, she sat on the edge of the mattress in the space between my waistline and hip. She dodged the tubes going into me and gawked at the heart monitor registering my beats in all their awakening mayhem.

Pika and Skittles instantly took perch on her shoulders, one on each, adorning her in green jewels.

"I can't believe this." She pressed her fingertips to the monitor's screen. "So many times I've listened and watched this awful machine. I *hated* it. But now…now I love it because it shows the truth. You're back." Taking my hand in hers, careful not to jostle the IV line, she sniffed back her fresh tears. "I have so much to say, Sully. So much to ask. Where did you go? Could you hear me? What brought you back, do you know? You don't need to worry about Drake, he's gone. And the police have been dealt with and—"

"Stop." I smiled gently. "I know…I heard you."

She froze. "You did?"

"Every word."

She blushed. "Are you angry with me?"

I winced. "I think the…question is, are you mad…at me?"

Her jaw tightened as she showed me honesty instead of lies. "I admit I hated that you went after me knowing you might not come back. That you forward planned your death by updating your Will and Testament. That you decided, without any consultation, that my life was worth more than yours."

"But don't you see?" I swallowed, slowly finding it easier to talk. "You *are* worth more. You have more…goodness in your little finger than I do in my…entire body."

"That's bullshit, and you know it."

I frowned. "I couldn't let him hurt you. I couldn't let him…hurt anything ever again."

"I know." She caressed my knuckles. "One day I might ask what you did to Drake, but not tonight." She risked a shy smile. "Tonight, I just want to hear your voice and feel your touch."

I looked at where our hands linked, willing my fingers to twitch around hers.

I grunted at the effort and sweat broke out over my forehead as I managed to squeeze her for a second before my ligaments gave up. "I can't move."

"I suppose it will take time for your body to regain its strength." She smiled. "But I'll help. Every step." Kissing my knuckles, she looked over her shoulder at the door. "I really should go get Louise, though."

"Louise?"

"Your doctor."

"You hired someone else?"

"You collapsed in Geneva, remember?" She shivered and looked away, her face haunted with memories. "I did my best with CPR, but the mercenaries brought you back to life with a small defibrillator. Once the ambulance crew arrived, you were transported to the hospital." Her shivers turned into a shudder. "I didn't like it there. Snowy and cold…populated." She risked a half-smile. "I requested to bring you home."

"You flew me back?"

What the hell else had this wonderful woman done?

"Campbell arranged it."

"But you did all that? You were with me the entire time? You kept breath in my body and—"

"I did what I needed to do to keep you." Her eyes narrowed with ferocity. "No way was I letting you go."

My chest clenched with her loyalty, glowing with a return vow. "I love you with all my fucking heart."

"Don't talk to me about hearts. That's what started this mess." She tried to laugh, but it was hollow. "God, Sully…seeing you collapse? It…" She bit her lip and looked away, doing her best to control her grief.

My body crawled with itchy frustration to touch her, heal her, eradicate those brutal memories. "I'm so sorry I put you through that."

A lonely tear ran down her cheek.

"Hey…" I fucking cursed that I couldn't capture that droplet and bring her down for a kiss. "It's okay. I'm here. And I promise I'm not going anywhere."

She nodded, swiping at her cheeks and forcing another smile. "I won't let you. I'll make sure Louise, her team, and Dr Campbell keep you right here with me."

"Where *is* Campbell?"

"Still here. He keeps threatening to retire, but I know he's waiting around. He doesn't want to leave until you're okay."

I frowned. "I want him off my island."

"He brought Jess back and Cal and Skittles. I know he betrayed you, but—"

"I don't want to talk about him." I'd woken a newly born man. Thanks to Eleanor, I had no imprisoned women and no nefarious guests on my shores, but I still had guilt for what I'd done and rage toward the man who'd gone behind my back and ultimately smeared the blood of *Serigala*'s creatures on both our hands.

"I understand that," she murmured. "We have plenty of time to catch up later." She kissed my knuckles again, raising my dead arm, stretching out frozen muscles and locked joints.

I groaned at the mixture of pleasure and pain.

She instantly lowered my arm. "Does that hurt?"

"The opposite. It's a relief to be in a different position."

Without a word, she brought my arm up again and rested it high on her lap. With exquisite care and worship, she massaged from my wrist to my elbow, all the way to my shoulder.

I grew hard.

I couldn't control any part of myself, but it turned out her touch was still an aphrodisiac I couldn't ignore.

"You have no idea how good that feels." I dug my head into the pillow, flinching as my cock kept swelling and pain lanced the tip.

She continued to massage me, and I continued to thicken.

I gritted my teeth against the growing discomfort but had to concede when she reached my neck and dug heavenly fingers into seized and tight muscles.

My sexual thirst overflowed. My bodily hunger snarled. And the pain in my cock became unbearable. "Stop." I swallowed. "Please, you have to stop."

Instantly, she tore her hands off me. "What is it? What's wrong?"

If I could blush, I would have. The unmentionable housekeeping of looking after someone in a coma wasn't exactly bedroom talk with the girl I wanted to pounce on and claim. "Eh, I'm guessing I have…a catheter in?"

Her cheeks pinked. "You do."

I forced a chuckle, proud that I could achieve yet another skill. "I'm hard."

"Oh, God. I shouldn't have touched you. I'm so sorry."

"Woman, shut it." I turned my head, thankful that I could do that even while cursing the lack of so many other things. "Kiss me."

"*What?*" Her eyebrows shot into her hairline. "There is no way I'm kissing you. You literally just said you're in pain."

"Kiss me." I couldn't stop looking at her mouth, despite the pain in my cock, regardless that I'd woken with tangled priorities of wanting sex over the ability to walk.

"You just woke up after being dead for six weeks."

"All the more reason to kiss me."

"I'm not kissing—"

"I'm already hard, Eleanor. The discomfort is already there. Kiss me…let me say a proper hello to you, and then you can fetch the doctor and put me out of my misery, okay?"

She paused. "I'll fetch the doctor now. She can remove the catheter and—"

"I need to kiss you." I sent every command through my limbs to sit up and grab her. I managed a few hand twitches and leg shuffles, but that was it. "Kiss me, goddammit."

"But—"

"I won't ask again, Jinx." I glowered. "Come here."

She shivered, and her nipples pebbled beneath my shirt. The material gaped as she leaned over me, giving me a glimpse down her cleavage to the weight and femininity of her chest.

Ah, fuck.

More pain shot down my cock.

This wasn't the smartest idea. I would suffer the moment her lips pressed on mine, but I would trade a million fires and a thousand drownings just to kiss her.

Kiss her after I thought I'd lost her.

Kiss her every hour of every day to make up for lost time.

"Sully, this probably isn't wise." She hovered over me, her soft breath minty and warm on my lips. Had she kissed me while I'd been under? Had I been able to taste her like I'd tasted icy berries, or had I slipped too far?

How did she know how to wake me? What possessed her to go against practitioner's orders and attempt to nurse me back with sensation?

She truly was a goddess who owned me life and soul.

"I don't care." I strained to sit up, willing my head to come off the pillow but only causing my heart rate to spike. "Stop teasing and kiss me."

"I'm not teasing. I'm deliberating."

"Kiss me." I focused on her stunning silver stare. I licked my lips, craving her. My balls tightened and another shot of pain ran hotly through my cock. "Kiss me, then get the doctor."

"What if—"

"I'm not asking, Jinx."

Her elbows buckled, and her mouth pressed hard against mine.

She moaned.

I groaned.

Pika and Skittles took wing.

Their feathers fluttered around our heads as I opened for her and my tongue slipped into her mouth. I hunted her, wanting to lick her, dance with her. I couldn't move any other part of my godforsaken body, but I could kiss her and remind her that our chemistry still blazed bright, that our bond and link had only manifested into something unbreakable.

When her tongue met mine, I sank into the wet eroticism of our kiss.

She deepened it, pressing my head against the pillow and brushing our noses together as we feasted and suffocated, switching from sweet hello to savage desire.

This lust was different, though.

It didn't just hold the singular urge to mate and join. It wasn't elixir desperate or selfish need for a release.

This had a different sharpness. A pain that spoke of separation and risk of never finishing our love story. It was still salted with goodbye.

Never.

I would never say goodbye again.

I bit her bottom lip, easing another moan from her chest.

She kissed me deeper, making me harder, ensuring pain became difficult to ignore.

A flicker of being locked in Ace's cage and at Drake's mercy came and went. Eleanor had found her way back to me, despite me sending her away for her safety, and I'd found my way back to her, despite the blackness of my end.

I'd promised her something when I'd lain broken and bleeding in that cage.

"If we survive this, Eleanor Grace…I'm going to fucking marry you."

"Is that a proposal?"

"It's a vow."

I smiled against her lips. "So, you dreamed that you married me, huh?"

She winced. "You died the moment I said I do."

"I won't do that next time."

Pulling away, her lips glistened and her eyes searched mine. "What are you saying?"

I longed to push aside the hair cascading over her shoulder, to hook it behind her delicate ears, to cup my fingers around her nape and bring her mouth back to mine.

Instead, all I could do was fetter her with words. "I have a new vow to give you, Eleanor." My heart rate picked up, exhilarating and exhausting. "The day I can walk on my own, I'm marrying you. You will say yes because there is no other option for us. You will promise to honour me, cherish me, and accept everything that I am, because I refuse to let you go."

The room swam, black spots appeared on my vision.

I clung to awareness, forcing words through fumbling lips. "You brought me back from death, Jinx. You fought for me, and you own me in every fucking way. I know I don't deserve you, and that I've done unforgivable things—things that you've wiped clean for me. I adore you in every fucking way a man should love his woman, but I'm warning you, if you don't marry me, then the contract between us will be reinstated."

I grew lightheaded and sick. The beeping of my racing heart

on the monitor grated on my temper. "You will remain shere as my prisoner because if you shink you can put yourself in danger for me. That you can shtand by my side even while I hurt you, drug you, and die on you…well, you don't shknow me well at all."

Her finger pressed against my lips. "Hush, Sully, you're slurring. You're tired. I'm going to get Louise—"

I bit her finger.

I sucked it into my mouth.

I convulsed with the pain of needing her and the pain in my cock from being so hard.

I needed her to agree. To say yes, she would be my wife because I couldn't survive with any other alternative. I couldn't fade again and not know she belonged to me body, heart, and soul.

But I never heard her answer.

I'd reached my limit.

My eyes rolled back.

I couldn't hold on to consciousness anymore.

I slipped.

But this time, I didn't slip into darkness.

I slipped into dreams where I was free to touch her, kiss her, fuck her, and get on one knee to make her my wife.

Chapter Thirty-Six

NO! NOT AGAIN!

I flew to my feet.

Dread galloped through my bloodstream. Panic that he'd fallen into a coma all over again ran rampant in my mind.

Doctor.

He needs a damn doctor.

Now!

Spinning around, I bolted toward the front door. If I was lucky, I could sprint to my old villa on the beach and grab Louise. If she was fit enough, we could run and be back here in fifteen/twenty minutes?

Too long!

God, why did I send them away?

Pika and Skittles took off, flying in front of me just as I reached the front door.

I ripped it open.

And smashed into Louise who ran in the opposite direction. Our bodies collided, our hands swooping upward to push against shoulders and boobs in our attempt not to fall on our asses.

Tripping backward, she grabbed my arms for support, her skin flushed with sweat, her legs covered in sand from running. She wore a simple purple dress that I recognised from the wardrobe that was fully stocked for a goddess.

Louise blurted, "Has he died—?"

"You're here—"

"Is he dead?"

"I was coming to get you—"

"What happened?" She pushed past me just as her two colleagues, Joe and Steph, appeared in the flickering tiki torches, running down the sandy pathway. She didn't wait for them, barging through the living room and into Sully's bedroom.

"Tell me what happened." Marching to his bedside, she grabbed his wrist and checked his pulse, all while glaring at the heart monitor. "I had an alert on my offsite unit. His pulse turned haywire. Did he have another attack like last time?" She assessed his vitals all while I jogged to her side and tried to control my worried breathing.

"You had a way to track him?" I couldn't take my eyes off Sully's unnatural stillness.

Don't you dare die on me now, Sullivan Sinclair. Not after asking me to marry your ass!

"Yes." She nodded impatiently, still looking at Sully's pale face and dark beard. "The heart monitor sends data to my phone via an app." She reset something on the controls, saying, "I came as fast as I could. I'm sorry if you had to deal with anything stressful while I wasn't here, but you need to tell me what happened so I know how to treat him."

"He…he woke up."

"He *what?*" She spun to face me, Sully's wrist still in her hand. "Was he coherent? Aware of his surroundings?"

I nodded stupidly. "Coherent and aware."

She beamed. "That's fabulous."

I had two emotions rioting through me.

Sublime joy and utter despair.

Tears I couldn't control slicked down my cheeks. "He woke up." I wrapped my arms around myself. "But he crashed only a few minutes later."

"What was he doing when he passed out?"

I blushed and looked away. "Eh, we kissed and—"

"You *kissed?*" She threw me a livid glance. "Dammit, Eleanor, you two have got to stop indulging in physical pleasure when his life is on the line." She rolled her eyes, muttering under her breath. "Sex before a heart attack and now a kiss straight after a coma. Jesus."

I trembled, fighting the highly inappropriate urge to laugh.

She hadn't meant her scolding to be funny, and there was *nothing* amusing about this if Sully had woken, used up the last of his strength, and died for good, but for some reason, my panic had turned into a jittery jester determined to make me insane.

I'm mad.

I've officially gone crazy.

If Louise wasn't here, I could've fooled myself into thinking this had all been the strangest dream.

Swallowing hard, I forced away morbid humour and shivery stress, sitting heavily on the bed. "Please tell me he's going to be okay."

"Louise, what do you need?" Joe, one of her Geneva team who'd been couch surfing for weeks, bowled through the villa followed by Steph who was young but smart.

"I can help too," Steph said. "Need an injection of epinephrine?"

Louise didn't reply, her entire focus on Sully. "Mr. Sinclair, can you hear me?"

Nothing.

The monitor revealed a healthy rhythm but no sign he'd heard her.

My entire body felt like jelly. Quivering, terrified jelly. "Come on, Sully. *Please.*" I clasped my hands, fighting the urge to touch him while three doctors hovered with urgency.

With her lips thin and mouth bracketed with strain, Louise did what I'd done when I'd woken to Pika's chaos and made eye contact with Sully. I'd pinched myself to try to snap out of a hallucination I wanted more than anything to be real. She pinched Sully to see if he was still with us or once again unreachable.

She pinched him so hard, she almost punctured the skin of his forearm.

The slightest blip on the heart monitor hinted his system felt that but was either too exhausted from previous conversation or too stubborn to wake.

I stayed silent while Joe passed her a small torch and she peeled open his eyelids, shining the light into Sully's bright blue pupils. She stared forever. She made all my doubt crest with new pain.

"Diagnosis?" Joe asked, his blond hair in disarray from springing from bed and racing through a moonlit island.

Louise didn't reply as she palpitated Sully's joints, ran her hands over the areas of healing bone and ribcage, and checked his temperature with a thermometer in his ear. Finally, she muttered, "He's stable. He's reacting to pain and light stimulus. That means his brain is functioning at a higher level, and he's successfully waking from his non-responsiveness."

My heart cracked like a delicate piece of china, shattering with hope. "So...even though he's under again, he's still with us?"

She nodded, swiping her auburn hair back into a ponytail. "There are stages to waking up. Some patients cycle through these for a while. Sometimes they're agitated and confused as they relearn motor skills and accept the overwhelming input from their senses. He might need to be restrained if he has difficulty with memory and behaviour. However, if he held a conversation with you, that means there is no speech or intellectual impairment, and he might already be in stage four."

"Is that good?"

"Stage four is classified for higher level responses. Talking, doing familiar tasks without too much difficulty. However, he might not be aware of his limitations and push himself too fast. He might also suffer personality changes which—"

"He sounded and acted like himself." I itched with the need to touch him, but I kept my hands braced together between my thighs.

"That's a good sign. At least his repeated attempts at cardiac failure haven't caused long term damage." She smiled and relaxed a little. The other two doctors headed back to the living room, the sounds of coffee being made floated back. "Did he mention how he felt? Any mention of pain or stiffness?"

I smiled. "You're going to scold me again."

She crossed her arms. "Go on."

"I gave him a massage. His joints are seized and muscles unbearably knotted. My eh...my touch gave him an erection."

"Of course it did." She rolled her eyes. "And..."

"He complained about discomfort with the catheter."

"That shouldn't make a difference. They're designed to work in a flaccid and erect penis."

My cheeks threatened to pink, even though I was fully capable of holding a professional conversation with a doctor who'd seen everything and touched everything that I had on Sully's body. Standing, I asked, "Is it possible to remove it? Now he's aware of his body again, he'll be able to do what's needed on his own."

"Was he able to move at all?"

"He moved his head a little. And managed a quick twitch of his legs and arms, but that was about it."

"In that case, the catheter should stay in. He's lost a lot of strength. It will take time to sit and move, let alone walk to a bathroom."

I glanced down at Sully and the unbearable urge to touch him rose again. This time, I couldn't ignore it. Sitting in the same spot where I'd been when he'd demanded I kissed him, I nestled between his waistline and hip and rested my palm against his naked wire and node stickered chest.

The moment I touched him, I felt calmer.

My fingers tingled. Heat gathered in my palm. The flow of our chemical connection returned, and I bit my lip to stop fresh tears. The heart monitor threw in a skip and patter, revealing Sully felt it too.

I choked on a thick sob.

A healing, hopeful sob that spoke of futures instead of goodbyes.

Louise squeezed my shoulder gently. "I'll go grab a cup of coffee and give you two a minute."

I didn't acknowledge her as she left. I couldn't look away from Sully's perfect lips and the peace on his face instead of tormented vacancy. If this was a dream, I never wanted to wake up. Then again, the thought of ever going back to sleep again, just in case this miracle popped, made me dig my fingers into Sully's chest with possession.

Pika and Skittles flew in from the open deck slider, swirling in the rafters, squeaking in their own language. It seemed they weren't ready to go back to bed either.

Smiling through my grateful tears, I looked up, tracking them as they soared so effortlessly, wishing I had wings to join them. I had excess energy bubbling inside me. The despondent depression I'd been in was lifting. The urge to do nothing had been replaced with the incessant need to do *everything.*

To jump and dance and dive into Nirvana. To swim naked in the rapidly lightening dawn.

I closed my eyes and sent a prayer of thanks.

Not to a god or goddess or any other deity.

Just thanks and indebtedness for being able to keep the man I loved for a little longer.

"You know…you are the most gorgeous girl I have ever seen."

"Sully." I gasped and looked down, focusing on vibrant blue eyes that sparkled with affection and something less innocent.

Something that made my breath catch and belly liquefy.

He moved his head on the pillow, the action making sweat bead on his temples as he looked at where I touched him, directly over his heart. "I felt you."

"I didn't mean to wake you. If you need to rest, go back to sleep."

He scoffed. "If I never sleep again, I'll be happy."

I laughed under my breath. "I was just thinking something similar. I don't know if I can sleep again because I'll be too afraid that you won't be here when I wake."

His eyes locked onto mine, dancing deeper, diving right into my soul and revealing just how much he wanted me. "Fuck, I missed you, Eleanor." He swallowed hard, gritting his teeth as his left arm twitched beside him. He let out a frustrated breath. "I want to touch you so bad."

Grabbing his hand, I raised his arm and splayed his fingers that'd seized from his long siesta. "Where do you want to touch me?"

Goosebumps prickled as he licked his lips. "*Every fucking where.*"

I *felt* that sentence.

Every word had fingers, running nails through my hair.

Every vowel had a tongue, licking between my legs.

I shuddered. "How is it that you affect me this much?"

His gaze dropped from my eyes to my lips to my chin to my breasts. "It's only fair." He gave me a pained expression. "I'm hard again and it hurts."

"I'm sorry."

"I'm not. I'd rather feel a thousand agonies as long as I never hurt you again."

"You never hurt me."

He scowled, his facial features not as stilted as before, moving with the same arrogance and authority that made me fall head over heels with a mercurial monster. "We both know I did." His gaze rose to mine before feasting on my chest again. "I know where I want to touch you."

I sucked in a breath, raising my breasts, revealing puckered nipples beneath his borrowed shirt and fluttery, turned-on inhales. "Where?"

"I want to cup you, pinch you. I want to feel your weight and—"

He choked as I sat forward and clamped his entire hand

around my breast. I closed his fingers around me. I added pressure so he'd feel every fullness and feminine part of me.

"Jesus Christ." His eyes snapped closed and the sheet covering his legs tented as his erection sprang to full attention.

"Wow, I really can't leave you two alone for five minutes."

I jerked and let Sully's hand fall. The weight of his arm and the lack of mobility meant it crashed to the bed and bounced.

He groaned as the IV line caught on the sheets.

"Oh, God, I'm so sorry, Sully." I stood and bowed over him, rearranging his arm so it lay nice and straight alongside his body. He chuckled through tight teeth. "It's fine. I'm fine. Stop fussing." He looked past me, narrowing his eyes at Louise. "You must be my doctor."

"I am." She came closer, studiously ignoring the stiffness between Sully's legs and the fact that we'd been caught fondling after I'd confessed to sex and a kiss—both that'd had disastrous results.

Louise gave me a look and rolled her eyes again. "You both need to learn some self-control." Her voice slipped from strict into bemused. "Honestly, don't even think about sex or any version of it for at least a couple of months."

"A couple of *months*?" Sully's shock made me chew on a laugh. "Yeah, that isn't going to work."

"It will take you eight weeks minimum to walk again, let alone have the stamina to enjoy intercourse."

"I'll be walking in seven days."

"Yeah, okay." Louise didn't roll her eyes this time but her tone gave all the sarcasm she needed. "If you do, you will literally be classified as a miracle in the medical world. Even people in a coma for ten days take weeks to be rehabilitated. You were out for a lot longer."

Sully's jaw clenched and pure determination glittered in his threatening stare. His chest etched with stark muscles as he gathered every shred of strength and eased a few inches off his pillow. His arms even moved a little, struggling to wedge onto his elbows only to slip away as he collapsed. "Tell me I can't do something and it only makes me prove otherwise."

Louise cocked her head. "I'm impressed." Moving closer to his bedside, she gave me a quick smile before slipping into professional mode. "What else can you move? Are you aware of your bodily functions? Do you feel the pressure of your bladder? What about any irregular electrical impulses in your limbs? Are your muscles contracted or at ease? Does sound bother you? What about your sight? Restored to full ability or hazy?"

Even my ears rang with her questions but Sully seemed to be evolving from a man who could barely talk into a quick-witted, vastly intelligent scientist who I had no doubt would prove her diagnosis completely incorrect.

He would walk well before two months had passed.

And when he does…he's marrying me.

"I can wriggle my toes. I am aware of my bodily functions. I want that damn catheter out and something to eat. I have a twitch in my left calf that won't stop and my right shoulder blade has a stitch. I can hear perfectly fine so would appreciate you keep your volume appropriate and I can see 20/20. Anymore questions?" He smirked, looking far too smug and entirely delicious.

He seemed so alive.

So…vivid.

How could he return so *him* when only an hour ago he'd still been a silent stranger sleeping beside me?

Louise returned his smile. "I'm glad you seem on the mend, Mr. Sinclair."

"I appreciate your care, Ms…"

"Maldon." Louise bent and touched his hand in official greeting. "Louise Maldon."

Sully nodded before looking me up and down. "I've answered your questions, now answer mine. Is Eleanor okay?"

"Me?" I frowned. "Why on earth wouldn't I be okay?"

Sully's gaze darkened to a self-condemning navy. "Let's count the ways. Last time I saw you, you were fighting off my brother. Before that you were fighting exhaustion from elixir. And before that you were fighting off your own heart attack while I tried to get us off this goddamn island."

"Wrong." I sniffed. "Last time you saw me, I'd just been on your lap and you had the audacity to die on me."

"Don't change the subject, Jinx." He glared at Louise. "Is she okay? Did I hurt her? Did Drake hurt her? Is there any long term damage?"

Louise glanced at me warily, most likely wondering what sort of messed up relationship we shared. Slowly, she answered, "Eleanor is made of strong stuff, Mr. Sinclair. She has spent every night by your side. She's stayed steadfast and hopeful and has been an asset to my team assisting in your care." Louise looked at Sully, spilling my secrets. "Her shock when you suffered tachyarrhythmia unbalanced her a bit and depression had set in with your prolonged state but…she's resilient and it won't cause lasting effects. Not now you're awake."

I scowled, wishing she hadn't passed on my own flaws and maladies. Knowing Sully, he'd hyper focus on my emotional well-being as well as my physical. He'd take on more guilt. He'd do his best to look after me when it was him that needed looking after.

I dared meet his vicious stare. He might no longer have goddesses in his control or sleazy guests to entertain but he was still a man used to power and obedience. "I'm fine, Sully. Don't make this about me—"

"It's *because* of you that I'm alive."

"And it's because of you that *I'm* alive."

"It's because of me that all of this happened."

"How are his legs?" I asked Louise, changing the subject, not ready to have a squabble in front of her. It seemed the longer Sully was awake, the more energy he had to expend. I understood the feeling. Every second that ticked past, I grew itchy. The desire to run and dance and swim hadn't left but now it'd morphed to more sexual desires. I wanted to be close to him. I wanted heat and wetness and every dominant, aggressive lust that drove us mad for each other.

Abstinence was going to be the hardest thing.

Celibacy when both our bodies hungered for touch and reaffirmation that we were alive would be yet another painful battle.

"Don't change the subject," Sully growled.

Louise chuckled and pushed me away a little. Bending, she grasped the sheet resting over Sully's hips. "May I?"

His glower switched to her. "To remove the catheter? Fine."

"Not yet, but yes, I will remove that."

"Then why—"

She pulled the sheet down, revealing Sully's erection had abated enough not to drag our attention directly between his legs and instead captured our stare on other parts of him.

I gasped.

Sully jerked, his gaze flying over the state of his legs.

I'd grown used to his wounds. I'd given him sponge baths and even carried in a bucket of water from Nirvana one night, hoping a rinse in his favourite waterfall would somehow cleanse him enough to wake up.

His face turned white with horror. "Fuck me."

"That's another reason you won't be walking within a week, Mr. Sinclair." Louise pointed at his shattered ankle, broken toes, and fracture tibia. Not that they were broken anymore. The cast came off a couple of weeks ago but the bruising still hung around and the withering of muscle around the injuries made it look far, far worse.

His other leg had suffered a broken femur and the harpoon wound had finally knitted together, the stitches and adhesive had dissolved until only a red scar remained. No more blood or infection but discolouration and lack of exercise had left his leg in a bad state of disrepair.

He swallowed hard. "Will I be able to walk at all?"

"You should. In time." Louise slipped into a quick and digestible spiel. "Your injuries were extensive but your bones have knitted back together while you've been unconscious. I suggest you stay off them for another few weeks to ensure there are no new fractures, but the surgery on your ankle has stabilised the joint and there are no serious complications that I can foresee when you do start walking." She dropped the sheet with a gentle sigh. "Along with the trauma to your legs, you sustained a few cracked ribs from CPR. They might be tender as you begin to move. I must request that you listen to your pain levels and take rehabilitation seriously. The faster you push yourself, the more damage you will cause. Slow and steady is the quickest way to normalcy."

Pulling away, she smiled at both of us. "I'll call the kitchens to arrange some food. I'll be back soon to remove the sensors and, of course, the catheter." She left with a gentle squeeze on my hand as she passed by. "Good luck keeping him in bed."

I smiled before sitting on the edge of Sully's mattress. He surprised me as his hand turned upside down, his fingers wriggling for me to link with him. His willpower to no longer be villa-bound was impressive.

Placing my palm on his, we both sucked in a breath, suffering the familiar tingles and longing.

"Thank you, Eleanor," Sully murmured. "For everything."

I squeezed his fingers hard. "Thank *you*...for coming after me to Geneva and for not dying on me."

He flinched as if I'd said something that caused physical pain. That couldn't happen.

I couldn't allow his thoughts to stray to the past. What was done was done. It was gone. Time had ticked forward and I'd erased what I could. From this day forward, I didn't want to talk about his brother or his goddesses or any of the violent crimes I'd read online about him in Jakarta.

We needed a fresh start.

Bracing myself for his temper, I said quietly, "Can I ask you a question?"

His gaze caught mine, still brittle from me thanking him. Brittle because he believed he didn't deserve thanks. Too riddled with condemnation to move on.

When he didn't answer, I scooted closer and pulled my hand free from his. Before he could argue, I cupped his cheek instead. His skin was warm instead of cold. Where I touched hummed with love and connection. "When you were unconscious, what was it like?"

His eyebrows raised as if he hadn't expected that. His jaw worked as he swallowed and chose his words carefully. "It was dark."

"Were you aware that you couldn't wake up?"

"Yes."

"Was it scary?"

"Petrifying."

"So for six weeks, you've been locked in a black cage that you couldn't escape."

He flinched again. "I suppose."

"Could you hear me? Feel me?"

"Sometimes. Not always. Sometimes…the dark would become too thick and I'd lose myself to it. For a while, I was too deep to do anything. I wasn't even aware I was still alive."

My whole body ached for him. I couldn't imagine anything harder. To be denied company and care. To be dead to a world you couldn't return to.

"What's this about, Eleanor?" He pressed his cheek into my palm, twisting his head to kiss me gently. "I'm back now. Whatever I lived through is over."

I smiled, glad he'd fallen into my trap. "*Precisely.*" I stroked his jaw before slipping my fingers through his longer, wilder hair. The length was a deeper ebony after not being exposed to sunlight and salty oceans for so long.

He frowned even though he shuddered and a groan rumbled in his chest as I petted and stroked. "I don't get your point." His lips twitched. "I just woke from a coma and my brain is broken. Give a man a break and speak plainly."

"Your intelligence levels surpass most of us, even if you've just woken up."

He turned his head again, nipping at my wrist as I continued caressing his hair. "Black and white, Jinx. Spit it out."

"See, there's the thing, Sully. There *is* no more black and white." I dropped my hand, ensuring he focused entirely on what I was about to say. Not an ultimatum, but a suggestion. A request given from the heart but enforced with rigid determination because it was for his own good. "You heard what I said while you were still unconscious. I sent away the girls, the guests, gave your animals a new sanctuary, and deleted everything I could from your old life…with Cal's help of course. I did that without your permission, and I'm still not entirely sure how you feel about it, but…just like you're no longer in that dark oppressive cage, your past life has gone too. I need you to let it go. Let *all* of it go. If we stand any chance at being happy, you can't keep recalling what you did or what happened between us before this precise moment. Promise me, you'll stop. That you won't let it eat away at you."

"You're under the impression that I care what I did." He narrowed his eyes, looking eerily similar to the man who'd told me humans couldn't have two sets of rules. One for mankind and one for animals. The one who used such black and white rules to exploit his own species.

This was too heavy a conversation to have when he'd just woken, but I could see the shadows haunting his gaze. The sins he still carried. The belief that he still didn't deserve me or have a chance at true joy.

"I think you do care…far too much."

"About you yes, but not about anyone else." His tone was cool, wary.

"I'm sorry but I see straight through your lies." I smiled to soften my barbed sentence. "I know who you are now, Sully. I know that you bury that part of yourself because your trust has been broken far too many times and you've seen the worst of what humans are capable of. But…I've read your emails. I've seen the generous donations to cancer research and philanthropy that you do. Your company is the best in the world for its aid to struggling countries. You gift breakthrough medicine instead of charging a fortune for it. You've taken other big Pharma to court over withholding drugs that can eradicate certain diseases and won. You're a good man—"

"Stop." His hand raised a little off the mattress, gaining more height than last time, his strength already surpassing anything I'd hoped. "I understand what you're trying to do, and I appreciate your attempt at wiping the slate clean, but allow me to put your mind at rest."

He waggled his fingers again, waiting for me to place my hand in his. The moment our palms kissed, he squeezed tight, making me wince with his newfound power. "First, I'll tell you how I feel about you releasing my goddesses, removing the guests, and rehoming my rescues."

I tensed at the unrelenting authority in his tone. I waited for his annoyance and admittance that I'd overstepped. That he would buy more girls soon and intended to continue business as usual once he was healed.

"I'm grateful to you, Eleanor." He squeezed my hand again. "So fucking grateful that you untangled my life when I was prepared to do it myself. You were the reason I was able to wake up—knowing that at least a part of what I'd done wrong had been righted. You're correct that I couldn't keep doing what I did. That I can no longer take advantage of a life, regardless that that is how the world works for so many unlucky creatures."

He cleared his throat. "As for my donations, I won't give you a false picture of me and admit I have some secret superhero complex to cure and care for the human race. I don't. I donate because it paints my company in a better light, gives us more leverage in human testing, and increases our bottom line."

I opened my mouth to argue but he cocked his head and murmured, "Let me finish."

I pursed my lips and nodded.

"You might think you've figured me out after going through my correspondence, but I am still the same man who first bought you. Yes, my ethics have improved somewhat. And yes, I will no longer use loopholes for my gain. But despite my new appreciation for *all* life and not just animals, I still find mankind abhorrent. I still despise overpopulation. I still believe the majority are spineless, selfish bastards that are a plague upon resources. However, there are enough who strife for equals rights for all— enough who aren't greedy, vain, and cruel. So because of them, because of *you*, I will respect certain boundaries that I didn't follow before."

He licked his lips, his gaze focused and fierce on mine. "As for not reliving the past, I can't promise that. I deserve to feel guilt for what I've done. I don't believe I've paid enough penance, even at the hands of my brother or the past six weeks in a black hole. You can't take it personally if I struggle to accept your unconditional affection for me. You can't ask me to forget because I don't *want* to forget. I want to be *better*. I want to remember, so I don't make the same mistakes because I fucking refuse to put you or any creature of mine in danger again. Do you get that? Can you accept that? You have my word that I want to be happy. I want to be happy with *you*. It might take time for me to forgive myself, but as long as you are there, then I know I can be the best kind of man because *you* make me better and you've already given me more joy than I've ever known."

Stupid tears rolled down my cheeks. I broke our touch, swiping at the droplets.

The past few months since meeting Sully, I'd cried in horror, terror, grief, and hope, but now...now, I cried with pure relief. I cried because this was a fresh beginning. Slightly messy with history and possibly tricky as we learned our new paths, but we were together.

I'd earned his trust.

I'd captured his heart.

And he'd just taken every last piece of my soul with his brutal confession.

Sully tried to raise his hand to touch me. His face etched with torment as he struggled to raise his palm to hip height. "Eleanor...don't cry. I didn't mean to—"

"I'm sorry." I swiped at my tears and placed my hand back into his. I raised his knuckles to my lips and kissed him. "I love you, Sullivan Sinclair. I love you so much it damn well hurts."

The tension of our honesty shattered, and his body turned sensual instead of strict. "I'm glad it hurts because I've never been in such pain." He arched his eyebrow at the tenting sheet again. "I won't last eight weeks not having you."

Looking over my shoulder, checking to see where Louise was so she didn't catch us breaking her rules, I wrapped my free hand around Sully's thickening cock.

He bowed off the bed, muscles seizing and his throat elongating with cords of power. "Jesus fucking Christ."

I rubbed him once before letting go. "I'll trade you sexual favours for motor improvements."

His eyes flashed a glowing turquoise as he glared at me. "What sort of favours?"

"Oh, I dunno...a kiss if you manage to sit up. A hand job

when you can stand."

"I'll do both today."

I laughed under my breath. "Honestly, I believe you would." Sitting back, I shook my head. "But we should take it slow. You have an important date when you can walk, remember?"

His chest rose with a sharp inhale. "You're saying yes?"

I grinned. "You didn't ask a question. You just told me."

"That's right. I did."

"So you don't need an answer. I'm marrying you the day you can walk."

He turned serious, his brows sinking low, shadowing complicated eyes. "I've stolen you once, Eleanor. I won't do it again unless it's something you want."

"Will I be your prisoner if I say yes?"

"Absolutely. All mine until death do us part."

"And will you be mine? Will you wear a ring so everyone knows you belong to me?"

"I'll wear one on every finger if you need me to."

I laughed again. "Will you permit me to travel? Will you come home with me and meet my parents?"

"If you're okay that we come back here afterward, so we can avoid the world, then yes. But only if you agree to come with me to stuffy board meetings that I can't get out of when I fly periodically to the States."

"Fine."

"Fine." His gorgeous lips slipped into a heart-stopping smile. "Let's get me walking then, woman. We have a wedding to attend."

Sullivan

Chapter Thirty-Seven

"I'M GIVING MY CHEFS a raise. They can have every penny I own."

Eleanor laughed beside me, the stress that'd carved into her cheeks and highlighted her weight loss had softened thanks to our shared meal. Her hair had been twisted into a rope and pinned to the top of her head with a pencil from my desk. Pika sat on my pillow, chattering away to himself where I'd been rearranged into a sitting position, while Skittles preferred to perch on Eleanor's knee where she sat cross-legged beside me.

The remains of our lunch lay between us.

After the intensity of our conversation, I hadn't been able to stop the tug of sleep. I'd fallen into a dreamless rest, unaware that six hours passed while Eleanor and my doctors watched over me as my body gathered its weakened endurance.

I'd woken to the scents of food—delicious, nutritious food—and my stomach had threatened to leap from my torso and grab a knife and fork without waiting for me to fully rouse.

It seemed every time I fell asleep, I woke a little stronger, a little more coherent and normal. And now that I'd eaten, I had visions of walking from this villa and jumping into Nirvana before the day was through. Fuck my legs. A swim would be beneficial as long as I didn't drown if I fell asleep again.

"I ate too much." Eleanor sighed. "Your chefs are magicians."

I glanced at the remains.

So many bowls had barely a dent in their delicious contents. My stomach, that'd felt as hollow as a cave, had filled too quickly. It ached in discomfort, stretching ribs that'd healed but still liked to remind me that they'd been broken and fixed without my knowledge.

"Dessert?" She spooned a mouthful of palm sugar syrup along with two tiny tapioca and rice balls into my mouth.

To begin with, I hadn't been down with her feeding me like a fucking invalid. However, she'd ignored my grumbling and selected a delicious rosemary-roasted mushroom and placed it onto my tongue.

The intimacy of sucking food off a fork and holding her stare as she locked onto my mouth had caused yet another fucking erection. At least this time, no catheter twinged my tip—thanks to Louise removing it—but if I was this reactive to Eleanor while still coming out of a coma, how the hell would I endure eight long fucking weeks?

Sexual favours for progress.

Chewing on the sweet confectionary, I ran my tongue over my lips and chuckled at the way Eleanor's breath hitched and nipples pebbled beneath my shirt. It wasn't just me struggling, and that gave me far too much satisfaction.

"You know…eating counts as progress." I swallowed and kept my voice for her ears only. "I deserve a reward. How about I eat *you* for the rest of my dessert?"

Her cheeks pinked; the spoon she wielded clinked against the porcelain bowl. "Louise will kick me out if we don't behave."

"Louise can watch for all I care." I did my best to shift, needing relief from the aching throb between my legs. To be fair, everything throbbed. The bones that'd knitted together and the muscles that'd resented not being exercised in six weeks all drummed in time with my heartbeat. If it wasn't for the pain meds that Louise slipped into my IV, I probably would've lost my appetite the second I started eating.

Exhaustion was yet another factor in my discomfort. The heaviness of my eyelids, the fog creeping over my mind. Just eating and talking felt like I'd swam around my island twenty times and then scaled Nirvana another forty.

I wasn't used to being so weak.

I despised it.

"Your first step…" Eleanor whispered. "When you take your first step, you can have me for dessert."

Goddammit, could a man die of denied gratification? I honestly didn't know how long I could stand such insufferable desire. "Done. I'll take a step, fall to my knees, press my mouth against your pussy, and stick my tongue—"

Another mouthful of sweet tapioca and palm syrup filled my mouth. Eleanor gave me a smug smile, effectively gagging my erotic declaration.

I chewed while narrowing my eyes at her.

The Indo dessert typically had sweet potato balls, but I preferred the chewy texture of rice and tapioca. I didn't really have a sweet tooth, but my main chef and his team of kitchen wizards had put together every delicacy that I favoured.

Three huge trays had arrived, groaning under the weight of coconut crisped kale, lentil patties with mint chutney, satay jackfruit tacos, pumpkin and pine nut paella, chipotle charred cauliflower, spaghetti squash with spicy guacamole, and a huge bowl of tropical fruit salad that I had a tendency of ordering when working late.

Tasting each element was a shock to my system. The salt was intense, the cumin and coriander spices pungent on my tongue. After having nothing, my taste buds clung to each morsel and dissected it until each mouthful made me moan with utmost pleasure.

"I'll hold you to that, Jinx," I growled. "I'm going to be inside you within a week, see if I don't."

My cell phone rang on the sideboard across the room, making Pika squawk and fly over to peck at the vibrating screen.

"Promises, promises." Eleanor placed the spoon back into the bowl and elegantly unwound her legs to slip off the bed. "If you keep staring at me like that, it might be me pouncing on you."

Skittles fluttered after her, the absolute love on the little caique's face in-tune with my own besotted attachment and desperate desire for Jinx.

Christ, I loved her.

The feeling only seemed to increase until it wrapped tight fingers around my heart and stabbed me with nails of loss.

What would I do if I ever lost her?

I wouldn't fucking survive.

My hands curled involuntarily, stopping my blackening thoughts and dropping my stare from the girl I adored to the clenched fingers beside me.

More progress.

I tried to raise my arms as Eleanor accepted the call with her back to me. "Hi, Cal. Everything okay?"

Pika darted to the pencil in Eleanor's hair, biting the implement until it dropped from her strands and bounced to the floor. Her hair instantly cascaded down her shoulders, and she grinned at Pika as he flew back toward me, perching on my sheet-covered toes with a cheeky look in his black eyes. He'd done that deliberately. Almost as if he knew how much I loved Jinx's hair. How I envied him for playing with it. A direct taunt from a goddamn parrot.

"You're a bastard," I muttered. "But a lovable one."

Pika chirped, puffing out his little white chest. "Lazy."

"Yeah, yeah, I'm working on it."

He cocked his head as if judging why I hadn't gotten out of bed yet. I looked past him to Eleanor as she padded barefoot toward me and tapped a button on the phone screen.

Instantly, Cal's voice spilled into the villa. "You busy? I figured you'd want the good news. You were right to donate those funds in Sinclair's name to Naked Charms. They began a campaign with the money to shut down animal testing on their biggest competitor in the cosmetic industry. It's just been announced that all its lab mice, guinea pigs, and a handful of rabbits are being freed today. I've already arranged shipment for them to come to *Serigala* phase two."

I frowned at Eleanor. What the hell was she doing donating stuff in my name? What the fuck was Naked Charms?

"Oh, that's great news." She winked at me, totally aware of my silent questions but studiously ignoring me. "Thanks."

"Guess you'll have to tell Sinclair what you've been up to when he wakes. If you survive his tirade, remind me to shout you a drink. You have balls, girl. Wait till he sees the spreadsheet of where his latest outgoings have gone."

Eleanor ran her hand through her hair, keeping my stare but looking less sure. "Eh, well...I actually have something to tell you about that."

"Oh, yeah? Bastard didn't die, did he?"

"Bastard is well and truly alive and contemplating revoking your access to his funds," I barked. "What the hell have you been doing?"

"*Sullivan?*" Calvin's shock bled through the phone. "Holy shit, you're awake."

"It's official. You're fired. Stupid statements like that aren't tolerated." I chewed a laugh.

"If I had any doubts that you'd suffered personality changes after lying on your ass for six weeks, you've just put my mind at rest," Cal snickered. "Still the same ole cunt as before."

"Glad I could do something right and ease your troubled mind, seeing as I've been made redundant from my own company." I couldn't hold back my chuckle this time, unclenching my fist and managing to raise my arm just enough to beckon Eleanor to come closer. "Miss me or having too much fun *being* me?"

"Fuck yes, we missed you. We all did."

"Hi, Sullivan. I'm so glad you joined us again." Jess's sweet tone cut through the masculine ribbing between Cal and me.

All ability to joke evaporated. "Jess..." I swallowed hard as Eleanor sat beside me, placing the phone on my chest and leaving the speaker option on. "I wanted to say this in person, but I can't wait."

"Oh, what's wrong?"

Looking at Eleanor, I whispered, "Did you tell her?"

"Tell her what?" she asked too quiet for the phone to relay.

"About the money that I asked the lawyers to deliver in the case of my death—"

"No." She shook her head. "Cal knows. I left it up to him to tell her...if you passed."

"Good." Clearing my throat, I raised my voice so Jess could hear. "I owe you a huge debt, Jessica. What you did with Drake, I'll never be able to repay. You protected Eleanor when I couldn't. You protected me, knowing I wouldn't cope seeing him hurt her. You put your own life and happiness on the line for me...a man who never deserved such loyalty."

Something rustled down the line before Jess said quietly, "It's fine. You don't need to thank me."

"I do. I also need to say you're free. You're free to go home, travel, do whatever the hell you want. You're no longer trapped here. Our contract is null and void." I cleared my throat, doing my best to swallow around all the things I'd done wrong against this woman. "I know money can't erase what I did to you, nor delete the guests you had to entertain, but I'd be honoured if you'd accept four million dollars as my attempt at apology."

"Four?" Eleanor's eyebrows rose, her lips curling into a smile. "Getting generous in your old age."

I smirked and carried on. "I owe you everything, Jess. Along with the money, I also vow to deliver whatever you ask of me. You can ask today or a decade from now, and whatever you request, you shall have it."

Silence fell. Cal's cough sounded in the background before Jess said softly, "I appreciate your generosity, Sullivan. And I mean it when I say you don't have to give me money. What I did with Drake was out of friendship, but I will accept the funds, if it makes things even between us." A slight pause before she added, "I do have one request, if I may?"

"It's yours. What do you want?"

"Can I stay? Can I stay on this island with you and Jinx and…Cal?"

My eyes snagged Eleanor's. Her grey gaze shimmered with adoration, and her hand reached for mine, linking our fingers.

Skittles landed on her shoulder, and Pika roosted on my head, and it seemed like fate pressed a pause button for me to fully appreciate this moment.

To understand precisely what I was gaining by agreeing to Jess's request.

I wasn't just allowing another couple to live on my shores, to share in my gardens, or to indulge in this tropical paradise. I was saying yes to friends, yes to family, yes to *trust*.

A network of happiness.

A bond that extended past the woman I'd fallen for and opened up my darkened world with promises of something so simple and satisfying.

Something I've never had before.

Squeezing Eleanor's hand, I spoke to her as well as to Jess. "Of course, you can stay. This is your home. *Our* home. Cal's and Eleanor's and mine. We're family."

Chapter Thirty-Eight

THE FIRST FEW DAYS of Sully's recovery followed bursts of vibrant energy, vows of leaving his bed to go swimming in his waterfall, and unbelievable progress in both his motor control and strength, only to be followed by bouts of deep restful sleep that slammed into him without warning.

He hated succumbing to sleep. Cursed each time he woke and resumed the exercises Louise had given him. I understood his desire to return to his original capabilities, but it hurt to see him push so hard, to see the pain in his eyes, to witness the horror that he'd fallen asleep outside of his control yet again.

He didn't celebrate the victories he achieved. He didn't care that he could raise his arms, operate a fork, or push into a sitting position unassisted. To him, nothing was a success until he could swing his legs out of bed and walk on his own.

His temper flickered on the afternoons where the humidity levels crept to unbearable and the urge to be in cool water overrode his patience with healing.

I requested Arbi to come help the Geneva team. Lending a hand with Joe to lift Sully from his bed and take him to the bathroom. One afternoon, they positioned him on a chair in the huge pebbled shower with its open-air wall.

Once we were alone, I shampooed, rinsed, and trimmed his longer hair.

His hands roamed over my body, sometimes shaking from

the effort but never conceding defeat, all while I shaved his beard down to a five o'clock shadow.

I shivered as he leaned forward and pressed a kiss against my cleavage. While I carefully snipped and shaped his hair, he gritted his teeth, gathered energy he couldn't afford, and slipped two fingers inside me.

I'd exploded the second he thrust deep and drove his thumb against my clit.

My release vicious and starving for more.

My libido well and truly awake now that Sully showed no signs of leaving me.

With my orgasm pulsing through me, I'd contemplated sitting on his lap and inserting his erection inside me. We could reconnect in the shower with a chair holding us and dragonflies flitting in the setting sun.

But his eyes had closed, his fingers slipped from my body, and he'd slumped into sleep with Nirvana crashing around us.

I'd finished my barber session, turned off the shower and ensured he was as dry as I could, before slipping a black sarong around his waist for modesty.

I'd called Arbi and Joe in to carry him back to bed and dismissed everyone's help for the rest of the night. I'd fallen asleep beside him, cuddled close with the two caiques flying through the sliders to raid a hibiscus bush in the moonlight.

"Jinx…you awake?"

My eyes snapped open.

Still dark but with the sense that dawn wasn't far away.

I glanced at Sully. He lay on his back, one leg cocked and one arm thrown over his head. Huh, he could move in his sleep, hinting his strength was returning far faster than what Louise predicted.

If he's still sleeping, who on earth—

"Jinx." Cal waved from the threshold of Sully's bedroom. I sat up, grateful I'd fallen asleep in a silver nightgown that hid what needed to be hidden.

Instantly, my heart kicked. "Jess? Is she okay?" I flew out of bed, ready to run to my friend. Jess had been getting stronger too. Like Sully, she slept a lot, and small bursts of exercise drained her quickly.

"Yes, yes, she's fine." Cal pressed a finger to his lips. "Don't wake him. I have a surprise, follow me." He tracked through the star-speckled lounge, leading me to the front door and outside.

Cicadas buzzed, bats cackled, and the occasional owl hooted in the dark proving just because we slept didn't mean the night wasn't teeming with creatures who frolicked in a different playground than us.

"What the hell is that?" I chuckled, swatting at a mosquito as I followed Cal down the pebbled path to the sandy laneway. A vehicle waited, chrome and matte black with rugged tyres, and a big tray on the back full of discarded pots ready for seedlings. The side panels held the same logo for *Lebah* that I'd seen on the girl's uniform.

"It's an ATV. They use them for the gardeners to transport seeds and what-not around *Lebah*."

"And what's it doing here?"

He crossed his arms, a gloating smile catching the slowly lightening sky. "It's for Sinclair."

My eyes widened as understanding bowled through me. "So he can get out of the villa without breaking his legs a second time trying to walk in the soft sand."

"Exactly. He'll be going stir-fucking-crazy in bed. At least this way, he can just sit and enjoy the ride."

"It's a great idea! You should give it to him."

"Nah, you do it. When he wakes in a few hours, take him for a whirl. Come visit us, we'll have breakfast together."

I hugged myself at the thought of getting him out and about. Of feeling the sun on our skin after being cooped up for so long. The tyres were big with all-terrain tread which would allow us to drive on the beach and through the shallows.

"He'll love it."

"Good." Cal turned to walk back to the main hub. "I'll see you soon then."

"Hey, Cal?"

"Yeah?" He turned around, raising his eyebrow.

"Why are you up so early?"

He smirked. "I'm always up early. Normally, I'd hit the gym before work, but with my lungs still healing and Campbell still on my case, I just get up out of habit. I was taking a walk when the boat arrived with this morning's vegetable delivery, along with this. I asked for one to be sent from *Lebah* the day Sully woke up."

Dashing to him, I pressed a kiss on his cheek. "You're a good friend."

Was I imagining it, or did colour flush over his cheeks? The icy second-in-command who tried to warn me off Sully was finally melting. "Just want him up and running, that's all." Giving me a quick sarcastic salute, he stuck his hands in his short pockets and strolled into the dawn.

Chapter Thirty-Nine

A WEEK PASSED.

A week of torturous rehabilitation and bossy doctors preventing me from leaving my bed even though Cal had delivered a perfectly good ATV that could be my legs.

Eleanor had argued on my behalf, saying a trip around my island would be beneficial, however, Louise had been insistent.

She'd ganged up with Campbell when he came to check on me. They advised they'd restrain me for my own benefit if I insisted on being an idiot. That my system wasn't ready yet. That I had to accept that my beaches and oceans would be there in another week or so when my vitals were more stable and the frustrating habit of randomly falling asleep had ceased.

I hadn't liked it, but I couldn't deny the wooziness in my head or the throbbing of my legs. If being bedbound for another week cured me faster, than fine.

I could be fucking patient.

Despite his stoic support of Louise, Campbell had been wary around me. He'd kept his distance and didn't hold eye contact long.

I'd been stony with him. My voice curt and cold.

Our meeting had been awkward with far too much unsaid shit.

I was aware I owed him an apology after my temper when I'd demanded a second shot of Tritec. That I most likely owed him multiple apologies after he'd put his life on the line to heal me, administer a drug that killed me, and worked night and day to keep Jess alive.

But…he'd betrayed me. Our past was littered with duplicity, and something like that couldn't just be erased. *Can it?* The thought of letting down my guard to give sincere thanks would take a lot longer to forgive and achieve.

That first week, along with rigorous physiotherapy to get my arms moving, my legs operating, and easing out the stagnant knots in my muscles from clenching in my coma, Eleanor and I entertained two guests.

Cal hung out during the hours that Jess slept, and he used the ATV to transport her to my villa when she was up to some company. That afternoon, Louise let me leave my god-awful bed, and Joe and Arbi carried me like a fucking invalid to sit on a deck chair overlooking Nirvana's constant cascading symphony.

The four of us had shared lunch. Eleanor and Jess had chattered while Cal and I caught up on things I'd missed with Sinclair and Sinclair Group.

Jess fell asleep first, her eyes suddenly closing mid-dessert and my endurance broke not long after. I clung to lucidity long enough to say goodbye to Cal as he bundled Jess into the ATV to drive her back to his villa, and managed to kiss Eleanor before I was placed onto my back in my cursed bed.

As I fell asleep, I made a vow that the moment I'd returned to full capacity, I would sleep somewhere different every night. I would build a fucking tree house if it meant I never had to spend another moment in a bed that'd become such a shackle.

Despite my frustration at my body's slow recovery, each day brought accomplishments. Which meant, each day Eleanor owed me a sexual favour or two.

Eleanor busied herself in the kitchen, making us a lychee juice with lots of crushed ice. Dusk had fallen and the trees were alive with roosting birds all singing and squabbling for the best branches. Nirvana sparkled as the sky set fire to daylight and smouldered into twilight, leaving streaks of amethyst to bleed into black.

Humidity and island heat had been extra cloying today, and I was desperate for a fucking swim. Not that I could request that, seeing as Eleanor had sent the doctors away and it was just us. No way would I put her in the position of helping me if I fell asleep while swimming and tried to drown.

Carrying the drinks to me, she ducked under the mosquito

net and hopped onto the mattress before falling into a lotus pose beside me. "Here."

"Thanks." I took the glass and sipped the fragrant sugar, enjoying the delicious texture of ice hitting my tongue. Taking a few shards into my mouth, I crunched them before placing the glass on the side table and scooting higher up the pillows.

My legs splayed a little, obeying my command to move.

At least I had my faculties back. I could move each extremity, even if I didn't have the stamina to stand quite yet.

"You know...I achieved two things today that are worthy of sexual favours."

Her eyes swooped to mine, her eyelashes framing grey smoky depths, her lips pink from the chilliness of her drink. "Oh, really?" Her cheeks flushed as she wrapped her fingers around her dew-dripping glass. "What talents did you regain?"

I scratched at my five o'clock shadow, catching Pika's aerial acrobatics as he and Skittles darted in from outside, ready to find their own perch for the night after gallivanting around the island all day. "What will you give me?"

She grinned. "Depends how impressive the achievements are."

"I bent both my legs and can touch my toes."

She sipped her drink. "Fancy." Her gaze twinkled with sarcasm.

I growled under my breath, "I'll have you know that took effort."

"I have no doubt it did." She laughed softly.

"I don't think you're taking my successes seriously enough." I reached for her breast, only grazing the delicious weight before she moved out of my reach, her yellow sundress hiding her stunning figure. "Come here and let me celebrate."

"I don't know if that counts." She placed her drink on the opposite side table before coming close again and kneeling beside me. "I thought you said you'd be inside me within a week."

"Come here and I'll happily oblige."

"Do something worthy and I might consider it." She ran her finger down the neckline of her dress, dipping into her humidity-damp cleavage. "I'm dying a very slow death not being allowed to touch you."

Lust sprang from containable to maddening. "You *are* allowed to touch me. Wherever you fucking want."

"I can't."

"You can. You have all the power here." I leaned forward, trying to snatch her. "Come here and we can be cured together."

She ran her fingertip around her nipple, making it tighten beneath her dress. "I can't because I made a promise to myself."

"What promise?" I grew painfully hard. Too hard. I hadn't had a release since Geneva and living with Eleanor was daily torment. I couldn't tear my eyes off her hand or stop my fingers from wrapping around my aching cock.

"When we next sleep together...it will be our wedding night."

"What?" I laughed harshly, but it came out more like a snarl. "That's the same day I can walk unassisted."

"Exactly. Biggest achievement equals biggest reward." She dropped her hand, growing serious, changing the tingling thirsty tone between us. "In all honesty, I'm afraid of sleeping with you."

I froze. My hand fell away, and our eyes locked. "Why would you—" I cut myself off, understanding her point of view. "Last time we fucked, I suffered cardiac failure."

She bit her lip, nodding once. "I know the likelihood of that happening, now that you're healing and healthy, are slim, but..." Her eyes darkened with doubts. "I love you too much to risk losing you. If it means a few weeks of painful celibacy, then..."

"It's worth it for a lifetime of happiness."

"Exactly." She came closer, pressing into me and cupping my cheeks with both her hands. "I'm not saying goodbye to you again...I can't."

Our skin ignited. My cock threatened to come from no other stimulation. Electricity infected both of us, making her shiver and me shudder. Parts of me that'd always taken what he wanted, regardless of consequences, very almost won. My hands twitched to grab her and take her anyway. My desire was a dangerous, demented thing.

But as she tipped forward, and her mouth met mine, I gave up control.

I groaned as her delicate tongue licked my lips, then sought mine.

I met her with a sensual taste, closing my eyes and focusing entirely on where we joined.

This kiss was sweet and soft, but it crippled me in ways no other kiss had before.

This was her, my perfect curse-breaking Jinx, letting me into deeper parts of her heart.

This wasn't about desire or bodily gratification but the start of our forever.

It was the best fucking kiss of my life.

* * * * *

Thirteen days since I'd woken and each day, I was stronger.

I no longer passed out at inconvenient times. My body was back under control, and each session of physiotherapy meant my muscles rebuilt and strength returned.

After a gruelling session of standing and bearing weight on legs that'd taken their fair share of beatings, I sat at a temporary desk by the deck overlooking Nirvana. Eleanor had gone to visit Jess and taken the two parrots with her, my doctors were enjoying the afternoon off and planning their return to Geneva, Cal was busy overseeing the faulty sensors and snares ringing my shores, and I was alone to slip back into my role as CEO of Sinclair and Sinclair Group.

My time was no longer split between legal and illegal enterprises. I didn't have emails requesting week-long stays or in-depth details of depraved fantasies to code. No new goddesses to request or daily orders of their wants and needs to complete. It felt odd not juggling two very different companies. To no longer see the dark web page where my island promised deviant desires for hire.

Cal had removed the details of my islands, and Eleanor had taken care of feed requirements and vet arrivals for the rescues that I hadn't had the tolerance to visit yet.

All I had was jargon heavy emails, encyclopaedia-sized PDFs, and regular briefings with Peter Beck.

As the sun set on the thirteenth day since I'd been reincarnated from a heartless procurer into a man striving to be the best husband he could be, an email from an encrypted address arrived.

At first, I thought it might be from the traffickers who'd bounced my last request and then vanished. However, the address was wrong.

And the contents? Well, it was a threat, pure and fucking simple.

To: S.Sinclair@goddessisles.com
From: Sparrow@292840.com
Subject: Bonjour

To Mr. Sullivan Sinclair,

You have recently come to my attention.

I will be frank so you are not confused by the following.

Due to your dealings with a certain trafficking outfit, you are now next on my list. That company has recently been shut down, and its staff are enjoying a never-ending retirement, if you catch my meaning.

If you don't, allow me to elaborate.

They are dead.

The men you used to source, select, and ship women to your islands are now in pieces. Unfortunately for you, and their other clients, they kept comprehensive records on girls acquired, money received, and locations they were sent.

You, Mr. Sinclair, are one of the worst.

You have purchased thirteen women with a value of over four million dollars.

Is that what a life is worth to you? If it is, you must allow me the decency of teaching you that there are four million ways a man can die.

You are going to die.

I have the coordinates for your islands.

I am coming.

Cordialement,

Q

Q?

Who the fuck was Q?

What sort of cunt emailed such things with such high and mighty bullshit?

Fucking bastard.

I'd kill him.

Adrenaline flooded my veins as I grabbed my phone to call Cal and have him watch the horizon for more boats bringing war. My jaw clenched as I swiped on the device, my mind racing with battle enforcements and yet another fight that I had no energy to endure.

Goddammit, we'd just finished a nightmare. The thought of living through another one? Of losing Eleanor to yet another asshole who thought he could take what wasn't his?

No.

Fuck no.

Whoever this cocksucker was, he would not disrupt my happiness. I would not allow him to ruin everything I never thought I'd earn.

The man he wanted to kill was dead.

He was talking about a ghost, and the man I was now...I fucking refused to die (again) when I was so, so close to being happy.

I'd matured since and I could handle this without bloodshed. *I think.*

With a steady hand, I placed my cell phone back on the desk and clicked reply.

To: Sparrow@292840.com
From S.Sinclair@goddessisles.com
Subject: Re: Bonjour

I tapped my fingers against the keys, excuses forming, my black and white rules of humans versus animals, food versus souls, and the age-old bullshit of humans thinking they were special over every other living species on our planet.

I wanted to drive my fist into his jaw and demand he acknowledge that it wasn't just people who felt love and loss and pain. Cows did. Sheep did. A chicken wasn't just dinner but a creature who had its own language, hierarchy, and lifespan.

The urge to pummel this motherfucker who *dare* threaten me via email and speak as if he was some liberator of women made me want to ask if he ate meat and shove the hypocrisy down his fucking throat.

But...

He was right.

Buying another for my own gain was wrong.

I knew that.

I'd stopped that.

I'd learned my lesson, and now all I wanted was peace. To keep Eleanor safe. To live out our lives alone and together, away from the jurisdictions and inhumane beliefs of a polluted world.

No one, especially this Q bastard, would take that away from me.

To Q,

I have so much to say so I will keep this brief.
I don't trust encryption and normally write in code, but for this, I will type blatantly so you get the message loud and clear.

You are right that I bought those women.
You are right that it was wrong to do so.
And you are right that I should pay.
Unfortunately, you are too late.
The last girl I purchased ended my tyranny.
She awakened me and broke me in equal measure.
I fell in love, and everything fell apart.
Because of her, I willingly died. Not hypothetically or romantically. I literally died.
But she loved me enough to bring me back.
And the man I am now is not the man who purchased those women.
They have been freed. Every last one of them. Freed and compensated. I can provide evidence of their safety if it will appease you.
Ordinarily, I would take your threat and retaliate with my own. I am not a man that allows such things to go unpunished. However, in this instance, I understand where you are coming from, and I am on your side.
You have my word that I am reformed. That no other life will be taken by me. All I ask is that you accept my assurances and call off your manhunt.
I've paid my debt.
I am just a man doing his best to be worthy of a woman who saved him.
Thirteen girls were bought, eleven were released, and one has chosen to stay. The last girl I'm keeping, but only because she's kept me. She will be my wife, and I will lay down my life four million times over to protect her.
So, in light of that, allow me a tiny threat of my own.
Come to my shores, and you will not survive.
Threaten me again, and I will track you down and ensure you cannot hurt my wife or loved ones again.
Are we clear?
You have no reason to hunt me.
And I have no desire to hurt you.
Let this be over before it even begins.

Sincerely,
Sinclair.

Pika swooped into the villa as I pressed send, his little caw a precursor before he dive-bombed my laptop and attacked the letter S. His tiny beak managed to hook beneath the plastic, almost ripping it off before I could stop him.

"Oi. Quit it."

He just chirped and marched toward another alphabet. Almost as if he knew the bastard I'd been writing to, he eyeballed the letter Q and tore it from the keyboard.

"Hey!"

I tried to grab him as he tossed it to the floor then swooped into my hair and dangled down my forehead, his black eyes in front of mine.

"You're a jerk."

He bit my nose.

"You can help me kill that asshole if he dares come here."

"Kill." He squawked.

"Huh, new word." I plucked him from my strands and plopped him onto the desk. If he was here, that meant Skittles and Eleanor weren't far behind. He had a habit of flying ahead, giving me warning, making my heart glow to see her again and building impatience to be back in her company.

Unlike the other times when I waited for Eleanor to return to me, this time, I wanted her to stay away a little longer. Adrenaline still flowed brutal and blistering in my veins. I felt violent and vicious, and I didn't want to make her worry because I doubted I'd be able to hide the reaction this Q bastard had caused.

Raking hands through my hair, I opened a new email, doing my best to change my thoughts to happier topics. I called up an address that I hadn't had reason to message in a while. His diamonds came in regular shipments, ordered by my staff to his. It'd been a long time since he'd requested drugs to stem his condition or the one-off email from his father commanding something that would turn his empathic son into an apathic monster.

To: J.H@HawksridgeHall.com
From S.Sinclair@goddessisles.com
Subject: A favour

Jethro,

It's been a while.
I assume that a drug-free life is treating you well. How is your lovely Nila? We are due a catch-up, I believe.
As much as this is a social email, I also have a favour to ask.
It seems I have fallen into the same affliction as you and have the undying need to marry. However, I am lacking the required bondage.

Pika fluttered to my knuckles, balancing on the back of my

hand with his tiny talons as I continued to type.

By bondage, I obviously mean a ring.
Due to an unfortunate incident, I had to use your diamonds that were
stored here for other purposes.

"As bribery to stop mercenaries from fucking my goddess high on elixir."

Pika bobbed his head as if he completely understood and could read every typed word on the screen.

I smiled and continued, grateful that my stress from Q was fading.

Can your jewellers fashion an engagement ring and wedding band? Cost is, of course, no object, and I believe a twelve carat flawless stone will suffice with multiple diamonds inlaid on the band. The only request I have is that a feather be incorporated within the design.

"Can't exactly leave you and Skittles out of the marriage, can I?" I raised my hand and kissed Pika on the back of his head. "You get an honourable mention on the rings."

He squeaked and head butted my chin, raising on his claws and nibbling at my lips.

"Yeah, you're welcome."

Dropping my hand to the keyboard again, I finished,

Is three weeks long enough?
I apologise for the rush, but it seems this hankering to make her mine won't fade. However, you're a married man, so I'm sure you understand.
Keep in touch, old friend.
Stay well.

Sullivan.

I pressed send just as an email appeared into my account.
Him.

With gritted teeth and hate coursing in hot waves through my chest, I opened Q's reply.

To: S.Sinclair@goddessisles.com
From: Sparrow@292840.com
Subject: Re: Re: Bonjour

Mr. Sinclair,

I have taken the liberty of looking up the girls whose names are on file. It seems you are telling the truth.

Eleanor Grace seems to have bewitched you as well as the man who kidnapped her. The very man whose heart I ripped from his chest—while he was still breathing I might add.

He hurt what is mine and that is never tolerated. And it seems he was biding his time to hurt what is yours. He was intrigued by her so…you're welcome.

Understand, I will not just take your word for your mutual affection. I will require evidence that she is as in love with you as you claim to be with her. However, the details you have already shared check out.

Therefore, I will merely watch you instead of extend a visit.

If you are who you say you are, you are not my enemy.

But if you are lying, we will meet, and you will die, and the girl you claim to love will be free.

Be in touch with evidence at your earliest convenience.

Merci,
Q

Fuck him and his French arrogance.

The urge to look him up made me open a dark web search page and type in Q, France, vigilante.

"Sully? You're still working?"

I twisted in the chair, stiffer than usual and suddenly feeling the fatigue of sitting in a chair and typing when my body was still shedding the effects of six weeks of unbroken sleep.

I'd need Arbi and Joe to carry me back to bed soon, seeing as I was still unable to walk.

I closed the lid of my laptop and held out my hand for Eleanor.

Skittles fluttered around her, flying to attack Pika as he met her in the sky. Eleanor rolled her eyes as the two caiques squabbled like children. Her hair was loose and sun-kissed. Bronze interspersed with rich chocolate, and soft waves from island heat made me desperate to fist the strands and sink inside her.

"I missed you," I murmured, pulling her down for a kiss.

She bent and pressed her lips to mine.

Unlike our sweet kiss from the other day, I drove this one

straight into sin. I opened wide, I punctured her lips, I kissed her all while surviving the need to keep her away from a threatening fucking Frenchman who dared care about her safety.

Her safety was *my* job.

If anyone else tried to hurt her, they would be shark food and then shit on the ocean floor—by my hand, no one else's. Her protection wasn't his duty or honour. *It's mine.*

I bit her bottom lip, making her gasp and fold deeper over me.

I grew hard, as always, and the unbearable roadblock she'd put between us made me pull away before I climbed on feeble legs and tried to fuck her against the wall.

Breathing hard, she stumbled a little as I let her go.

I smirked. "Still think you can last until our wedding night?"

"Truthfully?" She blew hair out of her eyes. "I don't stand a chance, not if your kiss can almost make me come."

I dragged my eyes over her body, drinking in the shape of her, the golden skin beneath the untied cream kimono and the colour contrast of her turquoise bikini. I was jealous as well as turned-on. "Been swimming without me?"

"No." She scooped up her hair, securing it into a messy ponytail. "It's so hot today, I was tempted and went prepared, but…just like I'm waiting to sleep with you, I'm waiting to swim until you can join me."

"So considerate."

She grinned. "I aim to please." Backing toward the bathroom, she promised, "I'll just shower, and then I'll cook us a simple meal. Jess says hi, by the way. Veggie puff pastry pizzas sound okay?"

"More than okay."

"Great." Blowing me a kiss, she dashed into the bathroom. I waited until the sound of the shower splashing overshadowed Nirvana's constant roar before opening my laptop again.

Jethro had replied, but I clicked on Q's email first and prepared to respond.

To: Sparrow@292840.com
From S.Sinclair@goddessisles.com
Subject: Re: Re: Re: Bonjour

We are getting married in a few weeks.
I will send you the evidence you require.
Until then, stay the fuck away from me and my islands.

Sinclair

Cricking my neck and doing my best to eradicate the strain of dealing with a wannabe hero, I opened Jethro's email.

To: S.Sinclair@goddessisles.com
From J.H@HawksridgeHall.com
Subject: Re: A favour

Hello, old friend.

Consider the ring done.
I will personally oversee the creation and priority mail it as soon as it is finished.
In answer to your question, yes, my lovely wife is doing well. If you could bottle what she gives me, Sullivan, you would have yet another groundbreaking cure on your hands.
I've never been so fulfilled or so…calm inside.
As for your own affliction, welcome to the club. The club where you thought you were all-powerful, all-important, and all-invincible and figure out that you're none of those things.
She is.
You are nothing without her and will spend the rest of your life happily accepting just how second-rate you are compared to her perfection.
Don't worry, though…it's natural to feel like a bastard who doesn't deserve her. You might never stop feeling that way, but if she loves you, then you did something right.
And yes, a catch-up is definitely in order.

Jet

The shower turned off.

Eleanor appeared naked and dripping, wrapping a towel around her gorgeous figure.

Closing the laptop, I followed her with my eyes as she gave me a sexy smile and disappeared into my walk-in wardrobe.

Our walk-in wardrobe.

Our lives had begun blending together.

Her clothes hanging with mine.

Her toothbrush next to mine.

Her side of the bed reserved only for her.

We were entwining ourselves, carving out domestication and togetherness. Me and her against the world.

No vigilante Frenchman could stop that.

No demented brother could hurt us.

And who knew, perhaps, when I could walk again and she wore my ring, I would take her to England to meet a friend of mine. I would proudly introduce her to my singledom life and reintroduce us as a couple.

Because one thing was for sure, there was no me without her now.

Nowhere I would travel without her.

No bed I would sleep in without her by my side.

We were joined…for always.

Chapter Forty

A MONTH SINCE MY world changed all over again.

Thirty days where each morning Sully opened his eyes, grew stronger, and wrapped me in his arms at night.

It both flew by and crawled by.

Flew because Sully used every waking hour to regain his strength and mobility and crawled because every touch between us was a live wire set at a voltage determined to annihilate us.

Sleeping beside him.

Touching him.

Kissing him.

All incredible and needed after almost losing him, but I couldn't deny that refusing sex was the hardest thing in the world.

Watching him dry off after a shower.

Seeing him grow hard just watching me.

Both of us flinching when we touched because our connection caused physical pain.

My body *ached* for his.

His temper spoke of his need for me.

Our self-controls were fraying.

I wanted him.

So damn much.

But I'd meant what I said a few weeks ago. I loved him too much to lose him, and I was petrified of sleeping with him because last time…

That won't happen again.

I nodded, following my logic that the likelihood of Sully having another cardiac arrest after an orgasm were slim. Previously, he'd pushed his body to the brink and injected his veins full of poison. He'd detoxed and healed since then, yet…every time I inched toward him or buckled beneath the urge to open my legs and beg, a small panicked voice would shout in my ear.

What if?

What if he needed more time to be strong?

What if I was pushing him too much?

He already pushed for more than Louise liked. His physiotherapy usually ended with them yelling at each other.

The first day he'd stood without support, he refused to sit back down again until his legs buckled from the strain.

The first afternoon he took a step—assisted by Joe and Campbell—he refused to stop until he tripped and fell to his knees, possibly setting back his healing bones by weeks.

In the end, Louise gave up on controlling the timeline and permitted Sully to train himself. To use the weights for his arms, and the Pilate bands for his abs and quads at his discretion.

Each day, Sully broke barriers and rebuilt the muscle he'd lost.

He was so full of life now.

He smiled more than I'd ever seen.

He laughed at my stupid jokes.

His eyes glowed with less torment.

His thirty-three years had been erased and he'd transformed into a younger, less brooding man. They did say that life was put on hold while a patient lay in a coma. That no aging process occurred.

Well, Sully's six-week sleep seemed to have stopped all clocks and reversed the strain of his prior years. I'd like to take some credit for that—for teasing his heart open to trust and filling it with affection. For showing him he didn't need to hate himself or his kind. That it was okay to be happy when so many other creatures were not.

Talking of creatures.

Today, I had a plan and I wasn't entirely sure how Sully would take it.

"So…I can kidnap him for the afternoon?" I asked Louise as she packed her suitcase and oversaw Joe and Steph as they dismantled the monitors and sensors, slowly restoring Sully's villa into a home instead of a hospital ward.

"Yes. He can stand and walk a few steps—if someone is there to help bear his weight. Make him use the cane at all times, seeing as he refuses crutches. If he wants to stand for longer than a minute, position him somewhere he can either fall safely or hold on to something. Don't stay in the sun for too long and no drinking alcohol, even though he's no longer on antibiotics or painkillers. His system is still fragile and should be—"

"Who the fuck are you calling fragile?" Sully growled as he appeared on the threshold of the living room. One hand rested against the door jamb and the other fisted a bamboo cane with a sweeping handle in the shape of vines and palm trees. The tropical design continued halfway down the shaft, whittled with birds and flowers.

Jess and I had sketched it out a couple of weeks ago and asked one of the carpenters who was working on Euphoria's reinvention to carve it.

Turned out, the carpenter was a woodcarver, skills passed down from generations and he'd leapt at the chance.

Sully had accepted the gift and hadn't said a word. He didn't need to. His eyes said everything. They touched me, kissed me, fucked me, and married me all in one grateful stare.

"What are you doing out of bed? Someone was coming to help you." Louise stopped folding her clothes, glaring at her tetchy patient. "You're determined to kill yourself, I swear."

"Determined to walk, that's all." Sully swayed a little as his legs grew used to his weight. He'd slipped on an off-white t-shirt and a pair of khaki cargos. No suits or ties. No sign of the gatekeeper of Goddess Isles. His legs had filled in thanks to his daily exercises but the discolouration of healing bones and weaker areas hinted it would take months before he could do much more than stumble.

Moving to his side, I waited until he looped his arm around my shoulders. "We're going on a drive," I said. "I'm your chauffeur."

"Finally, a change of scenery." He bent and kissed the tip of my nose. "Where are you taking me? The beach? The restaurant? Lunch with Cal and Jess?"

"We can do all that if you want, but first…there's something I want to show you."

* * * * *

"Are…are you going to say something?" I asked softly as I

turned off the engine to the ATV and glanced at Sully.

With Joe's and Louise's help, we'd assisted Sully from his villa and into the ATV and we'd driven, just the two of us, down the private laneway from Nirvana, beneath sweeping palms and dense jungle to the large oasis where Euphoria was housed.

The virtual reality playground soared into the sky with its thatched roof and aura of hidden fantasies. It might look the same on the exterior but the interior was totally reformed.

Last time Sully had been here, he'd killed a few men and saved me from his brother, all while I'd been helplessly high on elixir.

His hands balled and his jaw clenched as he focused on the building and the memories. "What's there to say? I wanted this burned down."

I hadn't brought him here to relive nasty pieces of our past. I'd brought him here to heal a fractured part of him that'd died on *Serigala*.

"I couldn't let it burn. But...it's not the same as it was, I promise."

When he didn't reply, I turned on the ATV again and drove away from the front courtyard and Euphoria's main double door entrance, heading toward the side of the large building where open-air bathrooms had been turned into entranceways for animals of all kinds. A shower had been removed in one, and the big stone bathtub relocated in another, allowing wet areas for creatures who required access to water like the two injured otters who'd arrived three days ago.

Driving as close as I could to the villa, I once again cut off the engine and hopped from the quad. "Wait here. I'm going to get someone to help—"

"Don't." Sully grasped the side handle and gritted his teeth. "I can manage."

Rushing back to him, I wanted to argue. To find some way to keep him inside the vehicle until I could get someone to assist, but he already swung his legs out and sank his bare feet into soft sand.

He closed his eyes and groaned. "Christ, I've missed that."

And just like that, I couldn't share this moment with anyone else. We would take our time. I would carry him if I had to. But I wouldn't take any more of his independence away. "Lean on me."

His blue eyes met mine. For a moment, he looked as if he'd argue. His cane sank into the sand and he poised to push upright to stand. Inhaling sharply, he looped his arm over my shoulders and allowed me to take some of his weight as he unfolded from the ATV and stood trembling, getting his balance.

"Okay?" I asked gently.

"Okay." Stepping forward, his momentum was stifled and constituted a shuffle instead of a step. I moved with him, not complaining at our slowness or begging him to rest when his t-shirt grew damp with sweat from strain and island heat. Slowly, we made our way into the building and gradually became surrounded by chaos.

Sully sucked in a breath as he slammed to a stop, leaning on me as his gaze darted from the temporary pens holding the bandaged recuperating animals from *Serigala* and the latest arrivals of skittish lab creatures who were undergoing vet checks before they would be found comfy enclosures to begin healing.

Four vets had their hands full and no one paid any heed as we stood on the perimeter and let life ebb and flow around us.

A scruffy jack russell got loose from one of the vets, bounding over to us. He barked at Sully, sniffed his sand sprinkled feet, then bolted off before the male vet could grab him. He wasn't running from fear…it was a game.

A tongue-lolling play that I doubted any lab creatures had ever indulged in.

I didn't know how long we stood there as the soft hammering of nails and the rasps of a saw added background noise to chirps, snuffles, and wuffles, but Sully slowly lost his tension.

He eyed up the construction, his quick intelligence understanding what I was doing without asking a single question.

The workmen had started on the extension for a fully equipped surgery. Equipment and medical supplies had already been ordered. The vets who worked here had been given accommodation in the goddess villas along the beach, and Cal had been in touch with the rehoming outfit Sully used, to advise they would soon have a few cows and donkeys ready to go to a new forever farm.

I'd done my best to give these creatures a second chance.

And in a way…Sully too.

Finally, Sully cleared his throat and clasped me tight to him. His hand turned white around his cane and his body shuddered. Burying his face into my hair, he inhaled and exhaled, seeking comfort and strength before pulling away and murmuring, "What you've done here, Eleanor, surpasses what I could've imagined. I know you were worried how I would react with yet another rescue facility and you are right to be worried. Most of me wants to shut this place down before anything else gets hurt because of me."

He grimaced but continued, "Each time I try to help, I end up hurting instead. My good intentions seem to come with pain—"

"Don't be—"

"Let me finish." He glanced around the busy space before twisting me to face him. He stumbled but glared at me when I went to hold his weight again. "Stop babying me. If I fall, let me fall. I want to look at you while I say this."

It took everything not to help him but I let go and nodded. "What is it?"

"I need you to promise me something."

I narrowed my eyes, looking up into his intense ones. "Okay…"

"Tell me you won't allow me to get obsessed. I…I have a tendency of trying too hard when faced with an animal that's suffered. That's why I didn't have much involvement with *Serigala*. I'd visit but the day-to-day running wasn't my responsibility." He laughed coldly. "I take each case personally. I seek out those who hurt them. I plot ways to deliver the pain tenfold. I become consumed with the need to have them live, regardless if they've given up the fight. It's not healthy for me to be so involved. And you've just brought them right to my door. You've made their healing personal and…honestly, that isn't a good thing."

What Cal told me about the cats Sully rescued echoed in my mind.

"He stabilised them. Got attached. They haemorrhaged. Died a miserable, messy death and I guess he just snapped."

The cats were the reason Sully had gone after so many charlatans and cruel bastards of the world. He believed he killed those cats because he'd gone over the vet's expertise.

He carried so much guilt for so many things.

I wanted to tell him I knew about the cats and I understood why he struggled. Maybe one day I would, but not here. Not while he was still healing and the haunting in his tone hinted he was honestly afraid of what he was capable of.

Nodding, I whispered, "If you need me to be a voice of reason…then I will be."

"I need you to keep me from believing I know better than the experts and stop me from attempting to save their life when that life is over."

I nodded. "They don't have to stay. Once *Serigala* is rebuilt, they can be relocated."

Running his hands through my hair, he brought me close until our foreheads touched. "I love you so much. I love your golden heart and your empathy. Just please...promise me you'll keep mine in check." He bent and captured my mouth, kissing me swiftly and deeply before murmuring, "Don't let me hurt you, Eleanor. Don't allow me to smother you in my need to keep you safe. I can already feel it happening—the desire to keep you by me at all times. The fear of ever losing you. It will drive me to do reckless, dangerous things. I'm not kidding when I say I hurt those I love. I do it because I love too much. I don't know when to stop. So you need to promise me you'll make me stop if I don't."

I kissed him again, wrapping my arms around his waist. "We all have that problem, Sully. You're not a monster for wanting to keep me safe."

"I'm a monster if I would willingly slaughter entire cities to keep you."

I dared to smile. "No, that just makes you a man in love."

"The luckiest man to be in love with you."

We fell into another kiss.

Yet another promise cemented.

Yet another step to our forever.

* * * * *

"You won't be able to fly if you eat another thing, Pika." I laughed as the green fiend attacked yet another roasted chickpea from our dinner.

"He's getting fat," Sully chuckled, reclined on a deck lounger, cast in silver from the moon, he looked good enough to eat for dessert.

After our visit to Euphoria, we'd driven around the island and stopped off at the beach to drive slowly through turquoise shallows. As the sun set, his energy levels depleted and we returned home, grateful that Louise and her team had returned to their villas for the night, leaving us alone.

Sully had dozed on the lounger as I ordered some dishes from the kitchen and we'd eaten outside, serenaded by Nirvana and the night chorus of insects.

The remains of a shared meal of coconut chickpea curry and a tempeh nasi goreng waited to be cleared off the table. Sully had retired to read on his tablet, skimming over work documents that needed to be cleared by the board in the morning, and I'd found the cell phone I'd purchased in Jakarta when I'd attempted every which way to return to Sully before hiding it under a bush when I'd swum ashore and been snatched by Drake.

I'd charged it and waited for it to start up as Skittles fluttered to my shoulder, yawning with feathered fatigue. I scooted farther down my lounger, the rattan kissing Sully's so we lay side by side on the deck.

The comfort of just hanging out was almost as precious as wild lusty sex.

Sully reached over and took my hand as the phone finally activated and the menu appeared. "That's the device you used for your dad to follow and call the police?"

"Uh-huh." I clicked through the apps until I got to Facebook. I'd been delaying a long message to my parents and it'd gone past forgivable to rude. My mother wouldn't mind. She had no idea what had been going on in the background, but my father...he knew too much to be able to relax and not enough to trust I was safe.

Sully arched an eyebrow as he placed his tablet onto his lap and eyed up my profile. "So that's social media, huh?" He visibly shuddered as a picture of someone's steak bleeding on a plate with the hash tag *#gottabebleedingtobegoodeating* appeared.

"Yeah, it's not a healthy place to hang out." Bringing up the message bubble for my dad, I added, "I was never really into it— it's convenient for keeping in touch but I hate the drama and fakery."

"You know...you can stay in touch with your past, right?" He licked his lips, his eyes narrowing with sudden thoughts. "You're not trapped here, Jinx. I hope you get that. Yes, I prefer it to only be us, and I haven't exactly been shy in not wanting to share you, but...you had a life before me, and you can still have that life, even now we're together."

"I know."

"Do you, eh...want friends to come and visit?"

He looked so earnest and sweet, he broke my heart. "No." I shook my head, jostling Skittles as she bobbed with tiredness. "I'll tell you if—"

The phone suddenly vibrated and trilled in my hands.

An image of my dad's profile popped up.

"Oh, no...he's trying to video call me."

Sully sat straighter on his lounger, rolling his eyes as Pika flew to his head and nestled in his midnight strands. "What's wrong with that? He'll be worried about you. I know I'd be fucking losing it if I were him."

"But...we're not dressed." I eyed Sully's lack of shirt. Tonight, the humidity levels had stayed far too high for clothing inside the villa. Sully had slipped off his t-shirt and shorts and stayed in black boxer-briefs while eating dinner, and I'd slipped into a copper bikini with tassels dangling off the top. My hair was wild with island waves, and Sully looked positively sinful.

He smirked. "Better answer it. He knows you're online."

"I'll just go put some clothes on—"

Sully reached across and in a move too fast to stop, swiped accept. He gave me a quick wink. "It's time I met your father, don't you think?"

The screen loaded an image of my dad, his greying hair spiked from his hands, bags heavy under his eyes. He'd aged and guilt squeezed me for being the reason.

"Hey, Dad. I'm *so* sorry I've been an awful daughter. I should've called you weeks ago. It's not fair at all."

He cleared his throat, his eyes casting over me in my state of undress. "You finally answered. I've been calling this damn thing since you left that terrifying message on my voicemail."

"I know. I have no excuse. I'm unbelievably sorry."

"You, um, have a parrot on your shoulder."

I rubbed my cheek against Skittles, earning a quick beak kiss. "I do."

"Why do you have a parrot on your shoulder?"

I smiled. "Because she adopted me, and I stole her from Sully."

"Sully being the man who caused all this mess. The man who I read very disturbing things about online. The man many are calling a heinous murderer and a psychopath."

"A man who has a past but isn't a psychopath. A man I fell for." I winced, wanting to ignore the fact that he'd read the articles I had online, not sure how to brush such things away.

He scrubbed his face before muttering, "I think you have some explaining to do, young lady."

I smiled wider, hearing the switch in his tone from angry to miffed. "I'll tell you anything you want to know."

He huffed. "Those allegations...are they real? He won't hurt you?"

"He'd never hurt me in a million years, and as for the allegations, they're in the past. He isn't that same man anymore.

You'll just have to trust me on that and forget you read such things."

"I expect a deeper explanation soon, Ellie, but right now, I'm just so glad you're alive." Peering around me, he asked, "Where are you?"

The outdoor lantern painted us in a romantic hazy illumination and the splash of Nirvana most likely distorted some of the sound but at least he could tell I was in one piece.

I was alive, and lucky enough to be sharing my world with someone I'd almost lost.

"I'm in the archipelago still, at the coordinates this phone gave you. It's called Goddess Isles."

"And that man who you assure me won't hurt you? That pharmaceutical CEO who ought to be in prison if the newspapers have a shred of truth—"

"Sully, sir." Sully leaned forward, crowding into the screen. His naked chest probably gave my father incorrect conclusions of what we'd been up to. "And your daughter is quite right, I would never hurt her and those allegations online are no longer who I am. However, I will admit that I would hurt any man or woman who dare put Eleanor in danger. She's changed me in many ways, but I would still make others bleed if they put her life in jeopardy."

"*Sully*," I hissed. "Stop it."

He just shrugged and raised an eyebrow. "You have my word, Mr. Grace, that you have nothing to worry about from me. I love your daughter more than I've loved anyone."

"Eh…" My dad's wrinkled cheeks pinked as Sully nodded respectfully all while Pika stayed dozing on his head and Sully's eyes flashed with violence. "I don't know what to say to that."

Sully smiled, doing his best to shed his aggression and be magnanimous. "Let's just focus on the here and now. It's an honour to finally meet you."

"Eh…likewise, I suppose." My father swallowed, eyeing up Pika but deciding not to ask. "Um…you look different to your company photograph online. Clothing is preferable."

"Suits have a tendency to hide the real man, sir." Sully grinned. "And we're currently in the tropics, so excuse my lack of attire."

"Fine. And you don't have to call me sir. Ross is good enough." My dad sighed. "My name is Ross and, as long as you keep my Ellie safe, then…I guess the rest can be discussed at a later date." He wasn't happy and his many questions glowed in his gaze, but he'd always done his best at accepting my decisions and reserving judgment.

"Ross then." Sully squeezed my hand, unseen from my father's angle. "I'm the reason your daughter hasn't called, I'm afraid. I…wasn't well for a while and her attention was very gratefully on me. If it wasn't for her, I wouldn't be here talking to you."

My dad's gaze snapped back to me. "What on earth happened over there? And what precisely is going on between you two?" His shoulders puffed up. "I think…I think I would prefer a private conversation with my daughter, Mr. Sinclair. I need to know she's happy and taken care of."

"Dad, I'm fine. Honestly. I know I made you worry and you'll be utterly confused, but please accept that things are—"

"I understand your desire to speak to her away from me, Ross, but allow me to give you the information you require." Holding out his hand, Sully waited until I'd placed the phone into it before leaning back on his lounger and saying, "Your daughter and I met through unconventional means, but I have full belief that it wasn't chance but destiny. I know you have no reason to trust me, or believe a word I say, but I need you to listen when I say that I love her. I love her more than any achievement or asset, pet or person before her. I love her for her strength, her empathy, her stubbornness, and her kindness. I love her so much in fact, I've asked her to marry me, and she's accepted."

"Oh, my God." I clamped both hands over my mouth.

My father let out a noise as if someone had punched him in the gut. "*Marriage*? Bit soon, isn't it? Even if you do speak very passionately about—"

"Your daughter brought me back to life, sir. In so many ways. I know it's tradition for the guy to ask the father's permission, but I wouldn't survive if you said no, so…I'm telling you that I am going to marry your daughter, and I'm going to give her every penny I own, every island I control, and share every remaining year I have left on this planet with her by my side. You are, of course, welcome to visit at any time. I will cover any ticket cost you require. You may request to come tomorrow, if you want. However, I must warn you. I have an agreement with Eleanor that means she will marry me the moment I can walk unassisted. That day is almost here, sir. And I will not wait."

My dad choked, coughing no doubt on absolute shock. "What? Walk unassisted? What does that even mean? You can't just *marry* her. Is that what she wants? What about her travels and career choices? Her friends? Just a minute here—"

"Sully, give me the damn phone." I reached for it, but he held it out of grabbing distance.

"All this talk of love and weddings has ensured I need to go kiss your daughter now, Mr. Grace. Please be assured she is in the best of health and is safe and please…forgive me for this."

"Sully, no, *don't*—" I launched at him, Pika and Skittles darted into the sky, but I was too late.

Sully punched the hang-up button.

"Did you *seriously* just say all that and then *hang up* on my dad?"

"I did." He tossed my phone onto the lounger, and with a groan and gritted teeth, he swung his healing legs over the edge of his lounger and pushed into a standing position. Snatching my wrist, he hauled me up with surprising strength. "Come on."

I looked at my abandoned phone, wondering what on earth I could say to my dad. What would he think? Would he take Sully up on his offer? How did he feel about me marrying this egotistical fool who'd successfully stitched up my heart with every delicious word and sewed me to him for eternity?

Sully looped his arm over my shoulder. Without his cane, his steps were lumbersome and careful, his bones warning him not to exceed too much pressure.

I hugged him and acted as his crutch, guiding him around the dining table. "Where do you want to go?" I eyed up the edge of the deck and the crystal pool of Nirvana, silky and inviting beneath. We were too close. One wrong step and—

"I want to go swimming." Sully fell sideways, pulling me with him off the deck.

Sullivan

Chapter Forty-One

I WASN'T PROUD OF what happened next.

I didn't mean to pull Eleanor into Nirvana or instantly paw at her the second we broke the surface.

I'd grown hard while confessing my undying allegiance to my wife-to-be while talking to my new father-in-law. My cock had ached as my mind filled with indecent thoughts the longer I envisioned her as my wife with my ring upon her finger.

I didn't have any control as I hung up, grabbed my gorgeous goddess, and tossed us both into the pool.

The exquisite sensation of cool water against my sticky skin was a new kind of aphrodisiac—not that I needed any more stimulation.

I was almost out of control.

Clinging to the final shred of my sanity.

The tiny shred of decency so I didn't take her by force but well and truly mad with every lust I'd bottled up over the past month.

I *wanted* her.

Christ, I wanted her.

I needed her to cure me.

Sinking to the bottom, I grazed the boulders below with my toes, keeping my shoulders and head above water. Eleanor couldn't reach, and she kicked against me, trying to swim out of my rabid embrace. Water sluiced down her hair, darkening her coffee strands to obsidian; the moonlight turned grey eyes into glittering galaxies.

She was, in one word, incredible.

"Sully, I don't know what's gotten into you but—Oh, God."

She bowed in my arms as I ran my hand over her breast, undid the knot of her bikini against her spine, then dove my fingers between her legs.

She jolted against me as I shoved aside her bikini briefs and rubbed her clit.

"I need you, Jinx."

"But we made a deal—"

I inserted one finger inside her, just to the first knuckle, dipping in and out, learning I wasn't the only one in a constant state of arousal. Her wetness was so much thicker than the pool, so much hotter and sexier and *fuck me*, I couldn't wait.

Kicking off the bottom, I swam with her in my arms.

My pinned together ankle hurt the most, followed by the torn muscle of the harpoon scar and a slight throb in my femur and tibia. But the pain was nothing compared to a month ago. I was getting stronger. My heart hadn't skipped a beat in weeks, and I'd put the weight on that I'd lost.

There was no need to wait anymore.

No need to put ourselves through this torture.

"I'm not going to die on you, Eleanor." I bit her ear as I found the shelf by the shore and fell to my knees on the gravelly bottom. Turning her around, I ensured her legs also met stable surface before I pulled her back against my chest and untied the strings of her bikini on her hips.

Naked.

Fuck me, naked, and wet and all fucking mine.

"I need you. Christ, I've never been so hard in my life." I ran my throbbing cock up and down her crack. I almost came from that friction alone. I'd never gone so long without a release. Never wanted a girl this badly, only for her to deny me. "I'll die if you don't let me have you—you're saving my life literally by opening your legs."

She scoffed, her tone breathy and as hungry as me. "Twisting this around won't make me—" She bucked against my hand as I speared two fingers inside her. "God, Sully...you're—"

"I'm?" I bit her ear again, nuzzling her wet hair off her neck and sinking my teeth into her throat. "I'm mad for you? Starving for you? I'm driving my fingers inside you because I can't bear not to touch you?" I rocked against her, ignoring Pika as he skimmed over the water, investigating why I suddenly decided to try to drown my chosen mate.

"What if something happens—"

"Nothing is going to happen apart from the best fucking orgasm of our lives." I fingered her harder, rubbing her clit with my thumb, shuddering with greed as her inner muscles squeezed around my intrusion.

"Say yes. Say yes and I'll be inside you. I'll fuck you until you scream. I'll show you just how alive I am…thanks to you."

"But—" Her moan cut her off as I added a third finger. "Oh, fuck me…"

"Yes, please. Goddammit, yes please." I bit her neck again, so fucking close to taking her without her simple agreement. She wanted me. She would welcome me and forgive me.

But…I wouldn't do that.

I wouldn't be able to stop myself from coming tonight, but it was her decision if it would be against her ass or deep inside her.

She shifted in my arms, her hand shooting behind and latching around my cock.

"Holy fuck, Jinx." I thrust into her hand, driving every inch to slip through the fist she'd made. "Tell me if I can have you. Otherwise, I'll come right here, right now."

With the most erotic groan I'd ever heard, she murmured, "You can have me. Just promise—"

I didn't hear the rest.

Ripping my fingers from her pussy, I knocked away her hand and ducked to find her entrance.

She swayed in my arms as the water currents licked around us.

She screamed as I speared upright, impaling myself hilt deep inside her in one thrust.

"Oh, shit." Eleanor's cry echoed around my utopia, amplified by the pool and deafened by the waterfall.

This was impulsive.

This was reactive.

This was fucking fantastic and fleeting.

Gripping her by the nape, I thrust into her. My knees dug into gravel, and my other arm wrapped tight around her waist, keeping her prone and at my mercy.

She screamed again as I lost myself.

I dropped all barriers.

I cut through every rope and chain imprisoning me.

I drove every part of me inside her. My balls smashed against her clit. My teeth sank into her throat. And I gave myself over to the overwhelming need to mount and claim and ruin.

I wanted this to hurt.

I needed to feel pain because Eleanor had the magic to rip apart my ribcage and sink her fangs into my heart.

I might be taking from her.

I might be setting the feral pace and pounding every piece of me inside her, but she was the one who ruled me.

She always would, and I honestly didn't know how to fucking deal with that.

I snarled as my pace turned demented.

She groaned and gasped.

Water splashed around us.

Savage snarls tumbled from my mouth.

My heart reminded me that it'd tried to kill me a few weeks ago and could still achieve such a tragedy.

But I ignored it.

I ignored everything apart from the hot welcome of Eleanor and the fisting fury in my balls.

She felt so good.

Too good.

Fuck, I was lucky.

So unbelievably, goddamn lucky.

Eleanor detonated first. Her climax shattered her one vertebra at a time—snapping her rigid in my arms. Wave after wave of ecstasy pulsed through her body, milking my length.

"Christ, woman."

My own release began like a thunderstorm.

Black clouds.

Rumbling thunder.

Wind and rain and lightning bolts.

And it ended as a hurricane, slashing through my belly, ripping out my past, hurling me into the future, carving me out with every jet of pleasure.

I came longer and harder than I had in memory.

I jerked and gasped until black spots danced on my vision and I struggled to stay coherent.

I gave everything I was, and fuck, it was worth it.

The sense of peace that cloaked us as we switched from animals to lovers was thick and cloying and better than any anaesthesia.

Eleanor pulled forward, disengaging our link and twirling to face me.

She swam against me, cupped my cheeks, and kissed me.

We kissed as our breathing evened out and our tongues switched from hunting to caressing.

We kissed until her lips twitched and she whispered, "Well, you're still alive which I'm grateful for but..."

I pulled away, bewitched by her. Once again seeing the invisible crown she always wore. This time it dripped with waterfall droplets and moss from nearby rocks. She looked like a nymph, sea siren, and witch all in one.

"But?" I asked, unable to stop touching her, kissing the corner of her mouth.

My cock twitched for a second round but my stamina had reached critical fatigue. I'd be lucky to stay awake until we crashed into bed.

"It's night-time, Sully, and there are Komodo dragons in this pool." Laughing softly, she swam out of my reach and stood. Water licked down her breasts, swirling around her flat stomach, hiding the rest of her. "I like my toes, and I like that thing between your legs that most likely looks pretty tasty to a toothed lizard in the dark." Wading toward the shore, she blew me a kiss. "Let's go to bed...I have other plans for you."

* * * * *

I woke up with my heart in my throat and an edge of panic on my peripheral.

Sitting up in bed, I groaned at my aching body. Every part of me pounded from my toes to the top of my head. I'd overdone it last night. I'd pushed boundaries that I wasn't ready to cross.

But I would do it all over again because I'd finally had her.

We'd reconnected, and my lust had become another tool that I would use to get better as soon as humanly possible.

Sighing, I looked at the shadow beside me.

The lightening horizon said dawn was close by, giving enough light to reveal Eleanor still dreamed peacefully. She was naked with her hair strewn like velvet ribbon around her. Pika and Skittles snoozed on the edge of her pillow while Eleanor lay half on her stomach and half on her side, her leg raised, revealing the inner privacy between her legs.

My cock twitched.

My mouth watered to roll her onto her back and wake her up with my tongue buried in her pussy. But something had woken me. Something that still whispered on my hazy thoughts.

I'd had a nightmare…a vision of losing her in another bombing of *Serigala*. Only difference was, the bomb was dropped on this island. I'd lost her. I'd held her remains in my hands as her lifeless eyes stared back at me.

Fuck.

Rubbing my face, I pinched the bridge of my nose, cursing the fear still in my thoughts. I supposed it would take time for my mind to heal as well as my body.

Drake was dead.

That Q bastard was mollified.

Cal had restored the sensors and snares hidden around the reef.

No matter what happened, I would always protect Eleanor— by shield, sword, or my soul. If she died, it would be an impossible task for me to continue so I might as well die in her stead.

Cricking my neck and doing my best to dispel unhappy thoughts, I massaged the areas of healing bone in thigh and shin where aching had magnified. My legs still looked fucking horrendous, but I'd proven Louise's predications wrong by walking in a month instead of two.

Unfortunately, I couldn't deny that it cost me a lot. Christ, the walk from Nirvana—along the shore, and back into my villa—had taxed me to the point where I almost asked Eleanor to go get Cal to carry my ass.

If it hadn't been for her and the stick she'd found for me to use as a crutch, I would've happily slept outside with the Komodo dragons.

Sitting in the dark, I stared at her. I ran my gaze along the sensual curve of her back and the mounds of her ass. When we'd first met, I'd seen a stunning girl who'd enticed and intoxicated me. Now, I saw a queen who I kept falling in love with. Each time I found out something new about her, I slipped further. Each time she let down her guard and said something stupid or made a face or mocked me with sarcasm, I became hers until not a single shred belonged to me anymore.

Tonight, I'd walked farther than I had since Geneva with broken bones and a hole in my thigh, and I was closer to my goal. She'd carried a lot of my weight with no complaint. She'd accepted my flaws with no judgment.

She never said no to me.

No matter if it taxed her or shoved her well past her comfort zones.

She was mine, and I was sick of waiting to make it official.

Grabbing my phone from the side table, I settled back against the pillows and pulled up the contact details for an event planner in Java. Normally, I used their services for guest stays in mainland hotels before they were flown to my shores. Occasionally, I'd enlisted them to host a few of my corporate contacts if flying to the States wasn't possible.

Now, they had a new task.

From: S.Sinclair@goddessisles.com
To: Jaya@sempurnaplanning.com
Subject: Wedding

Hello Jaya,

Please arrange a celebrant, bridal gown fitting the girl in the attached photo, and basic decorations for a beach wedding in six days. Catering will be done in-house. Small ceremony. Vows will be supplied. Please ensure no expense is spared on the dress but the rest…it's merely perfunctory.

I have faith that you will deliver another perfect event.

A helicopter will collect you, the celebrant, and items at seven p.m. the night before.

Kind regards,

Sullivan Sinclair

A smile twitched my lips as Eleanor shifted beside me, her gentle sigh making my heart fist. She slept beside me still bearing the name Grace. Unlike so many unfortunate surnames, that one suited her. She was the very embodiment of elegance and beauty. But in six days, she would become a Sinclair.

Eleanor Jinx Sinclair.

Sharing in my sin for eternity.

I went to turn off my phone, only for it to vibrate with two new messages.

One from Jaya and her planning company confirming my requests and another one from a friend who had perfect timing.

To: S.Sinclair@goddessisles.com
From J.H@HawksridgeHall.com

Subject: Ring

Sullivan,

Your rings are finished and are flying to you as we speak. I took the liberty of fashioning a male version of the wedding band, so your wife-to-be has something to claim you as hers in return. There's something about seeing a diamond flash on your finger, knowing that it chains you to her, that soothes a man's soul. I know it did for me, and I expect the same for you.

Wish we could be there to share in your day, but I expect details when you visit Hawksridge next.

Until then, stay safe and congratulations to you and Mrs. Sinclair.

P.S. Nila sends her apologies that she couldn't design a dress in time.

Jet

Chapter Forty-Two

"SULLY IS ACTING WEIRD."

Jess chuckled from where she did her exercises on the deck of Cal's villa. "What do you mean weird? Isn't he always weird? You know…weirder than say a normal boyfriend working in an office who likes slabs of cow for dinner?"

Even though she broke her coma before Sully had, she hadn't gained her mobility as fast. She could stand and walk now, but not for long periods. Unlike Sully, who had the relentless need to walk on his own so he could marry me as fast as possible, Jess had a man who enjoyed doting on her.

It was Cal's fault she hadn't progressed as quickly, seeing as he carried her most places now that his own wounds had become background noise, and they'd fooled around for the first time a week ago. Jess hadn't gone into intimate details, but she had shared enough for me to blush next time I saw Cal. After all, we were goddesses who'd shared elixir, seen each other naked, and regaled tales of our Euphoria aftermath.

Cal, according to Jess, was surprising in bed. He had his own deviant desires but preferred to focus entirely on her until she was boneless from countless orgasms before tending to his own wants.

I'd wanted to ask how an orgasm felt, now she'd had a forced hysterectomy, but I kept such questions silent, especially after she admitted sleeping with Cal would have to wait a bit longer for her inner wounds to fully heal and her patience was already thin.

Thanks to Jess's divulgence, though, I now felt like I knew Cal on a deeper level. It stripped away the final wariness between us and firmly placed him in my favourite bunch of people. He might take a while to warm up to strangers, but he was loyal and kind, and I could see why Sully had kept him around.

I paced around Jess as she did squatting exercises, clinging onto the deck chair as she rebuilt withered thigh muscles. The big scar on her belly from Drake's bullet was hidden by her loose-fitting navy and white pinstripe dress.

"He can walk on his own now, did you know that?" I ran a hand through my hair, wishing I'd tied it off my shoulders with how brilliant the sun shone today. My candy pink sundress seemed far too heavy for the heat. "He still has to use his cane, but he can walk around the villa and partly down the path. If Louise and her doctors hadn't flown back to Geneva yesterday, she'd probably spank him and send him to bed."

My thoughts flew after the doctor and her team. I owed Louise more than I could ever repay. Thanks to her tireless efforts and in-home care, she was the reason Sully had returned to me. She deserved every priceless gift.

Luckily, Sully had been of the same opinion, and had paid her and her colleagues a bonus that could enable them to retire if they wanted. We'd all agreed to stay in touch and given an open-ended invitation to return to Goddess Isles for a vacation anytime she wanted.

Jess giggled. "If anyone is spanking that man, it better be you. He'd tear anyone else's arm off."

I smirked. "I think he'd tear even my arm off."

"Oh, you might be surprised." She winked. "To the world, he's the dominant asshole, cutthroat in every area, but when he looks at you...you could do whatever you damn well wanted to him and get away with it."

"Maybe on our wedding night, I'll tie him up and see how far that theory goes."

She laughed, wiping away the beads of sweat on her forehead. Sitting down onto the same chair she'd been using as support, she got her breath back. "Back to the topic. Why do you think he's acting weird just because he can walk on his own now?"

I sat across the table from her, snagging a piece of pineapple from the fruit platter that had shards of ice melting over it. "He normally ensures I know how he's progressing. He grabs me and shows me, in no uncertain terms, how rapidly he's taking back his strength. However, this morning...he kicked me out. He said he had a ton of work to do, for me to send Cal to him for a meeting, and that I should come see you and 'stay out of trouble.'" I air-quoted that last bit. "What the hell does that mean?"

Her eyebrows raised. "Dunno. But you're right, it does sound fishy." The barcode tattoo on her wrist flashed as she snagged a piece of watermelon and sucked on the juice. I glanced down at my matching one, running my thumb over the slightly raised ink lines.

She caught me looking. "Ever think of lasering it off? We could fly to Jakarta and get it removed." She eyed her own one, rolling her wrist to catch the sun.

I shrugged. "Is it wrong that I don't hate it?"

She shook her head, seriousness filling her stare. "I'm glad you said that. I thought I was the only one." She took another bite of watermelon. "I don't see it as a bad symbol. I never really did. Yes, the kidnapping part was awful and the not knowing where I'd end up was petrifying, but the moment I stepped foot on this island, I knew I was home."

I nodded. "I agree. This tattoo was given against my will, just like I was given to Sully against my will…but, thanks to those events, I found exactly where I was supposed to be with a man I was supposed to belong to." Raising my wrist, I waited until she pressed hers against mine. I laughed and winked. "Besides, it's like an unofficial friendship bracelet."

"Ha ha." She grinned, her hazel eyes growing wistful. "If Cal falls in love with me, we could all live happily ever after. Two couples. Four friends. Two parrots. And a hell of a lot of rescue critters."

My heart glowed. "I'd like that." Placing my hand on hers, I added, "And he can't fall in love with you if he's already fallen."

She blushed. "You think? I'm not so sure. I'm not expecting him to—"

"Oh, believe me. Even if he doesn't know it himself yet, he's smitten. Next time he hugs you, feel what his arms say. I knew Sully loved me just by his touch, well before he ever had the courage to say it aloud."

"Ah, Ms. Grace."

I whipped around in my chair.

A stranger stood in the doorway to Cal's villa. Tucked down the end of the guest villa's laneway, Cal's home had the last private bay before the island became wild with jungle. He was as far away from the main beach as possible, ensuring we hadn't heard a helicopter land.

Jess frowned but didn't stand, leaving me to pad barefoot toward the Indonesian woman with an ebony bob, dressed in a stunning white suit and the biggest sunglasses I'd ever seen. "Can I help you? You are?"

Where did she come from?

She had to have been invited. Otherwise, she would never have stepped foot on Sully's shore alive...but why exactly was she here?

Pulling the huge lenses off her dainty nose, she blinked pretty black eyes. "It's time, Ms. Grace."

"Time?"

"To get ready." She backed up, holding out her arm for me to follow. A dune buggy waited with Arbi acting as chauffeur. Ever since Cal arranged to have the ATV shipped over from *Lebah*, Sullivan had ordered a few dune buggies to make it quicker to get around the island now there was just the four of us—not including the discrete staff who ran this paradise.

"You too, Ms. Young. I took the liberty of bringing a dress for a maid of honour as well as a bride."

"A bride?" I coughed.

"Yes. For your wedding."

My head whirled.

My heart exploded.

Sully...

How had he done this?

When?

The woman grinned, enjoying my shock. "I'm Jaya, and I've been tasked with preparing you. The ceremony is in two hours, just before sunset." Beckoning again, she added, "Please, we don't have much time."

I looked over my shoulder at Jess.

She stood, but her eyes flared with worry at how far she could walk without falling flat on her face. Darting back inside, I hooked her arm over my shoulder, moulding her feminine curves to mine, so different to the hard planes of Sully's body. "So that's why he's been acting weird," I murmured.

Jess snickered. "He's keeping his promise."

"Seems so." I tried to fight the smile on my face but couldn't. I tried to stop my heart from running away with romantic notions and erotic conclusions but started to shiver with anticipation instead. "That man only managed to walk on his own this morning, yet he somehow organises to marry me by the evening."

"What did you expect?" Jess asked as we cut across the living room. "He's a god ruling his own version of heaven and you, my dear friend, are his chosen goddess."

Sullivan

Chapter Forty-Three

JAYA HAD DONE EXACTLY what I'd hoped.

The small arch she'd crafted from vines and palm leaves from my island framed the open-air altar where I stood. The celebrant— a middle-aged man with a bald head and iron-pressed grey suit— stood behind me. Cal waited off to the side in a charcoal suit, complete with waistcoat and cravat. I'd told him not to dress up, but my command seemed to have fallen on deaf ears. At least he'd obeyed when I'd asked him to video call Eleanor's father and wedge a small table into the sand so my laptop could record and transmit our ceremony.

Ross Grace had been polite—even after I'd hung up on him previously—and run to get a glass of champagne that he'd been saving for special occasions. He now waited quietly, watching my beach and the glowing sky, poised for Eleanor to arrive.

I'd yet to meet Eleanor's mother, but at least her father was in attendance. He could watch his stunning, amazing daughter swear her life to mine.

She was no longer his.

But I would share her occasionally because that was what good husbands did.

Jess appeared on Arbi's arm. The man who'd once had a job of keeping imprisoned goddesses in line and bowing to every sinister guest's request now had a much more important calling. He'd been tasked with being head of staff, ensuring food was plentiful for us and the locals who lived on neighbouring islands, the villas were maintained even while currently out of use, and being at the beck and call of the two women who remained here.

Jim Campbell wasn't a part of our wedding witnesses, having flown to see his grandchildren in Chicago at the same time as Louise Maddon and her team flew home to Geneva. Louise had returned with a personal payment, along with a bank deposit substantial enough to fund another wing at her hospital. A gift of thanks for her tireless work giving me back my legs and life.

Campbell had also left with a gift. A hefty sum that spoke of gratefulness for his care toward Jess, Cal, and Skittles. He'd left with my blessing. He no longer thought of me as something to exterminate and I managed to accept his reasoning for his betrayal.

I'd expected his departure to be our last interaction. However, he'd requested if he could return in a month. Now that elixir had been destroyed, girls released, and no future imprisonment planned, he'd second-guessed his retirement.

Regardless of our amicable respect, despite the treason and tragedy we'd both caused, I couldn't make up my mind if I'd welcome him back. He was still the reason *Serigala* was bombed and so many animals crucified. But he'd redeemed himself by saving others' lives.

Ah well, that decision could be made another day.

Today was my wedding and all I wanted to focus on was my wife-to-be.

Cal sucked in a breath as Jess continued her laboured stroll toward us. She shared most of her weight with Arbi, her face tight with strain. Determination to keep going and not give in sparkled in her gaze. Her blonde hair had been coiled and pinned, complete with a sprig of jasmine in the fairness. Her lips glistened with gloss and her smile seemed to stop Cal's heart as he jerked beside me.

Jaya had done well, choosing a golden dress that skimmed Jess's ankles with a floaty hem, adorned with just enough lace and decoration to be perfect without overshadowing the bride.

Not that anything could overshadow Eleanor.

She could wear kelp from the ocean, and she'd still look exquisite.

Speaking of the bride…where the fuck is she?

I fought the urge to fidget, clasping my hands around the cane wedged into the sand in front of me. I'd managed to walk unassisted. My endurance increased each day. However, my balance still came and went and I had no intention of falling on my ass as Eleanor walked down the aisle.

Pika sensed my building tension, nibbling at my ear with his beak. "Jinx. Jinx!"

I stiffened, looking at the tiny parrot on my shoulder. "Another new word, huh? Decided to expand your vocab, little nightmare?"

Pika narrowed his black eyes, that cheeky look that always heralded mischief appeared. He squawked and stomped his claws on my blazer, kicking up a fuss. The ribbon where I'd tied our wedding rings dangled preciously in his talons.

"Don't you dare drop that." I growled as he fluttered around my head, the silver ribbon in question swinging wildly.

Three rings hung from it, clinking together with flashes of flawless Hawk diamonds as Pika continued to zip and dip. The glitter reminded me of the first diamond I'd given Eleanor. Disguised as a guest's payment for the cave fantasy, but really, it'd been a troth of my love for her even then. Eventually, I'd commission that stone to be turned into a bracelet or necklace—another piece of jewellery for the woman who owned me in every way.

"It was a mistake giving that damn bird a fortune in rings. What if he flies out to sea and drops them, just to piss you off?" Cal muttered, his gaze locked on Jess as she continued to close the distance between us.

"He wouldn't." I held out my hand, keeping one fisted on my cane and the other acting as a perch for the chaotic caique. "Would you, Pika?"

He chattered and chirped, sitting on my forefinger and spearing his wing into the sky to preen. The rings continued to swing, almost as if he'd been a thief and pilfered them, instead of being my ring bearer.

Soft waves licked around my ankles, soaking the linen suit I wore.

I'd stood in my walk-in wardrobe for longer than I wanted to admit, staring at the racks of severe, regal, and CEO suits that hung on hangars ready to be worn. Ties of every colour waited to be chosen. My uniform of my past felt familiar and appropriate for an event as special as a wedding.

But…as I'd reached for the usual dark and dense fabric, I'd stopped. The man who wore suits for power as well as protection had died in Geneva and not come back. I was marrying Eleanor today with a much lighter soul and not nearly as many sins that needed to be hidden within a stifling suit.

Today, I was free and I'd chosen simple linen trousers, rolling up the cuffs to reveal bare feet that patrolled the sands of my Elysium. A white shirt tucked in with buttons undone around my throat to let humid air lick around my chest, and a blazer that held a simple orchid pinned to the breast pocket.

I was underdressed for my own wedding but it felt like the perfect choice because I was underdressed in all manners when it came to Eleanor. The only decoration that'd felt appropriate was the dangerous purple flower that'd started me on this journey. A path full of deceit and corruptibility, using sex against women and possession against life, but it'd ended with four hundred bottles of elixir being destroyed by Mrs. Bixel in Geneva at my command.

Those who deserved to die had died—including me.

Those who deserved to be freed had been freed—including Eleanor.

Life had untangled the mess I'd caused and I'd never been so fucking grateful.

"You look amazing," Cal murmured as Arbi relinquished Jess to him the moment she was close enough.

She smiled as her eyes glowed with affection. "You don't look so bad yourself." Throwing me a glance, she added, "You either, Sullivan."

I nodded, unable to tear my eyes from where the sand kissed jungle, desperate for Eleanor to appear and begin her journey toward me. Two men caught my attention in the distance, alert and ready to protect, patrolling my shores.

Radcliffe and his team from Quietus had traded in their murder-for-hire and accepted new positions as my security team on *Batari, Monyet,* and *Serigala,* protecting the people and animals I held most dear. The team who'd failed to shield my scientists on *Monyet*—when Drake stole elixir—had been dealt with, the families of the guards who'd died in my employee had been heavily compensated, and I'd paid off Google Earth to obscure my archipelago, so no other man like my brother could spy on my islands and drop a bomb of destruction.

I'd done what I could to protect me and mine, and it helped knowing Quietus had my back.

Jess whispered, "You should see her, Cal. Wow."

My skin instantly puckered with goosebumps. Impatience flared through me. Pressure filled my stomach and lust thickened my cock.

I hadn't even seen her yet and I already wanted to tear off

whatever she was wearing and consummate.

Licking her lips, Jess spoke to me, almost mocking in her smug laugh, "If you manage to stay standing when you see her, Sullivan. I'll be beyond impressed."

My heart switched its heavy chug for a possessive gallop.

Come on, Jinx.

I miss you.

"Shit, she's here," Cal muttered under his breath, wedging his elbow into my side, pointing at the beach farther down.

My gaze instantly searched for her, but at the last second, I squeezed them shut.

I closed them because I needed fucking strength.

If I looked before I'd locked my knees and braced against my cane, I would do exactly what Jess predicted and fall into the shallows the moment I set eyes on my soon-to-be wife.

"Fuck, *sir*. You're screwed for the rest of your life," Cal snickered.

Gritting my teeth, I looked up.

I tracked to the shoreline where Eleanor had appeared and all my fight to stay standing abandoned me.

Fuck.

Just...*fuck*.

Her grey gaze caught mine, holding me upright even as my legs threatened to buckle. I swayed and clung to my cane, dropping the hand holding Pika to double fist the carved handle.

Pika squeaked and flew around my head but he was insignificant.

I couldn't tear my eyes off the fucking gorgeous creature coming toward me. The girl I'd purchased. The goddess I'd fallen for. The woman I would spend the rest of my godforsaken life worshipping.

Her hair had been left loose—that glorious, aphrodisiacal hair glistening and tumbling around her naked shoulders. Skittles fluttered beside her, a green jewel glinting in the sun, hinting that Eleanor's beauty wasn't just outward but to her very core.

She'd gained the trust of a shy bird all by being her. She'd stolen my pet of fourteen years because of her empathy. And she'd ripped out my heart just by fucking existing.

She was wrong that it was *something at first sight* with us.

It wasn't something.

It was love.

Pure, buckling, brutalising love.

I'd just been too shit-terrified to admit it.

Almost as if Jaya knew our story, she'd rejected the traditional white pomp and overly beaded gown, leaving Eleanor almost naked in refinement.

Her gown was sleeveless in the same soft simple linen as my suit. It clung to her body, revealing sensual curves and barely hiding the shadows of her nipples beneath. The tightness flared from her hips, falling in swathes of uncoloured, untampered fabric.

It mimicked the colour of the silver-golden sand she padded barefoot over, a diamond anklet glinting around her leg, the train of linen leaving a sweeping path behind her.

Parts of the skirt had been torn and left dangling in a way that hinted at a girl shipwrecked on my shores, gowned in the sails of her broken chariot, island bound and all mine to plunder.

"Breathe, man." Cal chuckled as I stumbled.

Opening my mouth, I sucked in fragrant orchid air and the salty tang of my sea.

And I couldn't fucking wait.

Why was it tradition for the bride to walk to the groom?

Why was I forbidden from meeting her on her journey and interrupting her path because that's *exactly* what had happened in life. Our paths had collided, entwined, and changed course.

The architecture of romance and finding your perfect mate didn't follow fucking rules, so why should I?

Digging my cane for purchase, I strode to claim my goddess.

Chapter Forty-Four

PAIN.

Delicious, consuming body-clenching, heart-suffocating pain.

I drowned in it. I succumbed to it. I would feel such pain for the rest of my life simply by looking at this man who was almost mine.

Sully had transcended from a mere god to a resplendent demon.

He had the magic to make me wet just from a stare, the power to stop my heart just from a touch, and the ability to bring me to tears just by the way he staggered toward me, refusing to wait for me to join him at the altar, abolishing tradition and scribbling out the rules just because he could.

The finger snap for the celebrant to chase him had all the characteristics of a conceited royal who bled power. His sniff of expectation for Cal and Jess to follow echoed with habits of his past. But beneath that arrogance lurked a newer, fiercer scandal.

A lecherous man who would always retain the outward exterior of cruel and impeachable but had somehow let me into the den of his heart. A den where he let down his walls, permitted me to see him, allowed me to cultivate the goodness deep within.

He didn't speak as he met me on the shore.

The jewelled kayaks that I'd used to run away had been hidden along with the loungers and umbrellas for banished guests. The beach was as empty as an uninhabited island and we were both dressed as if we'd been washed up with no belongings or past between us.

How had Jaya known?

When she'd pulled out the torn gown and promised me it was perfect for today, I'd been sceptical. Weren't all brides supposed to glitter in beads and rustle in lace? I'd felt underdressed, bare, completely at Sully's mercy as I'd padded barefoot within his sand.

No high-heels would've worked here. No fancy pantyhose or nail varnish.

From the moment I'd arrived, I'd traded shoes for nothing and the metaphor in that arrowed into my heart. Shoes weren't needed here because my path had ended. I didn't need to walk over glass or hardship, no need to traverse the roads of careers or stress.

I was home.

And every step from here on out would be with Sully by my side.

Skittles squeaked as she landed on my bare shoulder.

Pika fluttered after Sully, dragging a silver ribbon with three rings blinding in the sun.

And Sully took my hand in his, the rolled-up cuffs of his trousers damp from the sea, his hair messy and shoved back with an impatient hand, his five o'clock shadow soaking up the daylight and narrowing all my attention on his perfect kissable lips.

Those lips had said such vile things.

But they had also said the sweetest.

His left hand stayed locked around his cane as the celebrant caught up with us, wiping away the sweat at his temples, and rolling his eyes at Sully's broken tradition.

"Are you ready to begin?" the celebrant asked.

Sully swallowed and waved the man away. "All you need to do is the binding part, nothing else."

Cal chuckled, and Jess rolled her eyes, and I...I couldn't look away from the intense sharpness, the utter snarl within Sully's stare.

Whistling once, Sully let my hand go and waited for Pika to descend and wrap his claws around his finger. Leaving his cane speared into the sand, he pulled the ribbon free and unthreaded the three rings.

Silently, he passed the largest one to me.

I captured it in my palm and held it up to the setting, fiery sun. Every minute the sky darkened with cracks of crimson and splashes of sienna, bathing us in sinful red. The band I held was made of thick yellow gold. Heavy to hold and frosted with brilliant diamonds, sweeping over the top, following the contour of a quill and the bristling of a feather.

I looked up, understanding instantly. "For Pika and Skittles."

His lips fought a grimace and a grin. "You're not just marrying me, you're marrying everything that I hold precious. I will never trust anyone as much as I trust you to care for them as I do. I will never love anyone as much as I love you to share the same empathy toward animals who have been mistreated."

I bit my lip, stemming a silly wash of tears.

I would not cry today.

I would not ruin the soft lashings of mascara or blur the perfect image of Sully in his perfect linen suit standing on his perfect sunset beach.

Taking my hand, Sully splayed my fingers and pushed the huge cushion cut diamond onto my finger. It was triple the size of the one he'd given me after the cave fantasy and just as flawless. The yellow gold imprisoning it glittered with inlaid diamonds down the band.

"That is to show the world that you are mine. A gaudy, monetary reminder that it is my honour to provide for you, shelter you, and shield you." He ran his thumb over my knuckles, using me as his support when his legs threatened to sway. "Most of our life will be spent here, hidden in the Java Sea where we have no need of others. But, on those rare occasions when we mingle, I want every man and woman to see that ring and know that you are worshipped, adored, and own me fucking body and soul."

Jess started crying. Cal sucked in a breath.

I just clung to Sully, drowning in the oceans in his eyes and the absolute treasure I found there.

"I don't know what the traditional vows are. I have no idea what I'm supposed to say to you to make this official, but—" He cleared his throat, giving me a sexy grimace. "I love you, Eleanor. I love you so much, but I know it's merely a fraction of how much I'll love you as we grow old together. There is still so much to learn, so many habits to uncover, so many quirks and ideals to share. As we get to know each other, I'm afraid of how deeply I'll fall in love with you. There is no one else. There never was and never will be. You are my one and only, and that is my oath to you. Accept me, and you accept my drive to keep you safe. Love me, and you agree to be loved every day I am alive and beyond. Marry me, and you are mine forever. You are not only my friend and lover but you are my conscience, too. I promise to always listen to you. I promise I won't go too far. I trust you to indulge me when I'm overbearing and trust you have the temper to put me in my place when I need it. I *trust* you, Eleanor, with everything that I am."

He confessed to a level of devotion that any girl could ever dream of, and he delivered it elegantly and threateningly. His eyes glowed with domination all while his face softened with reverence.

The longer we stood bound together, the more his troth made my heart race to be alone, to touch him and confirm that this was real. This wasn't a falsity or a fantasy. My reality had become euphoric without any need for tricks.

The celebrant coughed behind his hand. "If that's all, Mr. Sinclair? Perhaps, Ms. Grace would like to say a few words."

Sully shot him a scowl but smiled guiltily at me. "Sorry if I went a bit dramatic." He cupped my cheek and ran his fingers through my loose hair, unable to stop himself from tugging a little and shooting shards of electricity down my spine.

I gasped as my inner muscles clenched.

Our proximity crackled with passion. The constant hum that always ignited between us had created its own force field, sizzling and thirsty with sparkling wattage, ensuring I would *never* stop wanting this man. "It wasn't dramatic," I whispered. "It was perfect. I don't have anything nearly as wonderful to say. You've wowed me."

Tucking wayward strands behind my ear, sending another lick of yearning through my belly, he murmured, "You don't have to say a thing for it to be perfect. *You're* perfect." He smirked, showing hints of the elixir king who I'd first met. "But…it is your turn, Jinx, and I expect you to vow your life to me."

I blushed.

We'd come so far from that first day. That first thorn of lust that'd pierced our skin, had wriggled into blood and bone, ensuring we were both infected with a lifetime of commitment.

Smiling, I sucked in a breath and pulled my fingers from his. My massive engagement ring glittered, refracting the sun's spires of magenta, coming alive like a tiny fire upon my hand.

It did what Sully intended. It marked me better than any tattoo or brand. It bound me to his heart and his islands, and I would never take it off.

Exhaling my worry that I'd stumble over words or make a mess of my declaration, I spread Sully's long, handsome fingers and slipped the masculine wedding band over his knuckle.

As it slid into place, something clicked open inside me.

A key to a place within that I didn't even know existed. From that place came a warm river of knowledge that this was right, this was *exactly* as it should be. They'd been many moments of premonition while living in this fantastical world and fighting off hallucination horrors. Seer-like visions when Sully was hurt, about to be, or that he would derail my life far worse than I feared.

And this one? It granted a flash-forward into the future as well as a rewind to the past, and I stood in the crosshairs of so many decisions and destinations all forking out like a thousand needles on a compass. There were so many journeys I could've taken, so many people I could've met, so many adventures I could've chased, yet…none of those would've been right.

Yes, I could've had a good life. And yes, I could've been happy, but only because I wouldn't have known the absolute joy of finding *the one*.

Sully was the one.

No question or doubt.

He was the reason I'd been birthed at this exact time in history because there was more than just serendipitous chance that'd brought us together but a lifetime of reincarnation and unknown attempts to find each other.

I lost the battle not to cry as I continued staring wordlessly at the ring looping his finger. To have that symbol on him made me possessive, powerful, and filled to the brim with omnipotent conviction.

This was kismet in every brilliant shape and story.

"Sullivan Sinclair," I sniffed back my tears and looked into his stunning sea gaze. "I am no longer afraid. No longer afraid of making a mistake or saying the wrong thing. No longer afraid of missing out or not taking a gamble when I should. I'm not afraid because I know I can tell you anything, and you will listen. I can confide in you, and you will care. I know I can make mistakes, and you will be there to help me and laugh with me. Every new experience, we will share together. Every new gamble isn't a gamble because we are together, and that's unbelievably precious. I have no doubt you will get bossy and controlling at times, but I also have no doubt you will be generous and protective. I promise you I will look after you in every mood and malady. I will stand by you with your charities and your crusades for all feathered and furred. Like you, I know that the depth I feel for you now is nothing compared to how I will love you a year from now, a decade from now, a lifetime from now. You own me body and soul, Sully, not because of contracts or choices but because you always have. Just as I own you."

Sully's nostrils flared as he grabbed my hand and slid the third and final ring onto my finger. A smaller feminine version of the feathered diamond creation already on his.

With a soft shake of his head and a gentle chuckle, he murmured, "I just had an epiphany, my wonderful Eleanor."

"Oh?"

He stroked the double diamonds on my finger, thoughts clouding his gaze. "Ever since I met you, there has been one question that never had an answer. I thought I had it when I first told you I loved you, but...I have a much better response now."

"What was the question?"

Sully ignored me and turned to the celebrant. "Can you please bind us now?"

I shivered as the celebrant nodded and clasped his hands. "Do you, Sullivan Aiden Sinclair, take Eleanor Grace to be your lawfully wedded wife?"

"I do." His rumble sounded like the volcano I'd always likened his temper too. The quiet cracking of tectonic plates, the absolute threat of power ready to be unleashed at any moment.

"And do you, Eleanor Grace, take Sullivan Aiden Sinclair to be your lawfully wedded husband?"

"I have a middle name too. I'd like to add it, please." I glanced at the suited celebrant. "Jinx."

Sully sucked in a breath, swaying enough that he grabbed his cane and spread his legs in the sand for support.

I smiled, desperate to kiss him, wild to get him into a bed so we could finish our final vows with his body inside mine.

The celebrant sighed but repeated his question. "Do you, Eleanor Jinx Grace, take Sullivan Aiden Sinclair to be your lawfully wedded husband?"

"I do."

"In that case, I pronounce you man and wife. You may kiss the bride."

Sully jerked me into him, but instead of planting his mouth to mine, he nuzzled into my hair and whispered against my ear. "Who are you, Jinx? Who the fuck are you to destroy me, restore me, and ultimately make me the happiest monster alive?"

I shivered as his tongue licked the shell of my ear.

We had an audience. Waves licked around our bare feet, soaking our hem and cuffs. Two parrots flew around our heads, not appreciating that they'd been excluded, and eyes watched us as Sully once again broke tradition.

"Who *are* you, Eleanor?" he murmured.

And I knew exactly the answer he wanted.

The question he'd asked since the beginning.

The question that had dragged a whole suitcase of answers with it but never gave quite the right one.

I'm yours.

I'm your other half.

I'm your ever after.

I'm...

"Who are you, Jinx?" Sully asked again, biting the simple pearl dangling in my ear.

I had the answer.

The only answer.

"Who am I, Sully?" I kissed the whiskers on his face. "I'm your *wife*."

His entire body shuddered. His exhale made him bow into me. And his voice wobbled with awe. "Damn fucking right you are." Pulling my head back with his fist in my hair, he crushed his mouth to mine. He once again smashed apart any wedding expectation of a simple public kiss and made the beach ignite with roaring fire as his tongue plunged past my lips and plastered me hard against him.

His cane dug into my dress. His arms banded around me. And his kiss made me breathless and aroused all in one.

I met his hunting tongue with my own.

He groaned as I dropped all propriety and kissed him as savagely as he kissed me.

We kissed as if we'd survived the wreckage of life and were truly shipwrecked on this sinful paradise.

We kissed until Cal drifted away with Jess, the celebrant grumbled and returned to the helicopter, and my father turned off the video feed, leaving us all alone in the warm-licking shallows.

We kissed until even the sun bowed to our need, extinguishing itself into the sea in a flaming orb of blood and carnage, summoning the cloak of night to keep our kisses and our animalistic drive to ravage each other far away from innocent stars.

Sullivan

Chapter Forty-Five

MY WEDDING NIGHT AND my body had almost reached its limit.

How fucking sad was that? How fucking embarrassing.

Five weeks since I'd woken, and I still suffered so many effects from harpoon wounds and helicopter falls. I cursed my weakness, but I was also rather proud. I'd earned those bruises and scars in defeat of my enemies and the defence of those I loved.

I'd earned them.

I would wear them with pride, even if it meant having wild sex with Eleanor would tax every last power I had left.

"We're at my old villa." Eleanor glanced up as we slowly made our way down the sandy laneway. Thanks to everyone leaving during our wedding kiss, we had no transportation. Even Pika and Skittles had abandoned us.

Not that the short walk from the beach to Jinx's old villa was an issue. It was an honour to walk beside her as birds roosted and the shadows of bats flickered just out of sight. I hadn't intended to return to Nirvana tonight.

I'd…done something.

I'd gambled on a new recipe Peter Beck had been working on and set up a surprise for Eleanor. I had no clue how she'd take it.

"Let's go inside," I said, digging my cane into the sugary sand and doing my best not to lean too heavily on her. If I couldn't walk unassisted, then I'd married her under false pretences, and that would be blasphemy.

She was my wife.

She's my wife.

Fuck, I'd never get tired of that.

Slinking out from under my arm, she dashed to the door and pushed it open. Waiting for me over the threshold, she laughed suddenly, eyeing up my slow, steady stroll. "You broke so many wedding traditions today, I'm wondering if I should break one of my own."

"Oh? Which one?"

"I think the bride should carry the groom over the threshold." She ducked out of my reach as I swiped for her.

"Say such things again and I'll have to punish you for trying to emasculate me. That kiss before almost ensured I fucked you right on the beach—with or without an audience. I can't control myself around you, and I definitely don't need you carrying my ass across a stupid doorway."

She winked and darted inside. "Ah well, plenty of time for you to sweep me off my feet and complete that particular tradition later."

"I've already swept you off your feet." I grinned, closing the door behind me and wiping at the heat on my nape. "I'd say I was pretty successful at it, seeing as my ring is now upon your finger."

She held up her hand, catching the Hawk diamonds in the sconces around the villa. They glittered with every promise and pledge I'd given. "They're stunning, Sully. I love that Pika and Skittles are included." She wrinkled her nose. "Where are those birds anyway?"

I shrugged, moving slowly but steadfast into the living room. "Getting drunk on hibiscus probably." From here, I could see the surprise laid out on Eleanor's bed. Familiar black boxes with purple orchids stencilled on the top.

For the past three weeks, I'd worked fairly hard, emails and theories, new concepts and trials. I'd achieved a few things during my work hours that I hadn't divulged to Eleanor.

One, there were hints of a pandemic brewing that required swift vaccines and expensive research to inoculate mass populations. I'd tasked the scientists on *Monyet* to deconstruct the current viruses on hand to hopefully provide at least some immunity, if and when that pandemic spread.

I wasn't opposed for Mother Nature to kill off the parasites of mankind, but I also couldn't stand by if it was in my power to protect someone's loved one.

Not now.

After falling for Eleanor, she'd ensured I had a deeper well of empathy. Too fucking much really. I couldn't stop putting myself in other husband's shoes, watching their wife succumb to infection and disease, knowing I had the resources to at least give a fighting chance for improving people's odds.

Two, thanks to Eleanor's flippant remark about using Goddess Isles for couples with marriage problems, I'd asked Cal and Jess to look into how employing a few psychiatrists and counsellors could work and offer a sexual vacation away from the strain of arguments, domestication, and mistakes. I wasn't interested in opening my shores just yet but possibly in the future.

Euphoria could once again be used. A program redesigned to provide a safe space for couples to unleash their anger and hopefully remember why they loved each other in a virtual reality program away from any stress of reality.

Three, the destruction of elixir in Geneva meant no more of the overly potent, potentially suicidal drug now existed. However, I had been dabbling with another panacea in a flurry of emails with Peter Beck. I still used the aphrodisiac extract from purple orchids but had requested it be mixed with a different formulation.

Peter had finalised the sample batch and finished the initial round of paid testing. Each person who'd taken it—carefully monitored for heart palpitations or overloading of the nervous system—had categorically claimed it was the best stimuli on the market.

I'd tentatively called it *cinta*—Indo word for love. I supposed, in a way, I was still trying to rectify my wrongs. Previously, I'd bottled *nafsu* (lust), but now, I wanted to do the impossible and see if I could use a less potent drug that had the power to cause happiness instead of pain.

All those things had kept my mind busy while my body healed, but I'd kept them a secret for a reason.

I didn't want Eleanor to think I hadn't changed or that I still expected certain things from a wife who was no longer a goddess, but...we'd both enjoyed the fantasies. Taking her in that cave and fucking her as I removed my masks had both been highly memorable events.

I didn't need VR to keep our marriage bed exciting, but I wouldn't say no to fucking her with wings or chasing her across a prehistoric plain to pin her on all fours and mount.

Eleanor's breath caught as she noticed the Euphoria boxes laid neatly on the pressed white sheets of her bed. Giving me a quick glance, she darted into the bedroom and picked up the eye lenses. Spinning in place, she held up the box. "I thought Drake took all your supplies to Geneva?"

"Elixir, yes, but not the sensors. I still have supplies here and on *Monyet*."

She cocked her head. "Why are they here?"

Closing the distance between us, I placed my carved cane against the bed and took the box from her hands. "I told you once that I dreamed about you. That I saw you well before you were brought to my shores."

She bit her lip, her gorgeous wedding gown straining around her chest. The shadows of her nipples were darker, hinting, despite her apprehension, she was intrigued and turned on. "What's that got to do with Euphoria?"

"I want to show you. I want to take you into that dream. I want you to see just how much I loved you when you were a figment of my imagination and understand how fucking grateful I am that you're real."

She picked up another box, this one holding the earbud sensors. They weren't needed for tonight. In fact, no other sensors were needed apart from the eye lenses. I had everything I could ever want with her and had no desire to distort any of it. I wanted to smell her skin and taste her lips. I wanted to feel her when I touched her, and I wanted her voice in my ears as she moaned.

"What about the inability to escape when we're done? I know falling asleep frees the mind, but…what if something happens, and we need to end sooner?"

"Wise." I nodded. "I've always loved how quick thinking you are, but I've taken care of it."

"You're saying you've done something to the coding?"

Pulling my phone free from my linen trousers, I pulled up the Euphoria app and showed her the new cypher. Lines of text, symbols, and numbers. It wouldn't make sense to someone who didn't know programming, but to me it was a back door that would always be permanently ajar.

"Give me your arm." I held out my hand.

Hesitantly, she obeyed.

My fingers enclosed around her wrist, once again tingling with awareness and heat. Would that ever go away? Could I ever touch this woman and not feel her magic?

Gritting my teeth from my rapidly hardening cock, I drew a small circle around her barcode tattoo.

She shivered, her lips parting for a feathery breath.

"Touch here if you want to exit the illusion. It works like a safe word. A blind spot within the program where if you pinch your inner wrist for three seconds, Euphoria will shut down, and you'll be freed from the fantasy."

She swayed into me as I pulled her closer, cupping her nape and tipping her head back.

"Are you sure it's safe?" Her gaze turned silver with lust.

I ran my lips over her mouth, tasting the sweetness of her and the sin. "I've tested it. Last night. Three second pinch and you're free."

Pika and Skittles suddenly darted into the room, their antics bringing life and colour while Eleanor and I drowned within darker and darker desires. They fluttered through Eleanor's hair and nibbled at my ears.

"Go away," I groaned, wafting at the fiends.

Eleanor laughed quietly. "I think they want to visit Euphoria."

"Another time perhaps." I ran my nose over hers. "I'm finding it harder and harder to share you tonight."

"They'll be jealous."

"They'll survive."

Pika chirped and Skittles darted to perch in the mosquito net.

They brought meaning and affection to our life. They were more like family than just pets. But right now, they were a nuisance, and I was done waiting to consummate my marriage.

Gathering Eleanor close, I shivered with sexual thirst. "Fuck, I want you."

"Then take me. Right now."

I kissed her.

Hard.

She melted into me, allowing me to dictate the speed and depth of my taking. She was submissive yet wild. Responsive but untamed. I wanted to take my time with her. But violence bled through my veins, blending with our new marriage and the weeks of begging my body to heal so I could take her the way she deserved to be taken.

I adored this woman, but I wanted to slander her too.

I wanted to strip her, punish her, splinter her apart, and then fuck her until she screamed.

I wanted to remind her that I was both man and monster in my heart.

Bending my legs, I continued kissing her as we sat on the bed. Breaking the kiss, I grabbed the eye lenses and unscrewed the container. I caught her heated stare. "Do you consent?"

She ran her hands through her hair, making me wait for her answer. Slowly, she stood and grabbed the neckline of her sleeveless dress. Keeping eye contact with me, she tore the fragile linen, slicing at the tightness and stepping out of the full skirt, naked and fucking beautiful. Her diamond anklet sparkled around her leg, golden sand clung to her toes, and the willowy power of her body scattered my heart with warning that this woman was still my ultimate curse.

A curse that I would forever crave and have no antidote for.

Running her hand down the flat of her stomach, she teased her clit. "Does that answer your question?"

"Fuck, yes." I swallowed hard. My cock bumped against my zipper, and a different kind of pain attacked me. "Yes, it does."

"In that case, you are overdressed, husband." Reaching for me, she slid off my blazer, unbuttoned my shirt, and spread both down my arms to toss them on the floor. Giving me her hand, she pulled me from the bed and without looking away, unbuckled my belt, unzipped my trousers, fisted my cock in her tight delicious fingers, then slipped both pants and boxer-briefs to my ankles.

Pika and Skittles huffed and vanished into the living room.

Eleanor laughed as she held out her hands for the eye sensors. "Prudes."

I drank her in as she tipped her head back and placed one, then two lenses over her gorgeous grey pupils.

"Goddammit, I'm about to come just looking at you."

She smirked. "Guess you better load whatever it is you've programmed, so you can have your wicked way with me then." She cocked her hip, revealing the trickle of wetness dampening the manicured curls between her legs.

She'd had no elixir, no *cinta*, no potion apart from her love and lust for me.

She *wanted* me.

And that made me the luckiest son of a bitch in the goddamn world.

Rushing, I kicked away my clothing and inserted the lenses over my own eyes, blinking past the haze to focus on my bride.

The mirage I had planned for us would finally show her how

I saw her. It would show her the invisible crown she wore upon her head, constantly changing, always evolving the more she bewitched me.

In this fantasia, she would stand on the pedestal where she'd originally been dream-bound and unattainable. And she would witness my hunger, my utter fucking desperation as I yanked her off that pedestal and sullied her in every way I could.

She would see how I saw myself.

A lowly pauper who hid in the dark and dabbled in filth until she set him free. She'd feel my tongue on her pussy as I thanked her. She'd cry out as I fucked her with happiness.

She would learn everything that a man should keep private about the woman he'd given his heart to, and I'd give her every weapon against me by learning just how much I cared.

But I'd already come to terms that Jinx was my lifelong curse.

And I would happily die because of it.

She held out my phone, the load button ready to be pressed. "I love you, Sully."

I took the device, hovering my thumb over the button. "I'm yours, Eleanor. I always have been. Now, you'll see how true that really is."

My thumb came down.

The world went white.

And the goddess of my heart stepped with me into a playground where we were angel and devil, queen and king, cavewoman and Neanderthal.

A playground where a god and goddess lived happily ever after.

Chapter Forty-Six

I STOOD ON A PODIUM.

The fantasy slowly came alive around me, revealing a totally different world.

We were no longer on earth—this wasn't just a different time period or place. This hallucination wasn't based on our planet. The light was brighter here, as if we were closer to the sun. There was no wind or elements, and the cotton wisps of clouds danced within the ballroom's ceiling as if we were so sky-high that it'd formed its own weather patterns.

A castle.

A castle in the clouds.

A castle in the mind of my husband.

I blinked as I started to make sense of the huge room. Five-story high columns held painted cupid panels and arched windows from floor to ceiling. No drapes and no mullions, leaving the glass a perfect portal to the staggeringly stunning vista beyond. Spires of a white-washed citadel beckoned beyond, perfect crystal skies framed the cloud fortress, and the sun was too big to distinguish—it was just there. Golden and glowing, bathing all of us in beauty.

I was right.

We weren't on earth anymore. We were in Olympia or some other home of the gods or perhaps…in a dream.

Sully's dream.

The moment I thought about him, he appeared.

Inserted into the fantasy with a snap and solidness, he was a man dressed entirely in rags. He spread his dirty hands as he caught my gaze. His palms calloused and trousers torn at the calf. His muslin shirt held patches and frayed edges, and one sleeve had been ripped at the elbow. His bare feet no longer held sand from Goddess Isles but filth from trudging through mud and mistakes.

"Hello," he breathed, unable to take his eyes off me, drinking in my gowned body.

I looked at where he stared, and my heart hurt at the difference in us. Where he was penniless and dressed in poverty, I sparkled with every diamond in creation.

My arms were inlaid with precious stones, my wrists twinkled with gems. The sheerness of the fabric covering me was weighted with opals of every facet. Panels of silver velvet cascaded in a train, embroidered with sapphire thread and decorated with another million opals.

Beneath my dress, I wore no shoes, but my feet had been painted with henna scrollwork, my toes complete with lotus flowers and my ankles hidden in rosebud vines.

My hair was loose and longer than usual, grazing almost to my thighs, and I felt a magic tingling in my fingers. The electricity I'd suffered from the very first moment I'd touched Sully now hummed powerfully in my blood.

I closed my eyes and focused on the sensation, following the crackle through my veins, around my heart, and along every inch of skin.

Just like this wasn't earth anymore, I wasn't human.

Looking at Sully, I whispered, "What is this place? What am I?"

He licked his lips, still unable to look away from my body. "This is my dream. When I first met you."

"You saw me this clearly?"

"I saw your silver stare and empathic heart. I saw you on an unreachable pedestal, and knew you held magic that could kill me with just a touch. I went to you. I bowed at your feet, and instead of commanding me to leave, you welcomed me. You cared for me even when I didn't deserve it." He shrugged in his rags. "The rest—the clouds, the castle, the opals—it's an embellishment to show you just how in awe I was of you, to hint just how much I needed you, even then."

"And the magic in my veins now?" I held up my hand, gasping as micro shards of light appeared in my palm.

"That isn't fake." His voice lowered until it slipped beneath my gown and made love to me with seducing syllables. "That is just a manifested reality. When you touch me, I feel it. When you kiss me, it electrifies my very soul. You aren't just a woman to me. You never have been and never will be. You are a witch in every way that matters."

I tried to quell the rapidly growing lust for him. To not grow wet for his misplaced worship of me but instead focus on how handsome he was, even dressed in yesterday's heartache. "Sully, I need you." I held out my hand, beckoning him to my podium.

He took a step, shivering as he once again drank me in. "You take my fucking breath away."

I shivered, my nipples pebbling behind opals and my insides melting with need. "Then let me kiss you, and I'll give it back."

He smiled, rakishly and shyly. A combination that set fire to my desire.

"Do you want me, goddess?"

"I'm not a goddess, Sullivan Sinclair; I am your wife."

"*Wife*." His dirty feet brought him closer, each step revealing just how high my plinth was, just how above himself he'd put me. "My forever after wife."

"You saw me as untouchable."

"I saw you as perfect." He stopped at the bottom and looked up. His chin met my henna inked toes. His hands gripping the marble platform keeping me out of his reach. "I saw you as everything I wanted and everything I would never earn."

"I'm not perfect."

He nodded, reaching out to wrap his strong, filthy fingers around my impeccable ankle. "No, you're not." I moaned as he ran his hand as high as he could go, scraping nails to the back of my knee. "You're so much fucking better than perfect." Yanking me forward, he buckled my legs and caught me as I tumbled into his arms.

My opal dress ballooned around us, my hair obscured my vision, but his body was hard and safe against mine. His arms bunched as he swung me to the floor, placing me gently before him.

"You've made me the happiest man alive, Eleanor Sinclair."

I blinked as he brushed aside my hair and cupped my cheeks. He trembled as he ran his thumb over my bottom lip.

"I will never stop loving you, worshipping you, thinking up delicious fucking ways to pleasure you." He tilted my head to the side, exposing my throat so he could run his nose along my neck and dip along my collarbone. "Tonight, I wish to fuck you in every position. I want to make love to you until your voice is hoarse and your body is deliciously sore. I want to christen every chamber of this castle and wring your blood dry of countless orgasms."

I moaned as he unsheathed his teeth, biting me with threatening strength. "There is just one catch, my darling wife."

My brain tried to follow; I did my best to stop panting for more and focus on the ultimatum in his tone, but I struggled. He'd drugged me with words, and I was utterly ruined for more.

He chuckled as he captured my chin, his navy eyes glowing with self-loathing and heated hunger. "In order to pleasure you in the way you deserve on your wedding night, I have a request to ask."

I swallowed and shoved back some of my drunkenness. "What request?"

He held up his hand, splaying open his palm.

Empty.

I frowned. "There's nothing there."

"There is, you just can't see it with the fantasy. Touch it. We're not wearing finger sensors so you'll be able to feel it."

Carefully, I ran my hand over the invisible item. My eyebrows drew together as I followed the tiny glass bottle along with the squishy dropper at the top. I didn't recognise the shape, but sharp suspicions landed on my tongue. "Elixir?"

"No. Never that. Not again. I will never put you in such danger." Pulling away, he opened the bottle and pressed the dropper to suck a few droplets of whatever tincture was inside. All his actions were a pantomime, manipulating an invisible thing. "This is *cinta*. A much lower dose than elixir. It merely provides stamina to the user and highlights lust already in their system. It's been tested and proven safe."

"I'm wet enough as it is." I smiled. "I don't need any help sleeping with my husband."

"And I'm happy to hear it." His face darkened. "It so happens, I am rock fucking hard and struggling with self-control but…I am still healing and…" He swallowed hard before rushing, "Please don't think I'm requesting we take this because I can't perform or that I'm not out of my mind with fucking lust for you. I am. I will gladly throw this away if you ask. But…I am under no illusions that I'm not at my top capacity yet. I won't be able to give you what you deserve for as long as I want. I want to be able to use you without succumbing to this shitty weakness still inside me."

Crowding me, he wrapped possessive fingers around my nape. "I want to be on my knees between your legs, Eleanor. I want to be inside you as you scream. I want you to remember this night as the start of our beginning and not be governed by my pain—"

"You're in pain?" I flinched and tried to get away. "Then we'll stop. We can wait—"

"*Wait?*" He chuckled coldly. "I can't wait, Jinx. I'm going to be inside you in a few minutes, with or without help. I just wanted to be honest of my limitations and admit that I want you more than I can physically provide."

I stared at him.

How was it that his honesty made me love him more than his assurances that he was invincible? It made me lust for him and also want to honour him. He stood in rags all while he'd given me every penny he'd ever earned—legally and illegally—and now, he'd given me his utmost trust.

Trust by admitting his pain instead of hiding it. Trust that he wanted more than he could give.

Silently, I opened my mouth.

"You sure?" He grunted.

I just kept my lips parted until his hand came up with its invisible contents and a single droplet of sour sugar hit my tongue.

Keeping eye contact, Sully dropped a dose into his own mouth before screwing the bottle shut and tossing it away. It had never been tangible in this fantasy and now bounced on a bed that we couldn't see, rolling amongst boxes of Euphoria sensors in a villa by the sea.

I waited for the kick and hostile takeover of elixir.

My heart flurried with fear that I would once again be a prisoner in my own body.

However, Sully was right.

This time, it was a heatwave instead of an inferno. It began in my heart and travelled in my bloodstream to my clit. It smouldered instead of burned, it tingled instead of tortured, and I gave myself into it.

I moaned as my need for Sully amplified, and his fantasy made me wish to turn the tables on him. He'd come to me as a bankrupt beggar, believing he was destitute in soul and heart. Instead, he'd traded what he thought he didn't have and taken mine in return, leaving me with evidence that he wasn't destitute but rich. Rich in so much affection and commitment.

Falling to my knees, I looked up at him.

"What are you—?" His eyes flared as I reached for the curled-up waistline of his tattered trousers. With swiftness born from lust as well as love, I pulled them down and found his bare erection.

He groaned as I wrapped my fingers around him. His hands dived into my hair as I bent forward and inserted him into my mouth.

I wore a gown of opals and held the power of lightning in my fingertips all while I sucked the cock of my handsome husband.

"*Christ,* Eleanor." He thrust into my mouth, his ass clenching and knees locking. "Fucking hell."

I dug my tongue into the slit at the top, tasting his musk before rubbing the wet length of him down my cheek as I dropped my head to suck his balls.

"Fuck—" He jerked above me, muttering incoherent lusty snarls.

My hand went between his legs, and I pressed on that sensitive spot that I'd heard about but never tried, and I broke the monster I'd married.

"Jesus Christ." He crashed to his knees, tearing his length from my control. Fisting himself, he shuddered and staved off the first pulses of a climax.

I was hot and wet and itchy and wanting.

Whatever he'd fed us made me lose all inhibition as I crawled onto him, knocking him to the floor.

For a moment, he splayed on his back with me fully gowned on top of him. His hot heavy gaze met mine, and there was a precious, perfect moment of oneness. But then he smirked a vulgar, soul-slicing smile, and he shoved me backward.

I fell to the side, my skirts floating around my legs.

"You think you can rush me, wife?" He stood on his knees, looking down at me. Without looking away, he tore off the ruins of his shirt then dropped his fist to his cock and masturbated blatantly before me. "Your mouth felt too good, Jinx. You almost made me come."

I groaned and writhed on the floor.

"Is that what you want? Do you want to come?" He dug his thumb into the top of his cock and quaked.

I nodded, shamelessly grasping my breasts through the opals.

"You know what to do then, don't you?" He continued touching himself, vain and villainous. Switching to his left hand, he commanded, "Get on your knees, get out of that gown, and slide your deliciously drenched pussy onto my fingers." He held up his right hand, spearing three fingers upward just as he had when we'd first met.

I suffered a full-body quake.

Bands of release threatened to explode just from his crude gesture. Unlike elixir that stripped away my thoughts and control, this new aphrodisiac made me embrace all my badness, my wetness, and sexual power.

With shaking hands, I obeyed him.

Ripping at stitches and tearing at silk, I shoved off velvet and opals then kneeled before him naked. My chest rose and fell, my breathing noisy and needy. And Sully's savage stare corrupted me as I crawled to him, balanced on one knee then raised one foot to spread my legs.

I bared myself before him, utterly graphic and bold.

"Goddammit, woman, you'll give me another fucking heart attack." Sully reached for me, but I snagged his wrist and guided his hand toward me.

I rubbed his fingers through the lust dampening my inner thighs, then with our stare locked together, I inserted his fingers inside me.

He wasn't prepared for what happened.

Neither was I.

The moment his fingers penetrated my pussy, I ignited and shattered in sparks. The magic in my blood, that he'd coded and created, exploded outward in golden bolts. My insides rippled around his intrusion, my back bowed, my mouth opened, and I came apart as a woman and as his so-called witch.

The ballroom filled with magic. Blinding and binding, skipping through the air with chemistry. More golden sorcery siphoned around us as I came harder, deeper. A womb-deep clench that left me gasping for air as I slumped on Sully's hand.

Oxygen didn't find me but Sully's tongue did.

His mouth crashed onto mine. His lips claiming me, his teeth sinking into me, his tongue plunging in time with his fingers. He kissed me like an animal who'd reached the end of his rope. The chain that'd been lashed around his throat since he was born fell away.

Snarling into my mouth, he gathered me off the floor and twisted me onto all fours.

His hand locked into my hair, cricking my neck to continue

kissing me while he rose behind me and mounted.

He penetrated and took.

He fucked me like he had as the caveman.

Fierce and brutal, punishingly swift and sure.

"Take me, Jinx. Goddammit, take it all."

His impalement shoved me forward but his fingers around my hips brought me back. His balls slapped against my clit, and whatever drug we'd dabbled in flared and ignited.

"Fuck, Eleanor." He rode me. Hard. Fast. "*Fuck!*"

The noises of his flesh hitting mine filled the cotton-cloud ballroom. He plastered himself over my back, laying kiss after kiss along my nape, spine, and shoulders.

I cried out and gave him everything I was.

There was nothing to hide anymore. No secret I had to swallow or quirk I had to mask. This man knew everything, and he loved every part.

He loved me when I was human.

He loved me when I was immortal.

He loved me past beauty, past pleasure, and pain.

He loved me as I loved him.

For his soul.

The part of him no one else had touched, and the part that I would shield every day for the rest of my life.

My knees bruised as he took me like a primitive beast.

His grunts sent shivers down my spine.

His pawing made wetness slick around his cock.

But it was his voice that made me come for the second time.

"You are—"

Thrust.

"—*everything.*"

My detonation triggered his and he pounded into me, not being gentle, being downright mean as he fed me the gushes of his release. His fingernails dug into my flesh, leaving marks. His cum branded deep within me, so I knew exactly who I belonged to, and we rode an identical high, glowing with the same electrical alchemy that existed whenever we touched.

Hoarse and panting hard, Sully slowly stopped thrusting, locking his cock inside me. He didn't go soft. He didn't fall to the side thanks to weeks of unconsciousness and so many broken bones. He was too stubborn for that. Too wrapped up in me, his wife.

Biting my shoulder, he twisted me until I was on my back. My legs spread and his cock still impaled inside me. "Now that we've got the initial intensity out of the way, it's time I worshipped every part of you, don't you agree?" He drank in my nakedness. "I particularly feel like watching you come with your legs around your ears." Grabbing my calves, he rolled me up my spine until my legs bent and my knees pressed against my cheeks.

He looked down where we were joined. "Now that's a view, my kinky wife."

The girl who'd been sold to him would've blushed and tried to hide.

The woman who'd married him bared her teeth and murmured, "Go ahead, husband, make me come again. But after that, it's *my* turn."

He laughed.

A perfect brilliant sound that I would never get tired of hearing. Bending over me, he thrust deep and kissed me.

He kissed with a sweeping tongue and sinful taste as he began to ride and murmured, "We have the rest of our lives, Eleanor Sinclair. And I intend to pleasure you every moment of it."

Chapter Forty-Seven

To: Sparrow@292840.com
From S.Sinclair@goddessisles.com
Subject: Evidence

Q,

As requested, evidence that Eleanor Sinclair became mine willingly, happily, and is now my wife.
Please see the video link to our wedding.
Never contact me again.

Sullivan

To: S.Sinclair@goddessisles.com
From Sparrow@292840.com
Subject: Re: Evidence

Sullivan,

Congratulations to you and your wife.

My own fiancée has just seen your evidence and took great joy in informing me that she met Eleanor when they were first stolen. Her name is Tess, and she passes on her regards. She's glad Eleanor is safe and happy.

Tess would also like to assure her that she is likewise happy and about to be married.

To me.

Like you, I fell for a slave who set me free. Like me, I hope you value what you have.

I will not say we are similar, but it seems we have both found redemption through love.

'Sans amour, tous les hommes sont des monstres. Sans hommes, toutes les femmes sont libres.' *Without love, all men are monsters. Without men, all women are free.*

Au revoir,
Q

THE END

Letter from the Author

I have a little surprise for you.

First, I want to thank you for reading five books with Sully and Eleanor, Pika and Skittles. I hope you enjoyed their romance and managed to escape our world and step into theirs for a while.

A book is a bit like Euphoria, where we get to enjoy a fantasy that isn't our own for a time.

I have thoroughly enjoyed penning their tale and already miss those cheeky parrots and the deviant fantasies that Jinx and Sully will indulge in while I'm not there. In fact, I have enjoyed Goddess Isles so much, I'm not quite ready to leave them just yet and have decided to write two novellas that I will explain below.

Please note YOU DO NOT HAVE TO READ these novellas.

This is not a ploy for more sales or to drag out the conclusion you want. You may end on this book (Fifth a Fury) and know they lived happily ever after, playing in Euphoria, swimming in tropical seas, and rescuing countless animals. However, if you (like me) would like to step inside their virtual reality world again and enjoy a few deviant fantasies and erotic games, then I will explain what's coming next.

SULLY'S FANTASY – 28th July 2020

This book will feature Sully's utmost desires. It will be sexy and sinful and a perfect bite of heart-fluttery spice. The best thing? It will be held at Hawksridge Hall when Sully travels to introduce Eleanor to Jethro and Nila (*Indebted Series*), and also meets Elder and Pim (*Dollar Series*). It will have long length cameos of Jethro and Nila, along with old locations from the *New York Times Bestselling series Indebted*.

JINX'S FANTASY – 25th August 2020

This novella will feature Eleanor's hidden wishes. Once again, it will be a perfect length of smutty and sinful and will also feature old characters from my previous books. In Jinx's Fantasy, Elder and Pim *(Dollar Series)* will hand-deliver the yacht that Sully orders in **Thousands (Dollar Series #4).** There will be cameos from those characters along with nautical travel with Eleanor and Sully.

THESE HAVE NO RELATION (story wise) TO THE FIVE BOOKS YOU HAVE JUST READ.
YOU DO NOT NEED TO READ TO FINISH THEIR TALE.
ONLY READ IF YOU FANCY ENJOYING MORE OF THEIR COMPANY.

Sully's Fantasy and *Jinx's Fantasy* are merely sneak peeks into their lives as a happily married couple who happen to have freaky fun in Euphoria.

I must repeat myself: **YOU DO NOT NEED TO READ THESE NOVELLAS**. If you are content with this ending, and have read enough of Sully and Eleanor's tale, the novellas are not required.

As for other upcoming books from me, I have a new Dark Romance planned.

The Fable of Happiness

More information and release dates will be announced on my blog and newsletter.

Thanks so much for all your amazing support and kindness, and I hope you have a wonderful week.

Pepper xxxx

Pre-Order SULLY'S FANTASY

Releasing 28th July 2020

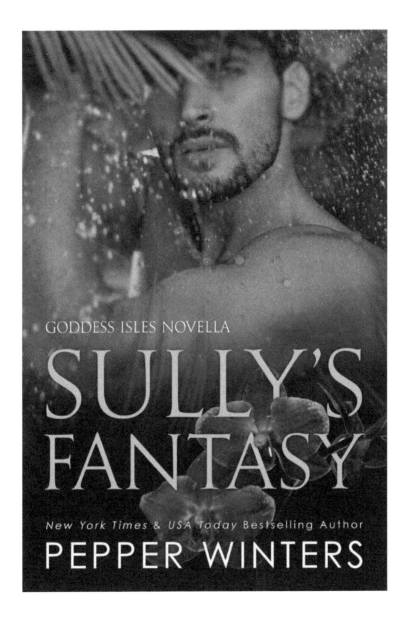

From New York Times Bestseller, Pepper Winters, comes a spin-off novella featuring Sully and Jinx from the USA Today Bestselling Series, Goddess Isles

"There was a wedding and vows and a happily ever after...but there was also lust and fantasy."

Sullivan Sinclair has high-powered friends as well as his new family. Invited to attend a masquerade at Jethro's Hawksridge Hall, he agrees.

Eleanor Sinclair has a new husband and untold wealth at her fingertips. While living on an island in the Java Sea, their lives are their own. However, a simple trip to England has both of them missing the tropics of home.

A monster and a goddess who have a special power to escape.
A fantasy that Sully dares to share.
A visit to Euphoria like no other.

Release Date: 28ᵗʰ July 2020

OTHER BOOKS AVAILABLE FROM PEPPER WINTERS

FREE BOOKS
Debt Inheritance (Indebted Series #1)
Tears of Tess (Monsters in the Dark #1)
Pennies (Dollar Series #1)

BOOKS IN KINDLE UNLIMITED
Destroyed (Standalone)

Dollar Series
Pennies
Dollars
Hundreds
Thousands
Millions

Truth & Lies Duet
Crown of Lies
Throne of Truth

Pure Corruption Duet
Ruin & Rule
Sin & Suffer

Indebted Series
Debt Inheritance
First Debt
Second Debt
Third Debt
Fourth Debt
Final Debt
Indebted Epilogue

Monsters in the Dark Trilogy

PLAYLIST

This playlist is a little different to prior ones.
I requested readers in my Facebook Group (Pepper's
Playground) to share with me the songs that they felt represented
Goddess Isles. Below are a few that they kindly gave.

Marshmello ft Bastille – Happier
Adele – Into the Deep
Billie Eilish & Khalid – Lovely
Katie Sky – Monsters
Daisy Grey – Wicked Game
Godsmack – Under Your Scars
Jack White – Love Interruption
INXS – Never Tear us Apart
Colbie Caillat – When the Darkness Comes
Illenium – In Your Arms
Chris Isaak – Wicked Games
Muse – Madness
Halestorm – Familiar Taste of Poison
Awolnation – Run
Massive Attack – Angel
Breaking Benjamin – Breath
Joji – Run
Geowulf – Saltwater
Deaf Havana – Evil
First Aid Kit – My Silver Linings
Hozier – In the Woods Somewhere
Imagine Dragons – Nothing Left to Say
The Verve - Bittersweet Symphony
R.E.M – Losing my Religion

ACKNOWLEDGEMENTS

Wow, another series done.

2020 started off tricky and just got worse. We're still in the midst of an event we never thought we'd see in our lifetimes and to have released a book series during this time came with its own moral-raising questions. However, I owe YOU a massive debt of gratitude for reading along with me, stepping into a tropical island where fantastical things are more common than reality, and sharing your lockdown and struggles with me.

I hope I delivered a tale you enjoyed and gave a small smidgen of peace from this crazy year. I want to thank you all again (so, so much) for reading.

A MASSIVE thanks to my beta readers who trudge through all my typos to see the story I'm trying to craft. Melissa, Heather, Nicole, Tamicka, Selena, Effie, you read along with me and keptp my motivation going. A huge thanks to Sarah and Scott for audio narration and for Will M Watt for doing a cameo. Thanks to Kiki and the amazing team Next Step PR for all their help. Thanks to the bookstagrammers, bloggers, reviewers, playgrounders, and anyone who takes the time out of their busy, stressful days to email or message me.

I'm ever so grateful and hope you stay safe and happy as we navigate our lives together.

I also have to say thanks to Dan Brown for the initial information on souls having a 'weight'. I was inspired by his book *The Lost Symbol*. However, studies on the weight of souls began in 1906. Please read this article for more details:
https://www.learning-mind.com/can-the-human-soul-be-weighed/

Thanks again,

Pepper xx

CPSIA information can be obtained
at www.ICGtesting.com
Printed in the USA
LVHW011758070820
662641LV00003B/466